Time of Death

*Other Five Star Titles
by Shirley Kennett:*

Burning Rose

Time of Death

A PJ Gray Novel

Shirley Kennett

Five Star • Waterville, Maine

Quote from "Oh, Those Family Values" published in *The Snarling Citizen* © 1996 by Barbara Ehrenreich

First Edition, Second Printing

Published in 2005 in conjunction with Tekno Books and Ed Gorman.

Set in 11 pt. Plantin.

Printed in the United States on permanent paper.

Library of Congress Cataloging-in-Publication Data

Kennett, Shirley.
    Time of death : a PJ Gray novel / by Shirley Kennett.—1st ed.
      p. cm.
    ISBN 1-59414-309-9 (hc : alk. paper)
    1. Forensic psychologists—Fiction. 2. Women psychologists
—Fiction. 3. Saint Louis (Mo.)—Fiction. 4. Serial murders
—Fiction. I. Title.
PS3561.E432T56 2005
813'.54—dc22   2005027040

*To my husband Dennis
for our past, present, and future together*

Acknowledgments

This book is the product of more than one mind.

When I wrote it, I relied on the invaluable assistance of Lee Lofland, a recipient of the Association of Chiefs of Police Medal of Valor. Lee is a former police detective with a vast background in crime scene investigations, in areas such as murder, rape, robbery, arson, narcotics, murder for hire, and ritualistic and occult crimes. All of those qualifications don't begin to describe the solid feeling of having Lee at my back with answers that keep my characters true to law enforcement principles and investigational techniques. Any errors in authenticity in this book are solely mine. Thanks, Lee, and if there's anything I can do for you, you know where I live—or can easily find out.

The author is one link in the chain between story idea and bookstore shelf. Some of the others are my agent, Eleanor Wood of the Spectrum Literary Agency; John Helfers of Tekno Books; Mary P. Smith of Five Star Publishing; and my editor, Hugh Abramson. Thanks to all of you for making me look good. I give credit to the International Thriller Writers, American Crime Writers League, Mystery Writers of America, and Sisters in Crime for providing in-depth knowledge and camaraderie. The Greater St. Louis Chapter of Sisters in Crime has been a wellspring of information and support. My special thanks to Laura Bradford, Vicki Berger Erwin, and Michelle Thouviner for those Saturday mornings in the bookstore café. To my sister Maxine Olmstadt, thanks for the time you spent reading my story and dispensing well-reasoned advice, and remember—you're only young once. My special thanks to Ed Gorman, a brave, daring, handsome, and all-around swell guy, for his encouragement over the years.

My husband Dennis and sons Tom and Tim were terrific sources of strength and encouragement while the pages of the manuscript mounted up. I couldn't have done it without you. Thank you, thank you, thank you. That's one for each of you.

Lastly, I wish to thank Babykitty for keeping me company in the middle of the night as I wrote this book, and for the occasional letters and symbols he inserted by walking on the keyboard to get to the cat treats. On some days, his contribution seemed the better part of my writing.

"At best, the family teaches the finest things
human beings can learn from each other—generosity and love.
But it is also, all too often, where we learn
nasty things like hate, rage, and shame."

—Barbara Ehrenreich, "Oh, Those Family Values"

Chapter 1

I'm surprised to see that my right hand trembles as I hold the knife.

With fear? No. I'm the one in charge here. I am not the slicee.

Shame? Maybe a little, that I don't have more socially acceptable things to occupy my time. Who decides what's socially acceptable, anyway? Probably there's some secret god to worship, the God of Successful Parties. I've made my humble little offerings at the altar, but not enough for the god to bless me into the kind of life I want: the house, the servants, upper arms that don't jiggle, the aura of class if not the real thing, adequate sex with hubby and a little something extra with the golf pro or the personal trainer or the stock adviser. Or with all of them, separately or in any combination.

If my offerings to the god weren't sufficient before, maybe some blood sacrifice will do it.

There's a little regret in the trembling of my hand, too. Regret that I didn't do this sooner. I've always known that if you don't climb the social ladder, you live on the droppings of the people on the higher rungs. I've just never done anything about it before.

Mostly my hand is trembling with excitement. This is going to work, I know it. I'm joining the ranks of rich bitches, and I'm doing it with my own cleverness and my own admittedly trembling hand.

I look around Old Hank's barn, checking my supplies. Hank's space heater, creating a bubble of warm air where I'm working. My telescoping five-hundred-watt halogen work light—ooh, watch out, that bulb gets hot! But it does lend an operating room flair to the whole setup. Scissors, gleaming. Sy-

ringe and needle, used and useless now, its ketamine contents spurted into the slicee's arm muscle. Stainless steel pans, oddly shaped, like little kidneys. A scalpel for delicate work. The rib saw. An anatomy book. A bottle of water. A heavy wrench to bash with, in case things get out of hand. The hammer and nails. And the knife from the sporting goods store. Yes, ma'am, that's one honkin' big knife any man'd be proud to own. *For what, I'd like to know. Gutting little Bambi, I suppose.*

Willing my gloved hand steady, I lean over the sedated form lying on a sheet-draped workbench. I would have preferred a stainless steel table, but bringing one in would have been far more trouble than it was worth. So, the old, oak workbench would have to do.

Showtime.

The first slice is reserved for his limp dick. I do the deed and plop the severed organ into one of the little stainless pans. A muffled gasp escapes me as his blood slips down his bare thighs and spreads between his legs.

Old Hank doesn't hear my soft gasp. In fact, I could stomp and holler and Hank wouldn't know. He's up at the main house, a hundred yards away, drunk to the gills. Earlier I left two fifths of Scotch on the porch, knocked on the door, and hid behind some bushes. The door opened and there stood Hank, silhouetted against the interior lights. I imagined his eyes gleaming as he picked up the bottles, and the puzzled look that must have crossed his face as it dawned on him that bottles didn't ordinarily walk onto his porch by themselves. He shrugged and went inside with his prizes. I figured that in less than twenty minutes he was dead to the world.

The neighbors all knew about Old Hank's binges, so they won't think it's anything out of the ordinary when he's found passed out in his own piss. That's Hank all right, Officer, hosed as usual.

Hank's house, barn, and chicken coop were an island of country life in the 'burbs. When Hank dies, there won't be a chicken around for miles. A live one, at least. Only those bloodless little corpses neatly arranged in the grocery's meat case.

Speaking of blood . . .

After the first slice, it gets easier.

I move my hand quickly, whimsically, angrily, leaving behind streaks of blood. The nose. The cruel lips. Plop. *The testicles.* Plop, plop.

The slicee's eyes are open, even though he's unconscious. It's just the way the drug works, but it's kind of unnerving. I turn the pages of the anatomy book, looking at the charts, then measure with the span of my hand down from the collarbone and out from his sternum to a spot on his chest. In a few minutes, I've got a rough hole dug. It's easy to do, if stitching the patient up afterward isn't a concern. I watch in fascination as his heart pumps beneath my questing fingers.

I check his breathing and sit down on a straw bale to wait. I'm not sure how long he'll be unconscious. Timing is important here. He might bleed out or go into shock. Maybe I gave him too much ketamine, and he's so far down the k-hole that he'll never climb back out. There's a good chance I've done too much damage during my inelegant intrusion into his chest, and his body will just give up trying to live.

I hope those things don't happen.

The pendulum in my head ticks off time, and then he begins to groan. I dash the bottle of water in his face. He screams as he becomes more alert. Must be like waking up in the middle of an operation to find that the surgeon's still fiddling around inside. I grab his face—what's left of it—with both hands and force his eyes in my direction. I want him to take a look at me. I want to be acknowledged. He's a bit past the acknowledging stage, but I settle for what I can get.

13

I lean over with the knife, put my weight behind it, and stab him in the heart through the chest hole, the window to his innards, the seat of his soul if he has one. I watch as the heart quivers and stops.

Didn't need the wrench after all.

Chapter 2

Dr. Penelope Jennifer Gray chose well when she selected soft-soled walking shoes that morning. Making her way over cobblestones on the Mississippi River levee, she placed her feet carefully. The early morning fog left a chilling film on her face. A degree or two less, and the cobblestones would be glazed with ice. She should be grateful for small things.

She'd gotten lost near Laclede's Landing, and not for the first time. The Landing was a dining and shopping area of St. Louis with a boisterous after-hours life. At six on a Sunday morning, the club goers were cleared out and the daytime crowd was still tucked into bed. She left her car in a no parking zone on Lucas Street with a "Police Business" card shoved into the front window above the steering wheel. A little traffic noise filtered down from nearby Eads Bridge, but it was muffled.

PJ could hear Detective Leo Schultz before she could see him through the fog. The sound waves of his voice seemed to have some kind of selective resonance with the suspended water molecules in the air, so that his voice carried when other sounds didn't. PJ honed in on his voice and came to a small knot of people gathered near a prone figure.

"About time you got here," Schultz said. His voice reflected disapproval of those inconsiderate enough to sleep in on a Sunday morning, PJ among them. She didn't take the bait. After a few seconds of posturing, he stepped aside to give her a view of the reason she'd been summoned from a warm bed.

A nude man lay only a few feet away on the cobblestones. Beyond him, the fog wiped the Mississippi from view. The

15

man's face, chest, and genitals were mutilated and bloody. His fingertips were sliced off, so that his hands appeared stubby. There was no large pool of blood underneath, but he was as pale as a vampire's victim. Small waves lapped at the man's feet, a watery caress for a man who was beyond comfort.

"ME's come and gone," Schultz said. "Basically we're just standing here, freezing, waiting for you to show up."

He wasn't giving up. She challenged him with her eyes.

"Probably stopped to feed your cat," he said.

"None of your business if I did," PJ said.

Anita Collings's voice cut in. "Hey, could we get on with it? There's a dead guy over there and he's the priority."

PJ looked over at Anita, prepared to tell her off. The sight of her junior team member's determined face, with well-defined dots of red on her cheeks and fog condensed on her eyelashes like drops of transparent paint on a brush, shifted PJ's crankiness. After all, they had been out here longer. She forced her muscles to bring up the corners of her mouth. The result was as she expected: Dave and Anita immediately returned the smile, and Schultz gazed at the white wall of fog over the river.

Dave Whitmore flapped his arms in an exaggerated attempt to warm himself up. "Could we do this back at Headquarters?"

"Oh, come on, it's not that cold." PJ grew up in Iowa, where the snow started mounting up early, ended late, blizzards weren't ice cream treats, and wind chills of minus thirty degrees weren't uncommon. By this time, with Christmas less than three weeks away, Iowa would be covered with some serious white stuff. She thought St. Louisans were winter wimps.

PJ walked over to the body and knelt down for a closer

look. The cobblestones were damp, and cold seeped through the knees of her jeans. The victim's eyes, open and with the flat gaze of death, held no enlightenment, and his mangled mouth told her no stories. There were ligature marks on his wrists and ankles. The small abdominal stab done to measure liver temperature was a gentle intrusion compared to the devastation in his chest. A softball-sized chunk of skin and flesh had been removed from his chest, directly over his heart. The ends of ribs protruded on each side of the hole, like flattened bits of chalk writing a story of savagery. It would be up to the medical examiner to begin the process of reading that story.

Studying the rough stubble on what was left of his cheeks, she noted that it didn't appear that he'd shaved in a while. She had the urge to take off her coat and put it over him, as if he needed more protection from the harsh elements than she did. The eyes drew her again, and she saw dried trails of tears that had leaked from the corners and flowed backward toward his temple.

Someone watched those tears with hatred or satisfaction.

PJ walked back to the group. "Who found the body?"

"Woman walking a dog. She had her dog off the leash— oughtta get a ticket for that—and the dog raised a ruckus. She called it in on her cell at half past five," Dave said. "Still dark then, but she carries a flashlight about the size of a baseball bat. Grabbed her dog and ran. She said she didn't get a really good look, but enough to know that the guy was dead. Officers Garcia and Leeds responded. Did you talk to them already? You probably passed them on your way down."

"I don't think I took the most direct route," PJ said. Schultz grunted.

A clattering sound alerted PJ to the arrival of the body removal crew. They'd pushed a gurney down the cobblestones.

Wouldn't it have been easier to carry the body than to try to roll the gurney uphill, rattling and shaking? She pictured the corpse in its body bag sliding out of the straps on the gurney and bumping its way down the cobblestones, and that brought something else to mind.

"There's not a lot of blood here, so this is probably a dump site instead of the murder scene. How'd the body get here?" she asked. "Did it wash in from the river?"

"The body hasn't been submerged in the water," Dave said. "Just ended up with the feet like that."

"Okay, so he was either carried or dragged from a car up there," she pointed uphill toward the road that serviced the levee, "or rolled down. Whichever way, that should mean evidence on the path down."

"Ahead of you there," Anita said. "Techs have a large area cordoned off where the body could've rolled or been dragged. They're going to wait until the sun burns off this fog a little to do a better search. Tromping through there now might damage evidence. The photographer's been grousing about condensation in his lenses, and he's put everything away until the fog clears."

"Do we wait around for that?" PJ said.

"One of us will, unless Mr. Big Time Detective says we can all leave," Anita said, looking at Schultz. He glowered back at her. "I'll interpret that as a no."

PJ had a good view of the two men working to get the victim into a body bag. They'd sized up the job, put back the standard bag, and brought out a heavy-duty one. It had two zippers and a flap that closed like an envelope. The men handled the body with atypical reverence, and in silence. PJ could hear the zipper closing. They grasped the handles of the body bag, lifted it up to the gurney and strapped it on— securely, she was glad to see.

The gurney clacked its way up the levee. Conversation stopped until it reached the top, a spontaneous expression of respect for the dead.

"I don't suppose there are any witnesses to the dumping," PJ said.

"None so far," Dave said. "But we can narrow the time the body was dropped. The security staff of the casino patrols this section of the levee a couple of times a day. As of 10:00 p.m. last night, this section of levee hadn't sprouted any bodies."

"Leaving us with a little after 10:00 p.m. to 5:30 a.m. There's a tall hotel near here, isn't there?" PJ said.

"Yeah, the Embassy Suites."

"We need to get somebody over there and see if any guests saw anything from rooms that face this way."

"I'll do it," Dave immediately said. "At least it's indoors."

"I think a couple of officers can handle that," PJ said. "It's a little too early to start knocking on hotel room doors anyway. No sense ruining their opportunity to sleep in." She directed a glare at Schultz, but it slid off him like an egg off a non-stick pan.

"The way the chest is carved up, all that stuff with the heart, that's our holdback," Schultz said. "So don't spread that around." It was his first contribution other than a grunt since she'd offered the olive branch. "The ME said the time of death was six to nine in the evening based on rigor progression and body temperature, but the cold weather, nudity, lying on cold cobblestones, and muscular development were giving her fits. Said she had to suck the goo out of his eyeball to confirm it, only it sounded real professional when she said it."

"Thanks. I needed that image." PJ tried not to think about what the victim's last hours were like.

"Nasty mutilations," Schultz said, nodding in the direction of the corpse. "Regular chop job. Think it's a homo thing?"

"Not necessarily," PJ said. "There are lots of mutilation murders with heterosexual killers. Women target male genitals for a lot of reasons."

"He's got no mouth," Schultz said. "Look at that face. I wouldn't be surprised if the autopsy shows his asshole's cut out, too. You know, the two places where a guy can take it. Fucking hard way to go."

PJ sighed. Working with Schultz was something of a trial. Living with him was even harder.

"Now can we go back to Headquarters?" Dave said.

"Yeah," said Schultz. "Everybody but you. You're staying with the techs."

Dave shot a glance at PJ, and she could see that he was hoping to be rescued from the task. She waved goodbye, thoughts of hot coffee already simmering in her mind.

When she got back to her car, there was a parking ticket tucked under the windshield wiper.

Chapter 3

In PJ's office, ideas were tossed as vigorously as a house salad in an Italian restaurant. As a psychologist and the civilian leader of the Computerized Homicide Investigations Program—CHIP—PJ knew that these early brainstorming sessions often produced information of lasting value. Their first hours on a case were usually spent around her battered old desk. She trusted the instincts of the people gathered there as much as she trusted her own.

It hadn't always been that way. As a female shrink with a background in computerized marketing research simulations, PJ had been an outsider who'd cried in a bathroom stall on her first day of work. Then, in case after case, she'd proven the value of her forensic virtual reality simulations. She'd been in horrifying situations and come out on top, if not completely unscathed. Even more significant to her were the acceptance she'd gained from her team members and the nascent love she felt for one of them.

Schultz answered his cellphone, and it was clear right away that it wasn't a social call. It irritated PJ that she regularly got news second-hand from a subordinate because she wasn't as plugged into the police pipeline as the rest of her team. Shouldn't whoever was on the other end of that call be talking to her? The silent phone on her desk said it all.

To derail those thoughts, PJ refreshed her coffee, even though her mug was half-full. She was out of creamer—Dave practically ate the stuff. She wondered what would happen if she bought individual packets. He'd probably rip open dozens of them. Sarcasm didn't work on him either—she'd tried. PJ had been driven to buying the stuff at a warehouse club. The sugar had been disappearing at an alarming rate, too.

After waiting for a few minutes as Schultz listened and interspersed a few "yeahs" and "no shits" on his end, she was getting impatient. Something that was said caused him to raise his eyebrows, and she wondered what that could be. She tapped her pencil rapidly on her desk, drawing a frown from Schultz. Anita's eyes were closed. PJ wondered if the woman could fall asleep that fast. At last, Schultz folded his cell. With that nearly imperceptible sound, Anita's eyes popped open and she was as attentive as ever.

Handy trick. She must be able to take twenty naps a day.

Schultz sat back in his metal folding chair—upholstered chairs for her office were perpetually on order—and puckered his lips. Her pencil resumed its *tap tap tap,* but he waited until he'd collected his thoughts.

"As far as ID goes," Schultz said, "there's been a missing persons report just filed that generally matches this man physically. Guy named Arlan Merrett was supposed to be looking over some business deals in Chicago since last Wednesday. His wife got home from Kansas City this morning. She expected him to have gotten home Saturday night, but he wasn't there. She checked his hotel and he never showed up. Never kept his appointments, either, according to a couple of pissed-off clients. She says he's never done anything like this and there has to be something wrong."

"Any chance he just ran out on the marriage?" Anita said.

"Not according to June Merrett, his wife. She says they were happily married. 'Ask anybody,' she says, 'they'll tell you.' Of course, wives always say that shit."

"He's out of town for several days and she never tries to call him at his hotel, not even once?" PJ asked.

Schultz's right shoulder went up in what passed for a

shrug but looked more like a muscle spasm. The twisting motion pulled his worn leather jacket, already gaping slightly across his belly, far enough apart that she cringed, expecting to be hit with a flying button. They all held.

"Some people aren't clinging vines," he said. "They can be out of each other's sight and not freak out."

"This whole business of the Missing Persons report falling in our laps just when we need it seems way too convenient."

"I'll take any coincidence I can get. There's probably a shitload of homicides out there that get solved because the killer gets a parking ticket or something."

"Or maybe the wife didn't try to contact Arlan because she wanted time for some hanky-panky of her own," Anita said. "What about this trip to K.C.?"

"Shopping at Country Club Plaza," Schultz said. "Mrs. Merrett likes the Christmas lights. Went to some kind of conference while she was there, she says."

"Lots of hotels around there," Anita said. "Wifey will play while hubby's away."

"We're getting ahead of ourselves, aren't we? We don't even know if the victim is Arlan Merrett," PJ said.

Schultz waved his hand dismissively. "A patrol car's picking her up now. She's coming in for identification."

PJ imagined a cheerful woman, arms filled with Christmas gifts from a pleasant shopping excursion, fresh from hearing motivational speakers at a conference, coming home to an empty house. Not too worried at first, figuring her husband just got delayed on a business trip. Then in a matter of hours, she's on her way to the morgue. PJ's heart went out to June, if that was her Arlan who'd been bounced up a slope on a gurney. She allowed herself to slide into June's despair, just a little.

Her pencil snapped in two.

"Easy, Doc," Schultz said. "That's city property."

Dave came in, cold air hitching a ride in the crevices of his coat, bringing a bit of winter to PJ's stuffy basement office.

"No blood on the street, but there was some on the cobblestones, not a lot, in a pattern that indicates the body was rolled," he said. "You know, like a tire with a patch of mud on it that leaves an intermittent track as it spins around."

PJ caught Dave up on the development with June Merrett.

"How is she going to identify him for certain?" he asked. "The guy's face has got to be hard to recognize."

"That's where things get interesting," Schultz said. "The clincher might be a scar he has on his back, high on the left shoulder, same place we saw one when the ME turned the body. That is, those of us who were here when the ME arrived saw the scar," Schultz said, keeping his eyes away from PJ, the object of his scorn. "The wife says a horse kicked him. We'll know after the autopsy. She's got a photo of the scar."

"What, she has a scar scrapbook or something?" Dave said. "Sounds fishy to me."

"Yeah. Of course, we could be looking for a jilted male lover," Schultz said. "Hell hath no fury like a woman scorned, and I don't think it matters what sex that woman is."

PJ noticed him looking pointedly at her—*Huh?*—and gave him a shrug of her own. None of her buttons shot across the room, although the extra twenty pounds on her frame tried their collective best.

"Hey!" Anita said. "What about a sex change operation gone really, really bad? Bad enough that the so-called surgeon got rid of all traces of the botched work, and the patient, too?"

"There could be something to that," PJ said. "There are known cases of transgendered people who didn't make it through the rigorous pre-surgical program at clinics. Driven to change, they'd do anything for sex reassignment surgery—even put their lives in the hands of an amateur."

"Shit," Schultz said. "So they got a few inches of dick they don't want. Maybe I should do a little Dumpster diving behind one of those clinics, check out the leftovers. Hell, I can sew on a button. I oughtta be able to sew on a dick."

That's it. That's absolutely it. What exactly do I see in this guy?

PJ smacked her hand down on the desk, rattling her Mickey Mouse clock. Her hand smarted a little, but it was a righteous pain. "Leo, that has to be the most insensitive and crude thing you've ever said."

"Amen, sister," Anita said.

The office door swung open a foot, and Lieutenant Howard Wall, PJ's boss, made one of his lightning appearances. His face poked through the opening. If he'd tried to squeeze the rest of himself in, the contents of the office would be at critical mass.

"The scar matches. Plus June Merrett ID'd her husband at the morgue. Claimed she recognized his eyes," Wall said, with a roll of his own. "ME wants another source of ID, but her word will do until we get dental records. Mrs. Merrett seemed subdued when she saw her husband, a lot less heated up than she was acting earlier. Then it hits 'em about three in the morning, and they fall apart." The door quickly closed, leaving PJ's mouth open. She'd been about to give Schultz a scathing lecture.

"Catching flies, Doc?" Schultz said.

"Play nice, kids," Dave interrupted, before she could respond. "What's the matter with you two lately, anyway?"

PJ felt heat on her cheeks and hoped the blush wasn't too obvious. As a psychologist, she should know better than to let Schultz get under her skin, especially in her work environment.

There *was* something wrong between them. Meanwhile, though, the sex was great. Schultz had hidden talents.

PJ cleared her throat. "That was a remarkably fast ID. Doesn't it seem like June Merrett was anxious to have her husband declared dead?"

"So she could take center stage with lover-boy?" Anita asked. "I mean, really, a scar photo?"

"So if it turns out to be Scarman, where's he been for four days?" PJ asked.

"He might have been killed right away and stashed someplace cool to slow down decay," Anita said. "Or maybe he really was alive all that time, and the killer took four days to do that damage."

The conversation fizzled as everyone considered what Anita said. PJ tried not to turn her vivid imagination loose on what could have happened to Scarman during four days of captivity.

"I don't think he was killed immediately," PJ said. "I noticed enough stubble on his chin that I think he's been alive for a few days without shaving."

"Maybe, maybe not," Anita said. "The skin shrinks after death and exposes more of the hair shaft that was buried in it. So hair appears longer, especially in the beard area, but there hasn't been any real growth."

Noises from the men's room across the hall intruded. Four people in the converted utility closet that served as PJ's office overtaxed the space's air handling capability. There was a layer of cold, uncirculated air at floor level. Starting about knee height, the temperature gradually increased. At the level of her face, it was enough to bead sweat at her hairline. She hated to think how hot it was at the ceiling. Smells were trapped at different levels, too. Doughnuts past their prime—long past. Stale coats tossed on a folding chair in the corner.

Mud and something else of questionable origin on Dave's shoes. Remnants of sausage biscuits imported from Millie's Diner by Schultz. On the positive side, there was a clean soap and herbal shampoo smell drifting over from Anita's spot.

PJ wished she could say the same for herself. She'd gotten up, tossed cold water on her face, thrown on yesterday's clothes, left a note for her fourteen-year-old son Thomas, and yes, fed the cat before leaving. She was suddenly conscious that others would be picking up the room's odorous mix, and she might be a contributor to it.

"Flip on that fan, would you?" she said to Dave.

"Officer Leeds had something to say about that scar business," Schultz said.

So that's who was on the phone. The buddy network. She was relieved that her boss hadn't bypassed her in favor of Schultz.

"He was there with Wall at the morgue. Mrs. Merrett said they had taken pictures of each other's bodies, all over. They'd have a little champagne, then take turns flipping through the photo albums, paint melted chocolate on whatever part showed up in the picture, and lick it off."

"She actually told Wall that?" Anita said.

"Scout's honor. How about that, Doc?"

"Not too surprising," she said. "Lots of couples have sex rituals that get them in the mood. In some cases, the ritual becomes so much a part of the act they might have trouble separating one from the other."

"Shovel on the shrink talk. Transgendered. Sex rituals."

She narrowed her eyes at Schultz, but he was unfazed.

"Get this. Mrs. Merrett offered to show the rest of the photos to the lead detective in the case. Wall told her that would be me, Dee-tective Leo Schultz. You think she's gonna come on to me?" Schultz said.

Dave burst out laughing.

"Hey, is that so funny? I hear she's not a bad-looking broad." Schultz ran his hand over the top of his head, a gesture left over from when there was some hair there to smooth.

Dave said, "Take along a camera. She'll probably want to get started on a new album."

"Damn straight."

"Could we get off this subject? Schultz, you and Dave get with Missing Persons and see what information they've got on Arlan Merrett. Also, check out the results of the door-to-door in that hotel and see if any witnesses have turned up. Anita and I will take on June and her body photos. Come back to my office when you're done. Wall's going to want an update. After that, I'll want to get started on some simulations."

"No fair about the photos," Schultz said. "June asked for me first."

Chapter 4

Schultz swung the door closed with a satisfying bang on his way out and headed off down the hall without a word to the others. Talking things over was useful—sometimes—but he needed time to process his own thoughts. He had a little time before meeting up with Dave, who was going to make the calls to check on possible hotel witnesses.

PJ sometimes complained about her office, but at least it was better than his situation. Three decades of mostly-devoted work and he didn't have an office to call his own. Maybe if he'd gone the administrative route, he'd be sitting in an office with a view of the Arch or at least the parking lot of the Municipal Courts Building. His work area was in a large room, desks bumped edge to edge, and there was no privacy. Worst of all, he shared his desk with a detective who usually worked nights. The man's name was Samuel Vinnert, but his strong southern accent and good-looking ass—or so the women said—tagged him as Rhett Buttler, with two t's.

Rhett accused Schultz of getting the whole "Buttler" thing started, which was true. It was his way of retaliating because Rhett left behind the scent of his aftershave on everything he touched on the desk.

Schultz settled into a wooden swivel chair that was a tight fit. There were shaped indentations in the seat for someone's posterior, but that someone wasn't Schultz. The chair screeched whenever it swiveled, discouraging use of that function. Each man who shared the desk had a drawer reserved for his exclusive use. There were no locks, so it was done by the honor system.

Yanking open his private desk drawer, he checked his box

of Little Debbie Zebra Cakes. Sure enough, one cellophane-wrapped package was gone. It was a classic example of Locard's Exchange Principal: "When two objects come in contact with each other they exchange trace evidence." Rhett left aftershave and took Zebra Cakes.

Morally freed by the man's transgression, Schultz opened Rhett's private drawer and pawed through the magazines.

Crap. Nothing new. What's a guy to do when he has to take a dump?

He slammed the drawer loud enough to draw the stares of the younger detectives in the room.

"Nothing to see here. Go back to your petty feuds and back-stabbing."

At the age of fifty-five, Schultz was a dinosaur to the up-and-coming, who wanted little to do with him.

CHIP swept all that away. He worked with a team where his contribution was appreciated and nobody patronized him as though experience equated to obsolescence.

He closed his eyes and let the images of the morning's events flow across the screen behind his eyelids. Schultz had a way of working that presented a logical front, but on the inside, he relied on hunches taken one step further: he was often able to sense a connection between himself and the killer he sought. He pictured it as a shining cord making its way from him toward a sinister, unknown destination. Each hunch he made, each fact he gathered, extended that golden cord out further into the darkness until one final connection made the cord shoot forward like an arrow straight through the killer's heart. Then all Schultz had to do was slide along the cord and he would land in a vat of evil masquerading as a human.

He told himself it was only a visualization of detecting techniques, but he knew there was more to it.

He tested the cord and found it coiled near his heart. Nothing to go on yet, so he reviewed the morning's events.

Driving downtown, mind clear, ready to work. Swirling fog, then the first glimpse of the body.

As he got closer, he could see that the body was male, muscular, with well-developed arms and chest, trim waist, and a washboard abdomen. The raw flesh where the genitals used to be raised gooseflesh on his arms and made his own balls crawl up a little higher in their sacs. The face was a mess from the eyes down. Fingers that at first glance appeared to be painted with red nail polish turned out to be missing the tips of the phalanges.

The killer trying to eradicate fingerprints to slow identification? The torn face could have resulted from a clumsy attempt to remove the teeth to prevent comparison with dental records.

Sitting at his desk in the overheated room, Schultz felt a chill of the heart.

He pulled a notebook from his back pocket and flipped it open to a clean page. He sketched a timeline and jotted down questions as he thought of them.

A rage killer who had the presence of mind to cover his tracks by making the body hard to identify?

Unless what appears to be a rage killing was cold and deliberate.

The wife's bullshit about licking chocolate—why wave that scar photo around if she was the one who tried to make the body hard to identify with specific mutilations? *Another piece that didn't fit.*

And another: where had Arlan Merrett been for the four days before he turned up on the levee?

"Looking good, Ernestine," Schultz said. He'd taken a walk over to Missing Persons to exert a little personal charm and make sure he got his hands on everything they had about Arlan Merrett. He was dismayed to see that Ernestine Bradlock was on duty, but it was too late to back out. She'd already seen him.

"Uh, huh, where's that book you borrowed?"

Shit. She remembered. He'd borrowed an expensive textbook from a forensic science class from her.

"Still reading it."

"You bastard, you lost it. I just know it. You've been avoiding me."

"I . . ."

"That book cost a hundred and ten dollars and you're going to pay every fucking penny of it."

"Hey, if I could just get a word in here," Schultz said. He leaned heavily on the corner of her desk. Most people would have shrunk back, but Ernestine held her ground. She'd worked in the Department of Corrections for fifteen years, until her back went out. A desk job hadn't sweetened her disposition. She was solidly built and could probably arm-wrestle Schultz to a draw. Even the short frizz of gray hair that topped her elegantly shaped head broadcast, "Don't mess with me."

"Get off my desk," she said. "Never know where those hands of yours have been. Somewhere filthy, no doubt."

"I lost the book, okay? I lost it. You happy now?"

"You're a careless son-of-a-bitch and a liar on top of that. Probably never read a page of that book."

True.

"I was halfway through with it. Look, I'm sorry. I'll pay you out of my next check."

"Fine." She flashed him a smile that was anything but welcoming. He recognized it because he saw one just like it frequently in the mirror. "Now, can I help you?"

Yeah, like a snake can help a mouse.

"I'm working on the riverfront homicide," Schultz said.

"Oh, the guy with no dick? Arlan Merrett? Don't see that every day. Whoever did it must've hated that man's guts."

"Thanks for the insight."

She pursed her lips, wrinkling the fine hairs of a barely-noticeable moustache, trying to decide if a retort was worth it. Schultz was spared. "If you hang around for a few minutes, I'll get you a copy of his file. I have to make a phone call first."

The phone call turned out to be making hotel reservations through a travel agency. She didn't try to hide the fact that her vacation plans took priority over his legitimate work request. Schultz kept his face neutral, but wondered what a woman like her did in Cancún, anyway.

Spend my money, I guess.

Ten minutes later, he was on his way back to his desk, a plump manila folder in his hand, and it had only cost him a hundred and ten bucks and downing a slice of humble pie.

When he got back to his desk, Dave was already there. He'd pulled up a chair and was looking over Schultz's notes.

"Remind me not to leave my diary out where you can get to it," Schultz said.

"There's nothing in your diary that I'd be interested in reading," Dave said.

"How do you know? There's some hot shit in there. Anyway, I got this file on Merrett. They love me over in Missing Persons."

Dave snorted derisively. "Didn't you borrow something from Ernestine? That woman probably hasn't forgotten her 1976 grocery lists."

Schultz slapped the file on the desk, ignoring his comment. "I'll take the front half," he said. He studied the photos Mrs. Merrett had provided, which included a couple of vacation shots with the two of them. Typical tourist photos, the happy couple in front of Old Faithful and in a tropical bar, sharing a drink from a coconut that had sprouted two straws. Seeing them together, he would have to say that based purely on looks, it seemed that Mrs. Merrett had married up.

They worked in silence for a time, as though Schultz's desk had a bubble around it that filtered out the noise and general commotion in the room.

Schultz came up for air fifteen minutes later. "White male, six feet two inches, two hundred pounds, thirty-nine years old, muscular, brown hair, brown eyes. Routinely jogs a fixed route at six in the morning seven days a week and works out with weights at a gym four days a week with a varied schedule. Born in Lawrence, Kansas, parents middle class, divorced when he was eighteen. Formed his company, Green Vista Properties, in 1996. The company renovates homes in marginal areas of the city."

"I have more info on that company," Dave said. "Profits were off the last few years. Merrett took on a partner last year, Fredericka Chase. She brought in an infusion of cash and some new ideas. Green Vista was one of the first to latch onto the loft district along Washington Avenue downtown, and they settled into renovating for the upscale market, half a million dollars plus. Lately Arlan did a lot of traveling, looking into taking the idea to other cities."

Schultz whistled. "I suppose June Merrett inherits her husband's share of the partnership."

"Nope. Fredericka gets it all, net worth about four million."

They mulled that unexpected bit of information over.

"Fredericka's dripping motive with that sole ownership of Green Vista. June might have motive if there's a lover lurking," Dave said. "Think either of those women could maneuver that solidly-built victim around?"

"June's less than average height and I'll bet her only exercise is opening her mouth," Schultz said. "Probably no powerhouse. What about Fredericka? I'm getting an image of a Swedish masseuse with biceps like pythons that just ate, the kind of woman you don't mess with if you know what's good for you."

Dave shuffled the papers spread out on the desk. "Says here she's five feet two inches, a hundred and two pounds."

"Oh, great," Schultz said. "Couple of suspects who probably can't lift a salt shaker between 'em. What say we visit Fredericka and see how she's taking the news?"

"We're supposed to get back to Doc's office," Dave said.

"Do you always do everything you're told?"

Chapter 5

June Merrett lived on Utah Place in southwest St. Louis, in the Tower Grove Heights neighborhood. The home was Victorian, about a hundred years old. Bare tree branches left shadows like forked lightening across the front walkway.

When PJ and Anita pulled up, a patrol car was just leaving. PJ remembered that someone had driven June home from the morgue. Anita rolled down the window so she could talk to the officer.

"Hey, Santo, how's the little one?" Anita said. "Fedelia, is it?"

"Fedelia's sleeping through the night now. The last four months have been living hell. I wanted to take nights just to get the fuck out of there, but I knew Inés would kill me."

"Yeah, you had that look the last time I saw you. Ready to spit nails but sticking it out to be nice to the wife."

"You got any pictures?"

Santo's face split into a wide smile. "Sure, got 'em right here."

Anita flipped through a pocket-sized baby book, making all the right noises, then handed the book back. "How's she taking it?" she said, with a jerk of her head toward the house.

"Like a drama queen. Hand-wringing, soggy tissues, the whole bit."

"Well, whaddya know. Wall said she was more like the ice queen. See ya," Anita said. Santo drove off, after a little nod of acknowledgement in PJ's direction.

"So now I'm the invisible woman," PJ said.

"He doesn't know what to say, you being a shrink."

PJ let it pass. Usually she got that kind of reaction from old cops, not the young ones. Stepping out of the car, she noticed there was a faint buzz of traffic from South Grand, but the home didn't seem part of that world. PJ half expected to see a horse-drawn carriage round the corner.

The two women shifted so that Anita was in front, PJ to the side and slightly behind. It was Anita who carried the detective's badge, and besides, she looked more presentable than a rumpled PJ.

On the walkway, PJ had the feeling the shadows of the tree branches were impaling her, pinning her like a butterfly.

If I were Schultz, with all his portents and hunches, I'd be a little worried right about now.

Anita rang the bell.

Fortunately, I am a cool-headed woman of science.

Mellow Westminster chimes brought June to the door. She was wearing a flowing red silk robe with a tie loosely knotted at her waist. Her face was bare of makeup. Her features appeared tugged downward by grief, but it could just as easily have been worry or simply fatigue. Red-rimmed, puffy eyes seemed to tower over the lower half of her face, which trailed off with narrow lips and the tip of a small chin. Light brown hair fell straight to her shoulders. There were no slippers on her wide, ungainly feet. Her effort at a smile of greeting fell short.

In spite of her current appearance, PJ could tell that June was an attractive woman, certainly better than average looking. Her body was half of an hourglass, the top half. Below the waist, her curves flattened out. She reminded PJ of a lollipop: a thin stick with a round top.

Anita introduced herself and then "Dr. Gray, departmental consulting psychologist."

"I wasn't expecting anyone so soon," June said. "I just got

home from that awful place and I thought I'd lie down for awhile."

"We'll just be a few minutes, Mrs. Merrett," Anita said. "I'm sorry for your loss."

June hung her head, almost like the strings holding it up had been cut. "It's been such a shock. I suppose you can come in, then. Where's that nice lieutenant, what was his name?"

"Lieutenant Wall, ma'am. He's working on other aspects of the case."

"Please don't call me ma'am. Makes me feel old. Arlan started teasing me after I hit the big three-oh." Her eyes suddenly glistened. "Anyway, call me June."

"I'm Anita and this is Penelope." Anita offered her hand, but June was already retreating into the living room, leaving them to follow her.

The room had a cove ceiling, with lace curtains that cascaded from their rods and pooled at the base of tall, sparkling windows. The furniture was an eclectic selection, arranged so that there were two distinct areas. The area at the far end of the room near the fireplace had a sparse, masculine look to it, with a worn leather chair next to a reading lamp and built-in bookcases flanking a brick fireplace.

Near the door, the pieces were crowded close together. Occasional tables held collections of ceramic birds and a glass display cabinet on the wall contained more thimbles than PJ knew existed. There were three clocks spaced around the area so that wherever a person sat, the time was instantly available. There were no clocks near the leather chair at the far end.

Zoned living.

June settled into an antique Queen Anne chair with polished walnut arms and upholstery that looked like the original floral needlework. She pulled her red robe tightly around her and crossed her arms across her chest, a defensive body posture if ever there was one. PJ cautiously lowered herself into the facing chair, which was covered in yellow velvet. Anita, apparently not willing to risk sitting in a three-hundred-year-old chair, sat on a nearby contemporary loveseat.

Two large oil portraits hung on the wall opposite the windows. June and Arlan Merrett, locked in separate frames.

A metaphor for the marriage?

Arlan's was draped in black. PJ wondered when June had time to do that, and whether she kept funeral drape as a household staple.

June followed her gaze. "Handsome, isn't he?"

The portrait showed a man with all the right features, but somehow they didn't add up to handsome. The eyes seemed no more alive with humanity than the ones she'd seen that morning at the levee. She dismissed the thought, assuming that the artist wasn't up to the task.

"Yes, very," PJ said. She wanted June to do the talking, hopefully of the loose lips variety. "How did the two of you meet?"

June smiled, and her face relaxed into a natural pose that PJ suspected wasn't seen too often. She looked serene. Only June's reddened eyes gave away her new status as a widow. "We met on a cruise to the Bahamas. Would you believe it? Six days and five glorious nights. We came back engaged. That was eight years ago, and it's been a very happy marriage since then."

Anita, who seemed to be counting thimbles, seemed content to let PJ keep the conversation going.

"A celebration cruise?"

"Hardly," June said. The smile dropped away, and it seemed like gravity was operating at double strength on her face. "My parents had died three months earlier. Father was a pilot, a good one, but his small plane went down in bad weather. They were going to Jefferson City to raise money for some politician. It was very oppressive around here after their funeral. My older sister May took the situation very hard. I had to get away for awhile. You know, take a mental health break, if only for a few days."

I could use one of those myself. Or a string of them. PJ needed some time to think about her relationship with Schultz. For the past couple of months, they'd been living together part time at her house, but she still didn't know what she thought about that. Her son Thomas had taken to Schultz, although not from the first, and the two had a strong bond. She was the one with reservations. It seemed like she needed more space than he did. There'd been conflict over that recently, and flashes of anger, like the mood Schultz had been in earlier.

"You weren't close to your parents, then?"

"Oh, I didn't mean that. It's just that I've always been better at coping with things. More practical, I guess."

"Tell me about Arlan," PJ said. "Let's start with what he did for a living."

"Arlan's a brilliant real estate developer. He's a step ahead of everyone, always seems to know what's going to be hot next. His company, Green Vista, did the first conversions in the Loft District." Some enthusiasm had crept into her voice. "He's been doing so well lately that we were planning to trade up our house. We can afford a lot more than the half a million we paid for this place when we were first married." She gestured around her, with a vaguely disdainful look.

Let's see, I could probably fit my house in here five times over.

PJ thought it was odd that June ventured into personal

things like the price of her house, given the circumstances. The woman's moods seemed to be all over the place. She was persistent in talking about her dead husband in the present tense, as though he would be walking through the front door any minute, which didn't gel with the reddened eyes. What had the officer said when he was leaving?

Drama queen.

"So he was a successful businessman. Did you work outside the home, June?"

"Oh, no, Arlan insists I stay home. We're old-fashioned that way. I do a little volunteer work at the city library."

June stopped and looked down at her hands, which were busily moving in her lap, rotating her right hand around her left thumb. As though she'd just found out what her hands were doing, she stopped the motion and folded them together in her lap, right hand resting lightly across her left palm.

Good little girl. Remember your ladylike behavior!

PJ let the silence stretch, an auditory elastic band. Anita sat placidly, her eyes having moved from the thimbles and found a comfortable resting place on the oil portraits of the lord of the house and his lady.

"Arlan's a very happy man, happy with his marriage and with life in general." June continued as though she'd rewound to the point conversation faltered and was recording over the gap. "He brings me gifts for no reason at all, flowers or a bracelet."

"Did the two of you have children?"

June's nostrils flared and her lips collapsed into a thin line.

Uh, oh, sensitive territory.

"We aren't ready yet," June said. "We're still enjoying our life as a couple. There'll be time for that. Being thirty years old isn't the barrier it used to be."

This is getting downright spooky. She's still planning a family

41

with him? Frozen sperm or something?

PJ decided to see how deep the denial went. "I guess a family isn't in the future, since Arlan's dead."

June blinked. "I know that. Of course he's dead. That's why you're here, isn't it? Listen, I'm really tired now. Could I finish this up with you later?"

Anita cleared her throat. The soft questioning was at an end.

"We'll be leaving soon," Anita said. "I have some questions I need to ask. Just doing my job. When was the last time you saw Arlan?"

"We had breakfast together last Wednesday, about eight o'clock. I made my special blueberry topping and he made Belgian waffles. That's the kind of thing we liked to do. After that, I left for Kansas City to attend a workshop on storytelling. Volunteer work at the library, you know? I attended all the sessions and picked up a lot of tips. I did some shopping, too. Anyway, Arlan was supposed to leave later that afternoon to meet some clients in Chicago, but he never showed up. I left K.C. before dawn for the drive home. I'm an early riser, drives Arlan crazy. When I got home, the house was empty. I told all this to Lieutenant Wall. I gave him my hotel receipt and a couple of receipts from buying gas. I got a speeding ticket on my way home. I was listening to one of the tapes I bought at the workshop, and I must have lost track of how fast I was going. He said he would check it out. I guess that's my alibi, right?"

Anita nodded. "Do you know of any enemies Arlan had?"

June took her time and seemed to be genuinely considering the question. "I'm sure he's irritated others, because you can't get where he did in the real estate business without doing that. You know, people he aced out on a property deal or something. But hate him enough to kill him? I just can't see that."

"Was he involved in an affair with a woman?" Anita said. "Or a man?"

June seemed completely taken aback at the suggestion. Whether it was for the affair itself or the suggestion of a male partner, PJ couldn't tell.

"No, of course not. We have a very satisfying sex life. Arlan is a very physical man, proud of his body. I mentioned that to Lieutenant Wall." She retrieved an album from one of the occasional tables. "I got the album out this morning. We have this little thing we like to do before we have sex. Like foreplay."

When June opened the album across her lap, PJ was treated to an upside-down view of a man's chest, small nipples marking the sides of the eight by ten photo.

A ragged, softball-sized chunk had been removed from his chest, directly over his heart.

"There are matching photos. We each have a paintbrush," June said. "And a bowl of melted chocolate." She flipped to the next page, which revealed a photo of a woman's breasts, nipples hardened with arousal. "Everything from the neck down. It was Arlan's idea originally. He's so creative."

"We get the idea," PJ said. "Wall already explained it to us."

"Oh, so you understand."

Sort of.

June thumbed through the pages rapidly. Glimpses of bared skin flashed by, as in one of those flip-the-pages books that gave the impression of movement. This one was a body tour, though. An intimate one.

She stopped at an empty page. "Here's where the scar picture was. Left shoulder, on his back."

"We're going to have to take that album with us," Anita said briskly, as though she confiscated pictures like this from widows every day. "You mentioned a sister earlier, your older sister May."

"Yes. I'm sure you'll want to talk to her. May Simmons," June said, and went on to give her address and phone number. Then she lowered her voice conspiratorially. "May's a wonderful woman, and I would hate to give the wrong impression, but I have to mention that she's jealous of Arlan and me. Oh, I don't mean financially or anything like that. She just envied our love for each other. I've seen the way she looks at Arlan. Anybody can see what a handsome man he is. You noticed it right away," she said, jabbing her finger at PJ. "Her husband Frank isn't a dynamo in bed. She's said so herself. May's probably on the lookout, if you know what I mean."

"If May was interested in stealing away your husband," PJ said, "why would she kill him?"

"If she came onto him, he would've turned her down cold. You know that saying about a woman scorned."

It was the second time that day the saying had come up. One of Schultz's hunches in action?

"One last thing, June," Anita said. "Did you notice any unusual behavior recently? Secretiveness, phone calls at odd times?"

"He was being a bit secretive. But it's just because he's such a romantic. Today's our wedding anniversary, and I just know he's got a present hidden somewhere in the house."

Anita gathered up the album, thanked June for her time, and again expressed sympathy. She also asked if she could return shortly with the ETU, the Evidence Technician Unit, and go through the house.

"Arlan and I don't have anything to hide. You have my permission. I hope I can get a little sleep, though."

June walked them to the door and closed it firmly behind them.

Out on the sidewalk, Anita said, "Holy shit! What do you make of that piece of work?"

"I'll let you know if and when I figure the piece of work out."

The ETU van pulled up as they were walking to their car. Anita bagged the photo album she'd confiscated, turned around, and headed for the front door again. PJ felt a little embarrassed holding the large paper bag containing the album, like she was hiding dirty pictures in a brown bag to sneak a peak at recess.

It looked like June wasn't going to get her nap anytime soon.

Chapter 6

Schultz drove his reddish-orange Pacer along in silence, listening to Dave Whitmore talk about the case and struggle along the same twisting thought paths Schultz had just been down.

"Some of this doesn't make sense," Dave said.

"Only some? I hate these wacko cutup jobs. Gimme a straightforward execution-style shooting, I say. That I can wrap my mind around."

"Hasn't working with Doc rubbed off on you at all? We do the sophisticated stuff," Dave said.

"Lots of sophistication's rubbed off on me. Looky here, I have an air freshener." He spun the little green tree by snapping it with his finger. PJ had complained that his department-assigned vehicle didn't smell good. Probably had something to do with that drunken informant upchucking in the back seat last month. Schultz wasn't particular about the lifestyles of his sources if they told him what he needed to know.

Did I ever clean that up?

Dave folded his arms across his chest and clammed up for the rest of the trip. Someone else might have looked inscrutable, but Witless—a play on his last name—looked like a teddy bear that didn't want to go to the tea party.

They headed for Fredericka Chase's residence. She lived in one of the lofts that had been remodeled by Green Vista. The neighborhood had an on the go feeling to it, with people out walking in spite of the December chill. Cheeks reddened, cheerful voices calling out to neighbors, children gamboling at their parents' sides—it looked like Santa's Christmas Land to Schultz, minus the deep snow. Sunlight filtered down through high clouds that were rapidly dissipating, like the morning fog. Or maybe they *were* the morning's fog, raised to heavenly heights. There were wreaths everywhere, and the scent of pine made it seem like the entire district had been doused in toilet bowl cleaner.

Most of the buildings had been converted already, but there were a sprinkling of boarded-up ones that served as a reminder of the neighborhood's recent past.

Schultz groaned when he saw that her place was on the third floor. Arthritis made him reluctant to climb stairs unless necessary, plus his foot was hurting from the morning's stroll along the cobblestones. It had been months since the bones in his left foot were shattered by a bullet, but it still ached. He imagined he could feel the coldness in every one of the screws holding his foot together.

He commandeered the freight elevator from a disapproving janitor who thought he had the place all to himself on a Sunday morning, and rode up. The elevator space was about ten by ten, with a wooden floor roughened by decades of dragging heavy items over it. Schultz closed the bars and flipped the impressive lever to the "Up" position, denoted by a nearly worn off "p" on the controls. The "U" looked as though it had been whacked off with an ax.

Dave followed him into the old elevator and kept his eyes down. He was either trying to decipher the graffiti carved into the wooden floor or carefully keeping his eyes from roaming the walls looking for an inspection certificate.

"It's okay," Schultz said. "All we have to do if the elevator breaks loose is jump up in the air right before it hits bottom."

"I thought that was one of those urban legends. You don't really believe that, do you?"

"Nah," Schultz said, "but I thought it might make you feel better. Ah, here we are." Schultz pushed the lever, and the elevator shuddered to a stop about two feet below floor level. "You first."

Dave hauled himself up, tearing the cuff of his pants in the process, and turned around to offer Schultz a hand. Schultz worked the control lever forward and back, bringing the elevator up level with the floor, and strolled out. Dave kept his face straight but there was a little twitch near his left eye.

The freight elevator opened into a storage room filled with old fixtures that had been ripped out during the remodeling. Schultz passed an old cast iron bathtub with claw feet that sparked a memory of the first apartment he'd had after getting married, of making love with his wife in a tub just like that, tasting the soap on her skin, rivulets of water dripping from her hair onto his chest. Thirty years ago, and he could smell the Ivory.

Maybe June Merrett isn't so far out of line with that chocolate business after all.

PJ had a tub like that in her house. All he had to do was turn off the cellphones and get her in it. Their slippery bodies moving against each other, her little *yip* of excitement when he gently bit her nipple, the rounded, solid feel of her everywhere he put his hands . . .

Good thing Schultz had his back to Dave. Little Elvis was ready to leave the building.

He opened the storage room door and found himself looking down a hallway with matted blue carpeting and several doors in various shades of green. A window at the end of the hall, streaked with settled tobacco smoke, dimmed the sunlight to a sallow haze. The pungent odor of stale urine rose from the carpet, which felt unclean all the way through his shoes.

Schultz halted. His stomach had gone south and his heart was knocking at the back of his throat. His hard-on deflated.

A man's body was fastened in a sitting position in the chair with leather straps at the wrists, ankles, and around the chest. He was naked. His mouth was taped, and there was crusty dried blood on his chin that had dribbled out from underneath the tape. Patches of skin had begun to slide.

His son died in a place like this, a hallway much like this leading to the room where Rick Schultz was executed in a homemade gas chamber. Everything was the same, even the grimy window at the far end of the hall that had caught Schultz's eye before the image of his dead son was imprinted on his soul.

Dave nearly bumped into his back. "Hey," he said. "What's wrong? See anything?"

Yeah, you might say that.

"Nothing," Schultz said. "The piss smell took me by surprise. I thought this was supposed to be a classy place, half a million bucks."

"Bad janitor," Dave said. Schultz nodded. The joke wasn't half-bad, considering it came from Witless.

Striding down the hall, Schultz noticed none of the doors had numbers on them. Fredericka's address was number ten, and there weren't even ten doors. He was sure she lived on the top floor. Had he gotten the wrong building? He went all the way to the window and turned around. On his way back, he noticed that one of the doors had a peephole, just the thing a new tenant would install. He knocked on the door authoritatively.

"Police."

"One minute, please," came the answer. It seemed to come from right behind the door. He wondered if Fredericka had heard the freight elevator and was nervously checking the peephole. A woman living alone in this building had a right to be cautious.

The door slid open a crack, held in place by the stoutest door chain Schultz had ever seen.

"Police, here to see Fredericka Chase."

"ID, please."

Damn if she isn't polite while being suspicious.

He held his badge up to the narrow opening, moving it slowly across since she could only see a slice of it at a time. She waited for the full Panavision effect.

"Is there someone else with you?"

Schultz shot a glance at Dave, whose raised eyebrows looked like twin frowns. He held out his hand and Dave passed him his badge. He did the Panavision thing again.

The door closed and reopened without the chain. "Come in."

Stepping over the threshold, Schultz was bombarded with sensations. The space was as big as an airplane hangar, with a few columns scattered through it that Schultz hoped were adequate to support the high ceiling. Dozens of small, high-intensity lights hung from tracks that snaked over exposed ducts gleaming with a silver coating. Light from windows twelve feet high bounced from wall to wall, so that the very air seemed soaked with it. The wood floor must have required the sacrifice of a small forest.

A kitchen occupied one corner, all steel and glass, with a couple of stools next to a high counter serving as the dining table. There was a bed opposite the kitchen, with its supports nearly invisible so that the mattress appeared to float. Near it was an ultramodern oval tub built for two. Schultz's fantasy with the claw-footed tub surged into his mind, and he mentally ground it out with his thumb. There didn't seem to be any place for the business portion of a bathroom.

Might account for the piss smell out in the hall.

Petite Fredericka wore even more petite, low-rise shorts

and a barely there halter-top, showing more thigh and breast than a Colonel Sanders meal. Golden curls were corralled, more or less, into a ponytail. Creamy skin, a lot of it, and cobalt blue eyes that seemed immense for her face. Curvy above and below a waist that looked like Schultz could snap it in two. She didn't look a day over nineteen, although he knew from Arlan's file that she was twenty-seven.

Freckles. She's got freckles, for Christ's sake.

There was a blotch of yellow paint on her neck, and she held a paintbrush vertically to keep it from dripping.

"You're here about Arlan, aren't you? Be right back," she said.

The view from the back was just as good as the view from the front. A small butterfly tattoo on her left hip dipped and rose as she walked.

She dumped the brush into a paint can. On the wall was a floral design, the only splash of color on the too-white walls.

Making her way back over to the detectives, she looked around as if noticing for the first time that there was no place to sit except the bed.

"Sorry for the inquisition at the door," she said. "I'm just being careful. When I came home a couple of nights ago, I thought somebody might have been in the place. It must have been my imagination working as much overtime as the rest of me. So I had the peephole put in and got a really big chain on the door."

"Did you report it?" Schultz asked. He noticed there was a little redness around her eyes, like she might have been crying recently.

"Report what?" she said. "A creepy feeling? I'm busy today, can this wait?"

"We won't take much of your time," Schultz said. Dave

was looking at the bed, realizing that it was the only place in the room to sit. Red slowly rose up his neck and headed for his cheeks. It looked as though he'd have steam coming out of his ears soon. "Just a few questions about Arlan Merrett."

Although she must have known what was coming, Fredericka melted in front of his eyes, her shoulders sagging, her eyes lowering until her chin nearly touched her chest. She appeared unsteady on her legs. He was reaching out a hand to help her when she folded and ended up on the floor with her legs crossed.

"If you don't mind, I think I'll sit down," she said.

Dave followed suit, though not nearly as gracefully, leaving Schultz in the uncomfortable position of the teacher standing in front of the class at lesson time.

He shifted to face them both. Dave looked up at him expectantly, the corners of his mouth almost imperceptibly turned up.

Getting me back for that trick with the elevator, no doubt.

"It's so awful about what happened to him," she said. "Nobody I've known has ever been murdered. I heard it on the news when I got up. Is it true he was . . . ?"

"Stabbed? This time you can believe what you heard on the news, Ms. Chase."

"Call me Freddy."

Not in this lifetime.

"Ms. Chase," Schultz said, "could you clarify for me your relationship with Arlan Merrett?"

Her mask slipped again, and under it Schultz saw an emotion he couldn't pin down. "We were business partners. I moved here from Albuquerque a couple of years ago. We connected at a developers' conference. Arlan liked my ideas for the loft district, and I liked his business sense and ability to promote. Since we got together, Green Vista has become successful on a whole new level."

Rehearsed.

"Did you see each other regularly, maybe have something going outside the office?"

"We were together a lot but we weren't sleeping together. Arlan was happily married."

"Happily married doesn't stop a lot of men. Do you know if he was having an affair?"

"Not that I'm aware of. He was old fashioned. We worked closely, even traveled together sometimes, and he never even made a pass at me." She shook her head as if she just uttered the unthinkable.

"If he wasn't interested in you, was he interested in men?"

"No."

Schultz wasn't giving up on his gay murder theory, but he couldn't dig up any evidence to support it. Yet.

"Do you know anyone who might want to harm him?"

"Oh, Arlan had the usual assortment of business rivalries. Nothing serious. Nothing worth killing a man for. I can make you a list of the main people, but I'm sure they had nothing to do with it. In this business, Detective, people who are rivals end up collaborating on some project another time. It's the way this game is played."

"I have to ask, Ms. Chase," Schultz said. "Where were you yesterday evening, say between six and nine?"

"Let's see. I got my hair cut around three, then came home and worked all evening on plans and estimates for completing the remodeling of this building. You may have noticed the hallway isn't in prime shape to take clients through. It's going to be a lobby area with a marble floor, and just two lofts up here. We're blocking off some space and making it into a couple of offices. Residents can have a home office but not have it intrude on the living space. It's one of the signatures of Green Vista, and it's going to be very popular. Portable, too."

"What do you mean portable?" Schultz said.

"Adaptable. I'm already looking into suburban applications. You know those multi-building apartment complexes, with pools and playgrounds and workout rooms? Why not convert a few of the apartments to subdivided office space? Reclaim your living space by getting that cluttered desk out of your dining room and put it into a sleek space with all the business conveniences."

"Sounds like you've got the sales brochure already written," Schultz said.

"Oh, we're pretty far along," she said. "Local zoning boards can be so picky, though. I've been dividing my time between this project," she waved her arm, vaguely taking in the entire building, "and a couple of complexes in North County. I've got an apartment out there as a convenient base."

"Big plans."

"Like I said, Green Vista is moving to a whole new level of success."

"Getting back to your activities yesterday evening. Make any phone calls? Order food delivered, that kind of thing?" Schultz said.

She shook her head. "No, sorry, I didn't realize I'd have to account for my time. I went to bed around one in the morning, I think. Alone. I slept in this morning, didn't get up until a little after eight."

"Did you know that Arlan left you his share of Green Vista?"

"Of course. It was written into the partnership agreement.

54

He said his wife was well taken care of otherwise, life insurance I guess. He thought I'd contributed enough to our success that I deserved it."

"I take it that means your half would have gone to him if you'd died first," Schultz said.

A little color showed in her cheeks. "No, I have a brother who needs long-term care, round-the-clock care. My share would have gone to my estate to pay for that. Arlan was okay with it."

"In other words, you benefit whether Arlan dies first or you do."

"You could think of it that way. We weren't quite so mercenary about it."

Dave spoke up. "When's the last time you saw your partner?"

Fredericka's head swiveled toward him, as though discovering his presence for the first time. The movement reminded Schultz of a praying mantis swiveling its triangular head, eyes locking onto lunch.

"On Wednesday," she said. "We had lunch at Jake's Steaks, in the Landing. I remember it because Arlan had a margarita, and he usually doesn't drink until evening. In fact, I don't think he drinks often at all. Too many empty calories." She patted her perfectly flat abdomen as though to protect it from the very phrase.

"So did he seem worried about something and that's why he was drinking at lunch?" Dave asked.

"He *was* worried, I think. Probably because of the clients he was driving to Chicago to meet. He gave me the impression the clients were going to be disappointed about something. I'm sure it wasn't our designs."

"He was planning to drive after drinking?"

"He only had one drink, silly." She had a musical laugh

that floated up to the high ceiling like a brightly colored balloon. "We split up about two o'clock, and I came back here to work. I assume he took off for Chicago."

Schultz noticed that Fredericka's attitude had changed when Dave started doing the questioning. A lilt in her voice. A tilt of her head. A jaunty toss of her ponytail. The weakness she'd suffered a few minutes ago had dissipated. She rocked herself sideways on her bottom so that she ended up close enough to Dave's knee that a spark could cross the distance.

Fredericka rested her hand lightly and familiarly on Dave's thigh. Beads of sweat began erupting on Dave's forehead like pimples on a teenager. No doubt he was wondering where the wandering hand would go next. Cutting off speculation, Fredericka got to her feet in a smooth motion that looked like a flower unfolding. She was clearly trying to draw the interview to a close.

"Arlan was a wonderful man," she said. "A good businessman and a good husband. An old-fashioned gentleman. I hope you find whoever did this awful thing."

Dave got up, limbs flailing around for balance. "We're doing our best," he said. "Any problem if we look around a bit?"

A fleeting frown passed over her face, a cloud blocking the sun. She hesitated.

"Arlan didn't spend much time here, and I have work to do, Detective. I have a contractor coming in first thing tomorrow morning."

"Just for a little while, Freddy," Dave said. "For our reports, you know."

Schultz didn't know that Dave could come up with such a disarming smile. Dave had certainly never used it on him.

"Well, okay. I'm getting back to work, though,"

Fredericka said. "Say, don't you need a warrant?"

The wattage of Dave's smile doubled. "Not if we have your consent. We won't take anything, though."

She pursed her lips into a kissable circle before saying yes.

Any more of this and I'll puke.

She retreated to one of the kitchen stools and set up a laptop on the counter. Like a pair of hungry lions scouring the savannah, Schultz and Dave roamed the space, taking note of everything. They discovered a pocket door that practically disappeared into the wall, and it led to an expansive room with a toilet, sink, shower, and dressing area.

"I knew she had to shit somewhere," Schultz said, once inside with the door closed. "This place is just a little too perfect, isn't it?"

Dave wasn't paying attention. He was looking at the U-shaped dressing area with one of those three-way mirrors surrounded by open shelving, hanger rods, and built-in drawers with glass fronts. All of them neatly filled. There was one small section of men's clothing, some casual outfits and a few suits. The nearby open shelving held folded men's dress shirts, socks, and boxers. Tucked below were four pairs of men's shoes, two dress and two casual. Schultz's eyebrows rose.

"Unless the lady's a cross-dresser, there's a man around the house." Dave said.

Schultz drifted over to that section and casually checked the items, which were in plain sight. "Size eighteen shirts, thirty-five inch sleeve. Arlan was a big guy, wasn't he?"

As they were leaving, Schultz asked about the presence of men's clothing. Fredericka was prepared with an answer, having seen them go into the room.

"Arlan stopped in to shower and change sometimes.

Work sites can be awfully dirty."

No doubt he needed someone to scrub his back, too. In an old-fashioned way, of course.

Chapter 7

Dear Diary,

These are things that happened to me, cross my heart and hope to die.

"Lazy bones, crazy bones," my sister chants. I press my fingers into my ears and pretend not to hear. She sees that our parents are busy in the dining room getting ready for Christmas dinner. She comes over and punches me in the stomach.

"Ow! I'm gonna tell!" I say, and my face screws up with pain. The punch is not quite hard enough to leave a bruise. Oh, no, she never leaves a bruise.

"Go ahead, crazy bones," she says. "You know they'll believe me over you. You might as well not even try. They'll punish you for telling lies again." She pinches my shoulder, hard. "You better save me your dessert and all of your cookies from the farm, or you know what will happen to you tonight."

I shiver thinking about it. I'm eight-years-old and skinny. Spaghetti legs, Mom says, spaghetti arms, all I need is some tomato sauce to make a good dinner. Mom must think that's really funny because she says it a lot.

My older sister is very strong. She can hold me down and pour salt water in my mouth, or cover my face with a pillow until I absolutely can't last another second without dying.

I hate Christmas dinner because my jerky relatives from Chicago are here. Grandpa Marshall, who gives me the creeps with his cold hands and beady eyes and I never want to be alone with him in a room again, is sick and can't travel. Maybe he'll die.

A good part about Christmas is the farm cookies. Dad picks them up every year. They come in a cardboard box tied with red string. Butter cookies shaped like reindeer, round cookies with cherries or nuts in the middle, cookies that are half-chocolate, cookies that look like half moons, gingerbread men. Mom never makes anything like that. Some old farm woman bakes them. If I'm fast enough, I can get some in my pockets before my sister sees me.

"Where's your new doll?" my sister says in her bully voice.

I close my eyes. Mom and Dad finally gave me something I want for Christmas, probably by mistake. My sister saw the happy look on my face. I wasn't fast enough hiding it. Big mistake.

"I don't know. I guess I lost it," I say, trying to keep my voice from showing that I still have it. "You don't like dolls anyway."

"You little shit!" She talks like that when Mom and Dad can't hear. "Gimme that doll!"

"No! You have presents of your own. You don't need mine. You don't even like dolls!"

She comes right up next to me, so I have to look up to see her face. I look right up her nostrils. They don't look any better than mine, I'll bet.

"Listen, you freak," she says, "Don't you ever talk to me like that. I'll have to tell Mom and Dad how bad you are. Maybe they'll send you off to live with Grandpa Marshall!"

She sees the fear shining in my eyes and knows she's got another thing to tease me with. So far I'd hid that from her real good, that I was scared of him and his big, scratchy hands. He wouldn't think of putting those hands on her, no, of course not. He'd get in trouble if she said anything. With me, he knows everybody will think I'm making things up again.

"Hah, hah, hah, you'll go live with Grandpa Marshall," she sang. "Then I'll have everything to myself the way I did before you were born. Everything was so much better before you came along, crazy bones."

I've heard that a thousand times. A thousand times a thou-

sand. What makes it so bad is that maybe she is right. I might be a freak. When I look in the mirror, I'm not sure what I see, me or a freak. Mom and Dad think I'm a liar because of all the things I've said about my older sister. "What are you talking about? Your sister's sweet as pie. Everybody knows that."

Hating myself for every step I take, I go into the bedroom. I pull the new doll out of my most secret hiding place, the one she hasn't found yet.

I walk back into the dining room, my feet dragging but pulled along like she's tugging on my leash. Which she actually does, sometimes. Puts Jingles' collar and leash on me and takes me for a walk, outside, where everybody except Mom and Dad can see.

Her hands are mean to my doll, and then she throws it on the floor.

I kneel down next to the doll, with her head hanging sideways and her new outfit torn. I wrap her in a washcloth to keep people, especially my jerky relatives, from seeing her bare front.

If only other people could see how mean my sister is. But they only see her shiny hair and her pretty face and her woman's body and that she moves like a cat, real smooth.

They don't see what's inside her the way I do. Her black, black heart. If I could, I'd rip it out of her and feed it to Jingles. Whenever nobody's looking, she pulls Jingles' ears or tail and then shoves him at me, like I did it. I would never hurt him. Jingles is nervous around me, and it's not my fault.

But she's my sister, and I'm supposed to love her. I guess I do, kind of. She's a lot easier to love when she's not around.

She didn't have to do that to my doll, though.

Chapter 8

Alone in her office, PJ dialed her home number. Thomas picked up on the second ring. He must be waiting for a phone call, and chances were excellent that it wasn't from her.

"Oh, it's you," her son said. "When can I have a cellphone like the rest of the universe?"

"When the rest of the universe pays the bill," PJ said. "You could at least ask me how my day's going."

"Hi, Mom, how's your day going?"

"Rotten, thank you. I left some meatloaf in the refrigerator for your lunch." PJ glanced at the time. It was nearly one in the afternoon.

"I just finished breakfast," Thomas said. "We need more eggs."

Again?

"Orange juice, too."

"I'll make your grocery needs a priority," PJ said. "They'll come right after winning a car on *The Price is Right*."

"Huh?"

"Never mind. I wanted to make sure you finish your homework before you start on that RPG stuff."

Thomas had discovered MMORPG—Massive Multi-player Online Role Playing Games. One in particular, *The Gem Sword of Seryth*, had captivated him. He'd gotten so wrapped up in it that his intermediate grade report included a couple of D's. The private school he was attending, Jamison Academy, was piling on the homework as the first semester came to an end. The workload was high, and the expectations even higher. She knew Thomas was up to it, though, and getting him into the academy gave her peace of mind.

After an incident in which Thomas was threatened with a knife outside his public school, PJ'd had enough. Paying the tuition made money tight in other areas, but both of them would rather eat macaroni and cheese and Ramen noodles than have Thomas try to cope. Her brilliant, gentle, sensitive son was thriving at Jamison.

"Yeah, I'll get it done."

"Remember, you have a math test."

"Mom."

It was time to change the subject. "Are you seeing Winston today?"

Winston Lakeland was Thomas's best friend. He'd been on the waiting list to get into Jamison, too, but Thomas was the last one on the list to get a slot. Both of them were hoping for a vacancy to turn up soon, for some family to move or some kid to flunk out. In the meantime, the boys saw each other on weekends. And online.

"Later. I think he's still asleep. When will you be home?"

The question jabbed PJ right in the extra organ that rode atop the hearts of single parents: guilt.

She made a quick guess and padded her answer. "By eleven."

"See ya."

He hung up, not waiting for her response. She figured he didn't want to give her too much time to think about the homework versus RPG situation.

PJ swiveled around and faced the high-end Silicon Graphics workstation that was the magnet that brought her to St. Louis. The department had obtained the equipment under a federal grant and quickly realized it was necessary to hire someone who knew what to do with its visualization capability. When PJ arrived, the boxes were literally gathering dust in a corner. She'd quickly set it up and installed the software developed in her marketing research job.

As a marketing analyst, she produced simulations of grocery stores, car dealerships, whatever the client wanted. People participating in the study entered the scene virtually and shopped, picked cereal from the shelves, or test-drove cars. It could be a product's shelf appeal that was being tested or whether a dealer's showroom enticed buyers to come inside. The big difference between her past and current work was in motivation: make a profit or put a killer behind bars.

She began by scanning in crime photos of the levee and the access road. Her program took the setting and rendered it in simple 3D wireframe mode. Then she did the same with photos of the victim. Her software filled in any missing areas by extrapolation, combined setting and person, and set the whole thing in motion. In fifteen minutes she had a wireframe version of a male lying at the base of the cobblestone levee, river water slapping at his feet. His wounds were crudely shown at this point, but she had routines to make the blood and guts realistic.

PJ had a large library of standard elements she could add, so she plunked a car, a late model sedan, on the access road. She also added a driver, choosing from among the set of avatars she'd developed. Genman, for generic man. Average height, build, appearance—the face in the crowd. She also had Genfem, Genteen, Genkid, and Genbaby programmed and ready to use. She'd never had to use Genbaby, and hoped she never would.

She ran through a basic scenario on her monitor. The car traveled along the access road and stopped. The driver emerged by walking through the door rather than opening it. The trunk lid popped open. Genman pulled the victim out and tossed him toward the river. Instead of rolling, the victim floated smoothly down as if he were cushioned on air and stopped several feet short of the river. Water surged up the levee from the Mississippi, rose three feet into the air, and enveloped his feet.

The playback was rough even by PJ's lenient standards for a first run-through. It was going to be a long afternoon.

There were three apples and a stale Danish lined up on PJ's desk, and that would have to do for dinner.

She worked with the wireframe scenario of the dump site until there were no scenes of walking through solid objects, and then added the subtle shading of 3D rendering. The victim's face was now Arlan's, and his injuries were chillingly accurate. The computer used its database of information about St. Louis to fill in the downtown backdrop. After reviewing the playback several times, PJ felt there was nothing more to be learned by exploratory VR. That was the term for interacting with a virtual world only by viewing it on a monitor. The next step was immersion, in which she would enter the world she'd created as a participant, and everything would appear life-sized to her.

It took more than a powerful computer to provide an immersion experience. It took a Head Mounted Display, or HMD, and a device to control motion in the virtual world, usually data gloves. When PJ first got started, she'd had to borrow those items from a researcher at Washington University. The hardware she borrowed wasn't the slick commercial type, but she was in no position to be choosy. The HMD looked like an overturned kitchen colander with wires streaming up from it like spaghetti defying gravity. It had served her well, but eventually the researcher reclaimed both it and the data gloves to use in his own projects. Left with no interface, PJ had taken the salaries allocated for two long-promised computer assistants and converted them into a hardware purchase. She needed equipment more than she needed additional staff.

The results lay in front of her, still new enough that she stored them in their boxes when they weren't in use—a kind of honeymoon period. Later on, they'd be treated as casually as the other objects in her office, which meant hoping no one sat on them.

PJ ate the Danish, sipping her coffee and savoring the relative quiet of the building. It was late afternoon, and there was a lull before the evening activity revved up.

She pulled on stretch data gloves that allowed her to move around and manipulate objects in virtual reality, and even provided tactile feedback so that when she "picked up" a knife she could feel the grip in her hand. The gloves used wireless transmission, so she wasn't tethered to her computer.

The new HMD was a light, sleek, open-topped helmet with two liquid crystal screens in front of her eyes. The screens were very bright but low in power consumption, so small batteries did the job—no more cables to tangle. The flat screens blocked out the outside world, like having binoculars glued to her face. There were eye-tracking and head-motion sensors in the helmet, so the high-resolution images of the virtual world existed only where she was looking. The rest was the null world, nothingness. When she moved her eyes or head to scan a scene, the world at the edges of her vision was continually being generated, so that it appeared to have been there all along. The generation was done so fast that there was no way to jerk her head around and catch the world in the process of being built. She'd tried, of course, and wrenched her neck so that she couldn't turn her head for days without wincing.

To add to the realistic effect, the speakers inside the

helmet were programmed for 3D sound. That means the sound of a door slamming reached one ear slightly ahead of the other ear, just as it would in the real world, letting the person localize the source. The volume of the sound fell off realistically according to its distance from the person, too. The only thing that was missing was the shadowing effect of having some object between the person and the sound.

From the beginning, PJ had incorporated decision-making into the simulations, artificial intelligence that let the computer extrapolate sketchy events into complete scenarios. Sometimes she was leading the simulation, and sometimes it led her. What the computer came up with sometimes gave her valuable tips that nudged the investigation one way or the other. Not all the time, though. Although the computer had a huge reference database available, it didn't have the judgment to use that information wisely. Taking things too literally meant that aliens or mythological beings sometimes popped up in a simulation as the computer was speculating on what could have happened. Her whole team had gotten a kick out of the angel who flew in and rescued a person from a burning building, or the time a killer had used X-ray vision to stalk his victims.

For her first immersion, she decided to be a FOTW, fly on the wall. She could observe what was going on, but not affect the action. She switched on the helmet, putting herself in the blue surround of the null world.

"Run riverfront," she said, and added a password. Voice activation certainly beat jabbing her fingers around blindly on the keyboard hoping to hit the right key to start the simulation.

The scene leapt to life from one blink of her eyes to the next. She was standing at the edge of Leonore K. Sullivan Boulevard, looking east toward the Mississippi. The fog that had given Arlan Merrett's body a natural shroud was absent. A waning, third quarter moon and a few of the brightest stars were visible in a sky washed out by city lights. To her right, the Arch glittered coldly, steel streaking upward and then hurtling down, like a rocket that couldn't escape the earth's pull. To her left, the floating casino moored at Laclede's Landing was a fountain of light and life, with indistinct figures moving in and out. Two bridges, one on either side of her, carried a small amount of traffic to and from Illinois— small only because of the day and hour. The cars were either headlights or taillights, with no vehicle detail shown. She could hear the noise of the passing cars. The Landing was a jumble of restaurant and nightclub signs. Most of the windows in the multi-story Embassy Suites Hotel had curtains drawn, but some were bright rectangles. Anyone looking down from those windows should be able to see if a car was moving around on Sullivan, if not specifics.

A low rumble of engine noise alerted her to the approach of a car traveling toward her. She curled her right forefinger slightly, changing the path of the optical fibers in the data glove. The programmed response was to walk across the street in the direction she was looking. When she reached the other side, she straightened her finger. Moving around using the gloves was something that even Schultz picked up with a little practice.

The car, a black four-door Taurus, rolled to a stop. The moon, reflected in the car's hood, seemed submerged in a deep, black pool. The killer was a man dressed in dark clothing, and he was checking that all was quiet around him. Although PJ was standing close by, he didn't react to her— she was invisible to the characters in the scenario. PJ moved up to the car and stood next to the trunk, where she expected the body would be.

The killer stepped out, but instead of moving to the trunk, he opened the rear door on his side of the car.

What gives? The body's always in the trunk.

She walked around to look in the rear passenger's side window. Sure enough, there was something large and dark lying across the back seat. The killer grasped a pair of handles, one on each side, and tugged, grunting with the effort. Once the object started moving, it slid easily over the upholstery. PJ hurried around the car to see what the killer was doing. He was pulling on the handles of a body bag.

Of course! A corpse is awkward for one person to handle, and leaves blood and other evidence in a car, but a bag has handles and sealed seams to contain blood. Some even have wooden slats on the bottom, between layers of plastic, to make a stretcher. Instead of dealing with a freshly killed body flopping around and bending in the middle, all a person had to do was pull one end of a stretcher, letting the other end drag. The stretcher-bag could even be tilted and levered into position, as the killer was doing now, using the side of the passenger seat.

In no time at all, the bag was on the street, aligned parallel to the car. The killer opened the long zippers, tilted the stretcher up on one side, and out rolled the body, down the levee toward the river. Blood was left on the cobblestones, as in the crime scene photos, but none on the street, where the stretcher was. The killer zipped up the bag and maneuvered it into the back seat, an easy task now that it was empty, and drove away.

The simulation fit the facts of the crime scene and added an important piece of speculative information. PJ ran through it again, putting herself in the role of a female killer. Arlan was heavy—she felt the computerized resistance when she tugged the handles of the bag—but feasible to move with a woman's programmed strength.

The killer could be a woman, at least as far as disposing of the body was concerned. Abducting Arlan, keeping him captive, and doing the killing was another story, and she'd deal with that some other time.

Ideas were forming in her mind of a two-person killing team. Two people could be united in their motivation for wanting Arlan dead and scheming together to get rid of him. For example, June and a lover who wanted to marry her. Or people with differing motivations could have come together and formed an alliance of convenience, perhaps for business reasons. The whole elaborate setup that made it look like Arlan was killed by a psycho could be nothing but a smokescreen, intended to direct the attention of the investigators away from a couple of business partners who just figured they could divide Arlan's cut of the profits between them. A quite ordinary, greed-motivated killing dressed in the handiwork of a serial killer.

PJ peeled off the gloves and removed the helmet. She folded her arms on her desk next to the remaining apple, lowered her head onto her arms, and fell asleep.

A persistent pinging sound woke PJ. She raised her head and looked around, trying to determine where it was coming from. She hadn't set an alarm. She was alone in the room. Logic, of which she was barely capable, left the computer as the source.

An animated graphic of a smiling face greeted her on the screen.

"Oh, God, I don't think I can take perky," she mumbled.

"Merlin here. What's the buzz, Keypunch? You are awake, aren't you?"

"For heaven's sake, Merlin, it must be the middle of the night."

"It's 9:02 p.m. Sunday evening. Am I not welcome? You in the middle of some hot and heavy sex?"

PJ stretched, noticing a kink in her neck. She'd promised Thomas she'd be home by eleven, and it looked like she was going to make it only because Merlin woke her up. "Hardly. At least let me get coffee started."

She shuffled over to the coffee maker, grabbed the carafe, and stepped out into the hall to get water. The women's room was down at the end of the hall, which to PJ looked like a very long trek. No one was around, so she went into the men's room across the hall from her office. She'd been in there once before, when she cornered Schultz in a stall and had an argument with him.

The place smelled as though it had been freshly vacated by a man with intestinal flu. Or maybe it smelled that way all the time. Wishing she'd walked down the hall after all, she filled the coffee carafe at the sink and made a quick exit.

With coffee brewing and her head rapidly clearing, she sat back down to converse with Merlin. They went back a long way, the two of them. She'd met him when she was in college, twenty years ago, although she'd never *met* him in person. He called her by her old college nickname, Keypunch Kid, which she'd earned by her proficiency and accuracy using a keypunch machine to punch programs and data into cards that were fed into the computer. Keypunch machines were anachronisms in the current technological climate. Merlin chatted with her, encouraged her, got her through rough times, and served as a sounding board for her ideas. A mentor who popped in and out of her life.

They'd started talking when online communication was the province of geeks, and moved forward as the technology did. Sometimes ahead of it. Currently they talked over secured VoIP, voice over Internet protocol. PJ had slyly suggested adding video, but Merlin predictably declined.

"So what's new, dirty old man?" she said.

"I resent that. I bathe on a regular weekly basis. Besides, I asked you first."

"You took advantage of me when I was groggy," PJ said. There was one apple left on her desk, so she picked it up and started munching it.

"Not the first time, won't be the last. I say again, what's up?"

"A new case. You've probably read about it in the papers. Oh, I forgot, you don't read newspapers."

"I prefer more direct sources. Heh, heh."

PJ pursed her lips. She'd wondered dozens of times before how Merlin picked up the threads of stories. She pictured him as a spider with the Internet as his web, information thrumming along the strands to the center, where he felt the sensations with his eight feet.

"Keypunch? You fall back asleep?"

"No, I was just imagining you as a spider."

"You definitely need to get out more."

"Hah! If only," she said. "I seem to spend more time in the company of the dead than the living."

"I told you Schultz wouldn't make a good lover. But did you listen?"

PJ chuckled. "Stay out of my sex life."

"Is there any to stay out of?"

Not much, lately. "Changing the subject, have you heard of the body found on the riverfront?"

"The guy with no dick? I thought we were staying out of your sex life."

"Merlin!"

"Yeah, I've heard about that murder," Merlin said. "Are you sure you're old enough to handle these sex cases? After all, there was the time when . . ."

"When I had to put back the beer I was trying to buy. That's beyond lame."

PJ knew there were legal issues with her discussing an open case in detail with a man she couldn't identify. She might have passed Merlin on the street and not known it. But all that was beside the point. He was a sympathetic ear, and she trusted him. She poured out all the recent events.

When she finished, he was quiet for a time.

"June could have hired someone to go to Kansas City for her to establish an alibi. It would be tricky, but it could be done."

PJ sighed. "I felt sorry for June at first. Now I don't know what to make of her."

"Psychos can be very charming when they want to. You should know that."

Before she could respond, her office door burst open and Schultz strode in.

"Good, you're awake. A bloody knife was found during the search of May Simmons's home," he said. "It's got her husband Frank's fingerprints on it and Arlan Merrett's blood. We found the murder weapon."

Chapter 9

Dear Diary,

These are things that happened to me, cross my heart and hope to die.

The earliest memory I have of my sister is from a time when I'm two years old. She is considered responsible enough to baby-sit for me while our parents have a getaway. All I know is that they are leaving and that I'm going to be alone with my sister. I hear my momma say that big word a lot, "responsible."

I'm terrified that I will die before they come back.

As soon as they drive away in the black car, she ties me in my booster seat. When I try to wiggle free, the rope or tape—I don't know now—cuts into my arms, so I cry. I am sitting across from her at the table, big tears rolling down my cheeks and my throat hurting from crying. She's eating something that I want, because I'm hungry, too. My parents are gone and I don't think I will see them again, or get something to eat because my stomach hurts.

When she's done eating, she leaves. Then I cry harder because I don't want to be alone. She's gone for a long time, a forever time.

When she comes back, she has a pretzel for me. I love pretzels. I like to bite them because my mouth hurts sometimes. Momma says I am a big girl, getting new teeth. I want the pretzel. She puts it on the table but doesn't untie my hands. I try to reach it with my mouth, I reach far and then stretch some more. My tongue touches the pretzel. That's when something bad happens. The chair with my booster seat on it falls over, and me with it. Suddenly I am sideways on the floor, still tied in the seat and screaming. Screaming.

Everything moves very fast when she pulls the chair up hard, and that scares me some more. But now she seems sorry. She cuts whatever is holding my hands and gives me the pretzel. I don't remember what happens next.

Later I am crying for Momma and my sister puts something in my mouth to make me stop. It smells bad and I choke on it. She puts me on the bed and pulls my clothes off. I stay there looking up at her as she moves around the room. I remember she's humming.

The next thing I remember is that I'm in the water in our pool. I'm holding on to a tube around my stomach that's holding me up. I'm inside it, like I'm the hole of a doughnut. If I let go, I will slip down into the water and never come up. I can't think of anything but holding onto that tube. I hate the water.

My sister is close by, moving through the water, forward and backward in the pool. I can't figure out how she does it. It looks like she's pulling herself through the water. I don't know how to do that. If I let go of the tube, I will go down under the water. She stops by me and presses my nose and gives me a big smile. I smile back because I think she's going to take me out, so I won't lose the tube.

She puts her hands on the tube and I'm very happy. Then she pushes down. The tube goes under the water. I'm holding on and I go down, too. I scream and water pours into my mouth. My eyes are open and I see her legs under the water. She's right there. I reach for her and the tube slips away from me. There is nothing holding me up and water is in my mouth and nose. I scream, but I only get more water in my mouth.

I feel her hands grab me. She pulls me up and puts me in the tube. I am spitting water out of my mouth and I can't get any air. I'm so sick and scared. She starts to go forward and backward in the pool again. I know that soon she will stop by me and push my tube down. I can't do anything. I can't get away. I'm sick and scared.

That's the first memory I have of my sister.

Chapter 10

PJ hadn't seen her son since early in the morning, and that was only a quick glance into his room, where he was sprawled across his bed. As usual, Megabite had claimed his pillow, causing Thomas's upper body to hang off the bed to avoid disturbing the cat. That was the image of him she'd retained all day.

She pulled her faded blue VW Rabbit convertible into the driveway of her home. It was a story-and-a-half on Magnolia Avenue, one of the smaller homes in the Shaw neighborhood. That made it affordable for a newly-divorced professional woman. PJ had started out renting the place, but fell in love with it and bought it when the owner decided to sell. It had wood floors, stained glass windows, a fireplace, and two bedrooms upstairs. The private yard had an intimate feel and beautiful perennial plantings that PJ had maintained. She could walk to Tower Grove Park, and often did when the pond lilies were in bloom.

And there was that driveway, allowing her off-street parking.

The house was dark, but a porch light had been left on for her around back. She touched the pane of glass in the back door out of habit, the pane shattered by a bullet that saved her from a psychopathic killer. Some people would have moved to get away from the reminder of an event like that, but in PJ's case, it strengthened her.

Track lights in the kitchen bathed the space in light. The smells of pizza and popcorn greeted her nose, and she smiled. *The smells of normality.*

Megabite appeared from nowhere and rubbed against her leg, meowing and showing off her honey-gold eyes. Obediently, PJ bent down to pet her. The cat rose on tiptoe and arched her back under PJ's hand. The young cat looked like different cats depending on the angle of viewing. Seen from the top, she was gray tiger-striped. From the underneath, she was pure white. Seen from the side, there was a horizontal band of orange fur on all four legs that neatly divided gray and white. The white tip of her tail was very expressive, and at the moment, it was expressing Food.

"Oh, Meg, I'm sure you've been fed a dozen times today," PJ said. Thomas loved the cat as much as she did. Being a teenager, he assumed that the cat needed to eat every hour, like he did. PJ put down a bowl of remnants of a roast beef sandwich. Megabite purred her approval and went to work.

PJ walked further into the house, looking for Thomas. The study door was closed, but there was a line of light underneath the door. She knocked and opened it, to find Thomas bent over the desk, working on the homework that was due the next day. Obviously he'd played around all day and left his schoolwork for the last minute. Typical, but she wished he'd get the important things done first.

Not that I did any better at his age. Then along came the to-do lists that run my life.

Feeling old and stodgy, she went over to him and tousled his straight black hair.

"Hey, you're messing up my look," he said.

"No, I'm creating a new look. You can be the first one in school to have it."

"Yeah, right. We're out of soda and frozen pizzas, and there's only one bag of microwave popcorn left."

PJ sighed. Sometimes her relationship with her son boiled down to a grocery list.

"I'll be back when I smell better," PJ said. "We can talk about the school week coming up."

Thomas grunted, but at least it was a social grunt.

The hot bath was wonderful, but PJ didn't linger. She tossed on a clean sweater and jeans over fresh underwear. She made a phone call and then went back downstairs with her hair dripping from a thorough scrubbing. Thomas joined her at the kitchen table. He was eating a granola bar.

"I'm going to be really busy the next couple of days. I just called Mick's mom," PJ said. "She said you could spend tonight and Monday night at her house and she'd take you to school with Mick. Megabite's going, too."

PJ found that having Thomas attend Jamison Academy had a side benefit. There was an active and supportive group of parents who looked out for each other's kids, called simply Parents Care. She'd thrown herself into it, because she liked the way others were concerned not only about academic success but the whole well-being of their kids. Mick was in some of Thomas's classes, and his mother Lilly Kane was a divorcée like PJ. The two women had gravitated together. The boys often spent the night at each other's houses, and usually Winston made it a trio. It was like having a co-mom, a tremendous relief for PJ, who had once had to ask her boss to recommend a babysitter.

"Okay by me," Thomas said, around bites of granola bar. "She makes eggs and bacon for breakfast."

"Do you make all of your decisions based in what kind of food is available?"

"Pretty much, yeah, unless there's girls involved. Mom, when are you and Schultz going to get married?"

So much for discussing the school week.

Schultz wanted to get married, and she wasn't ready for it. He'd surprised her with a ring, and when she didn't immediately say yes, Schultz assumed that she thought he wasn't good enough for her. As he put it, "Good enough to fuck, but not good enough to commit to." They'd talked it over, but she couldn't get him to see her reasoning.

She still hadn't left behind the pain of her divorce. It didn't help that her ex-husband Steven married a woman two decades younger than PJ before the ink was dry on the divorce decree. A few months later, Steven and Carla had a baby. PJ had wanted another baby, but Steven kept putting her off. Apparently, Carla was more suitable to carry the offspring of his loins.

That hurt.

Schultz had gone through major changes, too. His separation after thirty years of marriage had come as a shock to him, and was followed by divorce and his wife's remarriage within a couple of months—nowhere near Steven's record, but still a blow. And then the biggest blow of all, the murder of his only son.

PJ felt they needed time to work through those life-altering things on their own. From years of experience as a psychologist, she knew that decisions made right now might be rebound ones, to be regretted later. Schultz didn't worry about that. He just wanted to move on to happier times together.

She loved him. She loved his dedication, his caring for the victims and their families, his search for justice, his desire for her. Schultz had a hot core, even if the surface was chilly at times. He was a great father to Thomas, and that meant a lot to her. She wanted to spend the rest of her life with him. Just not yet.

If they got married, she couldn't be his boss. That meant either he left CHIP or she did. It was wrong already, just having the relationship that they did. She was probably breaking regulations every time they made love.

"It's complicated," she ventured, her eyes not meeting her son's.

"C'mon, Mom, that's bull. Do you love him or not?"

I just came home to take a shower and change clothes.

"Yes. I mean, I think so."

"So you should get married and we should move in with him. His house is bigger, and it's got this neat room on the third floor. I could live up there. You guys would have more privacy, too. I know you're having sex."

You do? What, I glow or something?

"Thomas, that's none of your business."

"In a way it is my business, Mom. Haven't you always told me that sex is for committed relationships, for marriage?"

Cornered.

"Yes, I strongly feel that way."

"So that's the rule for me, but not for you?" he said.

Redirect.

"Don't you have packing to do if you're spending the night at Mick's?"

The front doorbell rang. It was Lilly, to pick up Thomas and the cat and take them to her house. PJ had been saved by the bell. She enticed Megabite into the cat carrying case with a couple of treats, while Lilly talked silly baby talk to the cat. Megabite was a regular visitor at Lilly's house too, where there was company in the form of a couple of burly male cats, Peanut and Butter, brothers rescued from a shelter. Megabite had them wrapped around her paw, and Lilly too.

Thomas grabbed a duffle bag, dashed around collecting books and clothing, and was out the door into the winter night. He turned around on the front porch and smiled. It was the smile of someone older, of her son as the man he was on the verge of being. The smile of his gentle soul. She felt a surge of love that brought tears to her eyes.

I'd die for him. I'd kill for him.

"Love you, Mom. I studied for the math test."

★ ★ ★ ★ ★

A few minutes later, PJ went out to her car to retrieve a stack of notes. With the house to herself, she was going to work until her eyes wouldn't stay open, catch a few hours of sleep, and be back in the office before 6 a.m.

When she opened the door of her car, the dome light illuminated the interior. She froze. On the passenger seat was a box wrapped like a gift, complete with a red bow.

It looked so cheery sitting there. It might also blow her to smithereens.

Her hand still on the door handle, she hoped she hadn't done something already to trigger a bomb. Her heart beat against her ribcage like a bird fluttering its wings. Air slipped gently in and out her open lips, and she didn't dare blink. She pulled her hand away from the handle and stepped back, planting her right foot firmly, then drawing her left level with it. She moved backward across her yard that way, like dancing with an invisible partner. Her eyes were glued on the package she could see through the open car door. Ten steps back she stopped and took a deep breath.

Her hand moved to her pocket and retrieved her cellphone. She used it to call 911 and describe the situation, and then to call Schultz. Then, as calmly as she could, she walked down her driveway to the curb. No one was on the sidewalk, and there were no cars on the street that she didn't recognize as belonging to people who lived nearby. Her breath rose in frozen puffs as she waited. The house was between her and the car—was that enough protection, if the box was a bomb? What about her neighbors? There was nothing to do but wait.

A patrol car got there first, followed a couple of minutes later by a first responder from the bomb squad, who called for a removal unit. Schultz arrived like a bowling ball, knocking aside like pins anyone who got in his way until he reached PJ.

It took the squad only a few minutes to determine that the box wasn't going to explode. PJ was vastly relieved, and at the same time, a little embarrassed. Her street was lit up with flashing lights and men with protective suits were trampling her perennial beds and holding mirrors under her car, checking for bombs attached to the underside. The box was removed and sent off to be examined in the evidence lab. At Schultz's insistence, PJ's home was in the process of being swept for bombs.

PJ waved to Mr. and Mrs. Bickwallace across the street, standing at their front picture window looking like Grant Wood's *American Gothic* in pajamas.

Chapter 11

The air inside the car is getting cold. Soon I'll be able to see my breath in here. I don't want to run the heater, though, because an idling car on the street draws attention like a screaming kid in a five star restaurant. I'll have to tough it out.

Time glides by on ice skates, the measured swoosh-swoosh *of blade cutting ice matching the heartbeat I hear in my ears. Marilee is entertaining her gentleman friend and I'm out here almost seeing my breath while she heats up the sheets. For some people, the twisted ones, that would be reason enough to kill her. I have higher standards, though. Higher standards and, increasingly, class.*

Marilee's photo is on the seat next to me lying on the sheet of plastic I have thoughtfully covered the seat with, the photo I took when I was auditioning her for the part. I can't see it now because of the darkness, but I've memorized it. Brown hair the shade of oak leaves clinging to the tree in the middle of winter, average features except for an undersized chin. Twinkle wrinkles—the ones at the corners of her eyes when she screws up her face—should be covered with makeup, but in this photo are plain to see. She doesn't have smile lines, indicating that she probably doesn't smile much. Unremarkable body, but her tits haven't given in to gravity yet. They are her best assets, certainly better than those bovine eyes.

The door to Marilee's cramped frame bungalow opens and disgorges Polyester Guy. P.G. embraces her on the threshold and plants a sloppy one on her lips. I can almost hear the saliva churning from here. There's something about the way he walks, the easy, confident step of a man who's comfortable in his body, maybe a former athlete. Could be—the shoulders are still there, and a butt that would look better in a pair of tight jeans than the shapeless pants he's wearing. I'm pretty sure he looks better with his clothes off than on, and that's not something you can say about everybody.

She blows him a kiss, and P.G. departs in his Caddy of questionable vintage that resembles an ocean liner. I think he missed appealing to hot chicks with his ride by about thirty years.

I wait longer to make sure everything's quiet. Marilee's home is fairly narrow and deep, like a domino turned up on its side. The space between her home and the next is deeply shadowed. With my black, skin-tight, Lycra jersey and tights, I'll disappear when I get in there. An evil wallflower, that's me.

I'm not wearing underwear under my outfit. Makes me feel a little wicked. I tried underwear, marching around my house like a little soldier, trying out my new uniform. Got chafed. Now I trust the breathability of the fabric to keep me comfortable. That's something Marilee won't have for long. Breathe-ability.

The car windows fog up on the inside, and I rub a small circle clean so I can see the door and a little way down in each direction on the sidewalk. Clear.

I snap on three pairs of latex gloves and pull a ski mask over my head, and move stealthily to the house. There's an unpleasant smell in the air, garbage cans, some of them open, in front of each house. Tomorrow's pick-up day. Even muted by the cold, the blend of rotten meat, decaying vegetables, and probably somebody's dead hamster is enough to send a tremor of revulsion through me.

Mentally I go through my inventory, like in the barn. This time, I'm counting on surprise. A knife, that's all I have. The bare-ass minimum.

The shadowed space between the houses is a mouth that swallows me. I slide down the gullet and squeeze myself out into the cluttered rear yard. Understandably, I feel turd-like, but a quick shake and the feeling's gone.

Marilee is one of those people who prefers a cold bedroom, colder than the rest of her house. I already knew that, of course. I've been here before. Her bedroom window is open an inch, inviting in death's unwarmed breath. As I listen at the window, the ground is unyielding beneath my feet, setting a standard for me. I must not yield, or my goals will never be achieved. The shower's running. She's scrubbing away the traces left by P.G. I hope she uses mouthwash, too.

My fingers fit under the open window, and it slides up easily, a break for me. At this point, I'd like to say that I vaulted through the window with the grace of Catwoman, but the truth is I hauled myself up and tumbled into a heap on her scuffed wood floor. I return the window to its original position.

The bathroom door's open, and I can see steam condensed on the mirror. The smell of sex hangs in the air. It's too bad there's a glass shower door instead of a curtain. The urge to rend a shower curtain with a butcher knife, hear the screams, and watch the blood swirl down the drain is nearly overwhelming.

Chapter 12

Welcome to Gemswordchat, Vyzer_lok!
Now talking in the Mage's Secret Chamber. Enjoy your
stay.
gronz_eye has entered the room

    <gronz_eye> *whaz poppin dood*
    <Vyzer_lok> c u made it
    <gronz_eye> *hey i ever let u down*
    <Vyzer_lok> no but u never let up
    <gronz_eye> *ha ha 2 clever*
    <Vyzer_lok> we on 4 midnite
    <gronz_eye> *if i can make it mom on my case*
    <Vyzer_lok> yeah all i hear is shit about grades
    <gronz_eye> *me 2 man fuck that*
    <Vyzer_lok> u ever kjhakj;akdl
    <gronz_eye> *??*
    <Vyzer_lok> sorry man cat got on the keyboard
    <gronz_eye> *u were saying?*
    <Vyzer_lok> u ever find out more on those tunnels
    <gronz_eye> *yeah i think we can do it maybe a group of us*
    <Vyzer_lok> that would be like sweet i cant wait
    <gronz_eye> *my contact gonna come thru maybe soon*
    <Vyzer_lok> fckn sweet
    <gronz_eye> *u know we got to keep quiet about this no par-*
ents
    <Vyzer_lok> yeah u told me that like ten times hey can i
ask a guy i know?
    <gronz_eye> *shit no we cant risk it*
    <Vyzer_lok> he wont say anything i vouch for him
    <gronz_eye> *NO*

<Vyzer_lok> u dont have to yell

<gronz_eye> *listen i got this perfect setup just me & u and my buds*

<Vyzer_lok> ok

<gronz_eye> *just gemsword freaks my contact wont do it if i bring in anybody else*

<Vyzer_lok> i said ok dont get ur balls in a vise man

<gronz_eye> *c u at midnite im gonna get that vibrocrystal away from u*

<Vyzer_lok> yeah u & what legion of raging cyrroths? c u

gronz_eye has left the room

Chapter 13

The next day Frank Simmons was arrested for the murder of his brother-in-law, on the basis of the bloody knife found in his home.

PJ was still trying to fit that into her idea of a two-person murder team when she got news of the contents of the box in her car. It was another album of nude pictures, close-ups of small areas. A foreplay album. Arlan's distinctive U-shaped scar was present. A butterfly tattoo looked just like the one Schultz mentioned Fredericka had. Their fingerprints had been found on every page, and two of the pages were stuck together with Arlan's semen.

Who left the foreplay album for PJ to find? Apparently it had been spirited out of Fredericka's home the night that the woman had a feeling her place had been broken into. Someone obviously wanted to bring the love affair to light. So how did Frank Simmons figure into all of this? Was Fredericka playing around with him, too? She drew a diagram on a pad of paper, with arrows to indicate who might have been sleeping with whom. There were more arrows than in Cupid's quiver.

"Let's go to Millie's," Schultz said. He'd knocked on PJ's office door and opened it before she could respond. "I'll spring for a meal. 'Course, I might expect something in return." He raised and lowered his eyebrows rapidly. PJ's imagination responded to the suggestion of *something in return* and felt a rush of warmth below her belly.

The first time they made love, she'd wondered whether her over-forty body with padding on the hips still held any interest for a man. PJ had lost confidence since the divorce.

89

When she'd expressed her fears, Leo told her she was beautiful. He'd been worried about the same thing, since he didn't have the corrugated abdomen and muscular chest he'd had as a young cop. She told him he was beautiful, too, and she meant it. He was a great lover, playful, tender, and passionate, sometimes all three at once.

"I could use a break," she said. "I have a lot more to do here, though. I'll have to come back and work into the evening."

"Hell, me too. Detectives don't get regular sleeping hours, Doc. Regular loving hours, either." He tilted his head to point toward the hallway. "Coming?"

PJ pushed open the door of Millie's Diner and breathed in deeply. The scents of coffee brewing, sweet rolls baking, burgers frying, and onions sautéing entered her nose and went straight to the pleasure center of her brain. A smile spread over her face, and the wrinkles between her brows flattened out, leaving her with a smooth, untroubled forehead, at least for now.

It was dinnertime and most of the tables were occupied, but there were several spots open at the counter. She strode across the black-and-white linoleum and headed for her usual stool. The stools had round padded tops and chrome legs. She gave the top of hers a twirl to lower it enough that her feet wouldn't dangle. Schultz took her coat and his, and hung them on a peg that was already used. There weren't any empties, because Millie refused to put up more than ten of them. He settled into his usual spot, leaving one stool between them, the one that had uneven legs and rocked slightly. The one that the regulars avoided.

The windows that spanned the front of the diner were steamed up from the contrast between the indoor temperature, which hovered somewhere between bake and broil, and an outdoor temperature that had slipped below freezing. Millie's clientele had seen the large expanse of window glass as ripe for finger-drawn graffiti. Limericks, phone numbers, sketches inspired more by hormones than an artist's muse, and several hearts with initials graced the space. In a few places, Millie had obliterated freedom of expression with a towel.

A three-foot aluminum Christmas tree occupied a section of the floor underneath the pay phone, between two doors with "Women" and "Others" neatly lettered on in white paint. A spotlight with a rotating filter stood next to the tree, lighting it alternately with red and green. Above each door, a few Christmas cards were tacked to the frame. A sprig of plastic poinsettia in a small vase on each table completed the seasonal decorations.

Schultz spotted the proprietor, a woman in her sixties, and waved her over. "You can take our order anytime," he said. "We've been here fifteen minutes already."

Millie snorted, made a U-turn, and headed away from them.

"Hey, service here," Schultz said.

Millie made the rounds of the tables, chatting and refreshing coffee cups, taking her time. Finally she headed their way with a pot of coffee in one hand and her order tablet in the other. Schultz and PJ turned over the coffee cups in front of them, and a stream of coffee filled each. Not a drop spilled as Millie switched from one cup to the other. There was only one type of coffee—hot and strong. No vanilla crème, no hazelnut latte.

"Nice to see you, Dearie," Millie said to PJ, pointedly ignoring Schultz's remarks.

"Merry Christmas, Millie," PJ said. "I like your decorations." They were the same, tired items Millie used last year. Probably most of the Christmas cards were the same, too.

Some of those could be decades old.

"Thanks." Millie glanced at Schultz, and momentarily her lips flattened and nearly vanished, leaving a line across the bottom of her face that was as effective a rebuke as PJ had ever seen. "Would you like to see the menu?"

"Not today. I'll just have a cheeseburger, fries, and a strawberry milkshake."

"Strawberry, not chocolate like usual?"

"Red for Christmas."

Millie's eyes lit up. "Gotcha." Her head swiveled to Schultz. "What about you, you prevert?"

"That's pervert, for the educated among us," Schultz said. "I'll have the same, only make the burger a double, extra onions and can you spare a decent tomato, plus about twice as many fries as she gets, and a large Coke."

Millie stuffed her order tablet into her pocket and turned away.

"You know, that's the same order pad she had when she opened this place," Schultz said. "I've never seen her write anything on it."

"You really ought to be nicer to her. Christmas spirit and all."

"She's mad at me, which is nothing new. This time I think it's because I didn't send her a Christmas card." He sniffed. "Haven't ever sent one, but I guess she keeps hoping. She's got the hots for me, you know."

PJ sighed. Schultz's relationship with Millie was in a well-worn groove long before she came along. There was true feeling, though, at least on Millie's part. PJ'd seen a flash of it when Schultz got the news that his son had been killed.

"Probably jealous of you," Schultz said, "but she treats

you nice anyway. I give her credit for that."

PJ leaned toward Schultz, and lowered her voice. "Have you turned up anything new?"

Schultz checked that they were out of earshot of the rest of the customers. She knew he'd been burned once by blabbing details of a case in the diner, and he wasn't about to do it again.

"Arlan Merrett's ID was confirmed by dental records, not just the wife's say-so. The time of death is still estimated at six to nine o'clock Saturday night. Some of the wounds appear to have been made by a scalpel or similar instrument, but used clumsily. We're not looking for a surgeon. Cause of death was a stab wound to the heart, although the guy would have bled out anyway. The thrust through the heart was anything but subtle, probably made by a butcher knife. There were a few wood splinters in the victim's back, oak, so they tell me. Ligature marks on wrists and ankles. The skull fracture was postmortem, must have been when his head met cobblestones."

"Are you still going with the gay murder?" she asked.

Schultz shook his head, nearly knocking PJ's forehead because he'd leaned in so close. "I think Merrett was not only straight but screwing his partner who by the way inherits the business. That's in addition to licking chocolate off his wife's privates. Money and lust. All we're missing is power, for the big three. Merrett wasn't a botched sex change operation, either."

"Why are we sure of that?"

He shrugged. "Because the ME says so. Oh, and June's alibi checked out, at least so far. Several of the hotel staff recognized a photo of her, and said she was there for the entire workshop. A couple of the lecturers remembered her, too, because she asked a lot of questions. Would've made our job easier if they hadn't remembered her. Arrest wife for killing husband, neat and clean."

"Nothing was neat and clean about Arlan's death."

Schultz waved a hand. "I mean prosecution-wise."

A customer headed for the men's room, passing behind where they were sitting. Schultz cut off the conversation and slurped his coffee noisily.

Millie arrived with heavy white plates loaded with food, Schultz's actually overloaded. The buns had a sheen of grease and were pierced with toothpicks that held tiny American flags held out stiffly in a phantom wind. PJ could see crystals of salt riding her fries. A few sautéed onions had escaped from the cheeseburger and left shimmering grease trails across the plate. Her mouth watered and she realized it had been a long time since her last meal. There was a plump, perfect strawberry perched atop a dollop of whipped cream on her milkshake, and a small green bow on the tall spoon that came with it.

"Millie, you've outdone yourself," PJ said, waving the spoon with the bow.

Millie half-curtsied in a surprisingly graceful move. As she left, her eyes passed over Schultz as if he were a food stain on the wallpaper.

"Aw, now you're spoiling her," Schultz said. "She's gonna expect compliments every time we come here." He shook the saltshaker over his already-terminally-salted fries.

They continued talking in low tones, catching up on each other's news about the investigation. When they left, Schultz paid for both meals, spun a quarter on the counter, and left it as his usual tip. She slipped a dollar under her plate.

Schultz kissed PJ outside the diner—"I like a greasy woman"—and then swept her off to his home in Lafayette

Square, over her objections that she needed to get back to work right away.

His house was chilly, but he held her close on the sofa, his coat draped over the two of them, until she warmed up. She rested her head on his shoulder, letting his strength soak into her along with his body heat. PJ closed her eyes and let the corpse with the ruined chest and the sinister package with the red bow fade away, knowing her compulsion to see justice done would be back later.

His roaming hands excited her. She unfastened a button of his shirt, slipped a hand inside, and saw the hairs on his arms rise. She marveled at the power of her touch. Wherever their relationship ended up, she already evoked more of a response from Schultz than she had from her ex-husband for a long time before their divorce. Or had her touch ever been electric for Steven?

They moved to his bedroom, talking softly as if the world had let go of them.

She felt a surge of warmth for Schultz when she saw his room. He'd done something special for her. The room was as neat as she'd ever seen it—the compost pile he called his laundry was gone, and the dusty reference books were missing from his bureau. The wood floor shone, his mirror wasn't fogged with a coating that made her reflection blurry, and the dust bunnies had been herded into the last roundup. The bed was freshly made with linens that smelled like a sunny day, and there was a rose lying on her pillow.

Forty-two-years-old and I've never had a rose on my pillow.

Other women might get turned on by expensive jewelry or trips to Paris or gourmet dinners. Clean sheets and a three-dollar flower was PJ's aphrodisiac. She stepped close to Leo, wrapped her arms around his neck, and whispered in his ear.

"Very nice, Leo. Looks like you've taken lessons in hotel management."

He pulled away, clapped one hand over his heart, and the other rose to his forehead. He looked like a Victorian heroine about to faint, except for the stubble on his chin and the evidence of his arousal. "You've hurt me deeply," he said. "Deeply. Are you insinuating I don't live like this all the time?"

"I'm not insinuating," PJ said. "I know for sure." She needed to be close to him, touching him, part of him.

"Hey, I read in a magazine that women go for this shit." He moved behind her and began softly kissing her neck. His warm breath, even smelling of onions, melted the tension in her muscles and sent jolts of desire through her veins.

"I have to admit that under some circumstances, housecleaning can be erotic," she said.

"There's something missing, though."

"Mmm?"

"You, in my bed." He deftly unfastened her bra, and her breasts nestled into his cupped hands. She moved her hips against him slowly, feeling his erection pressing against her buttocks, and was rewarded with his sharp intake of breath.

"I want you." His words came in a hot rush.

She turned in his arms and slowly, thoroughly, kissed him. Thoughts faded, shoved aside by past images of their lovemaking and the tingling eagerness of her body. He pulled her shirt and bra up over her head and walked her backward until her legs bumped the bed. Somehow her jeans were at her ankles. She kicked off her shoes and stepped out of the jeans, and out of her panties. In moments his clothes, too, littered the floor.

His eyes drank in her nakedness and came to rest on her face. "I'm the luckiest man in the world," Leo said.

He wanted her in spite of the twenty extra pounds loitering on her hips, stretch marks left over from childbirth, and an ass that hadn't qualified as trim and tight in a long time. She was still desirable in his view. A surge of desire spread up through her like lava rising from a volcano. She wasn't just hot, she was incandescent.

"Less talk, more action," PJ whispered. Her stroking hand drew a moan from him.

A cellphone's distinctive ring invaded the bedroom. "Your pants are ringing," she said. Just then another phone rang.

"Your pants are ringing, too," Leo said. His hand slid between her legs, his fingers finding the knob that sent ripples of pleasure through her. "Don't answer."

The phones continued to buzz their urgency.

"Aw, fuck," Leo said. He reached down to the floor, pulled the phone from his pants pocket, and flipped it open.

"*What?*" he said. His voice still had the throaty sound of passion, but his angry tone was unmistakable.

PJ sighed, dug around in her jeans, and answered her phone.

Chapter 14

Schultz sat down heavily on the edge of his bed and stuck his legs into his pants. Another body had been found. Couldn't the schmuck who discovered the body have been considerate enough to wait another hour or three?

Why are we getting this call, anyway? We're not busy enough?

Out of the corner of his eye he could see PJ buttoning her blouse and putting on her shoes. Her phone call had been from her boss, Howard Wall, who could maybe be forgiven for the timing of his call, because he didn't know where PJ and Schultz had snuck off to, or that they'd done their sneaking together. His had been from Anita, calling from her car. Anita probably did know, because women talked about those things even when they swore they didn't, and she called anyway.

Fuckus interruptus. Latin for "a cop's life."

They drove together, in his car. Because he was pissed off, Schultz went slow enough to earn him several horn honks from people behind him. He also took the time to stop in a post office and mail a letter containing a check he'd written for one hundred ten dollars to Ernestine Bradlock. It was better than facing her in person again.

The victim's house was in the Bevo neighborhood, near the railroad tracks. There were two black-and-whites parked out front and the scene was already secured. A small group of neighbors, some wearing nightclothes even though it wasn't late in the evening, gathered behind the tape. He'd seen that look on their faces many times before. They were trying not to show how eager they were to see someone else's fatal misfortune. The ultimate reality show.

Schultz was the first detective to arrive. Dave was in Chicago tracking down the disappointed clients that were supposed to meet with Arlan Merrett. Anita was on her way to talk with May Simmons. It would be interesting to see what the woman had to say about the Merrett marriage and the fact that her husband had been arrested for murder.

After showing identification to the officer controlling access, Schultz and PJ plucked disposable slippers from the box on the front porch. After slipping them on—a process accompanied by grunting on Schultz's part as he bent over far enough to reach his feet—they went into the house. The front door had been knocked off its hinges. He noticed that the lock on the door was a lock in name only. It looked capable of keeping out a lamb, and that was probably stretching it. In the living room, a uniformed officer sat next to a distraught man on a tired couch that dated from the 1950s. Schultz and Julia, his ex-wife, had bought one exactly like it secondhand when they had furnished their first apartment. Next to the couch there was a blonde wood end table with spindly legs set out at an angle.

Check. Had that one, too.

Schultz looked around for the starburst wall clock and the green bubble glass hanging lamp.

Must be in other rooms.

The officer came over to them.

"Detective Schultz," the woman said. "I guess you caught another one."

"Yeah," Schultz said. The officer was a new face. "Name?"

"Officer Ran Suhao, sir."

"Officer Ran, bring me up to speed."

"This is George Huber, the deceased's fiancé. He's the

person who discovered the body. Mr. Huber visited the deceased tonight and later returned because he'd forgotten a book he meant to borrow. Marilee Baines is in the bathroom." At the sound of Marilee's name, Mr. Huber whimpered and buried his face in a handkerchief.

Schultz pulled on gloves for the search. "Here," he said, offering a pair to PJ. "Put these on. Keep your hands to yourself anyway."

Gloves appeared in her hand. "I carry my own now, thank you." She headed down the hall and he scurried after her, frowning.

Woman's getting uppity.

The officer followed them only as far as the bedroom door, so that she wouldn't have to let Mr. Huber out of her sight. "The ME isn't here yet, but the victim's been dead less than an hour, if my opinion's worth anything," she said as they approached the bathroom.

Schultz maneuvered himself in front of PJ. It wasn't to protect her from viewing the unpleasant scene, but he didn't want her accidentally messing with evidence. Just because she carried her own gloves didn't mean she was one hundred percent reliable at a scene.

The body drew his eyes the way the corpses always did. A naked woman was slumped to the floor of a shower stall. A wood-handled kitchen knife was buried to the hilt below her sternum. The ring finger on her left hand was missing, the whole length of it. Long wet hair was plastered to her skin, covering most of her face. The victim hadn't gone to her death easily. There were bloody smears on the opaque shower door and on the fiberglass walls, where the water from the showerhead didn't make contact. She'd tried to escape, but she was cornered.

An attacker coming at her and nowhere to go.

He closed his eyes for a moment, testing his intuition, letting the thread that would eventually connect him to the killer grope around blindly in the dark. There was a little tug on the line, but nothing he could grasp.

"Ran, did anybody turn the water off in here?" Schultz said.

"No, sir. It was off."

"Bathroom and shower doors open or closed? How about that bedroom window over there?"

"All open when we arrived. Be sure to look at the back of the bathroom door, sir."

Schultz swung the door closed. On the back, in blood, there was a crude diagram of a heart with a knife stuck into it.

"That's obviously why we got the call on this murder," PJ said. "It's a direct reference to Arlan Merrett's death. The knife in the heart, that's the holdback."

"I'd say that's jumping to conclusions. It could just as easily be a broken heart because of a jilted lover that has nothing to do with Arlan. This leads me to Mr. Huber, the fiancé out there."

PJ shrugged, as if to say he was entitled to his opinion, even though it was wrong.

"Mr. Huber," he said sharply. The man sat up, wide-eyed, a deer in the headlights of Schultz's voice.

"Y . . . yes?"

"Did you see anyone leaving the house, or near the house? On foot or in a car?"

"No. No one, not in the whole time I waited."

"You waited? You didn't find the door kicked in?"

"No, I did that myself. I don't have a key. I rang the doorbell over and over. I figured she was in the bathroom and couldn't hear it. After about five minutes I called her from my cellphone. When she didn't answer, I got frantic. She had to be home, because her car's parked outside and I just left her a little while ago. It was the open window, wasn't it? The way the killer got in? I begged her not to sleep with that window open, but she wouldn't listen."

Huber had had enough. He covered his face with his hands and his shoulders shook. "I begged her," he said from behind his hands.

"You may have scared the killer off." *That is, if you're not the killer.*

"Ran!"

"Sir." She was already at his elbow, somehow. "The killer might still be in the neighborhood. It's a long shot, but it's a shot. I want patrol cars saturating this area. Can you coordinate that?"

"I'll call it in."

Schultz was marveling at the woman's efficiency, in action and speech, when he heard a call from inside the house.

"Leo, you've got to see this."

When he got to the bathroom, she was squatting next to the shower. She'd raised the victim's head with a hand under the chin, and was gently clearing the wet hair away from the face.

"Damn it, Doc, I told you not to touch anything!"

"You didn't tell me not to touch any*one*. Look, Leo." She tilted the victim's face up to him.

A smiling couple, sharing a drink from a coconut.

"It's June Merrett," he said.

"Or someone who looks enough like her to be her twin." PJ took out her cellphone and dialed June's home. The phone rang for a long time with no response, and without switching to voice mail. Her suspicion grew that the woman lying dead at their feet was the same person she'd interviewed, a woman whose wackiness may have just been leakage of concealed, powerful grief. A woman whose grief she'd allowed herself to taste.

Schultz gestured to get her attention.

"She might be out, doing funeral arrangements or something," Schultz said.

PJ covered the phone, even though no one could hear her on the other end. "At this time of night? The body hasn't been released yet, anyway."

Schultz observed the corpse in the shower, his eyes lingering on the dead woman's breasts. PJ was about to give him an indignant nudge when he spoke.

"June's tits were bigger," he said.

"What?"

"This woman has smaller tits than June. Don't you remember her foreplay pics? In the album?"

"Well, yes," PJ thought back to the image of June Merrett pulling her robe around her when she sat down in her floral chair. *The lollipop.* "You might be right."

"Might be, hell. I know I'm right." He tapped his forehead. "The power of the trained observer."

PJ frowned, wondering just how much time he spent observing women's breasts, and how much of it was in the line of duty. She gave up on the call and folded her phone. "Better get someone over to check on June, in spite of your observational skills."

"Yeah, never hurts to have confirmation." He made a quick call asking to have a patrol officer check the Merrett house.

Schultz said, "So we probably have a look-alike here. Coincidence?"

"It would have to be a double coincidence, don't you think, with that drawing of the heart and knife on the back of the bathroom door?"

Schultz pushed the door closed and studied the drawing again. "I still say it's not conclusive. Mr. Huber out there could still be good for it. 'You've wounded my heart,' something like that."

Voices near the front of the house announced the ME and the ETU arriving and coming in through the scene perimeter.

"Didn't you say Anita was talking to May now?" PJ said. Schultz nodded.

"That's covered, then. I'd like to get back to the office and get some time on the computer. Meet me back there when you're done here."

"Go ahead; leave us out here doing the work while you go play games."

She put her gloved hand up to touch Schultz's cheek, and there in the bloody bathroom, he tenderly air-kissed it.

PJ's cellphone vibrated in the pocket of her jeans. She answered the call.

"June Merrett and her bountiful tits are alive and well," Schultz said. "The officers had to pound on the door of her house. She'd taken a sleeping pill. Probably took several pills. Can't say that I blame her. The woman's had a tough time."

"So we're back to coincidence that Shower Woman looks like June. With the drawing on the door, too."

"Yeah."

"Coincidence my ass. Find the connection, Leo."

"Way out front of you, babe. But I have to check some things first."

"Don't call me . . ." she said, and heard him disconnect, ". . . babe."

While she had her phone handy, PJ called June Merrett. There was something she had to ask.

A sleepy-sounding woman answered. Too late, PJ remembered that Schultz said June had taken a sleeping pill. PJ introduced herself.

Yawning, the woman said, "You were here before, weren't you? The police were pounding on the door a while ago. I can't seem to get any time to myself. Anyway, what can I do for you?"

"I'm sorry to intrude on your rest. Um, June, do you happen to have a twin sister?"

"Twin sister? No, it's just May and me. Although I did hear rumors."

"Rumors about what?"

"Oh, it's nothing."

"Tell me anyway, please," PJ said.

"Well, I did overhear my parents say something about an older child in the family. The way they were talking about it, it must have been some kind of scandal, maybe an abortion. I don't even know for sure they were talking about us—it was probably gossip about somebody else. My mother, Virginia Crane, came from a very wealthy background. When she married my father, Henry Winter, it was something of a shock to her family because he was middle class, and barely clinging on to that. I'm sure the Crane family had its little secrets. All those wealthy families do."

"What kind of secrets?"

"Well, Mother had a little brother named Ellis. He died when he was a year old. It was hushed up, but rumors started that he was a mixed race baby, and maybe his death wasn't accidental. *That* kind of secret. What's this all about, anyway?"

PJ weighed how much to say. How much had the officers already revealed when June came to the door after minutes of pounding? Probably not much, just checked to see that she was breathing.

"There's been another murder, June. The victim looks a little like you. I was just checking that you were okay."

"Looks like me? What does that mean? Was someone trying to kill me? Is that what the officers were doing here, seeing if I was still alive? Oh, no, first Arlan and now me. She's trying to wipe us out!"

"Calm down, calm down. Who do you mean by 'she'?"

"May, of course. May! She's jealous of us, I told you. You'd better ask her where she was."

"That will be checked out thoroughly, I can assure you of that."

There was a deep sigh on the other end of the phone. PJ pictured June standing there tugging her robe, bewildered that a murder victim looked enough like her that the police felt obligated to check on her well-being. There were times during PJ's divorce when all she'd wanted to do was stay in her nightgown, slink around the house, and crawl under the covers—and times when she actually did just that. It made her sympathetic to what June was going through.

And the police keep bothering her, on top of everything else.

PJ was embarrassed that she'd made the call. Her question could have waited until morning. "Why don't you get some more rest, June? I'm sorry about the intrusion."

"I'll try, but it'll be hard to get back to sleep now. I'll go check that all the doors are locked. Don't forget about May."

Chapter 15

Dear Diary,

These are things that happened to me, cross my heart and hope to die.

When I'm six, I bring home my report card from first grade. I'm smart, and I know it because me teacher tells me. At home, my parents don't think I'm very smart because my sister tells them that I do stupid things. She's making it up, but they don't listen to me. "She knows what she's talking about," Mom says. "You shouldn't question her, you're too little. You should be happy you have a sister who pays so much attention to you."

She pays attention, all right. That's because she's always watching for times she can do something to me, like smack me around. I don't give her any reason to. I stay away as much as I can. I'd like to go to a friend's house and spend some time with somebody who likes me. The problem is, nobody does. She tells them bad things about me, so I don't have any friends. Sometimes Mom and Dad have parties for me so I can meet friends. My sister helps out at the parties, of course, and the guests go home crying. I think they've about given up on the party idea.

"Lazy bones, never does anything," she says, and grabs my report card. It's not like I was waving it in her face. I had it hidden in my book bag, but she got it anyway. Every time she gets my bag away from me, she tears it a little, so it will look like I don't really care how I treat things that belong to me. I've gotten that lecture so many times I could mouth the words right along with Dad, but I don't dare.

"Oh, look how careless she is," she says, as she rips the carrying strap loose from my book bag. "Such a thoughtless child. Crazy bones, lazy bones," she chants as she holds my report card

up over my head so I can't reach it. Then she steps on my toes, hard.

"Oops."

She opens the report card and stares at it. I got high passes in everything, and an "exceptional" in reading.

"Give me back my report card!" I grab for it but she dances away.

"The teacher must have gotten you mixed up with someone else," she says. "These can't be your grades."

"Oh, yes they are! Give me that!"

"I'll just have to straighten things out. Where's that eraser?"

"I'll tell Mom."

"You do and you're dead meat, you little twerp." She said it like each word was a deadly threat, which it was. I didn't want to find out what it was like to be dead meat. I shut up about the report card but I made a face at her.

She found an eraser and undid all of Mrs. Sandauer's nice cursive writing. Then she wrote in different grades, like "Math: Can't count to three," and "Art: Not talented." In the comments at the bottom, she put "Very disruptive in class." Those things were so wrong. I tried to grab the card from her. I was going to rip it up. Better to have Mom and Dad think I lost it than to have them see it like that.

She grabbed my arm and twisted it behind my back. I tried to hurt her by kicking backward with my feet. The heel of my tennis shoe connected with her shin.

"Ow, damn it. Cut that out." She twisted my arm higher, so that I had tears on my face.

We heard Mom come into the kitchen and both of us froze. I didn't want to get punished for saying bad things about my sister, and I guess she didn't want to hurt me for real with Mom in the next room. She let go, and skipped away before I could get the card from her.

"Mom, look, a report card!" She dashed into the other room. I was right on her heels, but Mom already had the card in her hands. She was shaking her head.

"I'm so disappointed in you," she said. "I would have thought you'd have more pride than to bring home a report card like this."

I hung my head in shame. What else could I do? Then I got an inspiration.

"You could talk to Mrs. Sandauer, Mom."

That got her angry. "There's no point, is there?" she said. "She isn't going to change her mind. Her signature's right here." She shook the card in my face.

"Yes, ma'am. I'll try harder."

"Why can't you be more like your sister?"

Chapter 16

The team didn't gather until the next morning in PJ's office. Dave's wife sent in some biscuits and homemade jam. PJ's desk was sprinkled with crumbs, since everyone had gathered around it to eat. She didn't mind at all. Two excellent biscuits with raspberry jam rested in her contented stomach.

Her eyes landed on the picture of Megabite on her desk and it seemed impossible how long ago it was that she'd offered the cat a bowl of roast beef. PJ's hands, relaxed in her lap, could almost feel the comforting, warm feline weight and the vibration of her purrs. That's what she'd like to be doing now, settling into her favorite chair, Megabite hopping up to claim her lap, and cracking open a good book. Make that a good love story, one to take her as far from mutilated bodies as possible.

"Doc, what do you think of that?"

PJ blinked to find all three of them looking at her. *Think of what?*

"I think we shouldn't jump to conclusions," she said. It was one of Schultz's favorite phrases, and it could fit a lot of situations.

"See?" Schultz said triumphantly, banging his fist on PJ's desk. "She agrees with me. That's two against two."

He didn't seem to realize that two against two was a tie.

"Could we move on to Anita's report on May Simmons?" she asked. *When in doubt, change the subject.*

Anita straightened up in her chair, looking like a high school student about to give an oral book report.

"I first went over to the Simmons house about seven o'clock Sunday night. No one was home but the maid, who

110

said that the couple had gone to Powell Hall for a symphony performance. Apparently, neither of them was heartbroken about Arlan's death, at least not heartbroken enough to give up two hundred dollars' worth of tickets. So I took a break and got a few hours' sleep. I went back Monday morning. The knife had already been found. I talked with May for almost two hours," Anita said. "You need a roadmap in that place. Must be fifteen thousand square feet. When June said that her sister had no reason to be jealous financially, she was certainly telling the truth."

"So the sister married well, better than June did."

"Yeah, you could say that. Frank's the owner of a company that makes computer components."

"How about May?" Dave said.

"Takes care of the kids, shops, and occasionally volunteers on some fund-raising committee. She likes it that way, has no other ambitions. Frank wants her to do whatever makes her happy. He seems totally in love with her. I'm not sure whether May feels that way about him, or just about his money. She's a beautiful woman and could probably have her choice of wealthy men. All she'd have to do is wiggle her ass and light up her zillion watt smile."

"Hmm, sounds like you're jealous," Schultz said.

Anita shook her head. "I wouldn't mind having her T&A assets, but the lifestyle, nope."

"Is it so hard to believe that a beautiful, rich woman might actually love her husband and be faithful to him?" PJ said.

"Yes," said Dave and Schultz simultaneously.

"Men are so cynical," she said.

"Comes with the Y chromosome," Schultz said.

"One more thing about Frank," Anita said. "His left arm isn't normal. It's withered a little, reminds me of those tiny little arms on a T. rex, only not nearly as bad. The story is that

111

he was on one of those adventure vacations in the Australian desert and got bitten on his left forearm by an inland taipan, supposedly the world's deadliest snake. He was evacuated out on a helicopter and given the antivenin in an IV while still in the air, but he barely made it. He's got some kidney damage, too, but that doesn't show on the outside."

"So he has limited strength in his left arm?" PJ asked. Anita nodded. "Well, that puts a crimp in his ability to lug Arlan around, doesn't it? I may have come up with something interesting about getting the body to the dump site in my simulation, though."

"Moving on to the murder weapon," Anita said. "The knife was found in a drawer of a potting bench in an attached greenhouse. May asked her husband if he had an old knife she could use to cut roots when she was repotting. A couple of weeks ago, he left one in the drawer for her. Besides May, Frank, and the household staff, a number of people have been in and out of that home, including June, Arlan's partner Fredericka Chase, and about a hundred people who attended a Christmas open house a few days ago."

Schultz moaned. "We have a list?"

"Yeah. Looks like you're going to have to interview the mayor and the chief of police, Boss."

"Fuck that. Dave'll do it," Schultz said. "They already got a bad opinion of me from . . . never mind."

"Let Anita do it," PJ said. "She's got tact."

"Thanks for the vote of confidence, Doc, but I'd be happy to let Dave handle it," Anita said. Dave shook his head vigorously.

"Can't we narrow down that list?" PJ asked. "Any of those people at the open house could have taken the knife while they were in the house and then used it to kill Arlan, but how did the bloody knife get back into the greenhouse? Wouldn't it have to

112

be done by someone who goes to the house frequently?"

"Or someone who can break into the greenhouse," Schultz said. "Or who can hire someone to break into the greenhouse."

"Surely a house like that has a security system," PJ said.

"And your point is?"

PJ frowned. Homes with security systems still got burglarized. It wasn't an absolute protection, just a deterrent.

"Frank admits the knife belongs to him," Anita said, "and says it was in his basement workshop until his wife's request. His alibi isn't solid. He was home working on a presentation on his computer at the time of Arlan's murder. The maid retired to her quarters, as he says, about four o'clock. There's another maid who doesn't live in, and she left at three o'clock. The nanny was in the children's suite, and the last time Frank saw her was at dinner around half past five. There's a chef, but he left the house as soon as dinner was on the table. Always does."

"Take away the hired help and it's the same as Fredericka's evening. Working at home with no verification," PJ said. "How about his wife?"

"Out of the state," Anita said, looking at her notes. "She flew to Minneapolis on Friday because a friend who had cancer took a turn for the worse. May was in the hospital room when the friend died, and didn't leave that city until late Sunday afternoon. The friend's parents confirmed it. She spent Friday and Saturday night at their home, and is planning to fly back on Wednesday for the funeral."

"Shouldn't she have just stayed in Minneapolis until the funeral?" PJ asked. "Why did she come home?"

"Symphony tickets."

"Christ, she's either cold as hell," Schultz said, "or a tightwad."

"Or a music lover," PJ said. "Many people find music soothing, even when beset by grief."

Schultz looked at her, thinking that there were very few people who could get away with saying "beset by grief" and not sound pretentious or just plain ludicrous.

Who'd have ever guessed I'd fall for a shrink? Or that she'd have the slightest interest in me?

He admired the way her sweater skimmed her breasts and the v-neck displayed her long, elegant neck. He focused on the hollow of her throat, thinking of the way it sometimes vibrated when she spoke, the remembered thrumming of her heartbeat on his lips as he kissed her there when she was excited.

It wasn't just sex, although that was glorious with her. It was everything about her: intelligence, sense of humor, caring, the pride in her eyes when she talked about her son, the way she understood on a deep level his need to see justice done, and that she shared that need. Although he'd loved his ex-wife Julia, it was nothing like the primal connection he felt with PJ. His relationship with Julia now felt like three decades of practicing for the real event, for the love of his life.

Not that any of that made PJ easy to live with. No doubt she felt the same way about him. They were like two bolts of lightning that sizzled and crackled when they approached each other, but when they merged, they made one hell of a storm.

Anita and Dave drifted out to start working their way through the Christmas open house guest list. Schultz remained behind. He wanted to talk to PJ about the report from Chicago.

"You didn't hear a word of Dave's report," he said. "You had no idea what you didn't want to jump to conclusions about. I just didn't want to make an issue of it."

A defensive look flashed across PJ's face, and was quickly replaced by something approaching contrition. "No. I was daydreaming."

"Dave got together with one of the Chicago clients Arlan was supposed to meet. There were three men, but the other two didn't show. Looks like the real estate deal had something to do with pressuring other owners to sell so that entire blocks could be revitalized. The developers wanted to get their hands on all the property in the neighborhood before values started going up. Arlan was supposed to provide the persuasion money, and the hired strong arm tactics, to get the ball rolling."

"Okay, I get it now." She was looking off to the side, and still seemed distracted.

He should have let it go right then. He should have, but he didn't. "Christ, Doc, lives depend on our work. This isn't the fucking PTA. You can have your sex fantasies on your own time, which isn't the middle of a meeting. A meeting that you called, by the way."

"I get the point," she said. "I wasn't thinking about sex, anyway. That's your department. I've heard you've got a fantasy life with a whole harem of women to do your bidding."

"What the fuck? Who told you that?"

"Anita," PJ said smugly.

"Fuck, I can't say anything around that woman without it ending up in your ears!"

"Women *have* been known to talk to each other."

As if that was news.

PJ's eyes were shooting frozen rays. The temperature in the room dropped about eighty degrees, and he could practically hear his coffee freezing over. He should have let it go then, but he didn't.

115

"Yeah, but she's a cop, damn it," he said. "Her father's a fucking cop. Cops keep shit about each other inside the Job, or we couldn't fucking say anything."

Wrong. Shit. He saw by the look on PJ's face that he'd struck a major nerve. He fought down the tiny spark of glee deep inside that was a remnant of their first days of working together. *Big time wrong. How do I get out of this one?*

"You and your foul language can get the fuck out of my office," she said, "and go back to your little piece of real estate you can't even call your own because you share your desk with another fucking *cop*."

PJ was a cobra with its hood spread, and if he didn't act quickly, he'd get a toxic bite, and probably get kicked out of her bed, too. He raised his hands, palms facing her, in a gesture of either pacification or warding off.

Inspiration struck. He plucked the data gloves from their box, quickly stretched them over his large hands, and plopped the HMD on his head.

"Let's see your simulation," he said. "I'm not budging. I'm here to work."

Schultz waited, the darkened interior of the helmet blocking his view of PJ's reaction, wondering if his gamble would pay off. Wondering how long to wait in the darkness. It was hard to judge the passage of time. He began counting his respiration rate, adding six to his resting rate of sixteen per minute to account for agitation. He knew his resting rate due to long hours of boring surveillance when it was a game to make something out of nothing.

Sixty-two breaths later, the blue screens in front of his eyes came on, almost blindingly.

"I'll be the killer," he said, even though she knew his preference.

Originally highly skeptical of PJ's simulations, calling

them glorified computer games, he'd come to accept their value as another investigative tool—as long as they didn't replace interviewing real people and looking at real crime scenes.

Taking the role of killer was a natural for him because it was the way he worked an investigation, anyway, by putting himself in the killer's mind, thinking what the killer thought, and seeing what the killer saw. It gave his hunches a chance to ferment.

After Schultz, as the driver, had rolled the body down the levee, he did something he figured PJ hadn't thought to do. He walked around to the rear of the vehicle and opened the trunk. What was in there, if not the body?

The trunk light illuminated a small portion of the space, leaving the edges in darkness. A tarp protected the carpeting of the trunk. On it was a stained towel that, when he pulled it aside, revealed an assortment of knives, the blood nearly black under the dim light. There was also a plastic bag. Schultz lifted the bag, feeling its weight in his virtual hand. He brought it up into the moonlight.

"I think I found Arlan's dick," he said. He squinted at the bag and squeezed it. "And balls. Fingertips too, and maybe something that looks like a nose. The parts that weren't found at the dump site. I wonder where they are now."

Chapter 17

PJ got a call from June, who wanted to meet at a new coffeehouse on Grand named Dean's Beans. PJ arrived early and claimed a corner seating arrangement, two well-cushioned chairs with a low table between them, by plopping her jacket across the table. The scent of fine coffee wrapped itself around PJ like a welcome comforter. She sighed with enjoyment. She couldn't drag Schultz to a place like this. If it wasn't on the menu at Millie's Diner, he wasn't interested.

She didn't know what June wanted to talk about, but there was one big question on PJ's mind. Did June know her husband was having an affair with his business partner?

Dean, the owner, who looked only a few years older than her son Thomas, recommended a medium roast espresso. PJ hadn't had one in a while, so she took him up on it. She carried her cup and saucer back to the table, admiring the rich, golden cream on top. The aroma wafted up to her nose as she wondered what to expect when June arrived. The woman sounded so odd on the phone that PJ was beginning to wonder if grief—or guilt—had driven June over the edge.

June showed up carrying a brown envelope, and PJ hoped it wasn't more sex pictures. Not in Dean's Beans. Dean was probably underage.

June, indifferent about the menu selections, asked for a cup of coffee, then added six packs of sugar to the house blend she was given.

She and Dave ought to get together. Between the two of them, they could run this place out of cream and sugar.

Without preamble, June drew an eight by ten photograph from her brown envelope. PJ looked at it and blinked. It

118

showed nothing but a hand, a woman's left hand.

I knew it. I shouldn't have met her anywhere in public. The next picture out of that envelope is going to be someone's genitals.

"This was my ring," June said. "A real rock, a glacier, a four carat diamond in a platinum solitaire setting. A symbol of undying love. I used to love waving it under May's nose. After all, she'd been dumped."

Giving the photograph a closer look, PJ did think the ring looked impressive. "When was this, June?"

"About ten years ago. May was about to become the fiancée of a son of Boston old money. Then the family matriarch had a meeting with her, and after that, poof! No engagement. I never found out why. No one did, except May, and she wasn't saying anything."

She seemed to want to pour it all out, so PJ put on her psychologist's face, inhaled her espresso, and let the woman talk.

"I met my fiancé at a conference at UCLA," June said. "He had this idea about a technology incubator in the Midwest. He wanted to bring together all these top people, pay them scads of money, and let them research their little hearts out. I was happy to be coming back to St. Louis under those circumstances, sort of triumphant. May and I didn't always get along when we were growing up, you see."

I think that's been made perfectly clear. "Sisters often have rough periods in their early lives," PJ said. "Then they settle in and become good friends as adults."

June held her cup up to her face, then left it suspended there beneath her nose, as though she'd forgotten about it. Her mind was elsewhere. Finally she sipped from it and put it on the table.

"Frankie and I come home for the holidays. It's the first time he's meeting Mom and Dad." June continued as if there'd been no break in the conversation, and PJ noticed she was relating events in present tense again.

"The big moment arrives and he carries it off. May's so jealous even the whites of her eyes are green, and she can't keep her eyes off my ring. May sits across from us at the dinner table. Somewhere between the main course and dessert, I notice that she's not looking at my ring anymore. She's looking at my *man*."

A little color came into June's cheeks, and her voice edged louder.

Wind her up and let her talk. Actually, she's self-winding.

"I run my hand up Frankie's thigh to remind him who's wearing his ring. He kisses my ear, but I can see the gears spinning behind her eyes. She leans low to talk to him across the table, giving him a view of her two mountains and Paradise Valley. Really. She's so obvious, I figure Frankie and I are going to have a good laugh about it later that night."

There was silence for a time. "And did you?" PJ said. "Laugh about it later?"

"What? Oh, yes, of course we did. But during the next two days she's all over him, touching him on the shoulder, letting her hair fall in front of her face." June demonstrated, nearly landing her hair in her coffee cup.

"I almost think my parents are cheering her on, making a game of giving her opportunities to be with Frankie without me. It's a good thing we're staying at a hotel. At least I get him alone all night. After all, I've got breasts, too."

PJ hoped June wasn't going to demonstrate that, as she'd done with her hair. By now, PJ had a good idea where this was going. It was painful to listen to, especially with June reliving the experience.

"I'm busy packing away some Christmas gifts, and it occurs to me I haven't seen Frankie in a while. I go down to the pool, check the bar, finally check the hotel restaurant. The waiter points out their table, but the chairs are empty. I decide to check the little girl's room to see if May is putting on makeup."

Coffee forgotten, June reached out. She put her hand on top of PJ's, which was resting on the arm of the chair, as if using PJ for an anchor. She went on breathlessly with her story, rushing to the end.

"Inside I hear her. I hear them both. They're in the last stall. May's panties are on the floor and her legs are wrapped around Frankie. Her blouse is open and his head is buried in Paradise Valley. She looks at me and winks. Winks! I scream, and he keeps thrusting. The motherfucker keeps thrusting! I stand there until he finishes and pulls out. He sees me but he doesn't really see me, like I'm invisible or something. It's May he wants. I yank the ring from my finger and reach past May's ass. I drop the ring in the toilet and flush."

June had become the center of attention due to the volume of her voice and her subject matter, but in moments peoples' eyes flitted away. Other conversations resumed, and loners studied the newspapers or books they'd brought.

"So your Frankie didn't marry you," PJ said. Every now and then she had to prime the pump.

"He's May's husband, Frank Simmons. He was mine first. I just wanted you to know how her marriage got its start. That's why she's so jealous of the true love that Arlan and I have. Now do you believe me when I tell you that Frank and May are out to get us? First Arlan and then me."

June stuffed the picture of the diamond ring back into the envelope. Her face looked drawn, suddenly ten years older. She must have paid a high price emotionally revealing Frankie's betrayal of her and May's active part in it. Deep down, she probably still loved her sister, but there was a lot of static between that buried emotion and the surface.

PJ wanted to clear up something she'd been curious about. "Do you remember when we first met that you said you were sure that Arlan had hidden an anniversary gift for you in the house?"

June nodded. "I found it, too. It was lingerie, a sexy black lace teddy. True love, you know." She frowned. "He got it in the wrong size. He hasn't made that mistake in years. It was too small, and I had to exchange it."

Too small, huh? Bet I know who that gift was really intended for.

Looking at June, PJ was reluctant to question her about infidelity, but it had to be done.

"June, were you aware that Arlan and Fredericka were having an affair?"

June's eyes widened, but she said nothing for a long time.

PJ's espresso was lukewarm. She drank it anyway, four quick swallows, and settled the cup back into the saucer. "June?"

"I can't believe May would stoop to spreading lies like that," June said. "That's contemptible, even for her."

"There's another foreplay album, just like the one you and Arlan had. Only this one is for Arlan and Fredericka. I've seen it."

"I can't accept that. No. Arlan and I have true love. He only has eyes for me," she said.

Clearly distressed, June looked like she was about to flee both the idea of the affair and the table.

"So your husband never gave you any reason to think he was involved with Fredericka?"

"Having sex with the little nympho?" She sneered. "That's what he calls her, you know. He tells me everything. He resists when she flirts with him. If there are pictures of *her,* then May's behind it. She has to be. And the pictures are fake."

Before PJ could respond, June headed for the door, clutching her past in a brown envelope, her future in tatters.

Chapter 18

Schultz and Anita were sitting at the counter in Millie's Diner. The place was nearly deserted. One table was occupied with a quartet of Ladies Going Shopping, hands emphasizing their words, laughing, lowering their voices to gossip. All of them had ordered large salads and were now picking at the remains. Words from their conversation drifted up and hung motionless above the women's table until someone opened the door. The wind swirled the words over to Schultz. *Affair . . . Tacky . . . Fat ass . . . Adorable.*

Hunched over his plate, he was rounding up the last of his French fries and making sure each one got its fair share of the salt stuck in the swirls of grease on the plate.

"I thought you were loyal," he said.

"Where do you get off questioning my loyalty after what I did for you when you were accused of that hit-and-run?" Anita said, referring to an earlier case.

He waved away the reminder. "I know, I know, I'm talking about other shit."

"Like talking about you with Doc?"

"Yeah."

"She asked me. What am I supposed to do, lie?"

"Hell, yes," he said. "You've done it for me before."

"That was different. You were being framed then."

And I'm being framed now.

Anita frowned, and then wrapped her lips around her soda straw. She might have been thinking the same thing as Schultz.

He pushed on. "She asked you specifically what you knew about my fantasy life?"

124

"No. The subject just came up, that's all. We were talking about men in general."

"Can you just watch what you say from now on? You got me in a shitload of trouble."

"Actually, you're the one who got yourself in trouble, from what I hear. Making it clear that Doc's not part of the group because she doesn't have a badge."

Schultz put his head in his hands and groaned. *This is a nightmare! I don't stand a chance with these women.*

"How about we talk police work, Boss? You know, the homicides?"

"We already are. My love life's a dead subject."

"I've been looking into Shower Woman being the one who attended the workshop in K.C., like you asked. So far, no proof of that. Not even any prints at registration time. She was wearing winter gloves. Get this. She signed her registration slip and the gas credit card purchase left-handed, saying her right thumb was out of commission. The clerk saw the bandage sticking out from under the glove. Those signatures are inconclusive. Can't be ruled a match, can't be ruled a non-match to June's exemplars with her left hand."

"Marilee Baines could be a professional forger."

Anita snorted. "Gimme a break, Schultz. June has an actual bruise at the base of her thumb, several days old, turning yellow. Shower Woman doesn't. The K.C. hotel room has been cleaned and occupied, twice. No prints there, no nice long hairs, no fibers from her wool winter coat. Nada. The place prides itself on its exceptional housekeeping. June's alibi is still good."

"Shit. It was such a tidy package. June killed her husband because he was screwing around with Fredericka, and then killed the look-alike hired to create an alibi," Schultz said. "Cleaning up the loose ends."

"You've been reading too many mysteries, Boss. Things aren't that tidy in real life. Besides, if we're looking for wives whose husbands screwed Fredericka, the number is probably huge. I heard about her little love-fest with Dave."

"It would be faster to list the people who've known Fredericka longer than thirty minutes and *haven't* screwed her. Keep working on that alibi, Anita." He stood up and left a quarter tip.

"You and your hunches," she said. She put two quarters under her own plate, and when she thought he wouldn't see it, slipped another one under his.

Christ. All these women are in it together.

"Anita, where's Forest Park Terrace?" PJ was driving around in the private street section of the Central West End, having trouble finding the Simmons home. She'd finally resorted to calling Anita, who was working her way down the Simmons party guest list.

"I made a note about that in my report. I guess you didn't spot it," Anita said. "Forest Park Terrace is an old name, from the turn of the century. It's Lindell Boulevard now."

PJ sighed in exasperation. "Why does the Simmons home have a turn of the century address?"

"You'll have to ask them. The house is about a hundred years old. I guess they thought it was classier to keep its old address, impressive in gold ink on invitations, that kind of thing."

"Snootier, more likely. How do they get their mail?"

"Post office box, I suppose. Anything else, Boss?"

"Yes. Tell me how to get there. I just passed this huge gate with marble columns and a statue of a nude woman."

"That's Carrie. The statue, that is. The street you passed was Kingsbury." She gave directions from there.

"Got it, thanks."

The driveway was long and tree-lined, and the bare tree branches were covered with Christmas lights. The place must look fabulous at night, considering that it already looked fabulous during the day, without the benefit of holiday lighting. A gardener was working near the driveway, raking leaves that must have blown in from the neighboring house. He was young, early twenties, and had an amazing physique that drew PJ's eyes. When he turned toward her, she saw that his face was disfigured on the left side, maybe a burn scar. He wore his cap pulled low on his forehead. He was putting leaves into an open-topped compartment on the back of a utility vehicle, a kind of lawn tractor without the mower blade. It had wood rails all around the back end, like a large children's red wagon. She'd seen something similar at the Missouri Botanical Garden, but here it was at a private home.

Imagine having the resources to bring in a gardener and a cart for a few stray leaves.

The wind swirled the collected leaves, lifting some out of the cart. The gardener patiently went after them, and waved to her as she pulled up to the house. He had a smile that made it easy to forget the scar on his face. She smiled back.

There were marble columns on May's house that made the ones at the Kingsbury gate look like stubby imitations. Looking up while waiting at the door, PJ noticed a massive chandelier suspended above her head. She couldn't get over the fact that it was the front door light. The one at her house had one bulb and a little white globe that accumulated dead bugs.

The double doors must have been ten feet tall, and when one of them opened inward, she almost expected Igor, Dr. Frankenstein's assistant, to be standing there. Instead, there was a maid, attractive, thirtyish, and wearing a classic uniform of black and white, including a frilly white cap that covered her head. It was an outfit that would be at home in the 1890s.

"Is that a real mobcap?" PJ said. She'd meant to introduce herself, but the question just slipped out.

A slim hand patted the crown of the cap. "Yes, it is, ma'am. What can I do for you?"

"I'm here to see May Simmons."

"Missus May isn't seeing anyone right now. If you'll leave your calling card, I'll let her know you were here."

What century is this? Calling card? She could imagine what Schultz would say in this situation. Just thinking of his name brought back the exasperation she'd felt earlier, in her office. She hoped that the maid would think her reddened cheeks had to do with the weather.

"Uh, I'm Dr. Penelope Gray, a consultant with the St. Louis Police Department." PJ fumbled in her purse, extracted a business card that had bent corners and a stray pen mark, and handed it over. "Please let her know I'm here, and I'm willing to wait. Going to wait," she finished more forcefully.

The maid snatched the card from her hand and closed the door. Several minutes went by. PJ figured it would take that long just to walk through the house to deliver the message. Leaning against the marble, she felt its chill in the slanting December afternoon sun.

It would probably be August before this place warmed up.

Another five minutes, and the door opened.

"Sorry to keep you waiting, Dr. Gray. Missus May will see you right away."

PJ was barely in the door when May came down a sweeping grand staircase. She was wearing a long, black skirt with a lacy white blouse that had gathered sleeves, full cuffs, and a high neck.

Time warp. Abandon ship.

May approached PJ, who automatically extended her hand. May clasped it in both of hers. She had cold fingers.

"Welcome, Dr. Gray. It's been quite a strain, you know, with Frank being taken out of here in handcuffs."

"Sorry to disturb you. I'm wondering about the costumes."

"Oh, these? Mary Beth and I have been rehearsing for a play, a charity performance. We do stay in character quite a bit, as an acting technique. What must you think of us! Mary Beth, please bring us some tea in the drawing room."

Now there's a line I don't get to use. In my case, it's "Thomas, bring me some popcorn in the living room," followed by, "Get it yourself."

May ushered PJ into a large, formal room set up to receive guests. There were several sofas and chairs scattered about in a room that had a fireplace at each end. In one of them, a fire was burning, and the two women settled onto facing loveseats in front of the fire. The furnishings, unlike May's clothes, were modern.

While waiting for tea, PJ studied May's face, looking for a sisterly resemblance. It was there, around the eyes and in the aristocratic nose. But what was attractive on June was stunning on May's face. There was no weak chin, no lollipop shape. May could be a beauty queen. She certainly carried herself royally.

Mary Beth arrived with a tea cart and serving set of delicate china, translucent with gold edges. PJ took the small teacup in her hand and hoped she wouldn't break it. The cost of replacing it might bump Thomas out of private school for a semester.

May didn't look like a woman whose husband had been carted away in handcuffs with a murder charge hanging over his head. PJ couldn't see any sign of the strain the woman had mentioned. May was so concerned that she was busy playing dress-up.

"What can I do for you, Dr. Gray? By the way, what kind of consulting work do you do for the police?"

"I'm following up on the interview you had with Detective Anita Collings. I'm a psychologist helping the police develop criminal profiles."

True enough. Now that PJ had been unmasked as a psychologist, she felt free to assail May with shrink questions. "I have to say that you don't seem very disturbed that your husband has been charged with murder."

May waved a hand dismissively. "Oh, that's all a mistake, I'm sure. Our lawyer, Jack Nordman, is on top of it. Jack'll get the charge dismissed. My husband will be out on bail, and this will just make a good story to tell at our next social function. Very exciting, you know, having the police search your home. Puts us right up there with O.J."

"Except that O.J. went on trial, and you don't expect your husband to."

"If you knew Frank, you'd know the idea of him committing murder would be ridiculous. He's a kind, gentle man. Works with children's charities."

Psychos can be charming when they want to. Merlin said that, and it's true.

She noticed that May raised her little finger as she sipped from her teacup. The woman was too composed. PJ needed to get under that veneer of hers.

"What's your explanation for the bloody knife with his fingerprints on it then?" PJ said.

"I'm sure something will turn up. That's why we pay Jack the big bucks." She smiled sweetly. "I won't be home when Frank gets back; I have some holiday shopping to do." She looked pointedly at a wall clock. "We have reservations at Tony's tonight, though, to unwind from the stress."

"How are your children taking the news? Are they worried?"

The smile slipped away briefly, and then her face brightened. "They're fine. Nanny's taking them to see Santa today at Plaza Frontenac."

"Brian and Amelia are six and nine years old, Mrs. Simmons," PJ said, pushing harder. "They know enough to realize something's not right when the police haul away their dad. Don't you think they're worried?"

She shrugged. "I told them he was late for a business trip, and the police were helping him get to the airport. He does travel often."

"So you lied to your kids about the fact that their father has been arrested for murder? Don't they know June and Arlan Merrett? Do they even know Arlan's dead?"

At the mention of June's name, something flickered in May's eyes, something unpleasant. "Of course they know Aunt Junie, and that her poor husband is dead. What I tell my kids is none of your business, Dr. Gray. I'm lying to them about Santa, too. Are you going to arrest me for that?" May's voice had a snippy edge to it.

Ah, now we're getting somewhere.

"Of course not," PJ said, leaving out the fact that she couldn't arrest a person anyway. "I'm just speaking as a concerned parent. You can tell your children anything you want, as long as you're not severely beating them when you do it."

May's cheeks acquired a touch of redness that wasn't rouge.

God, I love my job.

"So you don't think your husband had anything to do with the killing?"

"No, I don't. He's just not that kind of man. He had reason to want Arlan out of his life, but he certainly didn't act on it."

PJ sat back, keeping the smug look from her face. She'd irritated May enough to make the woman incautious. This was information that hadn't surfaced during Anita's interview.

"What reason did he have to want to kill Arlan?" PJ said.

"For a psychologist, you don't listen very well. I didn't say anything about *killing* Arlan. I said Frank just wanted him to stop being a pest. Arlan had been trying to pressure him into investing in some out-of-town real estate deal. A scam, no doubt."

"Do you know any details?"

"I know that Arlan was trying to get him to part with two million dollars to buy some run-down warehouse. Can you imagine that? A warehouse! What would Frank possibly want with property like that? It's probably an insurance fraud thing, you know. Abandoned warehouse goes up in flames. Arlan's had some screwball schemes before and lost money. That's why it's embarrassing the way June talks about how prosperous they are. I mean, have you seen where she lives?"

"Yes, I have."

"Well, there you go. Her place is so tacky. Did you see that big oil portrait of her? I don't think she paid the artist well. He didn't touch her up enough."

No love lost here. PJ forged ahead, trying to keep May off balance. "Were you aware of the photo album that June used to identify the scar on her husband's body? The foreplay album?"

"The *what?*"

"A collection of revealing pictures of each other—very revealing—that they used to warm each other up for sex?"

"Oh, for heaven's sakes. Now I've heard everything. I can

see why Arlan might need a little kick-start, though, to work up any interest in June. And she actually admitted this to the police?"

"Seemed rather proud of it."

May shook her head. "I didn't think even June could be so depraved."

Probably not a good time to mention that June said pretty much the same thing about you.

"She also said that you were jealous of her, and should be considered a suspect in Arlan's murder. You, not Frank."

That was unexpected. May's eyes were as round as the saucer underneath PJ's teacup.

"So," PJ asked, "where were you on the night of Arlan's murder?"

Leo would be proud. I'm getting the hang of this.

"Jealous! What could I possibly have to be jealous about? She's the one who's jealous of us, Dr. Gray! Look around you. Don't you think June wants to live like this? She's so bitter she can't have any kids that she doesn't even send our sweet children birthday gifts. Do you know how hard it is to explain to kids that their Aunt Junie forgets, year after year? Next year I'm going to buy presents myself and say they came from her."

May raised her teacup to her lips, forgetting the little finger, and took an audible slurp. Her eyes narrowed and she lowered her voice to a conspiratorial whisper. "Did you know that my Frank used to be her boyfriend? She could have had this life, if she'd been able to hang onto him. As soon as he met me, he dropped her like the piece of trash she is. That's a motive, isn't it? Maybe she killed her husband and is trying to make it look like Frank did it. The police should be interrogating her instead of Frank."

"I'm sure the police are looking into that."

133

"Well, they'd better. No telling what that crazy woman will do," she said. May put down her teacup and patted her perfectly coiffed hair, as though she expected to find a renegade hair out of place. PJ could see her breathing deeply and visibly relaxing. She'd obviously caught on to the fact that PJ was deliberately and expertly rattling her cage.

Darn. Well, soldier on.

"You didn't answer the question about where you were, Mrs. Simmons."

"I told all that to the detective woman who was here earlier."

"Humor me."

"I was out of town. A dear, dear friend of mine passed away. Lung cancer, poor thing, and she gave up smoking years ago. The irony of it! I didn't get back in town until Sunday evening. I didn't even have time to get my hair done before Frank and I took off for Powell Hall."

"There's been another murder and the victim looks very much like June. So much so, it would be easy to picture the victim as part of your family. June said there were rumors about that. Do you have an older sister, Mrs. Simmons?"

It was new territory, something none of the investigators had asked before. Again May's hand explored her hairdo, then fluttered at the nape of her neck with nothing to do. She was silent.

PJ pressed further. "Where can I find your older sister? I'd like to speak with her." She picked up a button-sized, shortbread cookie from the serving tray and popped it in her mouth. It was smooth and buttery, just sweet enough, and practically melted on her tongue. May still said nothing, so PJ went for another cookie.

May sighed. "June's mistaken, Dr. Gray. Or delusional. I hate to bring that up, but there it is. It's just the two of us in this family. Maybe June had an imaginary friend when she was a child. It wouldn't be out of character."

Imaginary friends don't end up in the shower with knives in their hearts.

"Do you mind if I look around?" PJ said.

"It's a large home," May said. She seemed guarded, but it could have been the result of PJ's earlier sharp questioning. "The police have already done this. Is there anything in particular you'd like to see?"

The skeletons in your closet would be nice.

"Just the basics. The greenhouse, where the knife was found."

"It was sealed by the police. Are you authorized to break the seal, Dr. Gray? I thought you were a consultant, not a law enforcement officer."

Busted. "How about the rest of the ground floor, then?"

"Of course. I'm not sure what you'll learn from that, but I'll have Mary Beth show you around. I really do need to get on with my shopping."

The maid had changed out of her early 1890s outfit into a practical uniform of black trousers, white top, and white shoes that would have gladdened a nurse's heart. Once out of hearing range of the lady of the house, Mary Beth Paulson was friendly and informal. Chatting with her turned out to be more valuable than the tour of large, high-ceilinged rooms. The maid knew a lot about the interior design.

"I'm going into that some day, I'm not going to be a maid all my life, you know."

PJ was treated to a litany of colors, fabrics, and proportions.

PJ learned that while Frank seemed to genuinely treasure his beautiful wife and would love her even if they lived in a doublewide, May was a calculating social climber who had set her sights early on the name, the house, and lifestyle, and the perfect little kids, whom she relegated to the care of a nanny. On one subject, Mary Beth was emphatic: Frank was a nice guy and would never have killed his brother-in-law. He wasn't so nice to competitors. He was ruthless, but that was business.

PJ had already gotten a glimpse of May's self-serving attitude, and it wasn't much of a stretch to imagine her as part of a killing team if there was something in it for her. Motive was the problem. It seemed like killing Arlan would be slumming for her.

PJ and Mary Beth ended up in the staff kitchen, a cozy place no bigger than PJ's own kitchen but containing upscale appliances and granite counters. There was a separate area where Chef worked, and he scolded the staff if they went in to raid his refrigerator, so this place was a refuge. They sat on stools around an island with a gleaming sink. Mary Beth looked like she was glad to be off her feet for a time. PJ was more comfortable in the relatively modest surroundings in the kitchen than in parlors with grand pianos.

"What do you think of May's sister?" PJ asked.

Her companion hesitated before answering. "You can say what you want, there's nobody listening here. Is there?"

Mary Beth laughed. "Even the Missus isn't that paranoid. There's no hidden microphone in the flowerpot. It's just that I don't quite know what to think of June. She comes over often, but I think it's not so much to visit her sister as to visit the house."

"She's jealous, then."

"Not exactly. It's more like she's shopping for ideas, things May's done that she can adapt to her own life."

"Ever heard them fight?"

"Never."

"I noticed a control panel by the front door," PJ said. "Is that for the security system?"

"Yes, there are several of them in the house. Each room has a panic button, too, even the bathrooms and the walk-in closets. The kids get a kick out of pressing them. We have the cops out here at least once a month. Used to be more often. I've never heard Nanny lecture them about it, though. Those kids do pretty much what they want."

"She'll pay for that later, or at least the Nanny will," PJ said. "Is the security system operating all the time?"

"When the Mister is home, he makes a good effort, although he gets distracted about it sometimes. The Missus, well, a couple of times I've reminded her, and who knows how many times the alarm's been off that I haven't noticed. Not my job. You'd think people living in a place like this would pay more attention. Whenever I remind her, she gets stiff with me for a couple of days. So there's nothing in it for me. Makes my eyes tend to slide right by those panels, if you know what I mean. Besides, if a burglar got in here, I can't see that he'd make a beeline for the maid's quarters. Nothing valuable in there, with what I get paid."

Mary Beth got up and took a beer from the refrigerator, telling PJ to help herself.

Opening the refrigerator, PJ spotted a bottle of water that looked good. She'd been having way too much caffeine. Something else caught her eye, twin stacks of bright red egg cartons, six dozen eggs altogether.

"Wow," she said. "Somebody around here isn't too concerned about cholesterol."

Mary Beth laughed. "Would you believe that's only two weeks' worth? We get a new batch every two weeks, and throw out any that are left. The family doesn't use any other kind. Wouldn't dare bring anything else into the house. Chef put up a fuss, a little power play, because he didn't want the red eggs, that's what he calls them, pushed on him. But he's got the same kind in his kitchen."

"Really? What's so good about these? Should I be buying them, too?"

The cartons were old-fashioned cardboard, and had a distinctive hatching chick design on top.

Mary Beth took an unladylike gulp of her beer before answering. "They come from Old Hank's farm. It says so on top. Missus May's parents used to buy eggs from him, and she continued the tradition. Miss June does, too. In fact, it was Mister Arlan's turn last week to do the buying for both families. It was quite a ritual. The husbands never missed their turns. If they did, the wives would chew them out. You gotta wonder about these family traditions. Who'd get that worked up over eggs?"

"What day was Arlan's turn?"

"Last Wednesday, I know for sure. I remember him coming here with the eggs like usual, and being in a hurry because he was leaving for Chicago and wanted to get through downtown before rush hour."

"Do you remember the time of day?" PJ asked, trying to keep her voice casual.

"It was a little after four in the afternoon. I remember telling him I didn't think he had a chance of missing the traffic."

"Did you actually see him leave?"

"No, I had work to do. I left him stacking the eggs in the refrigerator, but how long could that take? He must have gone a few minutes after I saw him."

That was after he'd finished having lunch with his partner. Fredericka thought he'd left town immediately afterward, but instead he went on an errand to buy eggs.

It looked like Mary Beth was the last person to see Arlan Merrett alive, except for the killer.

Driving back to Headquarters in her Rabbit, PJ approached the stoplight at the busy corner of Lindell and South Grand, near St. Louis University, just when it turned yellow. It was lunchtime, and both car and pedestrian traffic was heavy. Grumbling about how she always seemed to be first in line at a stoplight because she didn't run the yellow or even red light like others did, she used the wait time to look through papers scattered on the passenger seat. Then she felt her car bumped from the rear, and begin moving. She was being pushed out into the intersection!

PJ smashed the brake pedal down as far as it would go, and fumbled for the emergency brake lever, which was between the seats. There were papers in the way, and her gloves, and her briefcase, and her sunglasses, and an empty White Castle bag. Her car groaned but kept moving forward. She heard horns honking, looked to her left, and saw a southbound truck bearing down on her on Grand. She heard brakes squealing—the truck's or her own, she didn't know. She glanced in her rearview mirror. The car immediately behind her was so close she couldn't see any part of it but its windshield, and it had no driver.

Disjointed thoughts and images ran rapidly through her head. *That driver's jumped. Jump? No, go!*

She took her foot off the brake and stomped on the gas pedal instead, hoping to shoot through the intersection ahead of the truck. The Rabbit lurched and responded, but not enough to avoid the collision completely. The truck clipped the back end of her car, sending it spinning toward northbound traffic. She shifted violently to the side in her seat, but was held in by the shoulder harness. Through the blur of motion, her mind focused on the shower of pebble-like pieces from the tempered glass of the broken driver's window, like crystals afloat in the winter sunlight, each with its own rainbow.

Chapter 19

I park a few blocks away on Waterman, near a school, and stroll over to May's place on Lindell. It's pleasant enough for a December afternoon, with sunshine lighting my way occasionally, as the clouds clot, skid apart in front of the wind, and then regroup.

Every time I take a swing at May, I miss.

It's like she'd got some invisible shield around her, a non-stick coating so that things would just slide off her, like water drops on a newly-waxed car.

I frame her for Arlan's murder by using her knife. Her knife, mind you, from her own greenhouse that Frank is barely aware exists. How am I to know that the stupid knife had his fingerprints all over it and May hasn't touched it? It's her greenhouse, her knife, ergo she's the killer. The police don't see it that way, though. Imagine arresting Frank! Why couldn't he have had an alibi, been thrashing around in a mistress's bed or schmoozing donors for his goddamned kids' charities?

And to think the disgusting prick was in the house when I replaced the knife. If I'd known that, I might have gotten double use out of that knife.

I approach the house, pretending that I'm walking to the bus stop at Lindell and Kingshighway. Metrobus Route 93, west-bound, 3:43 p.m. Checking my watch, I see that I could actually make the bus if I pick up the pace a little.

My coat from Goodwill smells a little funky. That used smell never goes away, the soaked-in perspiration, hopes, and disappointments. I find myself wondering about the coat's former owner. She may have walked in my same footsteps, heading for the same bus stop, wanting nothing more than to rest her tired legs and hoping that she gets a seat on the bus. I have a scarf over my head,

*the kind European peasant women wear, flat-soled black shoes,
gloves I literally picked out of a trash can, and a shopping bag so
worn the handles are taped on. Nobody even glances at me. My
clothes and my beaten-by-society, slumped shoulders are my shield
of invisibility, a different kind than May has but just as effective.*

*The Simmons home looms. I can see Frank's metallic blue
BMW 760Li jauntily parked in the circular drive. Bond was
posted, surprise, surprise, and the errant hubby whisked quickly
away from the jailhouse pervs. I make a confident left turn and
head across the lawn toward the backyard, like I'm heading
around the back for the servants' entrance. I feel no eyes boring
into the back of my head. In seconds, I am in the yard, walking in
the shadows of the home, heading toward the greenhouse that juts
out into an island of sunshine.*

*It's not the conservatory that would be expected with a house
like this. The green thumbs of previous owners had to do with
money, not plants. May had this one built a few years ago, a metal
and glass structure with expansive views of the grounds. It holds
an assortment of plants that she talks to more than her children.*

*When my plans started to take shape, I busted one of the
single pane glass panels with a rock. The gardener was accused
of kicking up a stone with his riding lawn mower. Frank was out
of town, deliberate timing on my part, so May had to take care
of it. She had the glass replaced, but, as I thought would
happen, didn't notify the security company. So all but one of the
panes of glass in that greenhouse have sensors connected to the
system. All but one big, juicy, removable pane of glass.*

*May is out shopping and the nosy, oh-so-smart police shrink is
out of the way. Frank's home alone, except for the staff. I'm not
worried about them. I know exactly where they'll be. Chef in his
kitchen, Nanny in the children's suite, Maid in the staff kitchen,
probably taking a nap, resting her head on the cool, exquisitely-
veined, green granite counter. The second maid only comes in three*

days a week for heavy cleaning, and this isn't one of them. I know all the details.

I check the target window carefully, looking for new foil wire that would make the glass part of the alarm circuit. None.

Out comes the putty knife. I'm getting quite good at this, even with gloves on. Removing the pane the first time was hard. It had been professionally installed and had these sharp metal triangles under the putty, which I now know are glazier's points. Faulty research on my part—I wasn't expecting those. I managed to keep from dropping them into the grass and losing them, thank goodness. After sneaking the knife back into the greenhouse, I put the glass pane back, complete with points and putty, hoping it wouldn't rattle or fall out.

I'm good at it now. Fast. Straight putty lines. I can get in and out of May's house so easily I might as well have put in a doggy-door.

The pane is out. I slip off my shoes and ease my way in. A cold wind eases in behind me, sending shivers through the orchids.

There are motion sensors in the house, but they are only turned on at night. I head for the back stairs, the one used by servants, making sure I don't run into one of the staff or a child who has temporarily escaped Nanny's grasp. My feet, clad in the same brand of stockings that May uses, know the way all by themselves. Upstairs, I head straight for the gun. May took shooting lessons. I know everything she does.

It's in her nightstand, unloaded because of the kids. The bullets are in the top drawer of her lingerie chest, under the push-up bras. I guess she thinks kids are unable to open drawers. Or have a fear of lingerie. It is rather startling to open that drawer and see those shapely cups in pairs, as if they're waiting for Noah to summon them. I leave the drawer open and scatter some bullets on the floor, as if they were handled in haste or fury.

I took shooting lessons, too.

Hugging the impressive down pillow from May's side of the bed, I approach the study. Classical music is playing. My heartbeat races with the delicate notes of the flute, the blood in my veins vibrates with the strings of the cello. Opening the door just a little, I check to see that no one else is in the room. Interrupting a meeting with, say, a group of cops buying new computer hardware would not be a good thing.

He can't see the gun. What he sees is me, holding a pillow across my belly. I squeeze the trigger. Down puffs out of the pillow, and a little "pop!" buries itself in the music's crescendo. A lucky shot, considering that I can't use my sexy, two-handed stance. A hole opens just below his hairline, and blood, guided by the furrows between his brows, flows down to drip on his papers. Before he can topple forward, I send another bullet into his chest.

Music falls on his dead ears.

I set the pillow and gun on the floor of the study and pull the door closed. May's going to have a nasty surprise when she gets home. Her gun, her pillow, her secret stash of bullets, her dead husband.

Can't fail this time. It's a swing and a home run. Even the police aren't so thickheaded as to botch this. They'll arrest May by dinnertime.

Out through the greenhouse, shoes on, glass puttied, quick, quick. I can't help giving myself a little hug of congratulations. Blocks away, I'll drop the old coat, gloves, and scarf I'm wearing into the school's Dumpster. Can't be too careful about things like down from the pillow or gun residue on gloves.

Rounding the corner of the house, I see May's black Mercedes SL600 Roadster coming west on Lindell. The timing couldn't be better. I should go, but I can't help myself. I linger nearby, ready to bolt through the neighbor's yard if I have to. The car turns in, and to my surprise, a hideous orange vehicle turns in after it.

She gets out. The carroty car's door opens . . . Fuck. Detective

Schultz. They walk inside together. Nothing for a minute or two, then a scream. She's laid eyes on her freshly killed beloved.

Damn. Damn. Damn. May's got a perfect alibi. The new widow was with a fucking cop at the time of death.

It's a swing and a miss, folks.

Chapter 20

Schultz was still at the scene of Frank Simmons's murder when he got the call. PJ had been in a car accident, and was in the hospital. Leaving Dave and Anita on site, he bullied his way through rush hour traffic to St. Louis University Hospital. The accident had practically happened on the hospital's doorstep.

He stopped in the first floor gift shop and bought a small stuffed kitten with an insipid, furry smile. Stopping outside the door to her room, he composed his face and cleared the anxiety from his throat.

She was in the bed closer to the door. The curtain divider was pulled back and the other bed was neatly made, waiting for the next occupant. Thomas sat on the edge of her bed, worried but brave. It was hard enough for Schultz.

"Hey, Doc," he said, "lying down on the job again?"

She turned at the sound of his voice, but winced slightly while doing it. The blanket pulled up nearly to her chin no doubt covered a multitude of aching spots. She patted Thomas's hand and asked him if it wasn't time for him to go.

"Mick's mom is waiting," she said. "We're imposing, so let's not push it."

"Okay, if you're that eager to get rid of me," Thomas said, smiling. "Get a lot of rest, Mom, and do everything the doctors tell you to for a change."

"I will, Sweetie."

"I guess rough sex is out for awhile," Schultz said, when he was certain Thomas was out of earshot.

She started to laugh, and then thought better of it.

"Bruises," she said. "Really, it's not that bad. I'm a poster child for seat belt use, though." She pulled down the sheet and lifted her pajama top. He raised his eyebrows and was about to make a smart crack when he saw her injuries. His hand traced the contusions on her neck, between her breasts, and across her abdomen.

"No deep injuries, internal bleeding, anything like that. If the truck had hit the driver's door, I wouldn't be here talking to you, or so I was told. I changed from the brakes to the gas just in time, and almost made it out of the way," she said. "My car's a goner. It was so old I only had liability insurance on it."

"Wall said you'd be out tomorrow. You're letting me stay with you."

She started to speak but he interrupted.

"No arguments, damn it," he said. "You don't have to be so fucking stubborn about your independence or whatever line of crap you're about to give me. You gotta let me do this."

Her face reddened. "I was about to say that might be a good idea until I can buy another car."

"Oh." He kissed her on the forehead, and gave her the stuffed kitten. She fussed over it, named it Marble for its tri-colored fur, and then asked for an update on the two murders.

"Three murders," Schultz said.

"Oh, no. Did someone get to the real June after killing Shower Woman?"

"Nope. Frank Simmons, out on bail. I hate it when my main suspect gets whacked. It makes it harder to prove he did it."

"Or to put him on trial," PJ said. "May's got a motive there. It doesn't look good in her circles to have a family member in prison for murder. No Frank, no trial."

"You never know, notoriety like that could be a plus.

Gives her some street cred. But May didn't kill him, at least not with her own hands. I was with her at the time of his death. I wanted to press her about that crooked warehouse deal in Chicago. When I called the house, the maid told me May was shopping at Plaza Frontenac. I found her car with a little help from the center's security guards and waited for her to come out. She was pissed. She didn't want to be seen there talking to the police, so I followed her home. Frank had just been killed. She found him in his study."

PJ's eyelids began to drift closed.

"Hey, you need some sleep," he said.

She pushed herself to stay awake and told him about Frank being June's fiancé first and then May's husband.

"Makes you wonder what else those sisters share," he said. "Motives are springing up like weeds in the family garden."

"Or the family burial plot. I'm tired now," PJ said. "You never know what they spike your drinks with around here."

He lowered the bed to its sleeping position. By the time he puttered around tucking in the blanket and fluffing her pillow, she was already asleep, with Marble's small ears peeking through her closed hand.

She had the same grasp on his heart.

Chapter 21

Welcome to Gemswordchat, Vyzer_lok!
Now talking in the Mage's Secret Chamber. Enjoy your
stay.
gronz_eye has entered the room

    <gronz_eye> *its on dood*
    <Vyzer_lok> SWEET
    <gronz_eye> *u owe me 10 bucks*
    <Vyzer_lok> can do when is it
    <gronz_eye> *friday*
    <Vyzer_lok> not at midnite i hope
    <gronz_eye> *whats the matter past ur bedtime*
    <Vyzer_lok> shit no i can make it
    <gronz_eye> *u take bus there cab home*
    <Vyzer_lok> tell me about the place
    <gronz_eye> *real tunnels creepy dim lights lots of forks and*
branches
    <Vyzer_lok> yeah u said that already I mean where
    <gronz_eye> *washington university brookings hall basement*
    <Vyzer_lok> no shit man ive been there
    <gronz_eye> *u been in the tunnels!!*
    <Vyzer_lok> no I took a class at wash u
    <gronz_eye> *thought u in 8 grade shit u cop or something*
    <Vyzer_lok> no cop it was like summer camp for com-
puter geeks
    <gronz_eye> *ok then*
    <Vyzer_lok> i heard about those tunnels theyre locked up
    <gronz_eye> *authorized only but im fckn authorized got a*
key
    <Vyzer_lok> how many players total

<gronz_eye> 5

<Vyzer_lok> whats the plan

<gronz_eye> *first test is u have to find which bldg & tunnel doors unlocked*

<gronz_eye> *inside will be the quest guide from gemswordmaster*

<gronz_eye> *all players have different quests but will cross paths*

<gronz_eye> *look 4 gems potions coins wands use them 2 battle others*

<Vyzer_lok> what do i bring

<gronz_eye> *u bring ur brain dood & my 10 bucks*

<gronz_eye> *u up 4 it*

<Vyzer_lok> yeah

gronz_eye has left the room

Chapter 22

The Pacer made its way out St. Charles Rock Road toward the suburb of St. Ann. PJ hugged her bruised ribs, unobtrusively, she hoped.

"You take that pain medicine?" Schultz said. Her movement probably hadn't escaped his attention, even though he was driving.

"Yes," PJ said, not bothering to mention she'd only taken half of it. She didn't want her mind fuzzy, and was willing to put up with the resulting discomfort. At least, in theory. In practice, she was hurting far more than she anticipated. Just folding her body enough to get into Schultz's car had caused her to bite her lip. "How far is it?"

"Geez, you sound like a kid asking if we're there yet. Interesting thing came up while you were in the hospital," Schultz said.

"One of many, it seems," PJ said.

"Anita went through June's neighborhood, interviewing the neighbors again. There were a couple of people she hadn't been able to get in touch with. One of them swears he saw June getting the newspaper on a morning she was supposedly in Kansas City. This man also saw her twice more during that weekend."

"Do you think he was seeing the look-alike, living in the house and pretending to be June?"

"Personally I think he saw June, being herself. Can I prove it? No."

"So tell me about all these people who had reason to shoot Frank." She'd missed that discussion while in the hospital.

"First of all, there's Arlan. You know about that one."

151

"Yes, he was pressuring Frank to get involved in some real estate deal. I doubt if Arlan reached out from the grave and pulled the trigger, though."

"Not Arlan himself, but maybe his representative on Earth. June or Fredericka or a hired assassin. You're gonna love the next one." He concentrated on his driving for a moment, as the Pacer seemed to have it in for some pedestrians on the sidewalk. He corrected the car's pull with one hand and shifted gears with the other. He was good at it. It was almost like the Pacer had become an extension of him. A really odd extension.

"May Simmons hired an interior designer named Thul Volmann," he continued, "and Frank didn't like the results. Frank spread his opinion around to his society friends. Volmann claimed that Frank cost him future business from the most profitable sector. There was a slander suit filed, but the Simmonses' high-powered attorney got the case dismissed."

"The famous Jack," PJ said.

"Yeah, him."

"Leaving a murderously-inclined designer," PJ said. "You know, the maid was interested in becoming an interior designer. I wonder if there's any link there."

"And I haven't even gotten to the good one yet," Schultz said. "Frank owned an apartment building he wanted to tear down for a commercial development."

"Let me guess. The tenants didn't like the idea."

"She's quick, ladies and gentlemen," he said. "The occupants formed a tenants' association dedicated to making Frank's life a developer's hell. They're a quirky bunch, too, and hot-headed, some of them."

"Are we sure that Arlan didn't have a hand in that tenants' association? Part of the pressure he was exerting on Frank for the Chicago warehouse investment?"

"Hey, I didn't think of that. This is one fucked-up bunch of people. It seems like they're all connected, and they're probably all guilty of murder. Well, capable of it and thinking about it, anyway. Anita and Dave are running down the designer and the tenants. They're having all the fun, while we're heading for some suburban farmer's place."

"Leo, I think we're dealing with people with different motivations for these killings, but a common interest in having the victims out of the way. Two people who pair up to kill, then go their separate ways. It's interesting what you said about they're all thinking about murder. Suppose we have a whole nest of killers."

"Personally I'm not even convinced about a team. I think we've got a loner here and we don't know enough to connect the victims."

They argued over that point for some time, the words becoming more heated as they went along, and the discussion straying into personal matters. Finally, PJ called a halt to it. She wanted to go over in detail what the Simmonses' maid had said about Arlan delivering eggs to the Simmons home on the day he disappeared. Eggs from Old Hank's farm, where they were headed.

"It was one of those weird family traditions, and they still go there for eggs today. Old Hank may not be able to keep the place much longer, though," PJ said.

"The land's probably worth a bundle. He should sell it and retire someplace without chickens. Give it a rest."

PJ shook her head. "If he has a choice about it, he'll probably be running that place until he keels over. There, that must be it."

She was pointing at a dilapidated sign that said *Hank's Chicken Ranch*. A blacktop driveway wound back from the street, passing through a heavily-wooded tract of land.

"Must drive the city fathers crazy," Schultz said, "having that undeveloped acreage just sitting there, not paying much in the way of taxes into the coffers. By the way, I gave the St. Ann PD a heads-up that we'll be on the property to talk to Hank and look around. I don't think they'll meet us there, but don't be surprised if a cruiser shows up. If we find anything, Lieutenant Wall will pick up the coordination."

PJ nodded. Turning into the driveway, they discovered that it turned to gravel as soon as they passed the first bend, out of sight of the street. They came to a fork, one side labeled *Eggs 4 Sale* and the other *Private—Trespissers Shot*.

"I like this guy already," Schultz said, yanking the Pacer's steering wheel toward the *Private* drive. He pulled up in front of a two-story frame house that showed the burden of its years. Window and door frames and porch supports all sagged. Different layers of paint showed through on areas of the house, like painting had been started and given up as too much work, several times. The porch steps were cupped upwards so that the nails at the ends of the boards were pulled halfway out. The faded blue shingles reminded PJ of blue hair on an elderly woman. In fact, the house seemed like a tired, old woman counting the years until she could rest.

Schultz got out of the car. "Stay here," he said, "in case the old geezer remembers where he put his shotgun."

She was about to object to being left behind, and decided it wasn't worth provoking Schultz.

This time.

She watched him move toward the porch, noticing that he was limping a little. His body had hard wear on it, like a car run too many miles with too little maintenance. Once, propped up on her elbow in bed next to him, she'd traced the record of his law enforcement service on his skin: smooth scars and rippled areas where muscle had been lost. Anita, indoctrinated in The Job from an early age by her father, had told PJ that career law enforcement officers accumulated injuries, some large, some small, like other people collect stamps or old movie posters. Walk into any cops' bar, she'd said, and ask for a show of old wounds. The veteran cops would all have a few, and stories to go with them.

PJ was no exception, although she was on the outside of Blue culture looking in. She bore the scar of a psychopath's knife and she had a scar on her soul, too, from killing a man.

Through the leafless trees, she could see a couple of buildings not far away. A conspicuous path headed through the woods in that direction. PJ rummaged in Schultz's car, not a pleasant task, until she found a fast food receipt and a pen. When she was out of the office, she carried a credit-card-sized wallet in her pockets along with her car keys and cellphone. A purse could get in the way, or, as Schultz had pointed out, could have its strap grabbed and wrapped around her throat. She was used to the arrangement, but sometimes it was a nuisance not having the resources of a large purse handy.

PJ, still heated from their earlier discussion, left a rather snotty note for Schultz, propping it up on the steering wheel. The path through the woods beckoned.

It actually felt good getting out in the fresh air and walking. She ached in more places than she could count, but as her muscles warmed to the task, it was almost a good ache. Her sore but working body was a reminder that the outcome of the attempt on her life could have been very different.

The first building, larger than she'd originally thought, contained chickens. It was an old-fashioned chicken coop, with a roosting area indoors and a fenced yard for chickens to scratch. The yard was relatively quiet, since most of the hens were dozing in the sun. There was a substantial buffer zone between the coop and the surrounding homes. The woods didn't continue far past the buildings, but beyond them was a pasture area that had probably held cattle in years past.

The barn had a feeling of abandonment about it. If the farmhouse was a tired, old woman, then the barn was a corpse long buried. There was an oversized door, wide enough to admit cattle. She went to the door and tugged on it. It swung open on creaky hinges.

It wasn't pitch black inside because the old roof had gaps that let in the sun. Shafts of light fell to the floor, filled with motes that looked more substantial than dust. There were massive beams far above her head, stained with what she assumed was pigeon shit.

The smell of rotten blood hit her nose, strong enough that she reeled back from it. PJ wondered if Old Hank killed chickens there. She pushed herself forward, remembering the little jab from Schultz about her staying in the car.

If chickens had been killed here, it must have been poultry's equivalent of Custer's Last Stand. There was a workbench near the center of the open space that was stained with blood. The dirt floor around the bench was churned up and reddish. Sluggish flies crawled across the surface of the workbench on the far end. It was December, after all, and while she might see an occasional fly indoors, there were more here than she would have expected.

Giving the bench a wide berth, PJ followed the wall of the barn, stepping on straw that at one time must have filled the barn with a clean, earthy scent. She didn't want to contaminate the place, but she had to see what the attraction was for the flies on the workbench.

Moldy chicken heads, no doubt.

PJ had to detour around a six-foot-high compost pile that

smelled strongly of ammonia. Light wisps of steam rose from the decomposition process of the chicken manure. Hank had probably gotten complaints about outdoor composting, so he would keep enough manure to use on a garden and have the rest hauled away. Flies must love it. For them it would be like living in a sauna that was simultaneously a buffet. Old Hank was growing flies as well as chickens.

She was almost there. The air was still and heavy, and she was reminded of her image of the barn as a corpse long buried. She was breathing the kind of air she imagined would be in an old wooden casket. The barn creaked in a hundred places, weathered wood rubbing against itself, as the wind blew outside. The air inside resisted or absorbed the wind's motion, so that she stood below the groaning rafters with not the slightest air movement at ground level, other than the wings of the flies, to stir the straw.

As she walked, new angles of the workbench and its surroundings opened up to her. Stainless steel basins littered the floor, some blood spattered, some containing odd-shaped chunks that didn't look like chicken heads. The closer she got the more activity she saw from the flies. A few more steps and she had a clear view of the end of the workbench. There was something nailed there, several somethings, with nails that were decades newer than the wood into which they were pounded. A scream built in her belly and was working its way toward her mouth when she heard Schultz's voice.

"There you are. . . . Holy shit! I think we found where Arlan Merrett was killed."

PJ swallowed her scream. "I think we found Arlan Merrett's missing parts, too," she said.

Chapter 23

PJ sat at her desk, aching. She'd like to go home, soak in a hot bath, and put her sore body to bed. She was caught up, though, in the drama of having found the place where Arlan was murdered and the prospect of finally putting together a complete virtual reality re-creation. She'd left Schultz, Dave, and Anita at the scene and gotten a ride back to Headquarters. She needed to do what she did best, and let them do the same.

The stale air in her office didn't seem nearly as oppressive as it usually did, in comparison to the air in the barn.

Her riverfront scenario had yielded a potentially valuable insight. Maneuvering the solidly built Arlan to the dump site would at least be possible for women as well as men. That included petite females such as Fredericka and males working at a disadvantage, such as Frank.

Frank! There had hardly been a minute to absorb the fact of his murder and to fit it into theories she'd been tossing around. The husbands of two sisters dying violent deaths within such a short time cried out for connecting the dots, but PJ was missing some of the dots. And how did Marilee Baines's brutal murder fit in?

Three deaths in three days, followed by a likely attempt on her life. It was shaping up to be a week for the record books in both her professional and private lives. Her relationship with Schultz was like background music to everything she did, except she couldn't figure out if it was harmony or discordance.

Who had tried to kill her?

The car that made contact with hers had left trace evidence, a scrape on her bumper, with paint embedded in it.

Forensics identified the paint as belonging to a blue 1991 Chevrolet Lumina. A car matching that description had been stolen the day before from a commuter parking lot in St. Charles. The stolen vehicle belonged to a construction worker named Antoine Card. Having no transportation since his car was stolen, Card hitched a ride with friends. He was at the site of a new subdivision development moving earth with a backhoe loader at the time his car, if it was his, was used to push PJ into traffic. The stolen car hadn't turned up yet.

The person who'd tried to harm her was still out there, maybe planning another attempt. Was it even connected with this case? It might be a relative or friend of someone she'd help put away for murder, or even something further back in her life. Perhaps evil Carla the home wrecker was after her for some demented reason. Taking away PJ's husband wasn't enough. PJ admonished herself for that little twinge of paranoia.

Take it one thing at a time.

Focusing on the first murder, she started making notes on a profile of the killer or killers. She still favored a team theory. The profile was a description of personality and lifestyle that can help narrow an investigation but never dictated it. A behavioral fingerprint. The place to start was looking at what the killer chose to do and what not to do.

Arlan disappeared sometime after four in the afternoon last Wednesday. He was killed Saturday night in Hank's barn, and dumped at the edge of the Mississippi in time to be spotted by a Sunday morning dog walker. He'd never made it to Chicago to meet with clients, and his car had never been found. Where had he been until the time of his death?

Arlan was involved with some shady real estate developers in Chicago, maybe the type who might arrange a murder if cheated or if there was a monetary advantage to having an associate out of the picture. In that case the killing would have been cold and efficient, a garroting or slit throat or bullet in the head, with no wasted effort. Certainly not the elaborate setup in Hank's barn. There was something very personal about that.

Someone watched those tears, with hatred or satisfaction.

Unless the whole setup was a ruse to make the police think a psycho killer was on the loose. She decided to set aside that consideration for now. If she was falling into the killer's diversionary trap, she'd have to extricate herself later.

The killer had to be organized and confident enough to abduct in daylight, emotionally involved enough to take out anger in the flesh. That pointed to a love affair, a marriage, a soured business relationship, a dysfunctional family. The problem was the killer could be experiencing any or all of those things with someone other than his victim. Some murderers can't bring themselves to attack the true target, and take it out instead on strangers carefully selected because they invoke the same sick feelings. The son whose mother sexually abused him and warped him for life kills wanton, dirty women—prostitutes—but not his mother, for whom he still has a sharply conflicted love.

The killer could be a stranger who chose Arlan for some twisted reason, and the swirl of suspects her team had been considering could have nothing to do with it.

Look-alike Marilee could have been chosen as the permissible target by someone who despises June, but couldn't attack her directly.

Frank, whose killing was straightforward and toward the impersonal end of the spectrum, could have been done by a killer who just wanted him out of the way for monetary reasons.

Focus! One thing at a time.

Spread out on her desk were photographs of the barn, sketches she'd made showing dimensions and relative locations of items, riverfront photos, and Arlan's autopsy report.

What was done to Arlan that wasn't needed in the killing, but provided some twisted, personal satisfaction to the killer? That was easy. Practically everything about his murder wasn't needed to kill him. Keep him captive for four days and then stage an elaborate operating room scene. Cut off his male equipment, his fingertips, his mouth, dig through his flesh to stab him in the heart up close and personal. Continue the mutilation by nailing the severed parts to the workbench.

Yet once the killer was finished with that ritual, Arlan's body was left at the waterfront like a dead fish. There was no attempt to care for him after death, like a mother who strangles her newborn but puts a nice outfit on the baby, booties on his cold, dead feet, and wraps him in a quilt. Two behaviors. Two killers?

So what would the killer's unique signature be?

Take your pick of half a dozen behaviors that weren't necessary.

Fingers, mouth, penis, heart. All components of expressing love. The killer could be taking away Arlan's capacity to love. Maybe two jilted lovers cooperating to get their vengeance. June and Fredericka? June did the mutilating of the second man who'd betrayed her, and Fredericka handled the dead fish disposal to get her hands on Green Vista. It made as much sense as anything else she'd come up with.

The ring of the phone startled her out of deep concentration. It was Schultz.

"Dave and Anita are still at the barn. I imagine they'll be there a while. Place is an evidence tech's nightmare. Or

161

dream come true, if you think of it in terms of the challenge. Forensics is finally hoping they'll get a break. I'm at the Simmons home."

An idea popped into PJ's mind. "Leo, do you think the barn could be where Arlan was held those four days?"

Schultz gave it some thought. "Nah. Hank was in there last Friday, adding shit to his compost pile. Even he would have noticed a man tied up in there. There's no place to hide."

"Well, it was a thought. How's May handling her husband's death?"

"She seems more worried about how the children are taking it."

"The selfless mom act," PJ said. "I thought she left most of the child rearing to the nanny."

"May talks a good show, that's all. She wasn't even the one who told the kids that Daddy was dead. Can you believe that? Delegated it to the nanny."

"How does Frank's death leave her financially?" PJ asked.

"With twenty million dollar trust funds for each of the kids and fifty million for her."

"Makes you wonder whether she's better off with or without him. She's a climber. She might think of it as an opportunity to move up a rung or two with an advantageous remarriage. I'll bet she's not devastated."

"She's been using that baby shampoo," Schultz said. "No more tears."

"She was with you at the time of the murder, but do you think she could have hired it done?" PJ said.

"Yeah. It could have been someone with free access to the house, and I don't just mean the Christmas open house guest list."

"You mean like the cook? The cook in the study with the revolver?"

"Ha, ha," said Schultz. There was a brittle tone to his voice. She was pushing too hard with her smart remarks. Neither of them had gotten a lot of sleep. Things were fraying around the edges.

"You said the maid didn't want to stay a maid all her life, right?" Schultz said. "Wanted to be an interior designer? We've confirmed the alarm system was off. Maybe she let in the killer for the price of a little shop in West County."

"I didn't read her that way."

"Oh, and I guess that my thirty years of reading people gets brushed aside just like that."

"Take it easy, Leo. You're under a lot of stress. Stress makes people leap to conclusions."

"Stress, bullshit. That's not a strong enough word for it. These people are dying right in front of our eyes. We missed Shower Woman's killer by minutes. Five minutes earlier, and I might have shot the motherfucker who got Frank Simmons."

"You're the one who always tells me it isn't good to dwell on the what ifs."

"Yeah, well, that advice was for you."

There it was again. The implication that she was a *non-cop* and had to be babied. Like being told for the umpteenth time not to touch things at a crime scene or to stay in the car.

She forced herself not to react. This wasn't the time to be working out their relationship. She had a job to do, and so did he.

"I've got something I want to bounce off you," she said, her voice level.

A bowling ball to the skull, maybe.

She told him about the theory she'd just come up with, about the killer wanting to wipe out Arlan's ability to love by taking away his fingers, mouth, penis, and heart.

"Christ, Doc, this isn't the Land of Oz. Next it'll be a search for a heart, a brain, and courage. Maybe I'd better put out an APB for the Wicked Witch of the West."

"You don't have to be sarcastic about it, if this profiling business is too much for you to handle."

"That wasn't sarcasm, babe, just a little reality check. Anyway, it seems like you're coming around to my first idea of it being a homo chop job."

PJ bristled. "Not at all. I guess it's no use discussing these things with you."

"Just like it's no use discussing marriage with you. You just start spouting all that shrink crap about rebounding. Well, rebound this." He hung up.

"And don't call me babe," she said.

Chapter 24

It was near closing time at the diner. As soon as Millie saw PJ, she said, "You sit right down, Dearie, and I'll bring you a piece of pie."

PJ nodded and took her favorite stool. Schultz's was empty, which was good because she didn't want to be around him right now.

The aluminum Christmas tree, alternately red and green as its illumination wheel slowly turned, was growing on her. The familiar scents and sounds started to loosen the tension in her shoulders and smooth out the worry lines in her forehead. By the time Millie placed a plate in front of her with a flourish, PJ felt almost human again.

The slice of apple pie was nearly six inches across at the wide end, warm, and fragrant. The scent of baked apples, cinnamon, and nutmeg was the essence of comfort. Millie had put a scoop of vanilla ice cream on top, and into that had stuck one of her toothpick flags. The ice cream was melting, sending streams of delectable cream down the sides of the pie. Melting had caused the scoop to lean to one side, and the flag looked in danger of drowning in cream.

We should all have such problems.

A mug of steaming coffee appeared at PJ's elbow as she was taking her first hearty bite. "Thanks, Millie."

"Schultz acting up again?" Millie said.

PJ nodded, her mouth too full to voice an answer.

"You pay him no mind," Millie said, shaking her finger as if she were lecturing the sugar container. "He's such a rotten lout. You know I always got to wipe the stool with disinfectant when he leaves."

"The floor, too," the two women said simultaneously, grins popping out on their faces, PJ's reluctantly.

"I'll just leave you to your pie," Millie said. "If you want anything else, the kitchen's open another fifteen minutes."

"I've got everything I need, thanks."

PJ missed Thomas. When this was over, she was going to have some days off with him and make Christmas cookies and apple pie with ice cream, and watch *It's a Wonderful Life* and *The Muppet Christmas Carol*, their two holiday favorites.

She hoped this case didn't drag on until it became a low-priority concern. So far, her CHIP team had a hundred percent solve rate. It was unreasonable to think it would stay that way forever, but deep down she hoped it would, and even deeper down hoped that her contributions would continue to play a major part in that.

She slipped on the data gloves and put on the HMD. The null world sprang up in front of her eyes.

"Barn," she said.

The interior of Hank's barn materialized, but the only light came from moonlight easing in through a couple of small windows. Not enough for an operating room atmosphere.

In a moment, a portable work light snapped on. PJ had built it into the scenario. Placed close to the workbench, it cast a stark spray of light across it, and made tall, dancing shadows behind her as she moved toward the center of the barn.

Arlan was already on the workbench, naked, hands and feet tied with ropes that were fastened over hooks on the bench. She thought back to photos of the bench, and it was true that there were hooks on each end, the actual uses for which she couldn't even speculate. She had scanned in the photos, and her software's artificial intelligence had selected them as logical ways to restrain Arlan.

At least he's not being held down by a succubus kneeling on his chest. I think I've finally gotten that mythology thing under control in the program.

As she approached the bench, she saw that a cloth was tied around Arlan's mouth. Cotton fibers had been found caught in his back teeth, so it seemed likely that his mouth was stuffed with a rag, at least at some point, to keep him from making a lot of noise.

Arlan's eyes shifted wildly and his head attempted to follow her motion as she circled closer to the bench. PJ was carrying a doctor's medical bag. She put the bag down on some straw and opened it. The halogen work light made the sharp objects inside gleam.

She pulled a scalpel from the bag and waved it in front of Arlan's face. His eyes, already round as golf balls, got even bigger, and he tugged on the ropes ineffectually with his arms and legs. Squirming around, he offered a moving target. If she tried to sever any body parts, there would be accidental wounds before she succeeded. The autopsy showed none.

Fishing around in the bag, she found a syringe. She jabbed the attached needle into the rubber top of a small glass bottle and filled the chamber. Approaching Arlan, she injected the ketamine into his arm and waited until he was still, which took about three minutes.

The canvas awaited the artist.

Following her memory of the autopsy photos, she lifted his limp penis, and, gritting her teeth, sliced it off. Another couple of slices removed his testicles. She lined them up on the edge of the workbench.

I'm definitely not letting Schultz run this simulation. He'd be afraid to fall asleep next to me.

Blocking out Schultz and his insecurities, she focused on what the killer was experiencing.

How would this make the scalpel wielder feel? A jilted lover could do this, a male or female lover. Maybe Schultz has something with that gay murder idea.

PJ went after the face next, trying for the effect shown in the autopsy photos. She found that she had to get a heavier cutting instrument from her bag, a small, pointed saw with mean-looking teeth.

There was so much blood. She glanced down at the floor, noticing that the dirt and straw were becoming mixed with blood. Her shoes were protected with paper booties wrapped in several layers of plastic bags. *No distinct footprints.*

Her first efforts on the face were tentative and the results didn't match the photos. Using a harder stroke, she dug through the cartilage of the nose and then unleashed a flurry of cuts at the lower face.

I think I'm going to be sick.

She took a few deep breaths, getting her revulsion under control and reminding herself that she was in her familiar office, not under a floodlight in a barn.

Is this how the killer reacted? With revulsion? I don't think so. I think this was anticipated and enjoyed, memorized and replayed in the killer's mind.

At the thought, her stomach threatened to reject Millie's apple pie. She shouldn't have soothed her feelings at the diner before going through the barn scenario.

The face was finished. It occurred to her that she was feeling more distress than Arlan. Ketamine was a dissociative anesthetic, meaning that Arlan's mind was separated from what was going on with his body. His mind was in the k-hole, to use the term that recreational drug users did, like Alice going down the rabbit hole. Thoughtfully, she turned Arlan's damaged face as far as she could to one side, so that blood and saliva would drain, and he wouldn't choke. She wondered if the killer did the same. Using ketamine might show concern for the victim's pain, an effort to shield him from a terrible experience. Or it could have been the only thing the killer could lay hands on that would keep Arlan from thrashing around too much.

Arlan's fingertips yielded easily to an instrument that looked like a scaled-down bolt cutter. It was time to excavate a hole in his chest. PJ used the same saw she'd used on the lower face, and the bolt cutter to deal with the exposed ribs. Bloody hunks of flesh went into a stainless steel basin. In a hurry now to get out of the horrible situation, PJ rushed through the process, hastily scooping flesh. The moment she saw a beating heart, she picked up a knife and stabbed Arlan, putting an end to his life.

Waiting for her own heart rate to slow down, she considered the body parts lined up on the edge of the bench. She knew they were supposed to be nailed to the wood, but couldn't bring herself to do that. She was too shaken by her experience.

"End," she said. The gory scene disappeared, replaced by a soothing blue she floated in for a time. Then she took off the HMD, peeled off the gloves, and sat with her elbows on the desk, her hands cradling her head.

When she finally looked up, Schultz was there, sitting across from her.

"You look pale. Been playing psycho killer?" he said.

"Whoever did that was one sick bastard," she said. Her voice was steady, but her hands trembled a little.

"Is that your considered psychological opinion?"

"Hell, yes."

His eyes were filled with concern for her. "You can leave

169

that crap to me if you want," he said, nodding at the HMD. "I don't get so emotionally involved in it."

It's my job, damn it.

"If you don't," she said, "how can you understand what the killer was feeling?"

He shrugged. "I just do. My hunches, I guess." He came around the desk and put both hands on her shoulders.

PJ flinched. Their last argument came flooding back into her. She wanted to yank his hands away, but the urge faded. He stroked her hair, then ran his hands down her arms, leaving warm paths on her skin that felt like she'd been painted with invisible heat. His large hands cradled her neck, his fingers tracing the outline of her jaw.

"I love you," he said in a low, intimate voice. "I'm sorry for the shitty way I've been acting. I'm taking things too fast. We're moving at PJ speed from now on." He kissed her neck.

"I know it's your job to study wackos like this barn killer. It's hard on you, but I support you because you're really good at this stuff. You make a difference."

PJ's pent-up breath escaped in a long sigh. Tears welled in the corners of her eyes. Hearing Schultz's affirmations had a powerful effect on her. He understood. She could let him be a refuge for her, a life preserver when the violence she encountered threatened to pull her under. Some inner resistance, a holding back that she'd barely been aware of, gave way. A wave of love swept through her, leaving every part of her body receptive.

"We're going to make this work, Leo." By *this*, she meant her emotionally-demanding job and their equally-challenging relationship. "It has to work."

He swiveled her chair around so that she was facing him. "You need to get this sick shit out of your mind, and I know just the thing." He tugged gently on her arms.

She was out of the chair and into his embrace. She'd still have to talk to him about the scenario, and the big questions that remained: where was Arlan kept prisoner, how did he get onto that bench, and how did he get to the dump site? But that was for later. She settled into the sensations of now, of feeling his arms surround her, of knowing that he wanted her and she wanted him.

Snuggled against his chest, she said, "This is nice. But my bruises ache and I'm still wearing my rib belt. I don't think I'm up to what you're thinking of."

"As long as you're not wearing a chastity belt, we're in business," he said.

He tilted her chin up and kissed her. She responded, pressing against him, and his kisses became more urgent. Her thoughts skipped away from homicides and body aches like rocks skipping on a lake, and focused on him.

He had a way of kissing that made her feel that she was the only thing that mattered to him then, the only thing that existed in his world. Their world.

She softly nibbled his lip and her hand drifted down, her fingers lightly touching the erection straining against his pants. He moaned, slipped his hand under her blouse, and squeezed her breast.

"You got a lock on that door?" he mumbled, holding her close.

"Yes." She pulled away with effort, reluctant to leave the heat of his embrace. The thudding of her heart and the *snick* of the bolt were the only sounds in the room. The men's room across the hall was mercifully quiet. When she turned around, he was sitting in her chair, his pants and boxers around his ankles.

"Ever done any lap dancing?" he said. Desire shone in his eyes and lit a fire in the center of her.

"I'm a quick learner. But we better hope nobody comes through here with a UV light," she said. "That chair's going to reveal bodily fluids."

"I love it when you talk dirty."

Chapter 25

My attempt to frame May is stalled but not defeated. Imagine that putz Schultz being there when May discovers the body. Since all's quiet on the May front, I turn my attention elsewhere. I decide that I can't get the fresh start I so deserve until I take care of old business.

Loretta Blanchette is a fourth grade teacher from Cape Girardeau who earns a few extra bucks working at a summer enrichment camp near there. I go to one camp after another, and the Summer Daze Springboard Camp is one of them. The campers, very few of whom want to be there, are getting a jump on the next grade level in math and science. I don't need a jump. I'm several grade levels ahead already.

Mrs. Blanchette either doesn't know of her students' desire to avoid humiliation at all costs, or enjoys putting them on the spot.

One rainy afternoon, she calls three students up to the board to work math problems. Class, we're having a math race. Isn't that fun? *I'm good at math, and left to myself I always get the right answers. When left to myself. Thunder booms outside and rain lashes at the windows as Mrs. Blanchette dictates problems. The other two students keep up easily, so she starts going faster. I fall behind, barely able to copy a problem without solving it before she moves on to the next.*

Looking out of the corners of my eyes, I see the other two students finish and raise their hands almost simultaneously. The race is over. I still have several problems to work. I keep at it, moving the chalk slowly as tears run down my cheeks. And then the worst happens. A hot stream runs down my leg into my shoe, and the twenty-eight eyes in the classroom that are not mine watch as my shoe overflows onto the floor. I won't go into what happens next, but it involves large quantities of hand towels from the bathroom and a trash can. *I still have five weeks left of camp, so for thirty-five more days, I go to her room, look at the trash can, and feel the stares of others.*

Loretta—I get a little thrill out of calling my teacher by her first name—is retired now, living in the northern suburb of Florissant in a matchbox of a house. I don't need any sedative for Loretta. She is small enough to be overpowered and nowhere near as formidable as I remember her. I dispatch her with a quick heart stab and she goes fast. A gasp, a moan, and she crumbles to the floor. I do the cutting on Loretta's kitchen table, one of those Formica-topped ones with gold flecks and chrome trim. I cut here and there, staying primly away from Loretta's privates, taking instead the finger adorned by a ring that flashed so frightfully and the eyes that laughed when I was driven to wet myself. I was hoping she would do the same, but no such luck.

I leave through the back door, because I'm not happy with that street light right out in front of Loretta's house. The less time I spend on her front porch with that orange light falling on me like pumpkin rain, the better. As I go down the steps in back, the next-door neighbor's porch light suddenly comes on. I shrink against the wall of Loretta's house. Have I made too much noise? Does the neighbor have supernatural hearing powers and has heard the blood gurgling in Loretta's throat? A blur of white moves down the steps and at first I think the neighbor has thrown something like a white basketball into his yard. Then the basketball barks at me.

A man steps out on the porch to see what all the fuss is about. He glances in my direction. I am not sure if he sees me, but the dog is heading in my direction, barred from viciously attacking my ankles by a chain link fence.

My heart is pounding. This is not part of the plan.

I cringe inside some bushes. The man calls to his dog angrily, yelling at him to do his business and leave that damned cat alone. The dog pees arrogantly on the fence and reluctantly tears itself away from the blood-scented intruder. Climbing the steps in desultory fashion, the dog continues to glare at me until the man scoops it up and shuts the door.

Circling around behind the neighbor's house, I break a window and shoot him just as he is about to make a phone call, using a gun that I bought years ago. I reported my gun stolen back in September, in preparation for a moment just like this. Details, you know.

I will have to get rid of these clothes along with my gloves, and go through my scrubbing routine, like I'm a doctor getting ready for surgery. There are ways to beat this evidence thing. It isn't until later that I notice a small tear in my Lycra jersey, just a few threads. It must have happened when I broke the window. There is no tear in my skin, no blood, but do I know for sure about discarded skin cells? No.

Was the neighbor—I'm thinking of him now as The Busybody—about to call the police, or just calling his sweetheart for a little Friday night action? Too late to ask now. That's unfortunate, but overall I'm pleased. One grudge settled, lots more to go.

If only I could just do that to May.

Chapter 26

Friday couldn't come soon enough for Thomas. He'd declined an offer to go to the movies with Winston on the dubious excuse that he wanted to spend more time on a book report. Winston knew something was up, but by his line of questioning, it was clear that he thought Thomas had a date. In a way, he did.

A date with adventure!

He figured he'd get a ride home with Mick's mom and ask her to drop him off at home because he had a lot of homework to do. Moms never questioned that, if it was said in a dejected tone of voice. His mother would be working late, and he'd call her at her office to check in and give the same story. Then he'd call her again later in the evening, say that his work had gone quickly, and that he was going to a late movie with Winston. She didn't like him going to the 11:00 p.m. shows, but after hedging, she would say okay because Winston's dad was going to be in the multiplex seeing a different movie. Also, she'd feel guilty for not being home more when there was a big case going on at work, and that would grease the wheels. In fact, he was counting on it.

His mom was treating him too much like a baby. Sure, he had more freedom than he'd had a couple of years ago, but it was too little, and it was coming too slow. It was like she wanted to keep him chained up and not let him have any fun. His mom always thought the worst was going to happen. She had a way of picking apart anything he wanted to do until some minor thing turned up that she could say no to. In the past few months, he'd really started to resent that. He could handle a lot more than she gave him credit for. And if he did get into a bad situation, he was smart enough to get out of it without any help from her. He was fourteen. In less than two years, he'd be driving. She'd probably find some way to keep him chained up then, too. He knew his mother loved him, but she just wasn't willing to let go, to let him get out there in the real world.

Besides, bad things happened to other people, not to him.

He was jostling with Mick and some other buddies on the way out of the academy, just a little friendly shoving, when Mick said, "Hey, Tombo, your mom's here today. Check out that retro car. That's not yours, is it?"

Schultz's reddish-orange Pacer sat in the parking lot, and his mother was leaning on the hood, waiting for him.

"Nah, that's my mom's boyfriend's car."

"That's a cop's car? He works undercover, then, right? You never told me that. An undercover cop. That is awesome."

Shit. Shit. Shit. Of all the days!

"See ya," Mick said, and punched him in the shoulder.

"Yeah," Thomas said, and punched him back. There was nothing left to do but make his way toward his mother. His pace slowed, his feet feeling as if they were suction cups.

"Come on, Thomas," she said loudly. "Get the lead out."

Groaning inwardly, he picked up his pace marginally. In too short a time, he was at the car, being clapped on the back by Schultz. Thomas tossed his backpack in the cramped rear seat of the Pacer and climbed in after it, feeling like he was diving into the deep end of the disappointment pool.

He scrunched down in the seat, which wasn't easy to do with his knees pressed against the back of the driver's seat. Parents who picked up their kids at the academy generally had new minivans or SUV's, not 1979 Pacers that had no air conditioning and pulled to the side when driving, so that progress down the road was kind of a zigzag. The car was assigned to Schultz by the police department. Thomas figured the detective didn't have a lot of influence there.

Schultz stopped for White Castles on the way home, which perked Thomas up a bit, or at least perked up his taste buds. White Castles were small, square hamburgers loaded with grilled onions and a miniscule pickle slice. He could shove an entire cheeseburger into his mouth. A double cheeseburger was two bites. Schultz got him eight doubles and an order of cheese fries. Thomas sat in the back seat, plotting ways to get out of the house, eating cheese fries and licking his fingers.

At home, the three of them ate at the kitchen table. They were soon joined by Megabite, who sat on the fourth chair and soulfully looked into each diner's eyes in turn until she scored bits of hamburger or melted cheese, no onions please. Thomas busied himself with his food, adding two large glasses of milk to the glop in his stomach, listening to his mother and Schultz try to discuss developments in their cases without giving away confidential details or being too graphic. If he'd been in a better mood, he would have enjoyed it, and probably plied them with questions. He noticed a box of fries sitting open and getting cold, in front of his mother.

"Mom, you going to eat those fries?"

She looked down as if she'd just discovered that the little sticks of fat were still there. "Oh, I guess not. I'm not too hungry."

He reached over and pulled the box in front of him, searched out the little package of salt in the bottom, and sprinkled it on.

"Sweetie, don't use the salt pack," she said in a distracted manner.

"Too late, Mom."

"Let the kid enjoy his food," Schultz said, unnecessarily

coming to Thomas's defense.

"Okay, then," she said, "just this once."

"Thanks," Thomas said. He didn't think she heard him. With any luck, the two of them would have sex and fall asleep. He looked over at Schultz, trying to imagine him in bed with his mom. He liked Schultz—liked him a whole lot—but that image was just too gross. He pushed it out of mind.

Thomas got up and started clearing the table of paper plates, napkins, and the open-ended boxes the White Castles came in. The two adults were absorbed in their conversation, something about a Shower Woman. He cleared his throat.

"Mom, I have homework to do. I'll be upstairs." He came over and gave her a kiss on top of her head. She wrapped an arm around his waist before he could get away.

"All right. Maybe we can do something together to-morrow. At least we got to eat dinner together," she said. She smiled at him, but the worry lines on her forehead didn't go away.

"Sure. Goodnight, sir," he said, nodding at Schultz. He hadn't settled on a name to call Schultz. Maybe soon it would be Dad.

At the rate Mom's going, I'll be old, like twenty or something, by then.

Megabite went up the stairs with him, staying two steps in front and keeping him in his rightful place.

The evening hours crawled. Thomas thought about contacting his friend and trying to get the tunnel adventure post-poned. There were other people involved, though, some of gronz_eye's buddies. They weren't going to switch every-thing around because his mom was spending the evening at home. He'd never live it down.

He couldn't even sneak out the window and go out, like all

of his buddies talked about doing and a tiny percentage of them actually did. He was on the second floor, and getting out required going past the adults. They seemed to have grown roots in the kitchen, where the back door was. He could try for the front door, but from where Mom was sitting, she'd see him go by in the hall. He ought to know, because he'd tried it before. Twice.

Maybe he could work out something with Winston, like getting Winston's dad to come over and pick him up and then sneak out of Winston's house. Winston's bedroom was on the first floor. He'd have to let Winston in on it, though, and he couldn't do that. He couldn't pull that trick with any of his other friends, either, because their parents kept an eye on them and would check with his mom about an impromptu overnight stay.

Fuck. I haven't got one friend who can cover for me, no questions asked.

He had to leave the house by ten thirty if he was going to make it the few blocks west on Magnolia to catch the Kingshighway bus, get off at Lindell, wait to make a connection with the Lindell bus, and end up at Washington U. by midnight. He'd plotted out the bus routes. He had exact change, and money for the cab ride back home. He'd thought of everything.

Almost everything. I didn't plan on my adventure getting stopped before it begins.

Reluctantly, Thomas started working on his homework. The cat leaped to the desk, seemed to swerve in midair to avoid the can of soda he'd brought, and executed a perfect landing. Folding her legs, she settled in next to him in the meatloaf position. His bedroom door was open just enough for her to leave if she needed to use the facilities. Every now and then, Thomas went to the door. They were still there, talking in low tones. No doubt now that he wasn't in the room, they were really getting into it on the homicide cases.

Don't these guys every get romantic?

At ten the phone rang. He checked the caller ID on the phone in his room. It was his mom's boss. A little hope started to bubble up in him, but he squashed it. It could be anything, like him asking for an update. The boss did that a lot.

The call didn't last long. His phone showed him that the line was no longer in use. And there were footsteps on the stairs! He bent over his books and chewed on a pencil, trying for the earnest student look. There was a knock at his door, and his mom entered.

"How're things going?" she said.

He shrugged.

"That good, eh?" She sighed. "I have some bad news. Schultz and I have to go in to work for awhile."

He plastered a disappointed look on his face.

"I probably won't be back for three or four hours. Would you be okay for a few hours? You can stay up and watch TV in your room."

"I'm not a kid anymore, Mom. We agreed that you'd start giving me more room. I am fourteen, you know. Besides, I think I'll just whip out this book report so I don't have to worry about it over the weekend." He tugged a paper out from under Megabite and held it up to illustrate his plight. Belatedly he saw that it was a math worksheet. She didn't notice.

"Doc," Schultz said from downstairs. "We gotta go. Geez, the kid's fourteen."

Go, Schultz!

The book report was a great idea. He'd just be in his room, working. Shit, maybe he had a future in improv. He saw the

181

decision forming on her face and decided to reinforce it. "I'll be fine."

"I'll lock up downstairs," she said. "Don't answer the door for any reason. You have my cell number."

Sweet!

"Just go do your job, Mom," he said.

"Thanks for being so understanding. I promise we'll have more time together soon."

He heard the door close downstairs. He had twenty minutes to make it to the bus stop. An eternity on kid-powered legs. Thomas wandered downstairs, found a quart of ice cream, and took it to his room to eat while he ran through his checklist.

Ten minutes later, he eased out of the back door, locked it with the key behind him, and set off jogging west on Magnolia. He sucked the satisfyingly cold air into his lungs and left behind long plumes of his breath, like a jet leaving a vapor contrail.

Chapter 27

PJ was on homicide overload. A schoolteacher, Loretta Blanchette, had been stabbed and mutilated in Florissant. It might be the work of the Metro Mangler, as the media was now calling the killer. As far as the public knew, the Metro Mangler had a thing for fingers. Stabbing in the heart, which the police had held back, connected Scar Man, Shower Woman, and Loretta.

There was a second murder in Florissant, the teacher's neighbor. Bernard Dewey was middle-aged, divorced, and had a job putting up billboard displays. And he was shot, like Frank Simmons. The Florissant police were looking into the two homicides, and she hoped they would be able to come up with something definitive to rule out the Metro Mangler. She didn't need any more corpses to worry about.

If they were all connected, then there were two classes of murders: one personal, bloody, and focused on mutilation; the other one, impersonal shootings. Two or more killers? One killer who did it dirty when it mattered to him and clean when it didn't?

There was a low rumble of conversation in her office, punctuated often by Schultz's strident voice. The three of them were discussing the lack of forensic evidence. The expanded drug testing battery for Arlan had turned up ketamine. None of the other victims were drugged. For murder weapons they had a total of three bullets from two different guns and one knife as evidence for five killings, plus whatever turned up from the barn, if anything. No fingerprints, no footprints, no fibers. No ripped buttons or earrings left at the scene. No discarded, bloody clothing. No skin under the victims' fingernails. No bodily fluids other than some sperm remaining inside Shower Woman, already determined to be from her boyfriend.

Blood spatter analysis of the kitchen floor where Loretta Blanchette was murdered revealed blank spots where the killer stood as the mutilation was done. The blood fell on the killer's feet instead of on the floor, so the blank areas should have been shoe-shaped and allowed the size of the killer's feet to be determined. Instead, they were ovals corresponding to a men's size 26 7E shoe. Possible, but more likely a deliberate attempt to disguise shoe size, such as plastic bags stuffed with padding and tied around the ankles.

There was one tantalizing piece of evidence from the location of Shower Woman's chest wound. The stabbing was done with an overhand thrust, but it could be a short person using an extended arm or a taller person using a bent elbow. The killer's projected height range was five foot two to six feet, too wide a range to be useful yet.

They were working with an extremely knowledgeable, or extremely lucky, perpetrator.

Just about every square inch of the corkboard on the wall across from PJ's desk was covered with tacked-up timelines and photos. She struggled to make sense of it.

Start with the first link in the chain.

"Who actually thinks Arlan was killed by his brother-in-law, Frank Simmons, who was arrested for the crime?" PJ said.

No hands went up.

"That leaves us with May, June, and Fredericka, plus the possibility of a sociopathic stranger."

"Glad you narrowed that down for us, Boss," Anita said.

"May and June really seem to hate each other," Dave said. "Although they try to keep everything peaches and cream on

184

the surface, like visiting each other so often. I can't see June killing her husband to spite May. My theory is that they killed each other's husbands, to get back at each other for old hurts."

"I could go for that except for one thing," Schultz said. "The look-alike. Someone went to a lot of trouble to establish an alibi for June in Kansas City at the time of Arlan's murder. The one who would benefit from that would be June."

"Unless May did it to cast suspicion on June," Anita said.

"I have a headache," PJ said.

"Maybe Fredericka wanted to do away with Arlan so she could inherit the whole business, and set June up to take the blame by giving her an alibi that looks phony," Dave said.

"You're saying that June really was in Kansas City and Fredericka or May located a stranger who looks like June so that neighbors would believe she was at home. Then the look-alike was killed to make it look like June was cleaning up, making sure no one could talk. I don't see how we can rule that out," PJ said. "I can't believe there was no trace in K.C. that could prove whether June was there or not."

"Nothing's turned up, but I haven't given up, either. Haven't given up trying to break Fredericka's alibi, either. Shit, what a mess," Anita said. "I hate this family crap."

"How does the teacher fit in? That's a finger-and-heart killing," PJ said.

Dave shuffled some papers. "I got some preliminary stuff from the Florissant police. Loretta Blanchette was a teacher in Cape Girardeau all her working life. After retirement, she moved here to be near a brother who was in a nursing home. The brother died last year, natural causes. None of our suspects has a Cape Girardeau connection. May and June went to private school here in St. Louis, and Fredericka grew up in New Mexico. No links."

"So the wacko stranger moves back into the suspect arena," Schultz said. The rest of the group looked glum.

"We're all tired," PJ said. "Why don't we knock off for tonight and see if the Florissant police come up with anything. Maybe we'll get a break."

Dave and Anita left immediately, as though they'd been waiting for a chance to get out of a discussion that raised more questions than it answered.

PJ looked at the clock on her desk. Mickey's white gloves said that it was 12:30 a.m. "Leo, I'm going to hang around for another half hour. I have some research I want to do. I'll take a cab when I'm done."

"The hell you will. Check out your chest. Somebody's already tried to hurt you. I'll drive you home. Come to think of it, let me check out your chest."

It felt good to smile. "Thanks. I'll ride home with you, but I'll take a rain check on that second offer."

"Got anything to eat?"

PJ opened a desk drawer. "I've got some Little Debbie cakes."

"You're kidding. That would be too good to be true."

She pulled out an unopened box of Zebra Cakes. Schultz snatched the whole thing before she had a chance to offer him an individual package.

"Woman, we are soul mates. See you in half an hour."

Chapter 28

Dear Diary,

These are things that happened to me, cross my heart and hope to die.

It's my ninth birthday and I should be happy. Instead, I'm in my room crying and I can't stop. Old Jingles is dead, and I saw it happen.

My sister's folded-up laundry is in a basket in the hall. She's supposed to put it away. It's part of her taking more responsibility and learning how to do things on her own. She's smart but never finishes anything. She has been to two colleges and dropped out before she got her first set of grades. Our parents are upset about that, and my sister hasn't found a husband either. She's twenty years old and Dad says she's a freeloader. Things have changed a lot in the past year. Some things happened that I don't know about and now Mom and Dad don't like my sister very much. One thing I know is that my sister hears people talking to her when there aren't any people around. There's been some talk about her moving out because she's getting really funny. I don't mean funny ha-ha.

My sister must have done something really bad because she's supposed to be their darling, their favorite who is always right. But not anymore. Mom had this strange talk with me and asked me about the things my sister did when we were alone. I didn't think it would do much good, but I answered truthfully. I figured I'd get punished, but she wanted to hear everything. Imagine that!

You know what, I think Mom and Dad are scared of her and they don't know what to do. They feel guilty about it, though. I've been scared all my life, and I'm a little guilty, too. I'm supposed to love my sister.

Mom is going to have a baby soon. She looks like she's carrying around a watermelon under her clothes. I hope it's a brother, because I've had enough of sisters.

Anyway, the laundry is in a basket and Jingles jumps in and makes a bed. When my sister gets home, she's really mad about him being on top of her laundry. She hollers and Jingles tries to sneak off to get away from her. Her face gets strange, kind of frozen, not like a person who's angry but she's saying angry words. I try to save Jingles, but she pushes me away. The second time she pushes me, I fall down the stairs and end up on the landing. My knee hurts a lot.

Mom and Dad hear the noise and come to see what's going on. My mother shrieks and Dad says some bad words. Mom tries to get Jingles away, but my sister balls up her fist like she does with me, and punches Mom in the stomach. Dad steps in and slaps my sister in the face, hard. I've never seen anything like that before. She comes after him with her hands out like claws. He picks up a vase on a table in the hall and smashes it over her head. She falls down and lies still. Mother is on the floor, holding Jingles, but his legs are every which way. Dad comes over and says he's got to do it and she says yes. Mom calls to me to close my eyes. I only pretend to. Dad turns Jingles' head around and he's quiet.

The silence makes me feel a lot better, even though I know he's dead.

Dad picks up my sister and carries her to her room. Mom comes down the stairs to check on me. I'm okay; I just have a hurt knee. I'm not okay inside, though.

Dad comes along and carries me down the stairs. He puts me on the couch and Mom gets a pillow and some ice for my knee. I hear Dad on the phone. Mom sits with me and pats my hand. In a little while, our doctor comes to the house. That's another thing I've never seen happen. He goes into my sister's room and later talks with Dad in the upstairs hall. I can't hear everything they're saying, but I heard that the doctor gave my sister a shot. I hate shots. She deserves it. She deserves a million shots.

Dad brings me a bowl of ice cream, chocolate chip, and tells me that he's sorry about Jingles. I want to tell him that I'm thankful for what he did for Jingles, but I can't find any words to say it. So I just eat my ice cream. Mom helps me up the stairs and into bed. When she's gone, I start crying.

I'll never, ever forget my ninth birthday.

Chapter 29

When Thomas got off the bus, he had a twinge of doubt. He could do his bus route in reverse and be back in his room in forty-five minutes. No one would know he'd left.

Except him. Nope, he was going through with it. If he had to leave the game early to get back before Mom got home, then he'd just make some excuse.

Thomas skirted the parking lot in front of Brookings Hall. It was well lighted and probably patrolled by car or bicycle. It took him quite a bit out of his way, but he managed to enter the Hilltop campus from the south side. He hesitated and ducked into the shadows between Brown and Busch Halls. Near midnight, there was no foot traffic near the buildings. Libraries were closed, and it being Friday night, the dorms were a lot livelier than the academic portions of the campus.

A student strolled by on the walkway, wearing a vest and carrying a radio. It was a member of the Bear Patrol, volunteers who walked the campus to help the university police. Thomas had read about it and hoped he wouldn't run into any Bears. Or maybe he was hoping he would. The young man stopped and looked in Thomas's general direction. Thomas was sure his nervous breathing or the blood roaring in his ears was loud enough to be heard. Just then a rabbit ran across the walk. Satisfied, the student moved on.

It was scary and exhilarating. And he hadn't even gotten to the game scene yet.

If he was caught, he'd be reported as a suspicious person, and no doubt held for his mom to come pick him up. The thought of that made him flatten himself even more against the cold bricks of the building. There were some bushes as part of the landscaping, but since the branches were bare, they impeded rather than concealed him.

He'd been told that his first challenge was getting into Brookings Hall, and then into the tunnels. Brookings had a gothic look to it. There were four towers that looked like rooks from a chess game, arranged in a square. On the north and south sides of the square were long halls. Stone archways were everywhere. Thomas prowled along the outside of South Brookings, trying any door he came across. On the fourth try, the door opened and he slipped inside. He was in a hallway lined with office doors. A staircase led him to a lower level, but there was nothing remotely resembling a tunnel entrance. He returned to the main floor and tried another staircase. This time, in a dimly lit corner, he found a door marked "Authorized Personnel Only" and tried it. It swung aside easily. It had to be the place, or it would have been locked.

Inside, he put an envelope on the floor with his ten dollars in it. There had been no instructions for paying gronz_eye, but sooner or later, the guy had to leave by this door, and he'd find it.

Ahead of him was a tunnel with pipes running overhead, some a foot in diameter or more. A string of utility lights wrapped in metal cages lit the way, but the light from one bulb didn't quite reach the next, so that the tunnel appeared to a series of light and dark areas. It was very warm, heat radiating throughout the tunnel from the steam pipes above his head. Beneath his feet was bare concrete, damp in places.

A few steps in, there was a wooden box about the size of a textbook on the floor. Thomas turned it over and over in his hands, unable to open it.

Great. This is going to be embarrassing if I can't even discover what my quest is.

His fingers finally slid a panel open by accident, and then

it was just a matter of time until he found the other sliding panels that opened the box. It was just like the game, only here it was in his hands.

Inside were two sealed envelopes, lettered in gold calligraphy. One of them read Vyzer Lok. So there was one person still to come after him. He removed his envelope and resealed the box.

Excited, he ripped the envelope open. Inside was a cryptic message.

Greetings, Vyzer Lok. Your quest is to find the Four Lost Keys of Durbane and bring them, and yourself, safely back to the entrance. No Vyzer has yet succeeded. The Keys do not want to be found, except for the North Key that may offer help or treachery. Good luck and beware.

Thomas stuffed the letter in his pocket and studied his surroundings. He could barely contain his glee.

One key wanted to be found. That meant it would have to practically fall into his hands.

He looked up, and scoured the pipes and the ceiling of the tunnel with his eyes. Nothing. He wondered about the other gamers who had arrived before him. One of them may have already retrieved the key, and he would have to battle for it with his wits. Or trade for it, if he located something that he didn't need but another gamer did.

Thomas set off down the tunnel. He was on a quest.

Thirty minutes later, Thomas had gone through several junctions of the tunnel, always choosing the path on the right to avoid getting lost. He wasn't actually very far from the entrance, because he was taking his time searching for keys.

His haul so far was four coins of limited bargaining value and his prize, a green fake gem the size of a golf ball. He'd also found a mummified mouse, which he'd brought with him in case it had some magic power in the game. He was getting discouraged. Time was ticking away, and soon he'd have to turn back, get off campus, and call a cab with his cellphone.

Then he spotted it, a glint of something gold. Rushing forward, he picked up a key that was partially concealed by a broken piece of concrete. It had to be the North Key, or it wouldn't have been so easy to see. There was no message with it, so he pocketed the key and moved on. He might not have to leave before the game was over after all.

At the next branch of the tunnel, there was a small door in the side wall that looked like it might lead to a storage room. Thomas fingered the North Key in his pocket.

The North Key may offer help or treachery.

A storage room might contain many items that he could use, including more keys, gems, or even a map. As far as he knew, he was the only gamer in the tunnels who could open that door.

The key fit in the lock. Thomas decided that at this point, with his time running out, he needed help. He'd take his chances on the treachery.

The door opened inward to a black space. The tunnel lights were too far away to light up the interior. Thomas put his hand on the wall inside the door, fumbling for a light switch. He found one, and snapped it on.

The room was small, a damp, musty place with old bookshelves stacked every which way, almost as if they'd been tossed in and forgotten. There were no obvious prizes for him. He'd have to search the room thoroughly, or ignore it as a dead end. He took a few steps inside, and when he did, he felt a rush of air behind him. The hairs rose on the back of his neck, and he had the strong feeling of being watched.

Then the door slammed and a heartbeat later the light went out.

Chapter 30

There was something PJ wanted to pursue but never seemed to find the time for it. She was determined to make some progress now that she'd been left alone in her office.

Call Thomas? She had her hand on the phone, but took it off. *He's probably asleep. Poor kid used up his whole Friday night on a book report.*

It was the rumor of the third sister that June mentioned that kept sticking in PJ's mind. Just because May dismissed it out of hand didn't mean there was nothing to it. She may have reason to lie.

It was hard to believe anything one sister said about the other. As hard as that was for PJ to imagine, she knew from her work as a psychologist that it wasn't uncommon. Sisters often saw each other as rivals for their parents' attention, for the clothes they sometimes were made to share, for the boys in a small pool of eligible dates. Thinking about that brought a smile to her face.

PJ grew up with a sister less than two years older than she was. She and Mandy did everything together, shared lipsticks, squealed over the same rock stars, competed against each other in academics and volleyball, and gave each other surprise birthday parties. Then along came Vince.

Vince Sellerman's family moved into Newton, Iowa, from Los Angeles. They might as well have landed in a starship for all the attention handsome, worldly Vince got from the local girls. He was seventeen, a year older than Mandy. Both sisters had a crush on him. Who didn't, in their crowd? He was the most exciting thing that had happened at Newton Senior High School since the Kolson brothers blew up the toilet in the teachers' restroom. But at fourteen, PJ was too young to even exist as far as Vince was concerned.

Mandy had a date with Vince and she and her friends were swooning with delight. PJ was feeling shut out, probably because she *was* shut out, told by the giggling girls to go play with the little kids. She started a rumor that Mandy had gone all the way with the football quarterback. In their circle, such things were the province of whispers and shock, something not done by nice girls. The rumor swept through the school and caused terrific hurt when Mandy not only heard it but also learned the source. PJ could still feel the shame that had overwhelmed her when Mandy confronted her. There was no such thing as an anti-rumor that would annihilate the rumor, or a magic undo command. Until Mandy graduated, kids still snickered behind her back.

For having been through it, the sisters were closer than ever.

Vince and Mandy married and had four children. Mandy had latent Earth Mother qualities, and was a wonderful, warm-hearted mother who managed her rambunctious family with love and a great sense of humor. Mandy confided that after hearing the rumor, Vince was particularly eager to go out with her. Standards in Los Angeles weren't quite the same as in the heart of the Midwest. Inadvertently, PJ may have been a matchmaker.

The things May and June said about each other had the same vicious elements as PJ's rumor about going all the way did twenty-five years ago. Juvenile and hurtful. But these sisters were still doing it to each other years after their adolescence, and neither of them seemed to feel any shame about it.

PJ shuddered to think what a trio of such sisters would be like. The duo was bad enough.

The parents were Henry Winter and Virginia Crane, married in 1956. The Crane family was very wealthy, very high society. The Winters weren't on any social register; they clung to the underside of the middle class like barnacles on a hull. Henry Winter was a hard-working dynamo of a man who wasn't afraid to get his hands dirty all the way up to the shoulders to build his manufacturing business. Virginia Crane was raised as a debutante whose idea of hard work was having a French lesson and a tennis lesson on the same day.

In PJ's opinion, there were two reasons a young woman like Virginia would marry Henry Winter. One was blind love. The other was defiance of her parents. Regardless of the reason, the offspring of the marriage had ended up with a thinly masked dislike and suspicion of each other.

There were records of the births of two daughters, May Flower Winter in 1967 and June Moon Winter in 1975. PJ wondered how June had suffered with a middle name like that. Parents could be so inconsiderate when it came to naming children.

No indication of a third daughter.

Death records revealed that both parents died in a light plane accident in 1997, while on their way to a political fundraising event in Jefferson City.

Survived by daughters May F. Simmons of St. Louis and June M. Merrett of St. Louis; John T. Winter of Denver, Colorado; Jasmine C. Singer of Hannibal, Missouri; and numerous friends.

Death records revealed that Virginia Crane had a brother who had lived only a year.

What was it June said? Virginia had a brother who died at the age of one and maybe he was murdered. A family secret.

The existence of the brother who died at a young age lent

credibility to what June revealed. If there was one secret on such a scale, perhaps there was another. It might be interesting to talk to the surviving aunt and uncle, do a little prying. PJ made note of their names.

It was 1:30 a.m. when Schultz came in. She'd run over her time estimate, but apparently he'd been busy.

"Brush those crumbs off your shirt and take me home," she said.

"Your wish is my command. Sometimes."

Chapter 31

Thomas screamed and spun toward the door, banging his shin on one of the bookshelves and tripping. Something landed on him in the blackness, something slippery and brittle that was all over him. Scrambling backwards, he pulled himself out from under whatever it was. With his back against the wall, he crouched, hands held out, ready to defend against what he couldn't see.

The light came back on. Blinking in the sudden brightness, Thomas stood up. The thing that had landed on him was a Halloween skeleton made of plastic, and it was coated with something that looked a lot like blood. The door was ajar, and he heard fading laughter out in the tunnel.

He shook his head. Apparently the joke was on him.

Some joke. I almost shit in my pants.

Feeling both ashamed and angry, he began retracing his steps. His shin hurt, and he kept replaying his moments of panic over in his mind, wishing he'd acted differently. How could he be so stupid?

All I can say is my ten bucks better still be there.

At one of the tunnel branches, a figure loomed suddenly in front of him, wearing a garish costume fashioned to look like a cyrroth from *The Gem Sword of Seryth*. A cyrroth was a fierce, shaggy mercenary with great strength but a tendency to double-cross anyone foolish enough or desperate enough to employ him.

As much in turmoil as Thomas was, he couldn't help admiring the authenticity of the costume, down to the sword that was permanently welded to a cyrroth's arm in a rite that marked its passage from welph to adult.

"Nice costume, dude," he said. "Don't think much of your joke, though."

"No passage without payment," the cyrroth said. His voice was deep and mechanical, like Darth Vader's. The costume must have a voice-morpher.

"I'd really just like to get out of here now," Thomas said in annoyance.

"No passage without payment."

"Yeah, I heard you the first time. Get out of my way, man." He gave the cyrroth a shove, but the creature stood his ground.

"Fuck you, asshole, get out of my way now!" Thomas advanced on the cyrroth again, the anger he felt when he discovered he'd been tricked in the storage room boiling over. "Now!"

The cyrroth raised his sword. Thomas was steamed, and if he could get hold of the guy in the costume, he was going to pummel him. He'd never been so riled up before. Normally he would have avoided confrontation, but this time he kept going, and made a grab for the shaggy chest.

The sword cut through Thomas's jacket and traced a hot line of pain across his left forearm.

Shit! This is for real!

The panic he'd felt in the storage room when the light went out returned tenfold. The sword was moving upward in a wide sweep, and when it came down, it would be heading for his neck. He looked around frantically for anything he could use to defend himself. Jamming his left hand in his pocket, he came out with the fake gem. He threw it as hard as he could, aiming right for the creature's face. It bounced off with no effect. Thomas raised his right arm to fend off the sword. It came whistling down and bit deeper this time. For a moment, pain immobilized him. Blood flowed down his arm inside what was left of his coat sleeve. He felt the wet warmth of it running down his side and smelled his own fear. His arm dropped to his side uselessly.

His other hand pulled out his cellphone.

Trying to shove his panic down, he flipped open the phone, making it chirp a few notes. The familiar blue glow of the numbers gave him an idea. Straightening himself up, he summoned his voice and began shouting.

"Yeah, I'm calling the police, you weirdo! You stay away from me. Get the hell out of here!" It was all bluff. His phone had no reception in the tunnel. "I'm taking your fucking picture, too." *Snap, snap.* He clicked a series of pictures. "The cops are gonna find you, freak!"

The distraction worked long enough for Thomas to dive to the side of the tunnel, roll, and come up on the other side of the creature. Then he ran like all the demons of Seryth were after him.

Chapter 32

Schultz pulled into PJ's driveway and went around the back of the house. It was nearly two in the morning and they were both tired. He was going to get a good dose of painkiller down her throat and put her to bed. The only thing they'd be sharing tonight would be a blanket.

They went upstairs. Thomas's bedroom door was closed. Schultz brought her a glass of water and watched her swallow the pills. She kicked off her shoes, got into bed fully dressed, and fell asleep in moments.

She'd made him promise to check the cat's food and water, and make sure the kitty litter was clean. He didn't feel like going back down because his arthritis was acting up and his screwed-together foot ached. It was a measure of his love for her that he was standing in the laundry room with a kitty litter scoop in his hand when he heard the noises from the downstairs bathroom.

He drew his gun and checked the kitchen. No one. Looking down the hall, he could see that a slice of light was coming from underneath the closed bathroom door. That door had been open before he went upstairs. He moved down the hall quietly and stood outside the door. There were drops of blood on the floor. Amid the bumps and shuffling coming from inside the bathroom, he heard a familiar voice.

"Ouch," Thomas said. "Damn it!"

"Son, you all right in there?" Schultz said. He hadn't holstered his gun yet. There was no response to his question. "Open the door, Thomas."

"It's okay," came Thomas's voice, a little shaky. "I just got a paper cut, that's all. You can go to sleep now. Everything's all right."

Schultz had heard better lies from street-hardened six-year-olds. "Open the door, son, or I'll break it down."

The doorknob turned and the door fell open a couple of inches. Schultz put one foot in the door to keep it from closing, and tapped the door open with the muzzle of his gun. There was no telling who was in there with the kid.

Thomas was alone. He stood in his boxer shorts with a package of gauze in his hands. "I can't get this fucking stuff to work right," he said. There was a clumsy bandage wrapped with gauze that was already slipping loose on his shin. His right forearm had a five-inch cut that had bled a lot. His left arm had a slice that did look like a giant paper cut. There were bloody towels in the sink.

"Let me see that, does that need stitches?"

Schultz took Thomas's right arm and examined the cut. It was deep, clean edged, and gaping apart.

"You'll need stitches, and we can't wait too long. Come on out into the kitchen. We'll get that covered and get you ready to go. You injured anywhere else? Feel dizzy or anything?" Schultz peered into his eyes. "Did you lose consciousness?"

Thomas headed down the hall toward the kitchen. Schultz gathered up the first aid supplies and followed him. After washing his hands, he gently cleaned both cuts and the leg abrasion with hydrogen peroxide, watching the liquid foam lightly in the wounds. On went non-stick four by four's, and then gauze dressings neatly fastened with tape in picture-frame fashion. The two said nothing while Schultz worked.

"That feels a lot better," Thomas said.

"You want to tell me how you got those?"

"I fell in my room."

"Uh huh, and I'm the tooth fairy. Out with it."

"Does Mom have to know?"

"Yeah, but there's no sense waking her up yet. We're going to talk about it, just the two of us. You didn't do those with a razor, did you?" Schultz indicated the cuts on Thomas's forearms.

"What?"

"Did you use a razor blade on your arms?"

"Oh, I get it. No, I didn't try to commit suicide. If I had, do you think I would have bashed myself in the leg first?"

Schultz kept a smile from leaking onto his lips. He'd been worried at first, but now he could see that Thomas was on firm mental ground. "Kids have done stranger things, you know."

"I didn't cut myself on purpose. I swear."

"I believe you. Tell me what happened, but make it fast. We need to get you to a hospital."

Once Thomas got started talking, everything came out in a rush. Schultz wanted to interrupt and shout at Thomas, grab him by the shoulders and shake the shit out of him for going through with something like this. As Thomas related his activities, Schultz went from indifference at a teenage prank like sneaking out to anger to nerve-numbing fear for what might have happened. "Where are your clothes?" Schultz said, a few minutes later.

"Upstairs in the laundry basket. You're mad, aren't you?"

"We're going to need those. There might have been some transfer from that time you shoved him. Have you ever seen that costume before, at a Halloween party, maybe?"

"Never. It was detailed, brown and hairy and had a mask with jowls like this." Thomas puffed out his cheeks and then pulled down on them, distorting his face.

"You say the sword was real. How long was it?"

"I'm not sure. Three feet, at least." Thomas looked down at his arm. "It cut right through my jacket, and he never really had a chance to get in a really good swing. I can imagine what would have happened next."

"Enough of that," Schultz said. He was doing enough imagining for the two of them. "How about his eyes? Did you get the color?"

"The eyes were covered with mesh to look like an insect's eyes. Cyrotths are crosses between—"

"I get the picture. You couldn't identify him, in other words."

"Not a chance. Not by voice, either. You're mad, huh?"

"Voice might be something we can work with. Maybe there's not a lot of these voice, what did you say?"

"Voice-morphers. Anybody can buy them on the Net."

Schultz frowned. He was hoping it would be something a little more exotic and easier to trace. "Let's see those pictures you took with your cellphone camera."

The pictures were dark and blurry. The security lighting in the tunnel wasn't bright enough to get a good shot. "These look like the Abominable Snowman on a moonless night," said Schultz.

"They could be enhanced. Don't you know about that?"

"Don't get smart alecky," Schultz said. His voice was sharper than he intended. "Of course I know."

"So you're really going to report this?"

"Hell, yes. The guy shoving you into a dark room is bad enough, but there's aggravated battery with that sword, and who knows how far that would have gone if you hadn't kept your head, no pun intended, and gotten out of there. This is one sick gamer, if that's all it is."

Thomas tried to get in a few words.

"Don't interrupt me. I got more to say. You're fourteen

and becoming a man and all that. Your mother is doing the best she can with you, but she's not here all the time and you're taking advantage of that. But you listen to me, you little shit. I'm watching you now too and you can't pull this crap on me, because I've seen too much of it. And unlike your mother, I'm not going to sit down and analyze your behavior. You try anything like this again, and I'll ream you a new asshole all the way up to your throat. Am I making myself clear?"

"Yes, sir."

"Come here, son," Schultz said. Tears threatened to well up in his eyes as he wrapped Thomas in a careful hug. "Thank God you're safe."

"Mmphh," Thomas said.

"Now," Schultz said, holding him at arm's length, "we have to go to the hospital and then downtown for some pictures of your wounds and get your clothes and cellphone pictures turned in. But first it's time to wake your mother up."

"She's gonna freak," Thomas said.

Chapter 33

Half an hour later, PJ was sipping strong coffee in the waiting area of the emergency room, listening to Thomas tell the story, and guessing the elements he was leaving out. She didn't mind that Thomas and Schultz were keeping the part about panicking in the dark between the two of them. Thomas had skipped over that in his description, but she'd inferred it from the circumstances. She welcomed the fact that Thomas had another person he felt safe confiding in besides her.

She reacted the way she assumed Schultz did: a mixture of relief, anger, and fear. After yelling until she wore herself down, she grounded Thomas for a month for sneaking out of the house. At the hospital, he was given a tetanus booster, stitches in one arm, and butterfly closures on the smaller cut on his other arm. He was brave, didn't flinch for the stitches, screwed his eyes tightly shut for the shot.

It was 6:00 a.m. on Saturday by the time she dropped Thomas off at home, where he planned to catch up on his sleep. She wished she could do the same. Instead, she went back out into the winter morning and drove to her office.

The hard drive had been removed from her home computer to be studied in an attempt to track down the gamer who'd lured Thomas to the tunnels. She wasn't waiting for the police to do their sleuthing. She wanted to talk to Merlin.

She contacted him on their encrypted VoIP connection, and he responded immediately. PJ wondered when he rested, because she'd never caught him groggy from sleep. It was good to hear his voice.

"I have to say I got cut off very abruptly the last time we

spoke," Merlin began. "You didn't even get the list of the day."

She rarely got out of a conversation with Merlin without one of his lists, which could be funny, serious, or both, but always on target.

"I believe we were discussing the Metro Mangler case."

"Not you, too," she said. "I can't pick up any paper or listen to the news without hearing that."

"You'll have to catch me up on the details. If you're still interested in my opinion, of course." He sniffed.

"That'll have to wait. First I want to talk about something that happened last night with Thomas. Or I should say, to Thomas."

She told him about the online gaming and the spillover into the real world.

"I have a bad feeling about this guy, Merlin. I think he'll try again, and keep trying until he really harms someone."

"It's enough to give gaming a bad name. I know some people who would be unhappy about that. They're purists."

PJ thought about the implications of what Merlin was saying. Sometimes his words required considerable interpretation, and she was never quite sure she got it right.

"Are you saying that the high-echelon gamers would resent this?" She was thinking that a game abuser might incur some retribution, in the same way that online chat leaders called channel operators, or ChanOps, banned or kicked people from a chat.

"Let's just say they'd have a vested interest in ousting a total wacko."

"My concern isn't for the integrity of the game. It's for the safety of my son, or someone else's child. I don't think you're taking this seriously enough."

"I have a different perspective on it as a gamer myself. I'm mainstream, not hard-core. Sure, this guy did something weird, but some gamers fantasize about their favorite games coming to life. There are griefers, too, cyberbullies who pick on others in the games. If a newcomer beats a regular, he might get threatened by griefers. That's petty stuff, but it can be upsetting."

"This one acted on his fantasy and he had a sword, Merlin. I don't think it's petty. You know what I'm asking. Can this guy be tracked down or not? I want a name and address."

"Tell me what you know."

She told him everything she'd pried out of Thomas, including the gaming sites and chat rooms he used, and said, "If the police effort comes up empty on this, I'm going after him myself. Somehow."

Merlin changed the subject and quizzed her about new developments in the multiple homicides. She spent time catching him up on the recent events.

"Let me see if I have all of this straight. Two sisters with issues that go way back. One husband under pressure from gangsters—"

"I didn't say that," PJ injected. "I said Chicago businessmen."

"Under pressure from *businessmen*. The other husband the object of a slander suit and the target of an angry tenants' association. A suspicious Kansas City alibi. A maid intent on a better life. A nymphomaniac partner. A bloody knife among the clay pots. A dead look-alike in the shower. Not one, but two, albums of dirty pictures. A teacher and her neighbor, the billboard man, murdered. An imaginary sister. No meaningful forensic evidence. An alcoholic chicken farmer. A diamond ring flushed down a toilet. A four-day gap in a victim's whereabouts. An attempt on your life. Hearts, fingers, male equipment. Have I left anything out?"

"Technically, Arlan's nose."

"All you need now is the secret diary."

"More like the secret decoder ring," PJ said.

"That's exactly the kind of humor you used to berate Schultz for, and tell him he was insensitive."

"Oh, God, am I doing that? Have I gotten insensitive too?" PJ was suddenly embarrassed about things she'd said in a light tone concerning the homicides.

Secret decoder ring. All those comments about the foreplay albums. The cook in the study with the revolver.

"You're just learning to cope with profound darkness the way cops do, that's all."

"Still." *I should know better.*

"Go back to the beginning," Merlin said. "And find out where Arlan was for four days. It might all come down to the disparity in his disappearance and his time of death."

PJ sighed. She had been concentrating on Arlan's murder. Ground zero. She just wasn't getting anywhere with it.

"You sound like a woman who needs a list," Merlin said. "One: Listen to your heart instead of your brain, for once. Marry Schultz. Two: Arlan was a strong guy and may have been capable of fighting off an attacker. Why didn't he? Three: Family secrets, but which family? Four: You might consider starting a foreplay album of your own. See above comment concerning Schultz. Five: The word for today is es-oterica. Take care, Keypunch."

Esoterica?

"Barn," PJ said.

This time the simulation began outside the barn. She wanted to explore how Arlan got onto that workbench, trussed and ready to carve. In her first scenario, a Genman worked to extract a naked, struggling Arlan from the back seat of a sedan. The car was parked about fifty feet from the barn, which was where the gravel driveway ended. Arlan's hands and feet were tied, but he was giving the killer a tough time anyway. After all, Arlan was a weight lifter and surely had a good idea that the person carrying him was up to no good. He'd be doing his best to get away. When would the ketamine that had shown up in Arlan's body be administered? While getting him to the barn, or when he was already in the barn?

Finally, the Genman retrieved a wrench from the car and whacked Arlan in the head with it to make him hold still. Arlan did have a minor skull fracture, but the ME thought it was from hitting his head on the cobblestones as he rolled.

The murderer then dragged the limp body fifty feet. There were no drag marks outside the barn. PJ cancelled the simulation and started again.

This time a Genman and a Genfem pulled up in a four-wheel-drive pickup, easily crossing the space between the end of the gravel driveway and the barn's door, even though it was rutted terrain. Much less distance to carry the struggling victim. Plausible, except that the only tire tracks on the ground between the gravel and the barn had been matched to Old Hank's pickup. The grass in that area was worn away, exposing loose dirt in a number of places. Fresh tracks from a 4x4's large tires, or even a sedan's smaller ones, would have been evident.

Maybe the killer parked far enough away to avoid leaving tire tracks and transported the victim in a fireman's carry. If the victim was unconscious and the killer had training in that type of carry, it would work.

Or Arlan was held at gunpoint and forced to walk into the barn.

If it were me and my feet were free to move, I'd run. The killer would have to shoot me in the back. No way would I go into that barn. But a strong man like Arlan might think he still had a chance to overpower the killer and take the gun away. Especially if the person holding the gun was a woman, maybe a petite woman.

"End," she said. Inspiration wasn't striking. There were too many variables. One killer or two, parked here, parked there, gun, no gun. She spread the barn photos out on her desk and went over everything again.

Chapter 34

Monday morning found PJ at her office an hour after dawn. She had the place mostly to herself for awhile, then the hallway gradually filled up. She got up to close her door and nearly ran into Anita.

"It looks like June Merrett really was in Kansas City at the time of her husband's death," Anita said. "She was at a dinner meeting with other attendees of the workshop on Saturday night. What we didn't know was that the restaurant made some menu changes that weekend. Brand new menus were used starting Sunday. The old menus were collected and set aside after their last use. June's fingerprint is on one of the old menus."

"Couldn't it have been left there on some other occasion?"

"The print was found on one of those plastic-coated inserts with the Chef's Special. That particular insert was new, and was only in place in the menus last Friday and Saturday nights."

"Good work, Anita. You stuck with it and it paid off."

"Well, I owe a lot to a K.C. cop named Ziegler. He did the legwork. I just kept after him."

"Schultz isn't going to be happy about this," PJ said. "I think he was hoping to pin all this on June."

"Yeah, he already shit a brick. Of course that alibi only holds for Arlan's murder. June's still up for grabs on the other murders."

Dave joined them and was brought up to speed. "Where does that leave us with the look-alike's murder?" he asked. "June didn't have to hire anybody to impersonate her."

"You've been looking at it from the angle of faking alibis,"

PJ said. "Suppose June had a lover or even a secret admirer. The admirer might kill Arlan in order to take his place in June's heart and home. If June then rejected him, the admirer might lash out at a surrogate—poor Marilee, whose death was a way to vent anger without actually destroying the object of his love."

Anita and Dave both stared at her for a moment, then spoke together: "Naaah."

"Hey, why not? I spent a whole thirty seconds coming up with that idea. It could even be a lesbian admirer."

"You're heading off the deep end, Boss," Anita said. "I've been wondering if we're going around in circles on these suspects because we should be focusing on strangers instead, like that I-70 Killer case."

"I haven't ignored stranger killings," PJ said. "I just can't get anywhere with the idea."

"So what have you got?"

PJ retrieved a rolled-up map of the city that was leaning against the wall and spread it across the desk.

"Arlan's body was found here," PJ pointed to a blue dot downtown on the riverfront. "But he was killed north of the city, here in St. Ann." There was a blood red dot about fourteen miles northwest of downtown.

"Marilee Baines was killed in the Bevo area, five miles southwest of downtown. Frank was killed in the central west city on Lindell," she said, pointing to a red dot about five miles west of downtown. "Loretta Blanchette and her neighbor Bernard Dewey were killed in Florissant, thirteen miles north of downtown."

"I guess you've tried drawing all kinds of patterns," Dave said.

"Yes. Too bad they don't form a big arrow or something," PJ said, referring to the area in which a killer operates—his home territory. PJ drew circles around the three city dots representing the homes of Marilee and Frank, and the riverfront where Arlan's body was found. Then she drew a line between the two county sites. "So it's two zones, one in the county, and one in the city. Residence and work, or the other way around."

PJ was warming to the stranger idea. "The biggest problem is how the killer selected these victims. Three of them seem closely related. Arlan, Frank, and Marilee. But Loretta and her neighbor have nothing to do with the first three."

"Nothing that we know of so far," Anita said. "That doesn't mean they aren't connected in the mind of a single person."

PJ nodded. "Agreed. Then consider the specifics of the deaths. Three heart killings, two mechanical shootings. Three men, two women. All of the victims are white. There's been no evidence of rape."

"No evidence to speak of at all," Anita said. "How about the killer being a member of law enforcement who knows what to avoid?"

"I noticed that idea was being tossed around in the media this past weekend, along with various reports of severed body parts turning up."

"We had to follow up on that body parts thing," Dave said. "Turns out it was chicken bones wrapped in clay and dipped in taco sauce. Some kids started it as a joke and now it's all over the city. An elderly woman had some in her mailbox and fainted. Somebody's going to have a heart attack if it keeps up."

"Did you find out who started it?"

"For once, we actually did. A kid ratted out his buddies on the original occurrence. But it's spread like waistlines at

Thanksgiving dinner. Calls are coming in by the dozens. We're telling 'em that if the fingers smell like food, it's probably nothing to worry about, but take them to the nearest station anyway."

"The Case of the Missing Chicken Fingers," PJ said. "Maybe we should hire Colonel Sanders."

Anita guffawed, shattering the Tinkerbell-like illusion of her appearance. "Good one, Boss. But that idea of the killer being one of us is seriously creepy."

"Does it have to be a stranger for this comfort zone idea to work?" Dave said, tapping on the circle drawn on the map. "Fredericka lives in that city zone." He drew his finger along the line between St. Ann and Florissant. "And she also has an apartment she rented in the county zone for a future real estate project. That's residence and work."

"Can we bring her in for questioning?" PJ said. "I'd like to get her out of her home environment and turn up the heat."

"Sure," Dave said with a grin. "I'm sure she'll come if I ask nicely."

Chapter 35

Schultz checked in with the Florissant police on the murder of the teacher and her neighbor. There had been two developments in the case.

Bernard Dewey died in his living room, wearing a robe and slippers. He'd pulled a phone into his lap and was about to make a call, but died with that intent. A window was broken and the shooter took aim through the hole. It was a low window, and there was nothing about the trajectory that refined the height range of the shooter. No footprints were found, but a piece of broken glass on the ground had captured a few black fibers. They were identified as a Lycra blend in common use for bicycling jerseys and other sportswear. No blood, no torn skin fragments.

The second thing to come to light was that Loretta Blanchette volunteered with parolees in a day-release program, tutoring several of them to get their high school certificates. Once a teacher, always a teacher. Two of the parolees hadn't reported in on the day of the murder, and were still missing. Interviews with other parolees confirmed that there had been some talk about how Miss B must have a lot of money because she dressed nice and drove a nice car. It wasn't a big leap from there to the two ex-cons interrogating Miss B to get money that wasn't there to give, getting disgusted that there was no treasure trove in the old lady's house, and killing her. The neighbor was just collateral damage when he happened to see them, or maybe they'd invaded next door looking for money.

Schultz had a hard time connecting the ex-con story with the fiber evidence. Ex-cons prancing around in cycling outfits? Maybe, but no clothing had been reported stolen nearby. And even if they couldn't find the stash of money they'd hoped for in Miss B's house, they would have taken anything that could be converted to cash. A modest amount of gold jewelry was in plain sight in the bedroom, and a laptop computer sat on a table in the living room. Still, enough doubt was raised that he couldn't put the killings firmly in the Metro Mangler column.

All that was percolating around in his mind as he drove to the Simmons home on Lindell. He wanted to have a conversation with the maid and see how big the stars were in her eyes about changing careers and becoming an interior designer. Or whether the stars were really dollar signs.

The marble columns and immense entrance doors gave Schultz the impression that the home was a fortress, not so much to repel enemies but to contain secrets.

The object of his interest opened the door. She was trim, early thirties, wearing black slacks and a plain white blouse. She was also wearing rubberized blue gloves that came nearly to her elbows and a jacket to protect her clothing. The jacket was damp in places, and she had cobwebs in her hair. Schultz displayed his badge and identified himself.

"Missus May is resting. She's not seeing anyone today. You can contact her attorney, Jack Nordman. Do you need his phone number?"

"No reason to disturb Missus May. It's you I'm here to see." Schultz had already planted half his bulk over the threshold, so that even the heavy oak door would have trouble budging him.

She frowned and took a step backward, as most people would if Schultz moved into their personal space, and that was the opening he needed.

"Now then, where can we talk?" He plied her with a soothing smile.

"I am rather busy." She held up her blue gloves.

"Only take a minute. Or we can talk downtown, if you'd prefer."

"All right." She stripped off the gloves and jacket and dropped them on the floor of the foyer. "Follow me."

"Doing some heavy cleaning today?" he said, as she led him through hallways of gleaming tile.

"You might say that. I was working on the children's play-room."

"How are the kids doing?"

She stopped and turned around. "Do you have children, Detective Schultz?"

Schultz blinked. He had a son whose face was beginning to fade from memory, permanently overwritten by an image of a gruesome death. And he also had Thomas.

"One son."

She nodded crisply. "Then you know what it's like to be a parent. I could count on one hand the number of hours Missus May has spent with her children since their father died. I think the only time she was really there for them was when she was birthing them. And even for that, she was knocked out."

"So you don't approve."

"I had a daughter. She would have been fourteen. Leu-kemia. It was us against the world. Her father was killed in Desert Storm, and we have no living relatives."

"I'm sorry."

She gave him a brittle smile. "It's just that some people don't value what they have. Or I should say they value the wrong things."

By now they'd reached a small kitchen. Mary Beth offered

him bottled water and took one herself. He accepted more out of courtesy than thirst.

"Let's talk about Frank and May," he said. "Did you think they had a solid marriage?"

She hesitated. "On Frank's part, I'd say yes. May's an opportunist. If she had an affair, there would have to be some advantage to it, some leverage she could get. But there was no other man as far as I know."

He noticed that it hadn't taken her long to drop the "Missus May" routine. A lack of respect had certainly taken root.

"At the time of Frank's death, you were in the house, correct?"

"That's in my statement, Detective. What is it that you really came here to ask?"

So much for my subtle approach.

"Did you let anyone into the house that day?"

"No."

"Or turn off the alarm system so that someone could get in unnoticed?"

"No. I was here when Frank was shot." She pointed to the counter where they were sitting. "I'd had a couple beers and gotten drowsy. I was up late the night before, reading a new design book. I put my head down for a bit, and the next thing I knew, there were cops in the house."

He studied her face. There was defensiveness in it, especially in her eyes and the furrows in her forehead, but no deceit.

"So tell me about this design business of yours," he said.

"It's something I've wanted to do since I was a girl. It started out as a kind of escape, I guess. My mom and dad fought a lot, and sometimes he hit her when he was drunk. I'd go in my room and lock the door. She told me to do that, just in case he decided he needed another punching bag."

She sat in silence for a minute, and he let her replay her memories. "I got a dollhouse for my sixth birthday. Pink and white and full of little chairs and tables. There was even a bathtub. I'd block out the noise outside my room and just move those little pieces of furniture around. Kept me sane, I think. So in a weird way I want to be an interior designer in honor of my mother. I've got some savings, and I've already taken some courses toward my degree."

Schultz had seen people motivated by stranger things before. He may not be able to wrap his brain around the motivation, but he intuitively knew that Mary Beth wouldn't do anything to taint her dream, like take blood money to betray her employer.

There was nothing here for him. He chatted awhile with her, shook her hand, and wished her well with her business.

Out in his car, he phoned PJ. He listened to the speculation concerning Fredericka, and learned that Dave was bringing her in within the hour for questioning.

One door closes, another opens.

Chapter 36

PJ sat nervously in the waiting room belonging to the principal of Jamison Academy. There was something about waiting to see the principal that brought back her own childish indiscretions. She found herself watching the clock, waiting for the bell to ring in the hopes that Kevin Archibald, the principal, would be tied up until school was over.

She'd gotten the summons while waiting to interview Fredericka Chase. *Mr. Archibald would like to see you immediately concerning your son.* Not words that a mother wanted to hear, least of all when the mother had several homicides hanging over her head. She'd dropped what she was doing and taken a cab, wondering why the principal wouldn't give her an explanation on the phone.

His office door opened. "Come in, Dr. Gray," he said.

Trying to remember that she was the parent and not the student being summoned into the inner sanctum, she followed the voice and was ushered into an office designed to impress. Wood paneling, a desk that went on forever, tasteful groupings of chairs, the deep tones of the Oriental rug, heavy brass lamps with green glass shades, the only touch of modernity a twenty-one-inch flat panel monitor so thin it looked like it could be rolled up as a window shade.

Mr. Archibald, whom she had only spoken to on the phone up until now, took a seat in a massive leather chair behind the desk, and waved her into a smaller version that faced him.

If I'd sassed the teacher, I'd be quaking right about now.

That is, until she got a look at the principal. He was much younger than she anticipated, maybe thirty-six. He was classically handsome, with a strong jaw, abundant, dark, curly hair that tumbled down over his forehead, brown eyes, and the build of an athlete. PJ pictured him in a muscle shirt and cute little shorts, and the mystique of the principal's office evaporated. While she could easily imagine calling him Kevin in a throaty whisper, addressing him as Mr. Archibald seemed ludicrous.

The girls must be falling all over themselves trying to get sent to the office.

"Dr. Gray, are you aware of our zero tolerance policy?"

"Certainly. Zero tolerance for drugs, smoking, bullying, sexual harassment, and weapons. It's a very attractive feature of the academy, and I fully support it."

She didn't want to think that Thomas had been involved in any of those things.

He nodded and opened a desk drawer. Drawing out a flat box about six inches wide and ten inches long, he placed it in front of him. "Then perhaps you can explain this package, which came in the mail addressed to Thomas, in care of the academy."

He opened the top of the box. Inside was a dagger with a jewel-encrusted hilt, nestled in a velvet liner.

PJ was speechless.

"It looks like gold and real jewels, but it's all imitation. However, the blade is functional."

"Thomas wouldn't bring anything like this to school. We don't own any daggers," she said. She felt as though someone were squeezing her heart. The moment she saw the dagger, she knew what was going on. "We have to find out who sent it and why."

"Exactly. That's why I'm turning this over to the police."

"I need to fill you in on what's happened with Thomas. The police are already involved. Seeing this," she tapped the box, "confirms my suspicion. Thomas is being stalked."

★ ★ ★ ★ ★

The dagger's box was a forensic dead end. There was a tantalizing partial fingerprint on the guard of the dagger, but it didn't turn up any matches in IAFIS, the FBI's Integrated Automated Fingerprint Identification System. Which made sense, if it belonged to some teenaged gamer.

There had been no progress in determining who had set up the meeting and terrorized PJ's son. Two court orders resulted in a phony ID for gronz_eye and the unhelpful information that a library computer had been used. No sign-in record existed at the library for the times the chat took place. Simple but effective. In a similar but trickier way, the gamer had erased his footprints from *The Gem Sword of Seryth* sites, where thousands of gamers interacted. PJ had visited the chat room several times from her office computer, but hadn't run across gronz_eye. Thomas, under her watchful eye, hadn't been able to locate him playing the game, either. The gamer had switched names, chat channels, game sites, and computers, and vanished into the cyberworld. He hadn't given up on Thomas, though.

Chapter 37

In spite of Dave's confident attitude about getting Fredericka to show up voluntarily, it was Tuesday afternoon before she finally arrived, leaving a trail of bug-eyed cops in her wake.

Dave was in the interrogation room with Fredericka. Schultz was content to watch from behind the one-way mirror. He missed PJ's presence, since he wanted to get her input as a psychologist. She'd disappeared, though, off taking care of school problems.

Schultz studied Fredericka's body language. She'd fallen immediately into the same behavior with Dave. She was wearing a short skirt that was a little scrap of leathery material, and a stretch top that ended in flirty lace north of her belly button. It was a wonder she didn't freeze to death, dressed like that in the middle of winter. Schultz had to keep reminding himself that she was a successful real estate developer. He'd seen her closet, and he knew she had business suits. Whether she ever wore them was another story.

These clothes were selected with Dave in mind.

Sitting across the table from Dave, she'd crossed her legs at the ankle. Sometimes her knees strayed further apart than the approved good girl distance. Aside from the blatant sexuality, she seemed relaxed and confident. Not the demeanor of a guilty person, unless the person had no conscience. It was only an interview that she consented to, not a real interrogation, the kind that would take place after she'd been arrested and informed of her rights. It could be that the heat wasn't high enough to melt her because of that. It looked like Dave was done with the preliminaries, so Schultz flipped on the speaker to listen in.

"We have reason to believe that you and Mr. Merrett were

having an intimate relationship," Dave said. "Would you confirm that?"

"Who told you that?"

"Photographs."

"Oh, did June find those? I never knew where he kept them."

"So that's a yes to having a relationship."

"Yes, it's a yes," she said. Her left hand strayed from her lap up to her bared abdomen. She drew her fingers slowly across the skin. "There wasn't any relationship, though. We didn't have all the trappings of an affair, like giving presents or sneaking away to bed and breakfasts. It was just, 'Hey, the report's done, wanna fuck?' "

"Who initiated this relationship?" Dave said.

"I think you could say we both did."

"Did you make an effort to bring an album of photographs to the attention of the police?"

"The foreplay pics? Nope. I don't even know where Arlan kept it. Kinky stuff, huh?" The hand had migrated to her neckline, where it was toying with the deep V-cut of her top. "So you've seen all those pictures of me?"

"Do you know of anyone who might want to take the album to the police?"

She shrugged, her breasts moving under the thin, stretchy material. "I said I don't know where he kept it, so how could I know who got their hands on it?"

"When was the last time the album was put to use, and where?"

"At my loft, at least a couple of weeks ago. Arlan brought the chocolate. We didn't bother with that very often."

"Would that be before you thought your place might have been broken into, the time you came home and had a creepy feeling?"

"Oh, yes."

"Since the album was last used at your loft, could Arlan have left it there?"

"I suppose. You think someone broke in to steal the album. It could have been among Arlan's things in the closet. I wouldn't have noticed anything missing. You're so clever, Dave." She reached across the table with the hand that wasn't occupied with her cleavage, rested that hand on top of Dave's, and let it linger there. Dave slid his hand out from under hers.

"Could we stay focused here?" Dave said.

"I am focused."

Anita arrived, and silently stood next to Schultz.

"You've already indicated that you were working, alone, in your apartment at the time of Mr. Merrett's death. Where were you on Sunday, from five until eight in the evening?"

"That's an easy one. I was making a presentation at a seminar at The Westin St. Louis Hotel on Spruce, downtown. When the seminar was over, a group of us women went to the health club for awhile, then to the hotel's restaurant and ate Asian food. We were there talking until the place was about ready to close. I got back to my loft, oh, I don't know, maybe ten thirty. I was tired, and depressed about Arlan's death, so I went straight to bed."

"You were depressed but you went to a health club and a restaurant?"

"The seminar was scheduled months ago, and the women were all business associates. I can give you their names. What was I supposed to do, sit around all alone and cry? Going out took my mind off the sadness."

Dave, taking notes, nodded. "How about this past Friday, between eight and midnight?"

Fredericka's hand gently rubbed the neckline of her top, and then slipped inside it, continuing her self-caress. She sighed. "Can't say much about that one. I was at home. And before you ask me, I didn't phone anyone or order food delivered. It was just me, alone with my body." She slouched a little lower, and her fingers were gently circling her nipple.

Dave shifted his chair and wiped his brow. "I'd appreciate it if you'd keep your hands in your lap," he said.

"Jesus Christ," Anita said. "Doesn't she know there's somebody behind the mirror watching?"

"Yeah, and I think she likes it. Looks like our boy needs a bucket of cold water," Schultz said to Anita. "Do you want to be the bucket or shall I?"

"I'd be happy to," she said. She went to the door and opened it without knocking. "Detective Whitmore, you've got a phone call," she said.

"Uh, thanks," Dave said. He didn't get up right away. Anita gave him a minute to compose himself.

"An urgent phone call, Detective," she said. Soon after that, Dave got up and left the room. Anita took his place in the hotseat across from the nympho, who had a disappointed look on her face. "Now then, Ms. Chase, maybe you could be more explicit about your activities last Friday night?"

Schultz clapped Dave on the back. "Way to go, tough guy. Maybe they'll study the tape of that one in the academy as a sample of how not to do an interview."

"Fuck that," Dave said.

PJ approached the two men just in time to hear what Dave said. In the mood she was in, she wondered if she should just turn around and go away. In her experience, if things were so bad that the Bear—the way she thought of tall, gently rounded, normally even-tempered Dave—was upset, that was not a good sign.

Turn around she did. She was behind in her simulation

work and didn't want to get involved in whatever Dave was so vehement about. Besides, there was someone she wanted to talk to even more than her two team members.

Settled in her office, she contacted Merlin.

"What's the buzz, Keypunch?"

She filled him in on what had happened since the last time they spoke. Law enforcement had been unable to find the gamer so far and the dagger at the school indicated that this guy wasn't going away.

"I thought it would be an isolated thing," Merlin said. "Like a practical joke. But I see that's not the case. If it's okay with you, I'll do some checking around."

"Of course it's okay with me. Why would you even ask?"

"Because I'm going to have to get very specific. At some point I'm going to have to reveal Thomas's identity."

She thought for a moment, not really sure of the consequences of what Merlin was asking. But she trusted him. "Do it."

"Sure thing, Keypunch. What's happening on the homicides?"

She gave him a concise summary, which helped to clarify her own thoughts. All the while, though, she was wondering what he meant by *sure thing*.

"So the maid didn't pan out as a suspect," Merlin said. "I'm glad to hear that. I've always had a thing for design myself."

"A thing? I can't picture you flipping through wallpaper samples."

"I didn't say what type of design."

"Oh," she said. "What do you think about the Florissant murders?"

There was no answer for several minutes. PJ was used to the long silences in her conversation with Merlin. She doodled on some papers on her desk, and stopped when she noticed she was drawing daggers.

"I'm inclined to think they're still connected with this case," Merlin said. "The parolees are a strong argument, but you have to go with your gut."

PJ nodded. "Heart and fingers. Or in this case, only one finger."

"Yes, a solo finger. A ring finger."

Why haven't I thought of that before?

"June and her diamond engagement ring," she said.

"Exactly."

"June has no alibi for that time period. But she doesn't have any connection to the teacher, either."

"So the teacher could be a target of opportunity," Merlin said. "An innocent victim whose purpose is to point the finger at June."

PJ rolled her eyes at the comment. "To frame her. That could be May's doing. May certainly knew the engagement ring story."

"There could be plenty of others who knew. I can see May gloating about it."

"So May is tormenting her sister and out to get her at any cost," PJ said. "Probably continuing a long-standing pattern of behavior but taking it up a notch. I like it. May could have killed Shower Woman as a way of saying 'this is what I could do to you, anytime I want' to June."

"And June retaliated for a lifetime of emotional abuse by killing May's husband," Merlin said. "Finally lashing out. A woman on the edge."

"It sounds good," PJ said. "Unfortunately, there's the matter of proof."

"Why spoil things when we're on a roll?"

"Unfortunately my coworkers get sticky about things like proof."

"Then get to work on it. What are you doing wasting your time talking to me? Don't leave without your list, though. One: Marry Schultz. If you can't do that, then at least live with the guy and get some regular smooching, albeit garlic scented."

"Onion."

"Can garlic be far behind? Two: Present behavior starts in the past. Set the Wayback Machine. Three: Chain Thomas to his bed at night, but not in a bondage sort of way. Fredericka is kinky enough for all of us. Four: Your hard drive will never be the same after the police give it back to you. It won't trust you anymore, after what it's been through. Five: The word for the day is still esoterica. Esoterica, noun: secrets known only to an initiated minority."

"I know what it means, you annoying man," PJ said testily, "but what does it mean when you say it?"

"Take care, Keypunch."

PJ wasn't leaving until she made some sense of her barn scenario. She had some ideas, and set to work with enthusiasm. Her conversation with Merlin had turned May into the top suspect. It required giving up PJ's notion of a killing duo, but that had gotten her nowhere. Schultz had never bought into the duo idea, for what that was worth.

She didn't have what she needed in her preprogrammed set of vehicles, so it took a while to add the item she'd glimpsed on the grounds of the May's home. It was a motorized garden cart with large, smooth wheels that left no tracks on the landscaping.

The null world, then a night scene.

PJ, as a Genfem, pulled a full-sized pickup truck into Old Hank's driveway. She followed the *Eggs 4 Sale* sign and came to a stop on the gravel turnaround some distance from the barn. There was a duffle bag full of supplies resting next to her on the seat, but she ignored it for now. Opening the truck's tailgate, she slid out two substantial boards and positioned them as ramps. Getting up into the bed of the truck was a clumsy maneuver for her. It wasn't the kind of motion she was familiar with in her scenarios.

In the truck bed was the utility vehicle she'd seen at May's home, the garden cart, barely fitting between the rear wheel housings. Only now it held Arlan, naked and unconscious in the wood-slatted area where the gardener had been futilely tossing leaves. The cart's engine was electric, so there was very little noise. She started backing the cart down the ramps. And promptly fell off. She had to restart the scenario a couple of times before she was able to get the cart down the ramps onto the gravel without overturning it.

Could May manage that? She could have practiced. Or she might just be more coordinated than me, which wouldn't take much.

The utility cart had turf tires. It left no tracks and fit easily through the oversized barn door. She drove right up to the workbench with it, got out, and set up her portable light.

Now for the second part of her plan. How did the killer, unless he was a strong man or two people, get the two-hundred-pound weight out of the cart and up on a tall workbench?

PJ retrieved the duffle bag from the interior of the truck. Inside it were rope and a manual winch, no surprise to her because she'd set it up that way in the scenario. Looking up, she saw that one of the structural beams of the barn was above the workbench. She tossed the rope up and over, again having to try a few times before succeeding. Then she fastened the two ends of the rope to a winch, and stretching over the cart's slats, worked the straps of the winch around Arlan's body.

It was amazing how much trouble the killer had gone through to stage this murder so precisely, and in a place associated with both May and June. Powerful needs must go along with it.

Family traditions.

Working the manual winch, PJ easily raised Arlan from the cart and swung him out over the workbench. She had a little trouble positioning him just right and lowering him, and in the process scraped his back more than once across the workbench. Oak splinters had been found embedded in Arlan's back, and it was easy to see how they'd gotten there.

PJ skimmed over the killing that came next, switching to an observer role and moving the simulation at ten times normal speed. In front of her eyes, a Genfem raced through the mutilations and dug into Arlan's chest. She had no urge to linger on that again. When Arlan was dead and his severed parts nailed, PJ switched back into being the killer. She reversed her actions, using the winch to put Arlan back in the cart, pulling the rope down from the beam, and driving back out to the truck. This time, because she was pulling forward up the ramps, she had a lot easier time of it. In a few minutes, the truck pulled away from the barn.

"End," she said. PJ felt exultant. It was something workable. She still needed a plausible connection between the kill site and the dump site, but the scenario had plenty of potential. PJ was surprised to find that it was eight o'clock at night. The time had sped by while she was working at the computer.

She called Thomas, who was watching a video at Mick's house.

"Hey, you're grounded. You're not supposed to be watching TV."

"It's in the room I'm sharing with Mick. I'm supposed to make him turn off his own TV? Close my eyes?"

Grounding wasn't as practical when Thomas was staying in another person's house as it was when he was under her thumb at home.

"Okay, no using the computer, no phone calls to anyone except me or Schultz, and no going out, like to movies with your friends. When you get back home, it'll be no TV, too. You can watch TV with Mick, as long as it isn't anything R-rated."

"Mick doesn't get to see that stuff either, so that won't be a problem," he said.

She quizzed Thomas on what he thought about the dagger arriving at the academy. While PJ was still there, he'd been summoned to Mr. Archibald's office and shown the dagger. He claimed no involvement with it, and she believed him. The principal did too, if she was correct in judging the man's body language.

"I'm getting creeped out about it, Mom," he said.

"Me, too."

"What do we do if the police can't find this jerk?"

"Let's let the law do its thing," she said. "And I've got something in reserve, too."

"I'm really sorry about this."

She was tempted to reassure him by saying everything was all right. But it wasn't all right, so she clamped her lips together on that. She'd already lectured him enough about it.

"We'll get through it, sweetie. We make a tough team, you know."

"Yeah. You and me and Schultz."

She hadn't meant to include a third party, but hearing it from Thomas, it did sound reassuring.

"I still have work to do, so I'll let you get back to your movie. Love you."

"Love you, Mom."

After hanging up, PJ used her computer to order flowers

sent to Lilly Kane. Mick's mother was being extraordinarily helpful, and PJ didn't know how she was going to repay her.

She called Schultz, trying his desk first, and was surprised to actually reach him there. Explaining her insight about May being the killer, she left out Merlin's role of talking it over with her. No one else knew about Merlin, and she preferred to keep it that way.

"So there are two things we need to do," she said.

"You know, when you say that, you usually mean things I need to do."

She flushed slightly, even though he couldn't see her. "You are the official cop portion of this team, as you so often remind me."

He sighed. "Let's not get into that now. What is it *we* need to do?"

She talked him quickly through her simulation. "This scenario would have a lot of credibility if we could find two things."

"One is the garden cart with Arlan's blood in it," he said. "The other?"

"Rope fibers on the beam above the workbench in Old Hank's barn. There is one teensy problem."

"Yeah?"

"I saw the garden cart in use at May's home after the murder. The gardener was calmly loading leaves into it. You'd think he would have noticed if it had been heavily bloodstained."

"It could have been scrubbed well enough that casual inspection wouldn't reveal any blood," Schultz said. "There could have been a tarp in it. Hey, maybe the cart was used to take the body to the dump site. You wouldn't need one of those stretcher-body bags. Just drag the body out of the cart and roll it. The cart could have been pushed into the river afterward."

"How about you go check out the cart, Dave goes to the barn, and Anita gets a search going in the river?"

"I can tell you right now that since this isn't body retrieval, we're not getting any divers until tomorrow, and that's if we're lucky."

"Okay, then, Anita gets a night off," PJ said.

Feeling that things were moving in the right direction, or at least a direction, PJ decided to follow through on the research she'd done about the parents of May and June and the mysterious third sister. It was time to put that theory aside or put some teeth into it. She got out her notes on the obituary with names of surviving relatives.

John T. Winter, the sisters' paternal uncle, lived in Denver. It was only a little after seven o'clock there, not too late to give the man a call. She looked up his phone number on the Internet, pleased to find it with minimal effort. She identified herself when he picked up, and asked if he was the brother of Henry Winter, the husband of Virginia Crane.

"Yes, I am. Henry died in 1997, though, if you were looking to get in touch with him."

"No, I'm calling to talk to you. Were you aware that both of Henry's son-in-laws have died within the past ten days?"

"Oh, god, no. Nobody calls me anymore. After Henry died, I lost touch. Was it another accident? My brother died in a plane crash."

"I'm sorry to say it was homicide, in both cases."

PJ gave the man all the time he needed to absorb the information. She didn't like being the one to bring him the news. "Mr. Winter, I'm sorry for your losses. This must be especially hard, hearing about both of these men at one time, and from someone who is not a member of your family."

"I'm all right, just stunned, I guess. Is there anything you can tell me about their deaths?"

"Very little, I'm afraid. I can say that Frank Simmons was shot and Arlan Merrett was stabbed."

"Jesus. No one called me." His voice trailed off. "Thank you for letting me know. I guess I'll get in touch with my nieces, see if there's anything I can do to help."

"May I ask you some questions, Mr. Winter? It could be of help in the investigations."

"Sure, anything. I just need to sit down first," he said.

PJ heard some shuffling that sounded like a chair being dragged across the floor. "You said that you lost touch with the St. Louis families after your brother died. Were you in close contact before that?"

"It depends on what you call close," he said. "Henry came out to visit me two or three times a year, and at Christmas, I usually went to St. Louis for a week."

"Was that from the time he first got married to Virginia Crane?"

"Yes, but Virginia and I didn't get along too well. I think I was a little too much of a reminder of our family's middle-class roots for her. I was a traveling salesman. Cash registers."

"Did Virginia ever talk about her little brother, the one who died when he was less than a year old?" PJ asked.

"Strange you should ask about that. She never did mention that to me, but my brother did. The boy's name was Ellis, I think. Died of the flu."

"There weren't any rumors about Ellis being murdered?"

"What? No, nothing I knew about. He got sick and died, that's what I heard."

"Only one more subject, Mr. Winter. How many children did your brother and his wife have?"

"Three."

PJ's heart nearly stopped. The rumor was true, then. "So there's May, June, and?"

"And April. I didn't know her very well. I was traveling a lot at the time. April was born only six months after my brother married Virginia. You know, like a shotgun wedding, only into a high-class family. Years later, when she was a teenager, Henry told me there were some problems with her, some behavioral problems, or problems at school. I don't really remember, and he didn't make a big deal of it. Doesn't matter, though. She died when she was twenty. A horse riding accident. I went to her funeral. May was a young girl at that time, second or third grade, I think. Little June was a baby then."

Not an imaginary friend. A real sister. Why would May lie and say June was delusional? To make June look crazy, apparently.

"Do you happen to have any pictures of April or of the entire family at that time?"

"I'm not sure. I can look through the old photos. If you're interested, Jasmine, that's Virginia's sister, would probably know a lot more about it. She and Virginia kept in very close touch. Listen, I'd really like to call my nieces now."

PJ checked her notes. "That would be Jasmine Singer, of Hannibal, Missouri?"

"Yes. Talk with her. She knew April well, I think."

"Thank you. I'll certainly do that. You've been very generous with your time, Mr. Winter. Again, I'm sorry for your losses."

Tempering PJ's excitement about confirming the existence of the third sister was the fact of that sister's death. Why would May lie when she said she didn't know of another child in the family? There could have been something traumatic about April's death that caused May to block out the experience of even having a sister.

Far-fetched. That would take some horrendous trauma.

Too bad April was a dead end.

Chapter 38

Schultz called the Simmons home. The maid answered.

"How's it going, Ms. Paulson?" Schultz said familiarly. Since their last conversation, he'd felt a bond with the woman who'd lost her child. The circumstances of her loss were different from his, but it gave them something in common.

"Please call me Mary Beth."

"Leo here."

"If you're wondering how things are going in the household now that Frank's gone, it's been very smooth. Almost like nothing's different. One fewer place to set at the table for dinner is what it amounts to."

"Not much grieving in evidence, then?"

"Oh, yes. But it's from the children, the poor things. They had a closer relationship with their father than with their mother."

"Do what you can, Mary Beth. Those kids are going to need support."

"Oh, we do. All the staff."

"Speaking of staff, what's the gardener's name?"

"You mean Jimmy Drummond? He's not on staff here. The landscaping work is contracted out to Green Vista."

Schultz's eyebrows rose. "You mean the company Arlan ran?"

"Uh huh. They have to maintain the grounds around their developments, and were constantly having to hire short-term help, so they decided to make the best of it and start a landscaping firm. Green Vista GroundWorks, I think it's called. They have GVGW on their vans. There's a manager, so Arlan didn't have to mess with the daily work. It was just a convenience for them."

How are these families tied together? Let me count the ways.

"So, Jimmy Drummond is assigned to May's account. Where might I find him when he's off duty?"

Mary Beth giggled. "I have no idea. I have a crush on him, would you believe? But I only admire him when he's on the premises. I don't follow him home."

"Okay, I'm sure I can find out where he lives."

"Maybe I should. Follow him home, that is."

Schultz said nothing. She wasn't going to get any advice to the lovelorn out of him.

"Do you know if the Simmonses own a garden vehicle?" he asked, thinking that it was likely the cart PJ had seen belonged to Green Vista GroundWorks.

"I think so. I don't have much to do with that, you know. But Jimmy walks to the storage building at the back of the property, in some trees. He comes out riding a wagon with rakes and stuff in the back."

"And he puts it away when he's done."

"Yup. Then he leaves in the van."

"Thanks, Mary Beth. You've been very helpful."

Schultz tracked down Judge Hector Martinez in the Central West End. The guy approved almost all of the search warrants Schultz took to him, which may have been because Schultz helped get the man's crack-addicted daughter into a treatment program and dropped in to check on her after that, making sure she stayed straight and continued her schooling. The young woman was in law school now.

Judge Martinez was in the downstairs dining room at Balaban's having white wine and what looked like grilled salmon. He also had a lady companion who was not Mrs. Martinez.

Judge Martinez seemed to be in a hurry to get rid of Schultz for some reason. He listened to the explanation for the warrant, interrupted saying, "Yes, yes," and signed it right there on the white tablecloth.

Schultz took a couple of officers and an ETU over to May's home. Mary Beth answered the door, and in a few minutes had produced a sleepy May in silk pajamas and robe down at the front door to acknowledge the serving of the warrant.

"You want to look at what? My storage building?" she said.

"Yes, ma'am. Specifically at your garden cart."

"I don't understand, but Detective, you didn't need a warrant. You could have just asked me. And you didn't have to wake me up for it. That shed isn't going anywhere."

"Just keeping everything legal, Mrs. Simmons. You know those lawyers."

She shrugged. "I'm going back to bed. If you have any questions, Mary Beth can come and get me. Again."

Schultz considered her demeanor. She showed no concern for anyone looking around in the shed. Either she wasn't the killer, or she was a brilliant actress, or a complete nut case.

There was a padlock on the door of the storage building that was removed by one of the officers with a massive bolt cutter, and bagged to be tested for fingerprints. The double doors opened, and Schultz swept his flashlight quickly around the interior. He didn't have any reason to think a bad guy was hiding in there, but it was procedure. The place was filled with rakes, shovels, and wicked-looking, long-handled pruning shears. And the cart.

It was about seven feet long. The carrying bin in the back

took up about five feet, leaving a couple of feet for a driver's seat and steering wheel. Shining his flashlight over the rails into the bin, he could see a little leaf debris but nothing else. No obvious bloodstains and certainly nothing to swab and test.

"Bring that spray stuff in here," he said to one of the crime scene technicians, who was getting set up in and around the shed. A photographer was at Schultz's elbow, already snapping pictures with a flash.

A tech named Vic Besle, according to his tag, came up carrying a bottle of Luminol. "We don't just squirt this everywhere. The chemical reaction can damage other evidence."

"Just use a little of it in one corner," Schultz said.

Vic seemed reluctant. Schultz made a grab for the bottle, which the tech quickly moved out of reach. "Hey!" Vic said.

"Gimme that!" Schultz said, getting impatient.

"Okay, okay, just one corner."

Vic reached over the wood slats, stretched a little to position the bottle, and misted Luminol into one corner.

Schultz flicked off his flashlight. In about five seconds, a ghostly, greenish-blue glow lined the slats and flared in the corner. The glow was the result of a chemical reaction between the iron in hemoglobin and the Luminol, a reaction that produced light.

"Looks good, but not presumptive," Vic said. "We'll need more testing. Luminol reacts with other things, like bleach or plant materials, which would seem to be an issue here."

"Since when did you guys start talking like that? Presumptive this and that."

"I'm a chemist," Vic said. "I'm moonlighting."

"Well, Mr. Moonlighter, I'd bet my balls that's blood. Photographer, get a picture of this."

Vic sighed and moved away.

Schultz's cellphone rang. It was Dave, from the barn on Hank's property.

"We had the St. Ann PD get in touch with Hank," he said. "The tough part was finding a ladder to get up to that beam. St. Ann brought in the fire department. They were happy to help out."

"Cut to it, Dave. Rope fibers or no fibers?"

"Rope fibers, Boss. Hank says he's never had a rope over that beam."

"Damn, we're making some progress here. Now if we only knew whodunit."

Was May the killer? The inner sense that Schultz relied upon wasn't jangling in the least.

Chapter 39

During high school, I don't have many dates. That doesn't bother me much, except that my parents are always wondering aloud why their precious baby isn't popular anymore. In seventh and eighth grade, I was the one setting the pace, getting asked out every Friday and Saturday night, having any boy I wanted, breaking hearts right and left.

Did I have to put out? Not seriously. The junior cocks never emerged from behind the prison of their zippers, although they certainly flung themselves against the bars. All the boys knew they weren't going to get past tit fondling with me. I did teach more than my share of boys how to unfasten a bra. Enjoy what you get, boys, then go home and jack off. *It should have gotten me labeled a cock tease, but my womanly tits were such hot property that no boy wanted to ruin his chances for a quick squeeze and suck by saying bad things about me.*

Girls that age today do oral sex on command, like trained dogs. Trained bitches. They're afraid if they don't, their guys will go find a better-trained bitch, and they'll be sitting home alone on the weekends, a fate worse than zits.

In my first couple of years of high school, I start to lose interest in all that groping. It's too much trouble to put on girl-clothes and shave my underarms and legs when sloppy T-shirts and jeans are so much easier and cover stubble. I have to wash my hair, too, and I put that off for days, until I have grungy hair. A boy kisses me and complains that I have bad breath. I guess I have grungy breath, too, because I haven't brushed my teeth for a week. Or is it two? My mother starts to notice that my shampoo and toothpaste aren't going away fast enough. I solve that by dumping a capful down the sink and squeezing the toothpaste tube down the sink, too.

So what happened to Miss Popularity? She faded away, a puddle drying up in the sun. A puddle with greasy hair.

Trying to prove to my parents that I can get a date for the senior prom, I take the initiative and ask Gregory Royalview, a boy who doesn't seem to have any other prospects. Then I join the other girls, talking about gowns, hairdos, and of course, shoes dyed to match, with clip-on bows.

On the night of the dance, Greg calls me and says he is going with someone else. I hadn't realized that it was me *who was the last resort. I thought that honor was his. I keep up pretenses in front of my parents. I secretly call a cab, give a vague excuse why my date isn't picking me up, and spend the night watching movies, excuse me,* films, *at a late-night artsy-fartsy theater across town. When I get home, my parents are asleep, and as far as they know, I've been to the prom. I hang up my gown in a plastic storage bag, but I never forget dear old Greg.*

No doubt about it, it's time to make Greg pay. I can't believe I've waited so long. It all seems so easy, and it feels good to let the inhibitions slip away and do whatever I want. This has nothing to do with becoming a Rich Bitch. It's just scratching an itch.

Greg and Cheryl Royalview are having lunch when I ring the doorbell. This is my riskiest effort yet. I can't stand on the porch in daylight too long, and I can't wear the black Lycra and keep my face covered. I'm potentially the object of any nosy neighbor's furtive glances, and I've already had to deal with The Busybody. It's such a thrill, doing this. I put my eye up to the peephole and have a sudden vision of my left eye transfixed by a long knife pushed in from the other side. In my vision, Greg says, "I told you I was going to the prom with somebody else! If you can't get that fact into your head, I'll just have to put a knife into it instead."

Instead of a knife, Greg's pale blue eye appears in the peephole. We look at each other, me looking for a gleam of recognition and him trying to figure out if I'm the type to do a home invasion.

Fortunately he is a poor judge of character based upon pupil and iris. The door opens and Greg, the little shit, doesn't invite me in. Didn't he recognize my eyeball? Was the whole thing so trivial to him that he can't even remember my name?

No matter, I force my way inside at gunpoint. Cheryl is the first to go, dispatched with a quick shot to the head. The red circle in her forehead is an imitation of the "O" her red lips form right before I pull the trigger. As a killing method goes, it's pretty basic, but my motto is if it works, do it again and again.

Greg, seeing his wife blown away in front of him, is understandably belligerent, but I'm prepared for that. I use a taser gun on him. His legs go out from beneath him, and while he's on the floor I quickly get rope around his wrists and ankles. It doesn't take long before the taser shock wears off, but by then he's spread-eagled on the floor, arms and legs tied to immovable objects. I straddle him and let my imagination take over. It occurs to some portion of my mind that I'm no longer hurting people only when they're sedated and can't experience it. Looking back on it, that seems too considerate. Besides, I've taken a liking to the process.

And in the new order of things, what I want, I get.

Chapter 40

PJ was about to call a cab to get home when Schultz dropped by her office with the cart and rope fiber news. She stood up behind her desk and did a little victory dance.

"Hey, babe, you can dance for me anytime," Schultz said. "How about I tuck some money in your underwear?"

She sat down heavily in her chair. "Leo, I've been meaning to talk to you about that, but I haven't had the time."

"About what?"

"Don't call me babe," she said.

He blinked. "You don't like it?"

"No, I think it's demeaning. It's also a pig."

He looked at her suspiciously. "Is this some kind of cops-as-pigs joke? 'Cause if so, it's a new one on me."

"I'm serious. Babe is an oink-oink pig in a movie," she said.

"I don't mean it that way," Schultz said. "I say it to be, you know, sweet."

PJ was getting annoyed. She hadn't expected this much discussion. She would ask, he would agree, and that would be that.

"It doesn't seem like you say it in a sweet way all the time. Even if you do, I'd prefer you find some other term for me, especially in front of team members." Irritation was plain in her voice.

"Well, shit, why haven't you said anything before? I didn't know it bothered you." Schultz responded in kind, and raised the stakes. He pointed at her as though lecturing a child.

There was no use trying to explain that she'd tried several times to tell him, only to be cut off by circumstances. "Do

246

you agree to stop?" The words came out in a very sharp tone. She was ready to escalate the cold war.

Schultz threw up both of his hands in surrender. "Hell, yes. If I slip up, I guess you can bust my balls."

"Not funny," she said, and sighed. Her anger bubble had abruptly burst. "Leo, let's put the brakes on this. I shouldn't have brought it up tonight. I could have found a better time, when we're both not so tired."

"I got rough edges," he went on, as though she'd handed him a live grenade instead of an olive branch. "I'm not all smooth and polished the way you are, Doc. You're just going to have to make allowances," he said. "Or not. See if I care." He got up and left the office, slamming the door on his way out.

Elbows on the desk, she cradled her head in her hands.

Handled like a true professional, Dr. Gray. Professional what, I don't know.

She straightened her desk, which meant rearranging the piles of clutter that were always there, made a phone call, and then looked up cab companies on her computer. Finding several, she closed her eyes, made a stab, and picked Laclede Cab. She was hoping there were cabs this late at night. St. Louis wasn't exactly the City that Never Sleeps. In fact, its bedtime seemed to be around 11:00 p.m.

Before she could make the call, her door opened and Schultz was there. He stared at the floor rather than meet her eyes.

"Come on, I'll take you home."

PJ asked if he would drop her off at Lilly Kane's house. She'd called and found Lilly watching *Casablanca* on TV. Schultz agreed but made her promise to take a cab home even though it was less than a dozen blocks to her house from Lilly's.

Over milk and crumb cake at the kitchen table, PJ talked with Lilly and caught up on her son's school week. Megabite spread out to her full length on the table in front of PJ, determined to sponge up as much attention as possible. The cat rolled over and ended up on her back, with her paws kneading the air, her tummy offered up. PJ obliged, running her fingers through soft belly fur like a comb, and being rewarded with a satisfied rumbling. If she held her hand just right, she could feel the cat's heart beating under her finger.

As far as Megabite was concerned, life was good.

PJ shared that assessment while she was in Lilly's comfortably cluttered home. She could hear her son's light snores coming from down the hall, and that was as calming as the cat's purr.

It didn't take long for Lilly's two cats, Peanut and Butter, to get into the act. After bumping their owner's chin several times, they sat down, tucked their paws in, and pretended not to be watching Megabite.

Lilly wanted to know all about the dagger incident. She didn't seem nearly as perturbed as PJ, and indicated that if the jerk came looking for Thomas while she was around, said jerk would have his reproductive equipment blown off. Lilly's ex-husband was a cop, and she'd learned to shoot, and shoot well. She also held a fourth degree Black Belt in tae kwon do. PJ found herself wishing that the jerk would tangle with Lilly.

Not wanting to keep her friend up too late, PJ left in less than an hour. She was ready for some serious pillow time. Her ribs were sore and so were her bruises, which were now a charming yellowish-green around the edges, while the centers were still purple. As her contusions changed color while healing, it was a reminder of the underlying process. Blood had been released from capillaries and trapped under her skin. The hemoglobin decays over a couple of weeks, and the

breakdown products give a bruise its progression of colors. White blood cells charge to the scene and slowly remove the products of decay, causing the bruise to fade and disappear. In her experience, white blood cells were the opposite of teenage boys, who create but do not take out garbage.

She phoned for a cab, waited a few minutes, and went out on the porch. The orange Pacer, looking a sickly mustard color under the streetlights, was still at the curb where she'd waved goodnight to Schultz. She found him sleeping behind the steering wheel, head back, mouth open, snoring for all he was worth. PJ knocked on the passenger's window and was rewarded by his sudden, jerky awakening during which Schultz smacked his knee on the steering wheel.

"What are you doing here?" she asked. She was touched that he'd waited for her.

"What does it look like?" he said gruffly. "Get in, I'll take you home. You sure gab a lot with your friend. I was expecting maybe ten minutes."

She used her cellphone to cancel the cab. At her house, Schultz followed her in without a word, and started fixing up the couch with a knit throw and a toss pillow.

"What's the deal?" she said.

"The deal is I'm sleeping on the couch." He kept his face averted, uselessly rearranging the throw and pillow.

"Suit yourself," she said, and climbed the stairs. Her legs were so tired she envisioned them sheathed in stone.

Thomas's room was directly across from hers, with the bathroom at the end of the hall. She flirted for a whole two seconds with the idea of soaking in a hot bath before deciding to just crash. She could already feel her head sinking into the pillow. Eyelids heavy, she turned into her room and snapped on the light switch.

PJ heard a sound behind her, but didn't process it very

fast. It was unfamiliar, sliding and metallic.

A sword!

She whirled around. Standing behind her was a costumed creature with shaggy, brown fur. It was wide at the shoulders and its face had insect-like eyes. Her breath stopped in her lungs, and her heart nearly stopped with it. Her body tingled with the sudden flow of adrenaline, and her stomach was on a free-falling elevator.

"I have come for Vyzer Lok and the vibrocrystal," the thing said in a flat, mechanized voice. "Where have you imprisoned him?"

The sword that was fastened to the creature's arm lifted menacingly. It gleamed in the light coming from her bedroom. PJ was defenseless, except for her words.

She was shaky and her voice came out in a whisper. "Why should I tell you?"

The creature froze in place. Evidently this wasn't part of its script. Then it advanced on her, the sword pointed at her belly.

"Leo!" That was all she had time to shout, because after that her whole attention was on ducking away from the creature, running into the hall so hard she smacked into the wall, and ending up in Thomas's room. She slammed the door and locked it. "Leo!"

The door splintered, and the sword protruded through, barely missing her.

No weapons here! Gun's in my room!

Frantically PJ looked around for something she could use. Everything was happening so fast. There was no time to think!

The blade withdrew from the door. In its place, a hairy hand tried to push through the door, but the hole was too small. PJ's eyes alighted on one of Thomas's prize posses-

sions: a *Star Wars* Millennium Falcon made of die cast metal. She ran to it and yanked the foot-long, heavy model off its display stand.

The sword smashed through the door again. This time, a large part of the center of the door gave way. She heard a snuffling sound, almost like it was trying to sniff out her location. She stood to the side of the door, and when the questing hand came through, she bashed it with the Falcon with all her strength. There was a yelp, and the hand quickly disappeared.

Cautiously she took a look through the hole in the door, just in time to see Schultz running down the hall yelling, a battering ram in boxer shorts.

She tugged the door open, and there was Schultz struggling on the floor, trying to pin the sword arm. Her heart thudding in her throat, now deathly-frightened for him as well as herself, she circled around so that she could get near the creature's head. She had to do something, and fast.

They were tangled together and moving rapidly. When she had an opening, she took it, and brought the Falcon down on the creature's head.

Schultz flopped off the still form, and lay on his back, his chest heaving.

"Jesus Christ," he said through gasps for air, "I'm getting too old for this shit."

"Did I kill it?" PJ stared at the unmoving, giant insectoid in her hallway. She felt tremendous relief that it wasn't Schultz lying there, wounded or worse.

Schultz rolled over, wincing, and felt for a pulse. "Nah, he's alive. Too bad. Go call 911. I'll keep an eye on him."

She started to walk away, holding her side. A diving roll wasn't the best thing for healing ribs and multi-colored contusions.

"Wait," he said. "Give me that spaceship, just in case."

"You're not going to do anything rash?"

"What? Oh, of course not. I got better things to do than fill out endless paperwork for squishing a bug."

On the way to the phone, her legs almost collapsed beneath her, and she felt nauseous. She'd allowed herself to think about what could have happened if the bug had encountered Thomas alone in the house instead of two determined adults.

Her mind awash with bloody visions, she punched 911.

Schultz asked PJ to get him his pants that were draped over the couch after she finished calling the police. He didn't particularly want to greet his fellow law enforcement officers in his underwear in the hallway of his boss's house. She was kind enough to bring his shirt, shoes, and shoulder holster, too.

Weapon in hand, he approached the unconscious bug and tugged on the head portion of the costume. It didn't come free until he groped around in the hair and found the zipper. With the elaborate mask removed, the two of them got their first real look at gronz_eye. It was a shock to discover that he was at least forty years old.

"Thomas will be interested to know that," PJ said. "Should I call him tonight?"

"It can wait. Geez, what's this guy's story, anyway?" Schultz said. "This costume must cost a month's worth of my salary. It's got to be custom made. Doesn't he have anything better to do than play online games, like have a life?"

"Maybe that is his life," PJ said. "He could have formed such a strong identification with this character," she gestured at the costume, "that he withdrew from the real world."

"I wonder if he has a wife and family and a regular job."

"He might. People with fantasy lives like this are amazingly good at hiding them."

He dropped the costume hood and stepped back a few feet, watching the man warily. Schultz held his gun at his side, but ready to use in case of trouble.

"I have to say I admired what you did here," he said. "You delayed him and did some quick thinking with that space ship. Then you stepped right up when I was fighting the guy and whacked him. That was brave."

"What did you expect me to do? Run away screaming and leave you alone to get sliced open?"

He shrugged. "I was winning. I would've had him pinned if you hadn't taken care of things first."

"Uh huh," she said. "Look, I don't want to get into some kind of pissing contest here, Leo. I don't have the equipment for it, for one thing. For another, I was scared shitless. I don't see anything brave about what I did."

"People doing brave things are always scared shitless. If they aren't, they're just plain stupid."

The doorbell rang. "Patrol car's here. You get the door and I'll make sure our bug doesn't crawl into the woodwork."

While the scene was being processed, Schultz phoned Dave, Anita, and Lieutenant Wall and left messages for them, explaining briefly what had happened. On the messages to Dave and Anita, he added that PJ was officially on recovery time and not to disturb her. All messages were to be channeled through him for the next twenty-four hours.

While he was on the phone, he saw the splintered wood door being carried out. It shook him up, knowing that she'd gone through that alone. As soon as she'd gone upstairs, he'd taken off his clothes, flopped on the couch, pulled up the blanket, and fallen asleep. He didn't know exactly what woke him up. It wasn't the fact that she'd yelled for him, which she said she did. At least, not consciously. He'd awakened with a terrible fear that something was wrong, fear strong enough to propel him up the stairs to check on PJ. He'd seen the figure standing in the hallway just as it plunged the sword through the door. Enraged with the idea that PJ might be on the receiving end of that thrust, he'd charged down the hallway, ready for a battle to the death. It sounded trite as he thought back on it, but that's exactly what he was prepared for at the time.

Then he saw PJ, or at least her feet, and relief flowed through him like a cool, mountain spring, dousing the anger that had been kindled when he saw the intruder. His training took over, and then it was just a matter of subduing another violent criminal. He was getting the upper hand when PJ's feet shuffled closer. Before he could shout at her to get away, she swung something at the bug's head, and the body underneath him went limp.

It was a brave thing for her to do, and he'd complimented her on it. What he didn't say was that it was a foolish thing. Her approach distracted him from what he was doing, and probably put both of them in greater danger. That sword could have sliced through her legs or across his throat.

He knew why she did it. It was the same reason that he charged the formidable-looking creature with no thought for his own safety: love.

I'd die for her. I'd kill for her.

When the bug was handcuffed and taken out on a stretcher, his face and form immortalized in numerous crime scene photos, and the last tech was out the door, Schultz took PJ upstairs. He needed to care for her, to do things for her, and she let him. He gently removed her clothes and pulled a nightgown over her raised arms. The sight of her bruised body disturbed him. It was too reminiscent of the battered wives he'd dealt with over the course of his career. He gave her Tylenol since her pain medication from the hospital had run out.

He put her to bed, took off his clothes, and crawled in next to her naked. He held her hand and stared at the dim shadows on the ceiling cast by a nightlight until he could hear her rhythmic breaths of sleep. Only then did he allow himself to close his eyes. In moments, he was asleep at her side.

Schultz awoke to pale light coming through the windows.
Dawn.

She was awake, watching him. "It's half past five. In the afternoon."
Sunset, then.

She cuddled next to him, and he noticed that she was naked, too. "Do I detect a certain naughtiness in your attire?" he asked.

"You mean my lack of attire. Definitely naughty." Her hand stroked him and very quickly, his erection tented the blanket.

"Mmm," she said, "looks like you're up to the task."

"What task?"

In answer, she put her leg over him and then sat up, straddling him. She slowly lowered her hips. He slid into her warm, moist embrace, and there were no words left to say.

Chapter 41

Schultz waited in his car while PJ went into a convenience store. They'd been heading to work when she'd spotted the store and asked him to pull in, saying she had to buy something that was none of his damn business. He knew enough to park and wait meekly in the car while she purchased whatever it was that women bought when they said things like that.

PJ walked out the door, but stopped and started fiddling with something in her bag. Schultz had taken the opportunity to fill up his gas tank, and he was still parked at the pump when she came out. He heard the roar of an engine, tires squealing, clutch popping. Swiveling his head, he couldn't spot the approaching vehicle, but he knew it was there. The sound was unmistakable.

I'm gonna get some punk for dangerous driving.

He turned the key and started the Pacer, while reaching for his radio. He was going to ask Dispatch to send a traffic cop. Schultz's days of writing tickets were long gone, but a guy could still have a little fun.

PJ stepped down off the curb into the parking lot. From out of nowhere, a black Blazer roared toward her.

It was too late to get out of the car and knock her out of the way. He'd never make it in time. He honked the horn, and she looked at him and waved cheerfully.

The Pacer was idling. He threw it into gear and lurched forward, leaving most of the car's rubber on the pavement behind him. PJ finally noticed the Blazer, and leaped back on the sidewalk in front of the store. The car pursued her, swerving crazily and almost losing control, and ended up ready to ram her through the plate glass windows.

256

The Pacer's front bumper crashed into the passenger's side of the Blazer. Both cars jumped the curb. The impact threw Schultz forward, but he'd only struck a glancing blow to the Blazer and he didn't completely lose control of the Pacer. His seat belt, something PJ had recently talked him into wearing, bit painfully into his abdomen but kept him in place. The Blazer's front end nosed into the window, and a shower of glass exploded into the store. The two vehicles came to rest.

Schultz looked at the driver, who was wearing a ski mask. Their eyes met. He couldn't make out anything, not the color of the eyes, nothing. The driver's gaze held his for several seconds, then suddenly the Blazer was moving. It was in reverse, dropped roughly off the curb, and pulled away from the collision site. The driver yanked the wheel around and sped away, missing the rear end of the Pacer by inches.

Schultz looked over at PJ. She must have tripped, because she was sprawled on the ground, the contents of her bag widely scattered. Two customers were on their way to help her, and the store clerk was in the doorway with a phone in his hand. Store customers were gathered around those who had been injured by flying glass. He hesitated, since procedure said his first duty was to protect and aid the injured, but there seemed to be plenty of help already at hand. PJ sat up, looked at him, and waved at him furiously to follow the Blazer.

That's my gal.

He backed off the curb, hearing a scraping noise from the undercarriage, and maneuvered to the parking lot's exit. There was a break in traffic, so he didn't slow down. He threw the Pacer out onto Chouteau Avenue, turned sharply, and sent the rear wheels into a wide slide. He corrected for it and stepped on the gas. He could see the Blazer ahead of him, and strained to get a look at the license plates. He called for backup, describing both Blazer and situation, and tried to keep the fleeing car in view without doing anything to endanger other drivers. Schultz fumbled for the magnetic rotating beacon to slap onto the roof of his car, until he remembered it was on the floor in the back seat.

A blue-and-white cruiser went by, its lightbar flashing. Schultz decided to leave the chase to the officers who had working lights and even a siren. He pulled over to the edge of the road. Still wired from the crash and the brief chase, he stepped out to inspect the damage to the front of the Pacer.

The bumper was mangled. The front portion of the hood had accordioned inward, and would need bodywork and painting. Fleet Services would, no doubt, total the car. Then there was a clanging that sounded like the Pacer's death knell. Leaning heavily with one hand above the wheel, breath pluming from his mouth, he bent over to see what the noise meant.

His entire exhaust system, from manifold to muffler, was lying on the street. Using his cell, he phoned Dave for a ride and then reluctantly informed Fleet Services that he needed a tow. Using the radio in his car, he found out that PJ had a skinned knee from her fall, was treated at the scene by a paramedic, and was on her way to Headquarters in a cruiser. Several people inside the convenience store had been hit with flying glass, none seriously injured. Another attempt on PJ's life. He sure hoped the driver got caught. It had to be the same person who'd pushed her car into traffic.

All in all, a crappy drive to work.

PJ went into her office and locked the door. Nearly getting run over had shaken her more than she'd let on to the officers at the scene. The earlier incident of getting pushed into traffic was definitely not an accident, then. She had almost convinced herself that the car that did the pushing had some kind of mechanical problem, like a stuck gas pedal. That didn't seem very likely now. There wouldn't be two stuck gas pedals. Besides, she'd seen the Blazer change direction and come bearing down on her, something she'd surely be seeing again in nightmares.

She thought about the suspects—persons of interest, really—one by one, and tried to imagine which of them was after her, and why. Something said to her during an interview, a careless remark, later regretted? Or perhaps she'd seen a clue and not recognized it, but whoever was after her assumed that she knew more than she did.

She looked at her notes and tried to remember word-for-word what she'd been told. Closing her eyes, she replayed all the visits she'd made, trying to remember details of her surroundings. The only thing she came up with was seeing the garden cart in use at May's house. That had given her ideas for a VR scenario, and led to the discovery of the cart with blood in it, blood that belonged to Arlan.

The gardener! He knew I saw him working with the cart. If he was involved, he might have thought I saw something suspicious on it, like a bloodstain.

She heard her doorknob jiggling.

"Boss, you okay in there?" It was Anita's voice.

"Yes, I'll get the door. Don't know how that got locked."

In the office, Anita eyed PJ closely.

"Nothing's wrong, Anita. I'm fine except for my knee." Her pant leg was torn and a little bloody, and inside was a neatly wrapped dressing put on by the ambulance attendant.

Probably thinks I was in here crying.

Before Anita could open her mouth to ask questions, PJ launched into her theory that the gardener was out to get her.

"The first attempt happened within a couple of hours of

me seeing the gardener using the cart," PJ said. "Then the blood-stained cart is found and somebody tries to run me down."

"Sounds plausible," Anita said. "I'll get some background on the guy. Schultz already got a start on that, I think. I didn't come in to talk about your recent brush with death, though, or even Schultz being an asshole, whining about his car."

That got a smile from PJ.

"I came to inform you of two more homicides."

"Oh, God," PJ said. "This is a slaughter. We've got to find the killer."

"You haven't even asked me if they're connected yet."

"Well?"

"Paired murders, like the teacher and her neighbor. This was a couple in Crestwood, off Sappington Road. Gregory and Cheryl Royalview. The wife was shot once in the head. Something interesting about her was that there was a condom in the trash, but the semen didn't belong to her husband. We'll be checking for a match in CODIS. The husband was mutilated, then stabbed about a dozen times in places that didn't kill him immediately. He bled out. He was awake for it, the ME says. At least until he went into deep shock. The killer got control initially using a taser gun. Think our killer has turned to rape, too?"

PJ puzzled over it for a minute. "It doesn't seem to fit, but this case already has so many weird elements, who knows?"

"There's a fine answer from the shrink," Anita said. "I could've made that pronouncement."

"There you go," PJ said. "You've found a new calling. I'm saying it doesn't make sense that a killer who's been so careful about leaving forensic evidence would suddenly leave the mother lode, his semen."

Anita nodded. "Eventually even the most careful slip up,

especially where sex is concerned. It would be great, wouldn't it?"

It occurred to PJ that they were talking about the rape and murder of a woman as "great." She winced, but had to admit it would be a break in an otherwise luckless case.

"Crestwood, that's South County, isn't it? Blows the dual comfort zone theory for downtown and North County."

Getting news second-hand didn't seem so bad when the deliverer was Anita. She had an open attitude and fully included PJ in every discussion.

At least the discussions I know about.

"So that means the sociopath is out?" Anita said.

"No," PJ said. "It could be someone who just defies profiling. As helpful as the techniques are, sometimes you just have to wing it. We could be dealing with other types of mental problems, such as a dissociative disorder resulting from early childhood trauma. Another possibility would be schizophrenia, which commonly shows up in the late teens or early twenties, and can have a genetic component. Both of those can involve violent behavior. Who found the bodies?"

"Greg's parents. By then the couple had been dead about a day."

"My heart goes out to them."

A child's death. Any child's death is an unimaginable thing. It must shatter a parent's life. Her thoughts tried to turn to Thomas's experience, to imagine all the ways that her son could have been hurt, all the ways that the episode could have ended tragically, but she firmly kept her focus on work. *Time for that later.*

"Do I need to go out there?" PJ asked.

Anita shook her head. "The Crestwood PD's on it and you can see the crime scene pics and autopsy information. Unless you're really eager to go, in which case I can give you a ride."

"I'd like to see my son and then get some rest. It's been a wild twenty-four hours."

"Go, Boss. Give Thomas a hug for me."

"He's not much into hugs these days. But I'll tell him you were thinking of him."

After Anita left, PJ worked a little longer in her office, hoping Schultz would show up and announce that he'd been assigned a new vehicle. With both of them lacking transportation, it was going to be hard getting around. In the morning, she'd rent a car.

Should have done that already. What was I thinking? I can't tie Shultz down ferrying me around.

She considered starting the development of a new scenario, Shower Woman's, and see if she could get some insight from that. The murder of June's look-alike might have information the team hadn't wrung out of it yet.

She was drained, though, emotionally and physically. There was no way she was going to make any significant progress tonight on something that required an ounce of creativity. PJ left a message on Schultz's voice mail, called a cab, and went to Lilly's house.

She woke Thomas up, even though it was eleven o'clock on a Thursday night and he had to go to school in the morning. Lilly fixed them both hot chocolate and left them alone in the kitchen. PJ had a long talk with her son about gronz_eye and didn't play down the attack at her house. He needed to know it all, and they talked like a couple of adults. She shared her concerns about someone being out to get her because of her current case, and told him how much she missed him. He accepted it all, but seemed saddened by it, and the attacks on her. For the umpteenth time, she wondered if she was doing the right thing having a job like hers and trying to raise her son. She was thinking of some way to broach this subject with him when he asked about the amount of damage she'd done to his Millennium Falcon model.

She left for home, traveling in another cab, the idea of walking the twelve blocks seeming about as possible to her as walking to Mars. At home, she climbed the stairs, her skinned knee stiff but her bruises, miraculously, beginning to feel better. She fell asleep clutching Schultz's pillow and smelling onions.

Chapter 42

Early Friday morning, Anita came by and whisked PJ off to a low-priced car rental company downtown. She wheedled her way into a rental only days before Christmas, and came out with the keys to a new Ford Focus in Sangria Red. Awed by the array of goodies on the dash, she pushed buttons, slid levers, and turned dials until she was familiar with the controls. Mirrors adjusted, she ventured into downtown traffic, wishing she had a CD handy to try out the player. All that was missing was the new car smell.

PJ felt a lot better this morning and ready to tackle two projects at work. One was the Shower Woman scenario, and the other was contacting Jasmine Singer, the maternal aunt of May and June. She was also expecting some progress reports today on an assortment of other interviews that had been done by Dave and Anita. Busy women don't have time to reflect on things like black cars bearing down or deadly, six-foot insects in the house.

She stopped at a bakery and bought two dozen doughnuts with red and green sprinkles for Christmas. At Headquarters, she had plenty of offers to help carry in the boxes, but graciously declined them all because she didn't want to pay off the helper in goods. Her team converged on her office and swarmed over the doughnuts.

"Hey, leave me some of those," she said. "At least one."

"Make some more coffee, will you?" Anita said.

PJ sighed and did as she was told. "Ready to get down to business now?"

"Sure, Boss," Dave said. "We've finally worked our way through the list of attendees at May's open house who might have planted the bloody knife. We had to make phone calls to

Europe and Australia to do it. Some of those people don't believe in 'home for the holidays.' "

"Let's hear the abbreviated version without the travelogue," Schultz said. He was using a napkin to catch the doughnut sprinkles, and doing a very poor job of it.

"We didn't come up with any leads. Nobody there saw anything suspicious. Background work on all the attendees didn't come up with anyone with a connection to Arlan, other than the people we already know about," Dave said.

"People like May and Frank," PJ said. He nodded.

"I've been talking to friends of May, June, and Fredericka, plus the victims' friends," Anita said. "All three of the women seem to have a lot of acquaintances but no best friends. There was a general consensus that Fredericka was having an affair with Arlan, but little else. None of these women opened up to anybody."

"How about friends of Frank? He hasn't been ruled out as Arlan's killer."

Anita looked at her notes. "A tough but fair businessman, a good father, a man with a lot of outside interests like music and art. He was the type who could have gotten very upset if Arlan was pressuring him into something illegal. He was a real straight arrow."

"Except that he was engaged to June before he married May," Dave said. "That's a weird triangle if you ask me."

"Maybe he was still screwing June, and her husband found out about it," Schultz said. "Could be blackmail. Arlan was trying to raise money for his pet project in Chicago. Maybe he saw a bundle of it because his wife spread her legs for her former fiancé."

"As kinky as Arlan was, I wouldn't be surprised if he liked that idea. Probably had a photo album of it he secretly collected," Dave said.

"Our cup runneth over with motives," PJ said.

"Next up, the Chicago businessmen," Dave said. "It's rough getting anybody to say anything, but from what I can gather from second and third hand sources, the guys were ticked off but not riled up. They just wrote Arlan off as a loser and moved on to the next project. Never thought much of him in the first place and didn't have high expectations."

"Okay, we'll scratch them for now," PJ said. "What about the tenants' association that was angry with Frank?"

Dave shook his head. "Tempest in a teacup. The tenants won. Frank had already backed off. They had no reason to kill him. With him dead, someone even worse might take over ownership of the building."

"My favorite guy is next," Schultz said. "Thul Volmann, the interior designer trashed by Frank. Still an open situation there. Volmann had hired an attorney and filed a defamation of character lawsuit. I spoke to the attorney, and he seemed to have Frank dead to rights. All Volmann had to do was let justice be done, but he may have figured monetary compensation wouldn't undo the damage to his reputation. People who work for Volmann say he's vain, dictatorial, and has a quick, vicious temper. Makes you wonder why they work for him. Anyway, I'd move him up a notch in consideration for Frank's murder. Connection to the other homicides seems nil."

PJ explained her theory about the gardener trying to kill her because she linked him with the cart.

Schultz shook his head. "I thought there was something to it because this Jimmy Drummond, the gardener, worked for a landscaping company run by Arlan. I found the guy and sweated him a little. Not only is he Mr. Upright College Student, but he's got alibis for the times that PJ was attacked, and they checked out."

The meeting wound down and the two men started telling raunchy jokes. That was PJ's cue to kick them all out of her office.

As he was leaving, Schultz pointed to the remaining two doughnuts. "You going to eat those?"

"Yes. Be sure to close the door on your way out."

When PJ checked her email, she found a message from Merlin, which was very rare. She didn't bother to trace the source of the mail and try to find out who or where Merlin was, since she was sure he'd use an anonymous remailer, probably several levels deep.

> *Keypunch,*
>
> *Where have you been hiding? You should tell your sweet Uncle Merlin. I haven't been able to get through to you, and thought you'd want to know some gamer friends of mine located the tunnel creep. He's Kevin Hannings, 4568 Tessabee Road, in Pacific, out I-44. They're a hundred percent sure of this. He's been banned from online gaming, period. Worldwide. Forever. Under any name he tries to come up with. I have to admit I'm a little curious how they did that, since I'm not confident I could. This has caused quite a stir among 'core gamers. People in assorted countries offered to come over and personally beat the shit out of him and then do worse things. Gamers have been known to have poor impulse control, so unless you're okay with having Hannings' guts ripped out and tied around his neck (that one won the vote), you should probably give Schultz the creep's name and address and have him picked up. Soon. Very soon. I believe several have already boarded their airplanes.*
>
> *Yours,*
>
> *Merlin*
>
> *p.s. I had to give out Thomas's game ID, so they know him now. I trust these people. I wouldn't be surprised if Thomas*

267

starts moving up in the rankings, though.

p.p.s. Thomas didn't happen to mention where Hannings got the costume, did he? I have two gamers pestering me.

PJ responded, giving a brief description of the events at her house and indicating that Hannings was already in custody. Thanking him for his efforts, she asked him to call off the gamers if possible, and sent the message on its way. She thought about what he'd mobilized on her behalf. Here was a person who cared so much about her and could call on help of every description from around the world if she asked. Selflessly. What had she ever done for him? Of course, some of Merlin's good ideas seemed to get away from him, but it was usually possible to control the damage. In this case, the only fallout would be that Hannings's neighbors might notice strangers casing the house for a few days.

Locating Jasmine Singer was easy. PJ enlisted the help of the chief of the Hannibal Police Department, who recognized the name immediately.

Aunt Jasmine, as PJ was already thinking of her, lived in a residential care home, but she wasn't one of the poor elderly scraping by on Medicare payments. She was a multimillionaire, and could easily have maintained her own home and hired whatever help she needed. She lived at Riverview Elder Care because she liked the company of the other active retirees, the security of living in a place with a twenty-four-hour staff, and the food. There was an on-site gourmet restaurant. The place apparently wasn't low end.

PJ phoned to ask if today would be a good day to visit. A staff member checked with Mrs. Singer, who said that she'd receive company after her nap, which was over at four o'clock. PJ made an appointment for a visit at four-thirty. On a map of Missouri, she picked a route. Highway 61 was probably faster, but if she took Highway 79, a two-lane road that paralleled the Mississippi River, she could stop at the city of Clarksville. Her son had brought home information from school about bald eagles that wintered there, fishing in the river below Lock and Dam 25.

She got the idea that she would take Thomas with her, even though he'd have to sit around in the lobby while she interviewed Jasmine. He would love the trip. It would be a Friday afternoon off school, and they could talk the whole way there and back. Excited, she immediately phoned Mr. Archibald at the academy to let him know she'd be picking up her son at one o'clock. The man gave her a hard time about pulling Thomas out during the school day, but relented when she made it clear there was an educational aspect to it.

PJ set to work on recreating Marilee Baines's murder in virtual reality. She had a few hours before leaving, and was already wondering if the trip to Hannibal was justified in terms of hard information for the case.

"Shower," PJ said. The null world resolved into a scene of a city street. Narrow homes lined the block, each with one or more banged-up trashcans out front. Quite a few cars were parked at the curb, since these homes had no garages and only a few of them had driveways. It was dark, with the light of the old-fashioned streetlights six houses in either direction barely casting a shadow as she moved. Once between two houses, she was invisible.

At the back of the house, one window had its curtains partially open. Light spilled from it, slicing across the yard like a knife. She approached the window carefully, staying out of the light. When she reached it, she squatted low to make sure no part of her head showed. On her feet were outsized, fuzzy bedroom slippers with smooth, leather soles, and her hands were sheathed with several pairs of latex gloves.

The window was open a couple of inches. She could hear water running in the shower. Cautiously raising her head, she peeked into the window. Inside was a small bedroom, inexpensively furnished but clean and neat. PJ tried lifting the window, but it wouldn't slide up smoothly. Probably a little stuck with layers of old paint above the two-inch mark. PJ reached into a pack around her waist, and found a knife patterned after the one that forensics determined was used on Marilee Baines. She used the knife to pry at the painted-over window track, then remembered that the police report said there'd been no pry marks at all, inside or outside the bedroom window.

"Stop, restart entering the back yard," she said. There was a dizzying moment as the scene reset itself. She went up to the window again, and this time, after carefully looking around for people looking out their windows, she wiggled the window back and forth slightly, then shoved it up. She felt the resistance of the paint holding, then breaking free. There was some noise, but neighbors had their windows closed due to the freezing weather.

Once the window was up, she had to act fast. Having practiced getting up into the back of the pickup truck in the barn scenario, she had no trouble controlling the Genman's motion to get up and over the low windowsill.

Inside, she quickly lowered the window so that if anyone did happen to look out, they wouldn't see Marilee's window standing wide open and become suspicious. She glided across the wood floor in her slippers until she came to the bathroom, which had vinyl flooring.

Now what? In spite of the bloody shower stall and some smeared blood on the floor, no bloody footprints had been found, either in the shower or in the bedroom. She ducked away from the doorway to think about it. There was a large mirror on the bathroom wall, and it would be possible for Marilee to see her coming, especially if PJ stood there thinking for a long time. The victim wasn't going to stay in the shower forever. The killer must have come prepared for this.

"Pause, free Genman," PJ said. Instantly the sound of the running water stopped, the droplets frozen in midair. Marilee, bent over scrubbing her legs with a loofah sponge, rear plastered against the steamy glass doors, halted in that inelegant position. Genman, free to move, stepped into the bathroom to look around.

And stood on a pink, shaggy bathroom rug.

Of course! Why didn't I notice that? There had been no rug at the scene, confirmed later when she examined the photos. The bathroom had been scanned into the computer, rugless, but its artificial intelligence had conjured a rug based upon stock photos of hundreds of bathrooms in its database. The majority of them must have had rugs outside the shower door, for wet feet.

PJ thought about what to do, stepped back out of the room, and then said, "Resume." She took off her slippers and left them right outside the bathroom, noticing when she did so another detail from the crime scene photos. There was a pair of slippers near the bed, similar to the ones she was wearing.

The killer staked this place out and knew a lot going in.

In her bare feet, PJ took a large step and planted her feet on the rug. She slid back the fogged-up doors and confronted Marilee. It was not a fair fight. PJ had a knife and Marilee had a sponge. With surprise on her side, PJ's first lunge was a solid strike.

Having seen the clear trend of how things were going, PJ

became a FOTW for the rest of the murder. It was mainly a matter of not getting scratched by the frantic and weakening woman. Although Marilee had defensive wounds on her hands and forearms in the autopsy photos, there had been no skin cells under her fingernails.

She watched Genman complete the killing, take the finger, and make the heart design on the back of the door in blood. Then she took over the role of killer again.

Her feet were bloody, but she carefully stepped into the waiting slippers. Then she reached into the bathroom, tugged on the rug, and when it got close enough, peeled off one of the pairs of latex gloves, tossed them on the rug, and rolled the whole thing up to take with her. It had a rubberized backing that did a good job of keeping in the blood.

Across the wood floor in her slippers, out the window, pull the window down to two inches, walk carefully out to the sidewalk with the rug. She stopped the simulation there. Somewhere on the street, the killer had a car parked, and would be away into the night, taking his bloody footprints with him.

Chapter 43

The cloudless sky was deep blue and the rolling hills north of St. Louis along the Mississippi River were covered with trees and tan pastures. A couple of turkeys took flight and skimmed over the roof of the car, looking like flying bowling balls and drawing "oohs" from both driver and passenger. With the car's heater pumping out warmth, it was easy to forget it was only fifteen degrees. There had been no significant snow in December, and Highway 79 was a dry ribbon following the contours of the land. It was a beautiful winter day.

The only cloud on her personal horizon was that the driver of the Blazer who'd try to run over her had escaped the police chase. She was no closer to knowing who wanted her dead.

Thomas was thrilled to go with her. The day trips they frequently took to explore the countryside around St. Louis had been at the bottom of the priority list recently. When this case was behind her, PJ was going to renew a lot of things that had gotten shoved aside. She was also going to think through her relationship with Schultz. She needed time to sort things out when dead bodies weren't turning up every day or two.

In Clarksville, PJ bought gas for the Focus and asked for directions to an eagle-viewing area. The attendant must get the question a lot, because he handed her a pre-printed slip of paper with directions to two different spots and told her it was early in the season but she might get lucky because of the cold weather. The eagles congregated around open water when the temperature dropped. She chose Lock and Dam 25, just because she'd never seen the setup before.

It was a little disappointing because the lock was inactive. There wasn't any river traffic at that time, and so it just sat there, ice coating the huge metal gates. There was a viewing platform with spotting scopes for the eagles. There were some, but they were far away on the other side of the river, and looked like dark shapes high up in the trees. There was no fishing activity by the birds.

"I guess it's siesta time," she said.

The wind coming in over the Mississippi was brutal. Even though they were wearing down parkas, gloves, and scarves that covered about every inch of their faces except for their eyes, they didn't stay long.

As they headed back to Highway 79, PJ and Thomas were a bit subdued. Aside from getting really cold, they hadn't accomplished anything.

"Mom, look," Thomas said. He was pointing out the front window. A magnificent adult eagle, its white head shining in the sun, had landed just ten feet above them in a tree branch. Its claws were curled around a wriggling fish, just snatched from the river. Holding the fish against the branch, the bird began to tear at it.

"Awesome," Thomas said.

"Awesome," PJ agreed. "But not for the fish." They sat there until the eagle spread its wings and flew away, then made their way through Clarksville, picking up some burgers for an on-the-move lunch.

Conversation fizzled out after the fries were gone, and they passed through the town of Louisiana driving along in comfortable silence. Half an hour later, PJ pulled into the driveway of Riverview Elder Care in Hannibal. They were fifteen minutes early, about as well timed as PJ could have hoped.

The grounds were beautifully-landscaped, attractive even in the dead of winter with plenty of evergreens. Instead of the decrepit old farmhouse she was expecting, the center was a low-slung creation fashioned of dark glass and slabs of black marble, a storm cloud fallen from the sky and settled on a hilltop. There was a circular driveway leading to the main entrance, but PJ found a visitor's spot in the small parking lot.

The lobby carried through with the glass and marble theme, but reversed to white. On the floor was white tile with a matte finish that PJ assumed was slip-proof. Off to the right was a solarium that held a large swimming pool. A few residents paddled around, and at one end of the pool, there was an organized exercise class. A receptionist sat behind a curved marble counter. She smiled at them and waved them forward.

"I should have brought my swimming suit," Thomas said quietly, so that only PJ could hear. "I could show those old guys in there some moves."

She nearly burst out laughing. Instead, she hooked her arm into his and propelled him along. He was dragging his feet, looking enviously at the pool.

"I'm Rhonda. You're here to see Mrs. Singer, aren't you?" the receptionist said.

"Yes. We're a little early, so we'll just wait over there." PJ pointed to a bank of upholstered easy chairs that looked like white leather and probably were.

"No need. She woke up from her nap a little early. I think she's very curious about your visit. Mrs. Singer doesn't have many guests. Actually, she just doesn't agree to see many."

PJ remembered the painful beginning to her phone conversation with John Winter, when she was the first to inform him of the death of his two nieces' husbands. She didn't want to be the bearer of bad news to Mrs. Singer. She already had an image of the woman in her mind: frail, crepe paper skin, eyes slightly filmy, sweet personality. Everyone's old grandma.

"You must be Thomas," said Rhonda, turning to her son.

"Some of the men headed off to the rec room a little while ago. I think they're playing table tennis. Would you like to join them?"

PJ saw the look that crossed her son's face. A swimming pool where he could show off his excellent water skills, maybe, but stuck in a room with a bunch of octogenarians batting a little ball back and forth wasn't his idea of fun.

"Actually, I have this book to read," he said, holding out *The Great Gatsby*, assigned at the academy. She'd been pestering him to get started on it, and now he was eager to use it as an excuse. Annoyed, she stepped on his foot out of sight of the receptionist.

"Ouch. I mean, I'd be happy to. Just show me the way."

"If you'd both follow me, please." The woman took off down the hall. They heard the rec room before they saw it. "In here."

The room was large almost to the point of being cavernous, high-ceilinged and lit by rows of skylights. Artificial lighting was taking over as an early winter sunset darkened the sky. There were several seating arrangements scattered around the room, some of them occupied with residents talking or quietly reading. One side of the room was lined with computers, and the rest of the place had many forms of indoor entertainment, including pinball machines, a self-service snack counter, pool tables, and table tennis.

"Heads up!"

A white ball went whizzing past Thomas's head. He ducked, and it clattered to the floor after bouncing off a plasma TV.

"Sorry."

They watched as play resumed. The men might have been octogenarians or nearly so, but they were active and thoroughly enjoying themselves. There was a rooting section that booed and applauded, and the players were good. They stood far back from the tables, and the moving ball was practically a blur.

"Hey, can you teach me how to play like that?" Thomas said.

"Sure, c'mon over, young man. Eddie here used to be a high school coach. He'll get you started."

"Bye, Mom. Take your time with your interview or whatever."

PJ and Rhonda continued down the hall until they came to wooden double doors. The receptionist knocked and then opened the doors to a sumptuous office.

There's no end to the surprises here.

"This is Dr. Penelope Gray," Rhonda said. PJ entered and the doors closed behind her. The only light in the room was an exquisite Tiffany lamp on the desk. The base looked like a twisted vine, and the stained-glass shade was ringed with blue and green dragonflies. Light glowed vibrantly through the shade. It took a few moments for PJ to notice the woman sitting behind the desk. She was diminutive, dwarfed by her massive mahogany desk. PJ guessed she was about sixty, with a crown of silver curls, wearing a conservative dark dress and a tasteful amount of gold jewelry.

"It does draw the eye, doesn't it?" the woman said, nodding toward the lamp.

"It's beautiful. Are you the administrator?" PJ asked. "I made an appointment to see Mrs. Singer. My business with her is private."

"Sit down, Dr. Gray. I'm Jasmine Singer."

PJ sat down, keeping her face lowered to hide her confusion. *This isn't everyone's sweet old grandma.*

"I don't just live here, I own the place. Most people are a little surprised when they meet me," Jasmine said. "Money can stave off old age, or at least the appearance of it, for a while. I'm seventy-nine. It shows up in some ways, though. The staff tennis instructor says soon he'll be able to beat me with one hand tied behind his back. I told him if he ever does that, call the funeral home because I'll be dead."

PJ smiled. She liked this brash, honest woman, and her sense of humor.

That's me, decades from now, I hope. Except for the money part.

She wondered how to begin, and if she was about to spring unpleasant news on her. Jasmine didn't seem to be much of a factor in her nieces' lives, so she might not be upset.

"Mrs. Singer," PJ began.

"Call me Jasmine."

"I'm PJ. Jasmine, are you aware of the very recent deaths of Frank Simmons and Arlan Merrett?"

"Yes."

"Then let me say I'm sorry for the losses you've experienced."

"I appreciate the sentiment, but I'd never met either of them, so it wasn't much of a personal loss."

"You didn't attend your nieces' weddings?"

"I was invited. I think the girls had stars in their eyes, figuring they'd get an expensive wedding present out of me. I told them it was too far for a frail old woman to travel," she winked at PJ, "and sent them each a toaster."

"They must have been disappointed about that. Not seeing you, I mean."

"It was a four-slice toaster. Top of the line. Same one I use myself."

PJ *really* liked this woman. "May I ask why you were estranged from your nieces?"

"You may ask."

"My questions may be very important, Jasmine. Do you know I'm working with the police on the homicide investigations?"

"The Metro Mangler. I know who you are, what you do, where you grew up, and the name of your son, your cat, your ex-husband, your CHIP teammates, and even who gronz_eye is. I know that you phoned John Winter in Denver, but not what you talked about. I know that you rented a Ford Focus because your car was totaled in an attempt on your life. I know that you bought gas and looked at eagles in Clarksville on your way up here today."

PJ was shocked. "You're having me followed?"

"Not until you called and asked to see me. When someone inquires about me, I find out all I can about them. There are plenty of people who are up to no good where the very rich are concerned. Not that you are, PJ. Would you care for some orange juice? I usually have some at this time of day." She pressed a button on her phone. "Rhonda, would you please bring in some O.J.?"

The trip was a waste of time. This woman's lips are sealed tighter than an envelope.

The orange juice arrived in crystal goblets. PJ took the offered goblet to be courteous and was glad she did. It was the best orange juice she'd ever had.

"I didn't come here to talk about May and June," PJ said. "I came to talk about April. John Winter told me he went to her funeral. What do you know about her death?"

"For one thing, I know that she wasn't in the casket that was buried that day."

PJ sat back, stunned, goblet half way to her mouth. "Who was?"

"A young woman named Elissa Nevers. Elissa was a maid in my sister Virginia's household. April killed her in a rage, claiming the maid had taken a necklace from her. The necklace was later found behind the dresser, where it had slipped. What she did to that poor maid was horrible. Even now I block it from my mind."

"Didn't the police investigate the maid's disappearance?"

"Not seriously. No one even inquired about her for a long time. She had no family. When a high school friend finally tried to get in touch with her, we said that Elissa had quit and left town suddenly, in the company of a young man she'd been dating. Elissa had done that very thing before and stayed missing for two years before surfacing in the Bahamas, working as a hotel maid. It was a stroke of good luck for us. The police lost interest when that fact came to light."

An innocent woman killed, possibly tortured and maimed, and there's something about it that's a stroke of good luck? PJ kept her face neutral, which was becoming harder to do. Her training as a psychologist came in handy at times like this.

"So where was April after the funeral? She couldn't continue living in the same house."

"Obviously. April came to live with me, at my summer home in Michigan."

"Weren't you afraid to take her in? Not to mention that you were hiding a killer from the law."

"Family secrets, dear. All the wealthy families are hiding something. Ours just happened to be a little bit more serious than some. Virginia and I were close, and I didn't hesitate when she asked it of me. I did take the precaution of hiring a doctor who lived with April and kept her under control with drugs."

Family secrets. Score one for Merlin.

"I think you should have gone to the police, have her arrested, and then gotten her committed to an institution.

What is it, schizophrenia?"

"You're good. No wonder you have such a high solve rate on your cases. We did think about April being committed, but it would have shamed the whole family. The newspapers would have loved the story. Also, I liked April. When you know her better, it's easier to sympathize with her."

PJ's favorable impression of Jasmine was fading fast. The woman was so concerned about image that she'd conceal a murder and let the killer avoid the consequences. And what could there possibly have been about April to trigger sympathy? That she was mentally ill, maybe. She might have led a better life if her parents had sought treatment for her early. No doubt that would have shamed the family, too. Thinking back on her earlier impression that Jasmine was what she wanted to be decades from now, PJ cringed.

"There's something else I think you should know about April. Virginia's husband wasn't the father. Virginia was pregnant when she married."

"The shotgun wedding," PJ said.

Jasmine's eyebrows shot up. "John told you that? May I ask what else he told you?"

"You may ask."

There was silence in the room, except for the ticking of a schoolhouse clock on the wall. PJ watched the short pendulum as it swung back and forth.

Jasmine shook her head. "John didn't have anything else to tell. Only a very few of us knew the secret."

Secrets known only to a minority—esoterica! Score two for Merlin.

"Who was the father?" PJ asked. Evidently Jasmine's lips weren't as sealed as PJ thought. Information was sailing out of her mouth.

Jasmine sighed. "I'll only say that April was the spawn of

rape. Virginia's probably thoroughly shocked in her grave with what I've said already."

"Where is April now? Is she still in Michigan?"

"That's the only reason I agreed to talk with you today, PJ. April murdered the doctor and ran away six months ago. With all the resources I can call upon, I can't find her. She's disappeared from the face of the earth."

Chapter 44

PJ wanted to think over everything she'd heard and remember every detail. Thomas wanted to chatter about his newly-acquired skill in table tennis.

She took US-61 home. It was dark and she didn't need the scenic route along the Mississippi. Her bright headlights tunneled through the night. After she saw a deer on the shoulder, she flicked off the buzzing thoughts in her mind and concentrated on getting home safely.

It was a tedious drive, punctuated by a stop at a fast-food restaurant to use the bathroom. She felt bad just taking advantage of the restaurant's restroom, so she and Thomas ate there, too. She managed to buy a salad but added a milkshake to it. Thomas ate two double cheeseburgers and looked around for more. Seeing him staring at her milkshake, she handed it over. All that accomplished was trading guilt over her indulgence for guilt over Thomas eating so poorly that day.

She resolved to keep better hours and maybe even cook an occasional meal. Using her cellphone from the parking lot, she told Lilly they'd be there in an hour to pick up Megabite and Thomas's things. Enough of this twenty-four-hour on-call business.

At home, she fed the cat, then called Schultz. Before he got there, she took a hot bath, swallowed a couple of Tylenol, and slipped on her flannel pajamas. The pajamas were faded from years of use, and the top was missing one of its buttons. She'd been getting around to replacing it for about three years. Physically comforted, she went downstairs to wait. Thomas passed her on the stairs carrying two apples and a bowl of popcorn up to his room.

"You couldn't be hungry again," she said.

"Yeah, I am. Aren't you?"

She shook her head. At least there was fruit involved. "Remember, you're still grounded. This would be a perfect time for *The Great Gatsby*."

She put on some coffee and cuddled with Megabite in the living room while it brewed. Either the cat was really happy to be with her, or just enjoyed kneading on flannel. Either way was okay with PJ.

Schultz arrived. Over cups of coffee at the kitchen table, she told him everything about her visit with Jasmine Singer. He listened with great intensity and didn't interrupt.

"So it's likely April Winter's the killer," he said. "At least, of Arlan and Frank."

"I don't know if we can say that for sure, but it looks like she might be lashing out against her sisters in an indirect way, by going after their husbands. Maybe for the life she didn't get to live. She was confined at Jasmine's summer home, and probably given drugs whether she was willing to take them or not."

"How about Shower Woman and the other five murders?"

"Seven murders, if you count Elissa Nevers and the Michigan doctor. I don't know. The killings that used the signature mutilation obviously have deep meaning to her. The others may have just been people who got in the way."

"Is it over now?" Schultz said. "She's done everything she meant to do?"

"You mean because there hasn't been a signature death in two whole days? If I were Jasmine," PJ said, "I'd be more than a little nervous right now."

"She's probably got that Elder Care place built like a fortress. After all, she's had plenty of time to prepare. She imprisoned April for thirty years."

PJ sipped her coffee and thought about that. Jasmine was enormously wealthy, so her "summer home" could well be a mansion, with every luxury and convenience, including connections to the outside world through books, TV, and computers. Without Jasmine concealing her, April would have ended up in an institution or in prison for murder. Did she do April a favor, even though her motive was to protect the family image?

"Jasmine as much as admitted that April was schizophrenic. Talk to me about that."

"The common age of onset is sixteen to twenty-five, which fits April perfectly. The one thing the public seems to know best about schizophrenics is delusions, like getting special messages from the TV or being singled out for persecution. There are also hallucinations, which can be seen, smelled, felt, or heard. Sometimes schizophrenics believe someone or something is giving commands for dangerous or violent behavior. 'My pillow whispers to me when I put my head on it, and it told me I had to kill Uncle Wally,' or something like that."

"You mean your pillow doesn't talk to you?"

"Not funny. Insensitive, too. People don't choose schizophrenia, Leo. Ten percent of them commit suicide, and for the rest it can be a miserable life. Social withdrawal, erratic behavior, unpredictability, the list goes on. Often they have drug or alcohol problems and can't keep a job. Antipsychotic drugs can sometimes help, but often there's a compliance problem."

"Jesus. As if young people didn't have a tough enough time already, some of them have to get saddled with this. Would a person with this problem be organized enough to carry out the planning for these murders? That barn scene was elaborate."

PJ hesitated before answering. "If she's taking her meds consistently to stay focused, probably so. But if she slips up on the meds, the killings will get less elaborate."

Schultz nodded. "Like Shower Woman and the teacher in Florissant—just bust in and kill. So what makes one teenager start hearing voices and others don't?"

"There's no single thing we can point to as the cause," PJ said. "Brain chemistry, genetics, even physical problems with the brain; each seem to play a part."

"Genetics. Didn't you say April was a child of rape?"

"Yes."

"As far as we know, April's mother didn't have the problem. So we could be looking for a schizo father." Schultz waved his hands around. He seemed to be on some track of thinking that hadn't occurred to PJ.

"Ten percent chance of inheritance."

"Oh. Not so good." His face fell briefly, then became animated again. "Still, what are the most common family secrets?" Schultz said.

"You mean besides murdered household maids?"

"Look who's being unfunny now."

"Hmm. I'd say spousal abuse," PJ said.

"And?"

"Child abuse. I see where you're going with this," PJ said. "Virginia would have been about seventeen when she gave birth to April. Maybe sixteen when raped."

"She could have gotten screwed by some high school punk or it could have been a family matter. Her father," Schultz said. He crossed his arms over his belly and leaned back. The chair creaked.

"There're a lot of ifs in that reasoning," PJ said. "Even if it's true, what good does it do us?"

"I don't know. Yet."

"It was devious to put the maid in the casket and bury her, claiming it was April," PJ said. "An uncle I've talked to attended the funeral. He was certainly convinced his niece was dead. That made it easier to hide April away with no questions."

"I suppose we're going to have to go for exhumation. The maid's family deserves that much, at least. What was the name again?"

"Elissa Nevers," PJ said.

"I'll get to work on an exhumation order in the morning," Schultz said.

"Jasmine is a devious woman. We have only her word that April's alive. It's convenient that the doctor who was taking care of her is dead."

"You thinking what I'm thinking?"

"That Jasmine is the killer and her whole story is a massive delusion?"

"Shit," said Schultz. "I was hoping you weren't thinking that."

PJ changed the subject and talked to him about her latest simulation, Shower Woman's murder. He thought the rug and slippers that kept the scene free of footprints were good ideas.

"Fibers from a thick pile rug were found on the bathroom floor," he said. "There were rugs in the linen closet that matched, so we didn't think much of it. April's going to have a bloody rug in her car. Not that it's still there, but forensics can compare fibers and match the blood."

"One thing that really worries me," said PJ, "is that if Jasmine is telling the truth, she hasn't found April in six months. How are we going to do any better?"

★ ★ ★ ★ ★

Schultz was wide-awake in bed next to PJ, who was asleep with Megabite curled on her stomach. He reviewed everything they'd discussed. Pieces were still floating around, not settling into place. Bringing April into the story made his special sense, cop's intuition or something else, perk up. The thread that he envisioned connecting him to a killer had uncoiled and was casting about for the link.

Where was she, this mysterious oldest sister who was wreaking vengeance on what was left of her family? What would be her next step? It could be killing June, May, and Jasmine, and then April might achieve some kind of peace, whatever her tortured mind would allow her.

Also pressing on his mind was the question of whether she was the person trying to kill PJ. April was a formidable opponent, maybe the most cunning he'd come up against. He wasn't going to let PJ out of his sight, and she could damn well complain about it all she wanted.

Chapter 45

Dear Diary,

These are things that happened to me, cross my heart and hope to die.

That's the way I used to start all my diary entries. Juvenile, isn't it? Some of those entries are so rambling and nonsensical it's hard to believe I was really like that. One thing that was interesting to see was the progression from printed letters in pencil to flowery script with hearts over the "i's" in pink ink.

I found this old thing when I was cleaning out Frank's office. I forgot I had a drawer in one of the file cabinets that contained some of my old things. Fortunately they were under lock and key, or my poor husband would have gotten an eyeful.

My last entry was when I was sixteen and in lust with my chemistry teacher, Mr. Boner. That was his name, I swear. He was so hot he burned brighter than the Bunsen burner flames in the lab. Late twenties, built like a gymnast, shiny, straight blond hair, pale blue eyes. I used to love to watch him move. I volunteered to be a lab assistant just to spend a little time after school with him, helping set up for the next day. I had him all to myself for a wonderful week, then that dweeb Maurice Serbin volunteered, too. Having Maurice around was like a dozen wet blankets. I could tell Mr. Boner was attracted to me. He was just too professional to do anything about it, and I loved him all the more for that.

Entries from that time are scorching, hot enough to singe the pages. I had a boyfriend at the time, who of course didn't know he was number two in my heart. Men are so dumb that way.

Then I just drifted away from writing in my diary. I'm surprised that I didn't throw it out, because by that time June was old enough to steal it. If she'd known about this little pink book with the tiny lock, she wouldn't have rested until she'd gotten her hands on it. That's the way she was. Nosy and obnoxious. If April hadn't died, she would have whipped little June's ass and made her not pry into things that weren't her business. Ha! That would have been something to see. Instead, I had to deal with the whining twerp. That's what June still is today, a whining twerp.

I just might keep writing in this diary. I can say anything about anybody, and not worry about whether it'll get me ahead or not. It's such a liberating thing to do, just saying things for their own sakes. Fuck. Cunt. Rim job. Motherfucker. Pussy fart. Look at me, I can use words that are frowned upon by polite society. I wonder what other society women scream out when they have an orgasm. "Thank you oh so much," or "Join me for tea next Tuesday?" What hypocrites. Whatever else I am, I'm never that.

Chapter 46

PJ slept late on Saturday morning. She'd been getting by on less sleep than her usual seven to eight hours, and her body staged a sleep-in. She awoke at eleven o'clock, alone in bed and hungry.

On her way to the kitchen, she checked on Thomas and found him asleep, too. A teenager's need for sleep was legendary, and there were at least a couple of physiological reasons for it. Hormones are released mostly during sleep, and there are also surges in brain growth and organization. Her son, a little thread of drool connecting his mouth to his pillow, was maturing in abstract reasoning capability and impulse control right in front of her eyes. She left him to it.

She spotted a DVD propped up on the table. It was the movie *Babe*, and on it was a note from Schultz.

What do you know, you were right. Babe is an oink-oink pig in a movie. Sorry for getting mad.

Just then, Schultz knocked at the back door and she let him in. He was carrying a stack of mail from her mailbox.

"Don't you ever pick up your mail out front?" he said. Not waiting for an answer, he went on. "Hey, did you hear about Fredericka? Green Vista is thriving under her sole ownership. She was on the TV news with a new thing she's got going, a planned neighborhood. All eco-friendly, solar power, row houses with small footprints to fight sprawl. That 'sit lightly on the land' crap. No doubt it'll make a fortune. She doesn't seem to miss Arlan's business advice. She looked good on camera, too."

"I'm sure she did."

"No, I mean good. Dressed up in one of those power suits she has. I guess she had to wear them sometime."

She gave him a quizzical look as he dumped the mail on her kitchen table. *He's studied her wardrobe? I guess it goes with his professional assessment of breast sizes.*

A hand-addressed letter stood out from the envelopes with computer-printed labels. She picked it up and slit the top. "Haven't you gotten a new car assigned yet?"

"No. I think they're punishing me because my old one got wrecked. Like it was my fault. I've been looking at that little red number you rented. You like it?"

"I'm considering buying one just like it."

He snorted. "It looks like a woman's car. Fits you just fine. I'll probably get some piece of crap assigned to me."

"Dare I say it would fit you just fine?"

Schultz broke out in a wide grin and clapped her on the back.

She pulled out the contents of the envelope. It was from John Winter, and it was a photo of two girls standing together at a beach in bright bathing suits. She flipped it over. In fine script on the back, it said: *April and May on vacation in Mexico. April is about sixteen, May about five. You can keep this.*

PJ studied the girls. May was a gorgeous child, tanned and lithe. Straight, shiny hair fell like a waterfall to her shoulders, light brown hair lightened further by the sun, sand clinging to her cheek. April towered over her little sister. She filled out her swimsuit, a modest one-piece, in all the right places. April was fair-skinned and wore a wide-brimmed hat that shaded the top half of her face. The short hair that curled out from underneath the hat was red. Tucked under one arm was a large beach ball. Although the logical thing to assume was that the girls were playfully batting the beach ball around right before the picture was taken, PJ somehow had the impression it had been more of a game of keep-away. In spite of the smile glued on her face, May's body language broadcast frustration.

She passed the photo over to Schultz, who also read the back and looked closely at the girls.

"You can see the family resemblance between May and June," he said. "But April looks like Sparkle Farkle."

"I wouldn't have taken you for a *Laugh In* fan."

"Rowan and Martin were my idols."

"I get the point, though," PJ said. "April looks as though she could have had a different father from the other sisters. Or her appearance could be recessive genes finally getting their day in the sun."

Feeling drawn to work after the indulgence of sleeping late, PJ left without breakfast, planning to get a quick meal at Millie's Diner. The place was busy when they got there.

"By the way, thanks for the DVD," she said. *And the thought behind it.*

"Oh, hell, I shouldn't have gotten so bent out of shape about it."

Millie drifted over to take PJ's order. She was beaming. "It was nice of you to send a card," she said. "I put it up in a real prominent place." Millie pointed at a Christmas card directly over the door to the women's room. PJ recognized her card, looking distinctly fresh next to the yellowed ones of previous years.

"My pleasure," PJ said. "I know it's late, Millie, but could I have breakfast instead of lunch?"

"Anything you want, Dearie."

"If it's not too much trouble, then, I'll have some pancakes and a couple of scrambled eggs."

"Coming right up."

"Would you two cut out this little love fest?" Schultz said. "I'm about to barf on the counter."

Millie gave him a withering look and stalked off.

"Before I forget, some guy's been calling at HQ for you," Schultz said. "Won't talk to anyone else, says he saw your name in the paper. I figure it's a reporter or true crime writer. Anyway, here's his number."

Schultz handed her a slip of paper with a greasy spot occupying two-thirds of the surface. The phone number was scrunched into one corner.

"I'm taking a run out to May's house after this," he said. "I want to take another look at that shed where the cart was found. I have this feeling we missed something out there. Wanna come?"

"Shouldn't we be trying to track down April?"

"Who's to say the answer isn't in that shed? Anyway, Dave and Anita and some guys from Missing Persons are on it. The Michigan police are real interested, too. They have a dead doctor on their hands and now a link to several more homicides in Missouri."

"I'm going to pass on going to May's house," PJ said. "I've got some work at the office."

They drove to Headquarters and Schultz headed off to bum a ride.

PJ dialed the phone number Schultz had given to her as soon as she arrived at her desk. A man answered and she identified herself.

"I'm glad you called, Dr. Gray. I saw your name in the paper on the Metro Mangler case, and I thought it might be easier to talk to a doctor than a detective."

She decided not to correct the impression that she was sure he had, that she was a medical doctor.

"I've got some information on the murder of Cheryl Royalview," he said.

A break. The hair on PJ's arms rose and she took a deep breath.

"Go on."

"I'm sure when Cheryl was autopsied, there was semen found. It wasn't in the papers, but it had to be there."

"What makes you think that? And what's your name?"

"I'm Jason Dearborn. Cheryl and I were having an affair. We made love that Tuesday night, the day before the paper said she was killed. Oh, God, it's so horrible."

PJ's excitement drained away. This sounded mundane, although she had to be thorough. "Do you have an alibi for the time of death, Wednesday, around noon?"

"I'm a vet, and I was at my clinic all day. Wednesday is surgery day. I was in surgery with my assistant from ten in the morning until three."

The fact that Dearborn was a vet revived PJ's interest. Vets worked with ketamine.

"Dr. Dearborn, I'd like to talk further with you. Would you come in to Headquarters? I can have a cruiser pick you up."

There was a long hesitation. "I'd rather not. I'm married, and I was hoping this could be kept quiet. I only called because I figured I'd be tracked down by DNA and it would be better to volunteer the information up front."

"How about meeting me at a place of your choice, then?"

"I guess that would be okay. I'll have to go after hours, since I'm at the clinic today. This doesn't have to come out, does it?"

"I'll do everything I can to protect your privacy." *I'm sounding more and more like Schultz every day. Say anything to lure 'em in.*

"How about meeting at Millie's Diner then," he said. "Around five o'clock? Do you know the place?"

Oh, great. "I know it. See you then."

★ ★ ★ ★ ★

PJ arrived early, intending to get situated and warn Millie not to recognize her. Dearborn beat her to it. When she came in, pulling off her gloves and stuffing them in her coat pockets, he made unmistakable eye contact with her right away. He was seated at a table near the window, where'd he be certain to intercept her as soon as she came in.

She went over to the table. "Dr. Dearborn?"

"Yes. Please call me Jason. You look prettier in person than you do in your newspaper photos. You have a strong face."

"Thanks," she said. *I guess.* For some reason, she didn't feel comfortable being on a first name with the man so soon. Or ever.

Jason Dearborn was about her age, with a roundness of face and body that reflected too many late night snacks. He had a prominent chin and nose, dark eyebrows, a small English mustache with an exaggerated curl at the ends, and was dressed entirely in black. He bore an uncomfortable resemblance to Snidley Whiplash. When he stood to greet her, she was surprised to see that he was not only her age, but her height too.

This guy must have some really endearing qualities or Cheryl Royalview was royally desperate. Maybe he's rich.

Setting aside her first impression, she was determined not to assume villainy on Jason's part. She was jumping to conclusions too much lately, a bad trait for a psychologist. *At least hear the guy out.*

Millie came over with a smile on her face that faltered a little when she saw Jason, but quickly recovered.

"How are you, dear—?" Millie began.

PJ interrupted her. "That's right, this is Dr. Dearborn. You two know each other?" She shook her head slightly, hoping Millie would pick up on it.

"I'm not a regular," Jason said. "Are you the real Millie?"

"In the flesh. What can I get you two today?" Millie flipped over coffee cups and flipped open her order pad.

"Dr. Gray?" Jason said, indicating that she should order first.

"I'll have the cashew chicken salad and iced tea."

"Excellent choices. You, sir?"

PJ's mouth almost fell open. Millie was actually writing in her order pad, playing her undercover role to the hilt.

"Grilled cheese platter and coffee, please."

Millie nodded smartly and headed off for the kitchen.

"Let's start at the beginning," PJ said. "How did you meet Cheryl?"

Dearborn answered her questions but didn't elaborate. There was nothing remarkable about the story. Lonely woman neglected by a workaholic husband meets obliging man. When the food arrived, he stopped talking until he thought Millie was out of earshot. Little did he know that Millie could be out in the alley behind the diner and still not be out of earshot.

They chatted about other topics while eating. Dearborn was a comic book fan, and they reminisced about old heroes. Everything seemed ordinary until he reached over and took her hand. Startled, she left it within his grasp, a captured bird in a cage of moist fingers.

"My wife has never understood my needs," he said. "Cheryl and I had a good understanding. It's terrible about her, but life goes on for the rest of us, I guess. After a decent period of mourning, I'll have to find someone else to," he looked around, but the nearby tables were empty. "To take control. Have you ever worn leather, Dr. Gray? I think it would suit you."

PJ's eyes widened and she reclaimed her hand. "I think we're done here," she said. "Check, please!"

PJ had lost the urge to protect Jason Dearborn's privacy. She called the team together, told her story, and asked Dave to do some background checking on him. "Do I detect a pattern here?" Dave said. "I'm getting stuck with all the sex weirdos."

Schultz volunteered to go with a tech to get a DNA swab from Dearborn.

"Where does he live? Or better yet, work?"

"He's a veterinarian, and I have his phone number," PJ said. "I don't know the address of his clinic."

"No problem," Schultz said. She handed him back the same greasy paper he'd given her, with Dearborn's number on it. "You know, you shouldn't go off meeting strangers. Somebody's out to get you, remember? You were supposed to be working in your office."

"I don't need your permission to follow up on a lead," PJ said. "I don't need a lecture, either. Anyway, Millie was around and probably had her hand on the phone the whole time we were in her place."

"That old broad's about as perceptive as a brick. I wouldn't count on her having your back. And what about when you left? The S&M guy could have given you a new nickname: Doctor Roadkill."

PJ felt her hackles rising. Dave and Anita were watching with interest to see who was going to launch the next volley. She couldn't allow her relationship with Schultz to interfere with her work—or his, for that matter. With effort, PJ put the whole thing behind her. Schultz sulked for a while, and then reverted to detective mode. The group had a long discussion about April and tossed around ideas for locating her.

"Schultz, anything come of your visit to May's place today?" PJ asked.

"I was hoping to find some indication that Arlan was in that shed for the last four days of his life. That hunch didn't pan out," he said.

"April had him hidden away during the missing four days," PJ said, thinking aloud. *Go back to the beginning and find out where Arlan was for four days, Merlin said. It might all come down to the disparity in his disappearance and his time of death.*

"You just now figuring that out?" said Schultz. "Unfortunately, that puts us no closer to finding her."

"I don't know about that. Maybe we should go back to the comfort zone idea. April probably owns a truck that was used at the barn, perhaps a black Blazer, too." She locked eyes with Schultz. PJ saw his nostrils flare at the mention of the Blazer. He was right. She shouldn't do anything careless. She wanted to be around for a long time to see Thomas far into adulthood.

If she died, Schultz would be there for Thomas. She knew that now, and it was a simple truth that was comforting. She smiled at him, and he smiled back, having no idea what was going through her head.

"So we drive around in all the kill sites and look for trucks?" Anita said. "Seems way too vague."

Dave said, "We can narrow it down by using vehicle registration records. What do we know about the truck?"

"Only that it had an eight foot bed," Schultz said. "To hold the garden cart."

"Well, that's something," Dave said.

"Are you kidding? There must be hundreds of those in the zones," Anita said. "And they could be inside garages where we can't check them out easily."

"Hundreds of full-size trucks with female owners about fifty years old?" PJ said. "Locate every resident who fits that description and check it out. Interview the neighbors."

The rest of her team looked skeptical. No one was taking up the battle cry. One of PJ's assets in her position was her ability to think beyond the constraints of police procedure. It was also one of her liabilities.

"The truck could be registered under a male name, or she could have sold it, or driven it into the river or something after it was used at the barn," Anita said.

"Driven it into the river," PJ said. "Arlan's dump site was on the shore of the Mississippi. We never knew why that particular place."

"Anita, you're a genius," Schultz said. "You get a gold star. Now go look for that truck."

"Yes, sir." She saluted and was out the door.

PJ was anxious to get home to see her son, but she wanted to work on something that had been bothering her. She had never worked out the link between her barn and riverfront VR scenarios. Schultz seemed determined to be underfoot, so she put him to work.

She did a little preparation, and Schultz donned the VR gear. She started the barn scenario after Arlan's body was in the pickup truck. Inside the scene, he was seeing everything first person, but on her monitor, she saw a three-inch-high Schultz open the truck's door and get in. PJ had never told him, but she'd scanned his picture into her computer and customized a Genman, so the little character really did look like Schultz, complete with the bald spot on top of his head.

He drove for a couple of minutes on generic streets. Speaking into a microphone, she told Schultz that he should take the second driveway on his left.

"Hey, I didn't know you could talk to me in here," he said aloud. "Wanna whisper sweet nothings?"

She didn't answer him. She was typing rapidly to keep a little ahead of the simulation, feeling her way along.

The time frame wasn't right, because PJ had no idea how long it would take April to get home. April's house was a box with a garage and a light next to the front door. *Genhome.*

She opened the garage door.

"Did I do that?"

PJ sighed. "I did. Stop asking questions. Go with the flow."

Schultz went through the process of backing the cart into the garage, then using the rope and winch to get Arlan's body out. He tucked the corpse neatly into the body bag from one of PJ's earlier scenarios. It came across as a gentle procedure, and PJ was reminded of the urge she had to cover Arlan's body with her coat as water lapped at his feet. Few people managed to inject any personality into VR, but Schultz was one of them.

PJ flashed to tucking Thomas into bed as a child, sweeping his long, black hair back from his forehead, planting a good night kiss there, and smelling his toothpaste breath on her face. Then she got another image of Thomas, this one horrible: she was tucking him into a body bag instead of his bed, and zipping it up over his bloodied face.

"Schultz!" she yelled into her microphone.

"What?" His hands went up to yank the HMD off.

The picture faded. Unnerving as it was, she thought it was her mind projecting what might have happened if gronz_eye had gotten hold of Thomas again.

Could-have-beens.

"Wait, it's all right. Let's wrap this up, though. I want to get home."

He drove the truck some distance away from the dump site, fiddled with the rope and managed to jam the gas pedal, sending the truck roaring down the levee, windows open for maximum water entry.

"So my truck is in the river. I'm stranded here."

"You walk over to Laclede's Landing and hail a taxi to go home. Say, how about that?"

"Checking the taxi pickups and destinations for that night?" Schultz said. "Could it be that easy?"

Chapter 47

The phone was ringing when PJ and Schultz got back to her house. She dashed to answer in the kitchen, calling out for Thomas that she was getting it.

When she picked up the phone, there was dead air.

"Hello?"

"Penelope Jennifer Gray," said a voice that sounded like it was under water.

"Speaking. May I ask who's calling?"

"Someone with a special interest in you and yours."

A chill climbed her spine. The gamer with the sword was in jail. *Now what?*

"You're out to get me, aren't you, Penelope?"

Schultz was across the room rummaging in the open refrigerator, his back to her. She went over and kicked him in the shin.

"Ow!"

She gestured at the phone. He immediately went to the living room to listen in.

"I'm not out to get anyone. Why would you think that?"

There was a watery-sounding laugh. "Very good, Dr. Gray. Always thinking like a shrink, turning my question back on me. I know you're trying to stop me. You're one of them, and they're always trying to get me."

"Stop you from doing what? Are you planning to kill someone?" PJ was shaking. She felt as though evil were creeping along the phone line and pouring itself into her ear. In her practice as a psychologist, she'd dealt with killers face to face. But that was in a controlled setting, usually in an interview room in a prison. Standing in her kitchen, with her son upstairs, with a caller who could be anywhere, was a situation that shook her to the core.

"Too many questions," the voice said. "How about this? Two questions are all you get. Someone may die, but I won't lie."

Someone may die. PJ tried to pull her mind away from going back to that image of Thomas in a body bag. *Why didn't I leave him at Lilly's? Or is he safer here with us?*

She was hesitating too long, her thoughts splintering. Scenes were streaming through her mind: Arlan's exposed heart, Shower Woman's blood on the glass door, severed body parts pierced with nails, the neat hole in Frank's forehead, Greg Royalview lying on the floor next to his dead wife, his blood draining from a dozen wounds.

"Tick, tick . . ."

"Who are you?" PJ asked.

"I'm dead."

Dead. April's dead but not really. One more question. What to ask?

"Where are you?" she blurted.

"Where I can see you. You haven't taken off that old blue parka of yours yet. You really should get something new. Maybe something bulletproof."

PJ heard a crash from the living room. It sounded like Schultz had dropped the phone. In a moment he was in the kitchen, gun drawn.

"Down, get down!" he shouted.

As she was dropping to the floor, he collided with her and shoved her under the kitchen table. Then his weight was on top of her, and she heard two *pops!* Glass rained down on the floor and chunks of the wall went flying, right where she'd been standing.

On the floor just a couple feet away from her was the

phone. A drop of sweat—or was it a tear?—slid down her check and onto the floor. Her heart was pounding against her ribs so loudly it nearly drowned out the voice, a voice that sounded drowned.

"Don't stand in my way, Dr. Gray, or you won't be standing at all."

Chapter 48

Schultz rolled off PJ and sat up, remaining under the table with her. He pulled out his cellphone, handed it to her, and asked PJ to call her son to make sure he was okay. She called her home phone and Thomas answered it upstairs.

"Everything okay?" she said, and listened briefly. She gave a thumbs-up sign to Schultz.

"Go in the bathroom, sit down on the floor, and stay put," she said to her son. There weren't any windows in the upstairs bathroom. The shots had come from outside, so there wouldn't be an intruder upstairs.

Unless there are two working together.

"Yes, naked," she said into the phone. "Don't give me any flak." She hung up.

Schultz crawled toward the hallway and took up a position where he could see both the front and back doors. Sitting alertly with his gun, he told PJ to call 911.

He'd heard most of the telephone exchange from the living room. It wasn't PJ's finest hour. She should have assumed she was talking to April and not wasted her two questions like that. If April was serious about giving two truthful answers, a couple of nice questions would have been "Who have you killed in the last two weeks?" and "Where are you going to be in an hour?" There was no guarantee a flake like April would live up to her promise to tell the truth, but what the hell, why not try? He was angry at the lost opportunity and angry that the killer was so arrogant she could take potshots at the police, lumping PJ into that category. Looking at the pockmarks in the wall where PJ had been standing made him afraid for her and Thomas.

His new family was being threatened.

Anger and fear didn't mix well in Schultz, like electricity and water.

"What the hell kind of questions were those?" he said. "Do you think you could have asked anything stupider?"

She glared at him from her spot under the table and said nothing.

"All right, that was harsh. Shit, I don't know what I'm saying. Sorry, I'm upset."

"And I'm not?"

Schultz was rescued from having to answer her question by the arrival of the responding patrol car, which must have been only a few blocks away. He went to answer the door. It was Officer Mel Leeds, who'd been first on the scene at the riverfront dump site.

"Keep this up, Detective, and we'll have to put you on our frequent callers list," he said. He bent down and spoke to PJ. "How're you doing under there, Dr. Gray?"

"I've been better," she said.

"You two stay put. My partner's watching the outside, and as soon as backup gets here, we'll set up a perimeter. Maybe the shooter's still out there, or maybe just his footprints or shell casings. We'll also make sure the house is clear. The ETU's on its way."

"My son is upstairs," PJ said. "I need to check on him. Now."

"Can't let you do that, Dr. Gray. Sometimes it's the family member who's the shooter. Goes outside, does the shooting, goes back in. It'd be dangerous for you to go up. Wait till the backup gets here."

"The hell with waiting," Schultz said. "I'm going up to check on Thomas."

Leeds frowned but didn't make any attempt to stop him.

At the top of the stairs, Schultz took a good look around before moving down the hall. There was a shower curtain covering the doorway to Thomas's room, since the real door had been hauled away as evidence against the gamer. The bathroom door was closed.

"You in there, Thomas?"

"Yeah. What's going on?"

"There were gunshots fired into the kitchen. You need to keep away from the windows, so stay in there for a little while."

"You're both okay, right? Man, this shooting and slashing stuff is getting to be a pain in the ass. Especially my bare ass on this tile floor. Can you get my PSP and pass it in to me?"

"We really are okay. The cops are downstairs. It won't be too much longer. What's a PSP?"

"PlayStation Portable. It's on the desk in my bedroom."

"I'll be a couple of minutes. You can sit on the toilet if that's any better."

"Gee, thanks."

Schultz went through the upstairs rooms, checking the closets, under the beds, the attic storage accessible through a small door in the wall of each walk-in closet. When he went into Thomas's room and flicked on the light, Megabite sat up, blinking. She stretched and jumped down from Thomas's bed, looking reproachfully at Schultz for disturbing her nap.

He grabbed the portable game, plus a T-shirt and boxers that were on the floor in the vicinity of the laundry basket. At the bathroom door, he passed the items to Thomas.

"Do I want to know what you're doing naked in the middle of the day?" Schultz said.

"Probably not."

Turning to head downstairs, Schultz bumped into PJ, who was right behind him. She shoved the bathroom door open so hard it smashed against the wall, catching Thomas nude, one foot into his boxers.

"Hey! A little privacy here," Thomas said. He quickly turned his back on PJ, preferring to bare his butt to his mom rather than his genitals.

"Sorry. I just wanted to see that you're okay."

"You saw more than that."

Figuring that PJ was about to launch into "You weren't born with underwear on, young man, I've seen it all," Schultz tugged on her arm.

"Come on, let's go talk to the officers," he said. "Everything's okay now." He caught himself just in time before calling her babe.

Chapter 49

Sunday morning, Dave came around at seven o'clock, picked PJ up, and drove her to the Embassy Suites Hotel at Laclede's Landing. He'd gotten a call from the hotel security manager.

The hotel's central atrium was filled with plants luxuriating in natural light pouring in from skylights several floors up. The sunshine was warm on PJ's shoulders, a pleasant change from being outside. The air smelled of flowers and the preparation for Sunday brunch. PJ thought wistfully of getting pampered in a hotel. Sleeping in, room service, relaxing poolside. And doing it again the next day.

The security manager checked their IDs and asked for Dave's weapon. He balked.

"I'm a law officer on duty. It's against procedures to surrender my gun."

"I'll take Dr. Gray upstairs alone, then," the manager said.

Dave frowned and gave in. In the security manager's office, his gun was put into a locker. The manager used a key in the elevator to take them to the top floor. When the elevator doors opened, they were surprised to see several guards dressed in foreign military uniforms in the hallway, and a woman wearing a colorful African wraparound dress.

"Who exactly are we seeing, Dave?"

"A man from Ghana. I guess with all this, he must be an important man from Ghana."

PJ was given a pat down in a private room by the woman in the hallway, who was efficient and unsmiling in spite of her bright clothing. PJ assumed Dave got his pat down right there in the hall. They were taken into the living room of a suite furnished as an office. A man in a dark suit and white shirt rose from behind a desk to greet them. The desk had nothing on it, not even a mote of dust.

The man would collapse on the spot if he saw the clutter in my office.

"The Honorable Hosni Naybet, Ambassador to the United States from Ghana," the security manager said, and left the room.

Dave stood rooted to the spot. PJ stepped forward, shook the ambassador's hand, and introduced herself and Dave. The ambassador was in his late sixties, tall, barrel-chested, and going gray at the temples. He looked like he'd been a physically powerful man in his youth and would still be formidable. His skin looked like the deep spaces between the stars at night and he carried himself with dignity.

"Welcome. Sit down, please," the ambassador said. "Would you like breakfast?"

"No, thank you." Dave had found his voice.

"I apologize for the security," he said. "Unfortunately, we live in a dangerous world."

He had a strong voice that PJ could listen to all day. He could be reciting a dictionary, and that would be all right with her.

"Why did you want to see us?" she said.

"I have some information in the case of the Metro Mangler, as the local media has termed the killings. A small thing, perhaps inconsequential, but you should be the judge of that."

He sipped from a mug of coffee that was about the size of a pint of ale. "I was here in the hotel the night of the first murder. I have a good friend in the city, and I get here when I can to visit. Not nearly often enough, of course. At about ten minutes after ten, I went to my window to look out on the river and the Arch, a view I always enjoy. A vehicle caught my attention, since no others were moving at that time on the frontage road."

"What type of vehicle was that?" Dave said.

"A pickup truck, traveling south. I have no information on the model, color, or license plate number. The truck came to a stop at the edge of the road. The driver got out and pulled a tarp from the truck bed, where it had been covering something."

"And could you see what that was?"

"Are you familiar with the 1950s movie *The Invasion of the Body Snatchers*?"

PJ and Dave both nodded.

"The item in the truck bed resembled a seedpod. Bigger than the ones in the movie, I think, but I was looking down from some distance. At that moment, my wife called me to the telephone. I moved away from the window to take the call. By the time I got back, the truck was gone. I left on a plane for Ghana later that night, and it wasn't until I got back here yesterday and read the local newspaper that I made any connection in my mind."

"It's likely that you saw the body of the first victim being dumped at the river's edge," Dave said. "Is there anything else you can tell us?"

"No, I'm sorry." The ambassador stood up, and it was obvious that their visit was over. "A horrible thing. I hope you find the killer soon. Dr. Gray," he said, turning to her, "I'm familiar with your work in virtual reality crime scene simulation. I've been urged by law enforcement officials and university faculty in my country to invite you to lecture, and if willing, to present a short workshop."

"I'd be honored."

PJ left him her card, with a request to call if he thought of anything else.

"Wait," Dave said. "What happened to the tarp that was covering the seedpod?"

Ambassador Naybet stared out the window, looking at the barges on the river, evidently reviewing the scene in his mind.

"The driver put it into the cab of the truck," he said. "On the passenger's side."

When Dave pulled around the back of PJ's house to drop her off, there were two cars in her parking area. A dark blue car stood next to her Ford Focus.

"What's that?" she said. She felt a stab of fright. *April?*

"I think about a 1989 Taurus," Dave said.

"No, I mean what's it doing here? Could there be an intruder in the house?"

"Would an intruder be so blatant about it? Give Schultz a call. He probably just woke up."

PJ glanced at him. He casually accepted that Schultz was sleeping at the boss's house. Sooner or later that was going to trip her up, trip them both up, and hard choices would have to be made.

She pulled out her cell and called her home number. Schultz answered on the first ring.

"Are you going to come into your house or sit out there and admire it?" he said, without preamble.

Not only was he awake, he'd been watching them.

"I think I'll stay here and make out with Dave." Dave's eyes widened, and she smiled to reassure him that she wasn't about to jump him. "You have a visitor in there?"

"Nope. You are looking at my newly-assigned vehicle."

"A 1989 Taurus," she said, hoping to dazzle him with her automotive knowledge.

"Tell Dave it's a 1987. Air-conditioned, radio, power win-

313

dows, cruise, tilt steering wheel. I have fallen into the lap of luxury."

"How many miles?" Dave said, loud enough for the cell's microphone to pick up.

"Hundred twenty-eight thousand. Practically new." She relayed the answer, ended the call, and thanked Dave for the ride.

The kitchen smelled of coffee and pancakes, and Schultz was setting the table.

"I need to get your consent to tap your home phone," Schultz said as he put syrup and butter on the table. "I think it's likely April Winter will call back."

"Sure. I'll let Thomas know he'd better watch what he says to the girls," she said. "That goes for you, too."

"The wire guy will be over in a couple of hours. He'll have a form for you to sign, keeps his butt out of trouble."

Over breakfast, PJ talked about her visit to the Embassy Suites Hotel. Schultz was suitably impressed that she'd been invited to lecture in Ghana.

"Nothing will come of it, I'm sure," she said. PJ was already exploring the idea, though, wondering what the life of a traveling consultant might be like, helping countries all over the world set up forensic computer simulation programs. She could take Thomas out of the academy for a year abroad and have him travel with her. If Mr. Archibald was satisfied with eagle viewing and Hannibal as an educational trip—they hadn't even had time to drive by Mark Twain's boyhood home—then she could imagine what he'd think of a trip around the world. Would she miss direct involvement in crime solving? She looked at the small craters in the wall where Schultz and a tech had dug out two bullets. She would have to hang a calendar over them.

The easy thing to do would be to turn away from this work.

Set up a private practice or join a clinic. Or go back to marketing.

She watched Schultz sop up syrup with the last bite of his pancake, and then swirl his finger around the plate, picking up the dregs. He licked his fingers.

Man saves a fortune on napkins.

Months ago, it would have bothered her. She would have had to stifle the urge to fix him, to try to make him more like her conception of the proper husband. Is that what had happened with her ex-husband Stephen?

I fixed him up nicely but the Other Woman got the benefit of it, and a baby, too.

She turned her thoughts loose and let them run down well-trodden paths of guilt and regret and anger.

Would I miss crime solving? Yes. The victims and survivors are counting on me, a little cog in the whole justice machine. I've caught the Blue bug, even without a badge.

She pushed the consulting idea aside. There was work to be done right here under her nose, never mind across the Atlantic. "How's the search for the pickup truck coming?"

Schultz snapped his syrupy fingers. "I was supposed to call Anita half an hour ago."

PJ stuffed her mouth with a bite of pancake to keep from saying anything when he wrapped his big, sticky hand around her wall phone. Anita answered right away, and he punched the speakerphone button.

"You're on the air."

"We got it," she said.

"That's terrific," PJ said. "Is the truck out of the water yet?"

"No. I thought they'd just send the divers in, but the Army Corps of Engineers had this gadget they wanted to use. It's a boat-towed metal detector that picks up iron and steel. All I

315

know is it's bright yellow and looks like a missile."

"Boys with toys," PJ said.

"Exactly. They fiddled with that thing for almost two hours, and then found the truck right where I told them to look."

"How did you know where to look?" Schultz said.

"Tire tracks about a mile from where Arlan's body was found. Somebody burned rubber, heading straight down for the river. I gotta go. They're about ready to pull it out of the water. I'll call you when the VIN trace comes back."

"Good work, Anita. Keep us informed," PJ said. Schultz hung up.

"I hate to bring this up," PJ said, "but how do we know that's the truck that the killer used? Somebody else could have dumped a truck in the river for any number of reasons."

"We don't know. The Vehicle Identification Number will tell us who owns that truck, and where that person lives. We go over there, bust in, and see if anybody looks guilty."

"With a warrant, I hope."

Schultz rolled his eyes. "You know, I wish you hadn't taken that training session on warrants. I preferred you barefoot and ignorant."

"I preferred you not speaking to me. What are the chances of that truck giving us any useful information?"

"You mean besides the VIN?"

"The victim's blood."

"Oh. I wouldn't count on that, even if the truck was soaked in Arlan's blood. The river water will wash it away. Even if there was a trace amount of blood somewhere, water degrades the DNA. DNA samples are supposed to be air dried and stored frozen in paper bags. Old Man River doesn't handle things that way."

"Fingerprints, then?"

"Even less chance. Fingerprints are ninety-nine percent water. The rest is salts from sweat and a little oil. Latent prints literally wash away."

PJ sighed. The truck wasn't going to be the breakthrough she was hoping for. The only useful item might be an address based on the VIN, and that could easily be phony.

"Don't give up yet," Schultz said. "Fibers or hair might be trapped in some tight spot where the water couldn't dislodge it. And there could be other evidence. A knife in the glove box would be nice. The blade could be matched to the wounds."

"Ooh, hair and fibers," PJ said. "CSI St. Louis."

"That stuff's important. Jurors watch CSI, too. They expect all that crap."

"I'll bet when the prosecution doesn't trot it out, jurors feel like the case isn't strong, even if that feeling is subconscious."

"You'd have a winning bet. Detectives and techs are collecting more evidence, too, because more can be done with it. Storage areas are ready to pop. Got any room in your basement you'd like to rent out?"

"Not for the kind of material you're thinking about." She thought about Arlan's body parts taking up residence next to her washer and dryer. PJ's cellphone rang. It was Jasmine Singer.

"We have more to discuss," Jasmine said. "When can you be in Hannibal?"

"Can't we do this by phone?" PJ said.

"No."

She looked at her watch. "All right, I can make it by one this afternoon."

Jasmine hung up with a decisive click.

"That woman's getting to me," PJ said. "But I can't wait to hear what she has to say."

"Why don't we leave now, then?" Schultz said.

"Lilly is coming over to pick up Thomas in twenty minutes. The boys are going to a movie this afternoon, then back to her house."

"And that keeps us from leaving because?"

"Because we'll be all alone in the house."

"Oh."

She came around the table, stood between his legs, and wrapped her hands around his neck. She pulled close to him and kissed the top of his head tenderly. His face was buried in her breasts, and his hands clasped her hips and then began exploring.

She pulled away.

"Hey, come back here. I was having a good time."

"Me, too, but Thomas is going to come roaring through the kitchen in about fifteen minutes, wanting to know when his movie starts and probably wanting to borrow money."

"That gives us ten minutes."

"Why settle for that when we can have two hours?" She rubbed her hand between his legs, feeling the stirring inside his clothing.

"Keep doing that, and we'll be all done in two minutes."

PJ was planning to use the drive time to Hannibal to have a Relationship Talk with Schultz, when he was trapped and couldn't get away for a couple of hours. It didn't seem like the right time, though. Their lovemaking had been languid and mellow, and that time was an island in a turbulent sea of grim events. She didn't want to spoil the afterglow with questions, so they rode in silence.

Could be I don't want to hear the answers.

She hadn't taken the route along the Mississippi. Gray clouds hung in pendulous layers and ahead of her, she could

318

see a dark haze that meant rain was falling. The temperature held in the mid-thirties but the roads would be icy by nightfall. It was hard to believe that above those gloomy clouds the sun was shining. PJ switched on her headlights and glanced at Schultz, who was watching the scenery so intently he could have been counting telephone poles. He was wearing his neutral face, the one he fell into when he was alone. In every line of that face, PJ could see his deep concern for the murder victims in his cases. The vulnerable people, the ones who died frightened, helpless, and in pain. The face reflected in the passenger's window was marked with those deaths, the whole collection of them he'd dealt with in his career as a homicide detective.

It was the way her face would be, years from now. She suddenly realized that Schultz must do the same thing she did: replay the scenes in his mind, reconstructing a victim's last hours or minutes, bearing witness to what the killer did on behalf of humanity. Hers was facilitated by her scenarios. His came from within. On the deepest level of their being, she and Schultz were the same.

She reached over and squeezed his hand. "I love you," she said for the first time.

The guard at Riverview Elder Care asked for Schultz's gun, pointing to the prominently displayed *Absolutely No Weapons Permitted* sign on the front door. Schultz showed his badge and then ignored the man. PJ reminded herself not to take him with her the next time she went to see an ambassador.

The marble lobby and leather chairs held no charms for PJ this time. The solarium was empty and dim, with rain pounding on its expansive skylights. Rhonda had the look of a woman who needs to eat more bran, and Jasmine's luxurious office seemed pretentious.

Jasmine got down to business right away.

"Detective Schultz, I don't recall inviting you. You'll have to wait in reception." Her finger went for the intercom button to summon Rhonda.

"You don't need Rhonda," PJ said. "He's staying, or we're both going."

Jasmine's finger stopped in midair. Her mouth looked for a moment like she'd sucked on a lemon. Then a smile took the place of the sour face. "You're welcome to stay, Detective. Didn't mean to get off on the wrong foot. Your presence merely took me by surprise."

Schultz tipped an imaginary hat. "No sweat. I often get that response."

Jasmine shifted her chair to marginalize Schultz.

She sees me as sympathetic. Or she doesn't like men. Or doesn't like this *man.*

With Schultz taking the snub unusually well, PJ didn't waste any time. She could be as direct as Jasmine.

"In our last conversation, you implied that there was more to April's story than you were willing to tell me," PJ said. "So let's have it. If you're just going to claim 'family secrets' again, this will be a short visit."

Ignoring the jab, Jasmine tented her hands beneath her chin and began to talk. "I believe we left off at the point where I said that April was conceived as a result of rape. My sister Virginia was sexually abused by our father, Marshall Crane. There had been an incestuous relationship, first with me as the older sister, and then with Virginia, who was nine years younger than I. Father had a thing for being a virgin buster, to be crude about it. He moved on when a girl got stale for him. Unfortunately, Virginia got pregnant before he lost interest in her. I think she was sixteen when April was born, or just turned seventeen. Virginia had a sweetheart, a young man of modest means whose biggest virtue was that to the day he died, he believed April was his daughter."

"Henry Winter and the shotgun wedding," PJ said.

"Yes. Virginia had sex with Henry when she was already six weeks pregnant. She did love him, but she was also a practical woman. He thought the baby was born a little early."

"So Virginia has her baby under the bonds of matrimony. I presume Marshall left her alone after that."

"Of course. She was stale goods, remember?"

Schultz snorted in disgust. Jasmine flicked her eyes in his direction, but only for a moment.

A family where pride and social status trumps the welfare of its children. The burden of protecting the secret fell to May. No wonder she lied to me about having an older sister.

"April was a difficult child from the beginning, but her parents adored her and made excuses for her odd behavior."

"Odd in what way?" PJ asked.

"Many ways. Even before schizophrenia took over April's life, she had violent tendencies and zero impulse control. I told you about Elissa Nevers's death. I omitted the murder before that."

"Let me take a wild guess. Marshall went after fresh flesh."

"How right you are. April was abused once, that we knew of, at age fourteen. She didn't get pregnant, thank God for little favors. After that, April was bent on revenge. I believe some of Marshall's pieces were never found."

"And the family covered this up."

"Yes. The story was that Marshall died in a dreadful accident overseas. Exploring in New Guinea and never came home. There was some kernel of truth in it. At least he had traveled there the year before. No one was very fond of Marshall, not even his wife," Jasmine said. Raising her eyebrows, she said, "Especially his wife Caroline. She's the one who bribed the police to accept the overseas disappearance story."

At the mention of bribery and police in the same sentence, Schultz spoke up. "Do you know who was involved in that? Wrongs can still be righted."

"Believe me, Detective, it's something that doesn't need to be stirred up."

"But—" he said.

Jasmine rode right over his voice. "Caroline set up a trust fund for her murderous granddaughter, fifty million dollars, supposedly. I guess it was her way of atoning for what her wretched husband had done. April came into her trust fund when she turned eighteen, and being the paranoid person that she was, immediately divided the money and established different methods of accessing it. Did I mention she was too smart for her own good? I've cut off three different paths to that money, but only accounted for a measly ten million or so. April has a lot of money at her disposal. She could easily hire someone to kill for her, but she wants to do it herself."

"So Marshall's murder bore similarities to Arlan's?" PJ asked. "You mentioned pieces?"

"From what I've been able to find out about it, yes. If you look at family photos, Arlan has an uncanny resemblance to Marshall. They could have been father and son."

That's why so much planning went into Arlan's death. She was killing her abuser all over again.

"Frank Simmons's death showed no reenactment of revenge," PJ said.

"If I had to hazard a guess on that one, I'd say April was trying, probably still is, to frame her sisters," Jasmine said. "If that doesn't work, I don't know what she'll do. She's a loose cannon."

PJ and Schultz looked at each other, knowing they were thinking the same thing: Shower Woman, hired to cast doubt on June's alibi, and then killed for her efforts. Lights were coming on in PJ's mind, illuminating the dark motives for the string of murders.

Arlan Merrett spent four days with April, and in her mind, he was Marshall all over again. What a living hell that must have been for him.

"April's lashing out at her sisters," PJ said, "because they lived a comfortable, unfettered life, while she rotted away in storage."

Schultz was nodding. "You do realize, Ms. Singer, that you're in grave danger? I imagine you're next on April's to-do list."

There was a sudden change in Jasmine's attitude. She'd been her usual imperious self, accustomed to having her wishes materialize into reality. At the mention that she was a prime target, the shell she lived in was crushed, and inside there was a frightened woman. In seconds, Jasmine's eyes overflowed and tears charted a path through her makeup.

I could almost feel sorry for her. She's just reaping what she sowed thirty years ago.

Jasmine pulled a tissue from a box on her desk, dabbed at her eyes, and pursued the drops on her cheeks. When she spoke, her voice was almost back to normal.

"I worried that someday this might happen," Jasmine said. "It was the price I paid for preserving the family name. It was my burden, and after me, it would be May's. Although I had thought that April would have an unfortunate drug overdose before May had to take up the mantle."

"So May knows nothing about this?"

"No, other than what she heard and experienced as a child, before April's 'riding accident.' May definitely believes her older sister is dead."

PJ had heard enough. Jasmine was self-centered enough to believe that *she* was the one who'd paid a price. *What about April, who should have gone on trial for the first murder she committed, of the man who raped her? What about all the people April had killed since that time? She would never have served a day in prison after her first murder. A high-powered attorney would have gotten her time in a treatment facility, which she surely needed. Excellent treatment might have alleviated April's rage and lessened the effect of her schizophrenia. Or not. At least she would never have had the chance to kill again, and again.*

"I think we need to get going," PJ said. "There's a lot to do, based on what you told us. I would suggest hiring a lot of extra security, Jasmine, and notifying the police here."

I'm surprised you've lasted this long.

"I have a couple of questions before we go," Schultz said. "What connection would April have to the murders of Loretta Blanchette, Bernard Dewey, and the Royalviews?"

Jasmine considered. "Blanchette was a teacher April had at summer camp. I remember the name because my sister got an unflattering report about April's performance at the camp. The rest, I don't know."

"Why are you telling us all this if your motivation for years has been to protect your family's secrets?" Schultz said. "With a pedophile and a serial killer as ornaments on the family tree, I doubt that you're going to be in demand for teas, golf dates, and charity events. May and June are going to experience the fallout, too."

Jasmine fastened her eyes on her desktop and didn't speak for a long time, long enough for Schultz to start fidgeting in his chair.

"I would like to say that I'm unburdening my soul in the

face of death, Detective. But it's nothing so lofty," Jasmine said. "The fact is that our roles are reversed now, April and I. She's free and I'm trapped in this facility. I don't dare leave. She's probably out there now, waiting for her chance and gloating. And that pisses me off; after all I did for her."

Chapter 50

From my vantage point twenty feet above ground in a majestic old oak, its arms spread wide to embrace me and my purpose, I see Dr. Gray and Detective Schultz leave. Snow falls gently on their bare heads, in Schultz's case, literally bare, and gives them crowns of six-sided stars. Snow dusts their shoulders as they walk to Dr. Gray's new car. Even the obscene redness of the car is muted by the floating snow, as though Mother Nature is embarrassed by the Freudian display. You'd think a psychologist would pick up on that, but it must be true that the plumber's faucets always leak.

They take the time to brush the snow off the car, passing the scraper from one to the other in a long reach across the windshield that reminds me of Michelangelo's painting on the roof of the Sistine Chapel, the one where God reaches out his hand to Adam. Since Adam is naked and equipped, he would have to be Schultz. That leaves Dr. Gray as God. As I watch, they shift into being those characters and back again.

They drive away, the car's exhaust making a thin stream of exhaust fumes, doing its part to hasten climate change.

The snow is beginning to cover me, too. By nightfall I will be nothing more than a bump on the oak's branch, which I suppose is better than being a pimple on the ass of the world. Having been one, I will be able to make a down-to-earth comparison.

I begin to see the individual snowflakes dancing in the wind, putting on a performance for me, and growing larger, too. As big as the oak's silent leaves, soon as big as toasters. That's when they talk to me. Falling things talk to me. Leaves, rain, waterfalls with their drops as big as my head, and snow. They all have different voices, but they all say the same thing to me: You deserve better. You deserve to be a Rich Bitch who can do anything you want, go anywhere you want.

And so I will. The God of Successful Parties can be wooed and won over.

Did I mention that my oak is close to the building? The hardest part was getting here, climbing up the side of the tree away from the surveillance cameras. Once up high, I might as well be invisible. Nobody looks up, including cameras. Maybe I am invisible.

This is the way it will happen. Time will do its skating-by thing again, and then I'll shake off the snow and move. After tying my rope to this heavy branch I'm on, I'll toss the other end over to the building. It has a grappling hook. The hook catches, I take up the slack in the rope. I've done this tree-to-tree in the woods, but tree-to-building is different enough that my body will be buzzing with adrenaline. Next I'll lower myself onto the rope like a sloth hanging underneath it, and work my way over to the building. My arms and legs are up to it, but what if I'm unlucky? What if the God of Successful Parties chooses that moment to sneer at me, and I tumble to the ground? I'll be on camera at the very least, caught and handcuffed at the very most. If that happens, if I get the handcuffs, I'll freak out. Handcuffs bring it all back.

No falling.

I've studied the architectural drawings so much they must be tattooed on my retinas. There's a vent shaft topped by one of those huge twirling metal caps, like a dome on a Russian church. Unscrew it, drop a rope, shimmy in. The shaft goes horizontal and I can crawl in it, just barely. Good thing I didn't eat today. Count the passageways, third left then fifth right, ends in an air return in her office. Kind of tricky here. The air return grid is a tight fit. If I drop it, maybe handcuffs.

No dropping.

Jasmine has no cameras in her office, I suppose because some of her business dealings aren't squeaky-clean. Or she doesn't like

Candid Camera keeping track of how many times she uses her private bathroom.

It's the best of circumstances. Jasmine has her arms folded on the table, and her head resting on them. She's taking a quick nap. Poor dear, I guess she hasn't been sleeping well lately.

I put the tip of a knife to her throat, make a small cut. A few red drops well up, and she startles awake. There's not much light in the office, she can't see me clearly, but she knows it's me. I pull the knife across her throat. Her scream turns into a gurgle.

As she dies, I make a few quick doodles with the knife, and then I'm out. Traversing the rope, I play back my triumph as the snow whispers in my ears.

Chapter 51

Schultz wished he was driving. It was hard enough for him to relax as a passenger, but when it was snowing, relaxing was out of the question.

"I can drive if you're tired," Schultz said.

"I'm fine," PJ said. "That's the third time you suggested that. If you have something to say about my driving, just come out with it."

"I get nervous when other people are driving in bad weather. I trust my reflexes."

"And not mine, I guess. I grew up in a small town in Iowa. I've slipped around on more snowy streets and little country roads than you can imagine."

"Don't take your eyes off the highway when you talk to me," Schultz said. "Why do you keep bringing that up, anyway? Your idyllic early life in Iowa?"

"Do I?"

"Oh, it comes up every now and then. You're not the only country mouse, you know. I grew up on a farm in Missouri."

She looked over at him, eliciting an annoyed gesture to keep her eyes on the road. "I never knew that about you. I thought you were a city boy."

"Well, I exaggerated a little. I only lived on the farm until I was nine. Then I moved in with my aunt in St. Louis."

"Your parents kicked you out at age nine? You must have been some little devil."

"My parents and my two sisters died in the fire that burned down the farmhouse. My little brother and I survived because he'd pestered me into going out looking for frogs."

"I'm so sorry, Shultz. I didn't know about that."

A cellphone rang. Both of them reached for their phones, but it was Schultz's that was trilling in his pocket.

"You can't answer your phone anyway," he said as he flipped the phone open. "You're driving."

She rolled her eyes, but at least she was facing forward at the time.

Schultz listened, then mouthed to PJ that it was Dave on the other end.

"Good news," Dave said, "times two. Searching the cab records for pickups at Laclede's Landing paid off. We got three between ten-fifteen and eleven o'clock that Saturday night. Two destinations were hotels. The third was a house in South St. Louis. The driver remembers it because it was a nice fare, but in the opposite direction of where he was hoping to end up, which was to the airport."

"You show him the photo?" The picture of the two sisters on the beach, the one PJ had received in the mail, had been passed around.

"Yeah. He thinks it was her, but that picture's thirty years out of date. She still had red hair, though."

"Shit, what a break." Out of the corner of his eye, he saw PJ turn to look at him. "Cut that out, you're making me nervous."

"What?" Dave said.

"Not talking to you. What else?"

"You're gonna love this one. Couldn't get any fingerprints or blood off the pickup truck, but we did get hairs that had gotten trapped well enough to outlast a dunking in the river. Some were caught in an exposed bolt head in the pickup bed, having been yanked roughly out. DNA says it's Arlan's. More hairs were caught in the driver's sliding headrest support, tangled and pulled loose when the person turned his head. Or her head, in this case. There were only two hairs, but it was enough for mtDNA testing. Whoever was driving had the same mother as May and June."

"Holy shit motherfucking Christ!"

"Yeah, no shit. It's all coming together."

"We'll be there," Schultz looked at his watch, "in forty-five minutes. I want to be there."

Schultz folded his phone. "Put the pedal to the metal, woman, we got her!"

"What about all the careful driving business?"

"To hell with it. We have to be in South St. Louis in forty-five minutes."

"Your wish is my command," she said. She pressed on the gas pedal and sent the rear end fishtailing, then regained control, going at a higher speed.

"I told you I was good at this," she said. "I'll have us there on time, unless there's an accident on the road between here and there that slows me down. Now explain what's going on."

Schultz went over everything Dave said. When he started on an explanation of mitochondrial DNA, she interrupted.

"I know all that. It's DNA found outside the nucleus of the cell in the mitochondria, little energy factories. A mother's egg has a bunch of them, sperm relatively few because they're so tiny compared to the egg. So the embryo's mitochondria come almost entirely from a single donor, the mother. The nuclei of the embryo's cells have two donors."

"I'm impressed," Schultz said.

"I'm not. Biology 101."

Damn, it took me a year to learn that.

It was nearly dark by the time they got to Morganford Road in South St. Louis. Snow was pelting the window with serious intent. Three inches had fallen in a short time, with no sign of letting up. Schultz had to call Dave back to get the address, something he'd neglected to ask about in the first call.

"We just passed Bevo Mill Restaurant," Schultz said. "Only a few more blocks."

PJ squinted out the window. It was hard to make out anything in the road, much less alongside it. "You mean that big thing over there that looks like it has arms?"

"It's a windmill," he said, "and a restaurant. It's hard to see the street signs. There's the cemetery. Turn left. Left!"

PJ turned, trusting that there was a street there. Almost immediately, she came to a roadblock and slid to a halt, the front bumper inches from a cruiser that had been parked on an angle, blocking the street.

Someone was tapping on her window. She fumbled for the button to lower it, not having had enough time in the Focus for her fingers to go there automatically. The glass slid down, and snow rushed in, speckling her face.

"We're about two blocks away from the house," Dave said. "Officer Daniels will park your car out of the way. C'mon out, we've been waiting."

A preoccupied Schultz walked away with Dave, leaving her standing alone. *At least I can follow their footprints.*

She gamely took off after them. The wind was bitterly cold and insistent, finding all the chinks in her coat's armor. She wasn't wearing a hat or scarf, so she pulled her neck and head down, turtle style. Hunched, eyes tracking footprints, puzzling over the fact that other footprints were starting to criss-cross the two sets she was following, she collided with someone.

It was her boss, Lieutenant Howard Wall.

"Howard," she said. "I'm glad I ran into you. I seem to have gotten separated from Schultz and I don't know where all the action is."

"The action hasn't started yet, and when it does, it will be the SWAT team going in. The subject's taking a little break from murdering people, watching TV, probably having a beer."

"So I do what?"

"Go in after the house is secure. Let the guys with the big guns handle knocking on the killer's door, Doctor. You notice I'm not up there at the front of the line, either."

I guess when it's safe to go in with paper booties, they'll call me.

PJ knew she was being illogical, but she resented not being there when April was captured. "So when does this knocking occur?"

"We're taking it slow. The house is under close observation, so she's not going anywhere."

"How do you know she's in there?"

"Neighbor saw her go in before the snow started and not come out. Like those sticky cockroach traps. We got her on thermal imaging. SWAT likes to know how many people are in a house before entering, anyway. She's in there, all right."

PJ's first experience with thermal imaging hadn't been much fun for her, except in retrospect. Schultz had brought in infrared goggles attached to a helmet, and said he could see through her clothing like X-ray vision. She kicked him out of the office. Later she found out from Anita that the thermal image included clothing and the only way he'd be seeing skin is if PJ was naked in the first place. Even then, the image was not detailed.

"You're saying it might be awhile until April is taken into custody," PJ said.

"Could be quite a while. I think the neighbor's houses are slowly being evacuated. Don't want any possibility of her running into one of them and starting a hostage situation.

Excuse me, Doctor," Howard turned away to talk to someone.

Excuse me, Doctor, I have something important to do. She made a face at his back. *Oh, get a grip. Let the police do what they're trained to do.* Suddenly ashamed of her pettiness, PJ's cheeks were flushed with warmth in spite of the snow.

Turning away from her distracted boss, PJ thought that May, June, and Jasmine should be warned to stay wherever they were until April was in custody. Not that she could say so in those exact words. She was sure Schultz wouldn't want news of this operation leaked out before an official arrest was made. Even then, it would probably be up to the prosecuting attorney to decide when and how much the women would hear of April's story.

Don't contaminate the witnesses or the process.

She headed back to her car, to sit in the relative warmth and make the phone calls. Roaming around, she couldn't find her car. Officer Daniels had parked it somewhere, and she didn't know where the officer was either. Ready to stomp her feet in frustration, she spotted Anita and hurried over to her.

"Any idea where my car is parked?"

"Not yours specifically, but there are several over there," she said, pointing to several cars lined up along the street outside the blockade formed by the cruiser.

"Thanks. Call me when I can get in the house, will you? I want to study any setups April has, like photos or items collected from her victims."

"Will do. Stay warm until then, Boss," Anita said. "Great work on this case, by the way."

"Thanks." Anita had already turned to go. The wind swept PJ's response away.

She found her car by remembering that the license plate

number had double-oh-seven, James Bond, in it. For cars of the approximate size and shape of hers, she wiped off the license plates with her fingers. Only when she was standing next to the Focus did she remember that she'd left her keys inside for Officer Daniels to use.

Shit! What now?

PJ cleared some snow from the driver's window, cupped her hands, and peered inside. The key was still there. She searched for the door handle under the snow, found it, and opened the door. Using the scraper thoughtfully put in the car by the rental company, she cleared a little of the front window so she could see what was going on outside. Then she got in and savored the feeling of being out of the wind. Snow covered all the windows and was already beginning to cover the area she'd cleared directly in front of the steering wheel.

Feels like being in an igloo.

PJ took out her cellphone, and then paused to get her thoughts together and plan something to say.

Something cold pressed against her right temple. She reached up instinctively to push it away, and her hand came into contact with the barrel of a gun.

"Hands in your lap, Dr. Gray." It was a woman's voice.

Fear stabbed PJ's chest like an icicle. Although she'd never heard the voice before, there was no doubt in her mind that it belonged to April.

To the woman whose murders, counted and uncounted, probably exceeded the number of fingers on both her hands.

PJ's hands dropped into her lap like stones into a pond. "Hello, April. I was wondering when I'd get to meet you." She kept her voice as noncommittal as she could. One wrong word and her brain was likely to be decorating the window of her rental car.

The rental car company will charge extra to clean that up.

PJ squeezed the shakiness out of her voice and tried to wrap some discipline around her thoughts. The barrel of the gun made a cold circle where it was pressed against her head.

A cold kiss. A last, cold kiss.

She wasn't dead yet, so April must want something from her or have something to tell her. *Or something to do to me. Don't think that.*

Unbidden and unwelcome, images of Old Hank's barn streamed through her head. Flies in the middle of winter. Blood soaked into the grain of the old workbench. Shriveled pieces impaled on nails.

Stop!

"What do you want from me?" PJ said.

"First, toss that cellphone into the back seat."

PJ didn't want to let go of it. It seemed like a lifeline to the world of sanity and safety. But she lobbed the phone over her shoulder and heard it land on the seat.

"Now," April said, "I want you to drive out of this area. Act like nothing is wrong. Honk the horn and it's the last thing you'll do."

Snow covered the front window like a grave blanket. "I'm going to have to clear the window," she said. "I can't see to drive."

PJ shifted toward the door, one hand on the handle. There was a sound near her ear that could only be the pistol's hammer being cocked. She put her hand back in her lap.

"Use your windshield wipers. I don't want that front window too clean, anyway. It's more private like this, don't you think?"

PJ switched on the windshield wipers. The wiper on the driver's side, which had less snow to clear, did a fair job. The one on the passenger's side tunneled under several inches of snow and dislodged some of it.

"Pull forward and make a right turn onto Morganford. I'm taking the gun away, but remember, Dr. Gray, bullets can go right through this car's seat and out through your chest."

The gun's hammer dropped harmlessly, and April withdrew into the back seat, crouching down. PJ breathed for the first time since she'd put her hand on the door handle to get out.

She started the car. The heater came on full blast and startled her. She adjusted it lower and turned on the headlights. The snow in the beams of her headlights blew almost horizontally, lashed by the wind.

PJ gasped when a gloved hand thudded on her window and a flashlight followed.

"That you, Dr. Gray? Didn't mean to startle you."

PJ sat still. She couldn't open her mouth or the scream inside would get out.

A whisper came from the back seat. "Answer."

"Dr. Gray?" The person outside made a gesture with her hand: Roll down the window.

PJ opened the window a couple of inches. "Oh, it's you, Officer Daniels."

"Yes, ma'am. I saw your headlights come on and thought I'd check to see that everything was okay. Wouldn't look good to have a car stolen from the crime scene with all these law enforcement personnel around."

PJ tried to force herself to laugh, but it came out as a choking sound. She patted her throat. "Catching a cold, I think."

"This is the weather for it. Good night, ma'am. Drive safely."

PJ closed the window, wondering why the officer couldn't see the fear she was certain was shining from her eyes like beacons.

"Excellent," came the voice from the back seat. "Let's get moving."

PJ drove in silence as April called out directions. There was almost no traffic on the street and the plows weren't out yet. The Focus clung to the road, traveling through twin ruts in the snow.

"So who's that back there in your house?" PJ asked. She felt she'd better start talking, engaging, charming, whatever it took.

"A prostitute," April said. "Can't draw in the johns with bruises all over her body from her last beating, so she's taking time off. A hundred bucks, and all she had to do for it was sit around in my living room and watch TV. She'll be lucky if some trigger-happy cop doesn't blow her head off. Did you hear that?"

"What?"

"Turn off the radio, will you? The voices are distracting me."

PJ reached over and turned the knob, even though the radio was already off.

"How much did Jasmine tell you? I was never able to get a bug into that office of hers," April said.

PJ hesitated. The less she revealed, the better.

"She told me that you had some problems living at home and went to her country home for awhile."

"That's it? No lies about paranoia, bad temper, seeing things?"

"No. I don't think Jasmine wanted to talk about you. I was the one who went there and pressed her for information."

"How did you find out about me?"

"June told me there were rumors of an older sister. I was curious."

I've got to be the one asking the questions, drawing her out.

PJ wondered if this was to be the last hour of her life. That made her think about Arlan, the stand-in for the man who'd raped both April and her mother. What had he endured in his last hours? She would have to be strong.

Fortunately, I am a cool-headed woman of science.

When the car passed under a streetlight, PJ glanced up to the rearview mirror. She caught a glimpse of April. Thin, almost gaunt. Red hair unkempt, gone too many days without a shampoo. Eyes constantly on the move. Lips pressed together into a line that sliced across her face like the stroke of a knife. She seemed to be listening to something, almost certainly was: the odd chattering of a schizophrenic mind.

Things might have been different if April had gotten early treatment. A better life for her, and people might not have died.

PJ tried to picture the face in the mirror as the teenager in the swimsuit in Mexico, holding a beach ball. At that time, April's schizophrenia hadn't stepped into her life like an elephant tearing up a garden.

With the rape, her life hadn't been a garden anyway.

It was time to test the waters. "Why are you so angry with your sisters, April?"

A stream of profanity flowed from the back seat. PJ waited it out, wondering if she'd get any answer other than that.

"I have to get them before they get me. Now that I'm out, see. Destroy them so completely they can't come after me and put me back there. I can't understand why the fucking police couldn't get it right. May killed those men. I watched her plan it and watched her do it."

"You mean May's husband and June's husband?"

"She shot her husband through a pillow. Feathers floated down and stuck in his blood. She's guilty. The little bitch was always guilty of something. She hid cookies from me."

"What about Arlan? Did she kill Arlan, too?"

"The goddamned knife was in her house! May had to punish Arlan. He did something really bad. But she murdered him and she should be in jail for the rest of her life. Locked up. They put me in handcuffs. Now it's her turn. Turn left at the next corner."

She's going to kill me for sure. She's giving away so much because she already knows I'm not going to tell anyone.

April continued talking, raging against May for a variety of offenses. A new image in PJ's mind drowned out the words from the back seat—tucking Thomas into a body bag instead of his bed, and zipping it up over his bloodied face.

Despair blackened the edges of PJ's vision. It was all she could do to keep her hands on the steering wheel. She wanted to reach back and yank the gun away from April.

I have nothing left to lose. When I get a chance, I have to take it.

"June was only a baby when you left St. Louis. What about her?"

"She got my life. May got my life, too. They both have to pay." April laughed, a sound that froze PJ's blood. "Auntie Jasmine's already paid. Didn't I ask you to turn off that damn radio?"

"Sorry. I'll take care of it now." PJ turned the silent radio off again.

"That's better. Right turn here. I could never forgive them for not helping me when I was locked up. You're supposed to love your sister."

Helping you? You were dead to them.

"April, did you know that your parents and Auntie Jasmine told everyone you were dead? They had a funeral for you and everything. May and June didn't know you were alive and being held against your will."

April's shrill voice was abruptly cut off. She didn't know, couldn't have known because all information that reached her was undoubtedly filtered. Jasmine was responsible for that, and it seemed like Jasmine was already dead.

The first of how many today?

"That's a lie. I'm not dead, I'm right here. They abandoned me."

PJ wasn't going to break through April's delusions. If it were even possible, it would take a lot more therapy than PJ had time for. They had just arrived at May's home.

The snow had let up as rapidly as it had started. Walking to the door, PJ noticed a few stars poking through thinning clouds. It would have been a beautiful view, the pristine expanse of snow and the heavy coating on the trees, like paint splashed on with a heavy brush. Beautiful except for the gun shoved in the small of her back.

PJ knocked on the door. April didn't want to use the doorbell that probably had multiple receivers around the house, and she stood off to the side of the tall doors. PJ gauged the distance April had placed between them, and judged it too far to get the gun away.

I'm only going to get one chance at this. Can't waste it. Wait for it.

PJ's stomach was in knots. She hoped no one answered the door. There were lights on in the house, but there might be lights on somewhere in the huge place all the time.

The door swung open and Mary Beth smiled a warm greeting.

Oh God, no, no!

Sensing April moving up behind her, PJ swung both of her arms up, trying to block the entrance. "Get out of here!" PJ shouted.

"What?" Mary Beth's eyes widened. She must have spotted the person behind PJ, and was backing away.

April ducked low and fired beneath PJ's outstretched arm. Mary Beth was hit in the chest. Blood appeared on her shirt and widened impossibly fast. Another bullet struck her forehead, and she collapsed.

PJ brought her arm down hard, but April wasn't there anymore. She was out of reach, still on the porch.

"Get inside," April said.

Her breath coming fast and shallow, PJ moved into the hallway.

And lunged for the security system panel, where there was a glowing red button that said *Emergency*. Her situation certainly qualified as one.

Her hand inches from the button, PJ felt a blow on her head, and sank to the floor alongside Mary Beth.

Chapter 52

Schultz watched as the team finally went in, to do what they called "serving a high-risk warrant," and what he called "Get 'em before they get you." He was across the street, closer than he was supposed to be, behind a car. The house, a Dutch home with a gambrel roof, was shrouded in snow. Even though the snow was easing off, wind was whipping around what had already fallen. The house looked no different from the rest of them lining the quiet street. Inside the other homes, family life went on with its ups and downs. Inside this one was a killing machine, the antithesis of life.

He wasn't feeling the jangling inside that he normally felt when the link connecting him to a killer had sprung into being, and he was this close. Adrenaline was creating a rush of sensation in him strong enough to drown out any of that awareness.

He heard the shotgun blasting the hinges off the front door. As the door fell aside, a flash-bang was tossed in. The loud burst of noise was muted a little by the snow. In seconds there were shouts of "Police!" and "On the floor!" and "Hands over your head!"

Schultz was in the house seconds after the SWAT team called clear, hand wrapped tightly around the warrant. He was there to preserve evidence and keep the SWAT intrusion to a minimum. They knew they were supposed to do considerable evidentiary processing, but it wasn't always the first thing on their minds.

They had an unarmed woman in custody, lying on the floor on her side, her hands cuffed behind her back. He shooed most of the team out of the house, leaving only a couple to handle the suspect. Coming over for a closer examination, he studied the woman. She was terribly frightened, crying, not at all defiant like he would have expected. That's when he noticed her hair.

April was Sparkle Farkle, red-haired from birth. This woman had noticeable black roots. Her red hair was a dye job.

Fuck. Another look-alike.

She'd be arrested and tested, but Shultz was willing to bet his left testicle that her mitochondrial DNA wouldn't indicate that she was the third sister. April was one giant step ahead, and that added fuel to the cold fire already ignited inside him about these murders.

With the familiar motion and patter of the crime scene techs around him, Schultz made his way systematically from room to room. Nothing seemed unusual until he got to the spare bedroom. It was disquieting, even for him, to walk in and find a body strung up with a hangman's noose. The body was pierced with enough knives that it could fairly be described as a pincushion.

There should be a large pool of blood underneath the body, but there was only shag carpet, brown flecked with gold, and dry. Looking closer, he saw that it was a familiar manikin, a Resusci Anne used for CPR training. He'd had a refresher course just a few months ago. There was a rope and winch setup suspending the body from a ceiling hook, looking eerily similar to the scenario PJ had come up with in the barn.

Without the beams twenty feet overhead. Without the flies, and without other things.

He spun the manikin around with his flashlight, and got another shock. Instead of the manikin's bland face with perpetually open mouth he was expecting, a photograph of May Simmons's face was glued in place and anchored by a knife through the forehead. The anger expended on the manikin made April's intent clear. He didn't even need a shrink to tell him what that intention was.

Schultz dialed the number at the Simmons house. The phone rang several times, but May finally picked up. He told her briefly that the police had just missed snagging the prime suspect, and that she should stay in her house with the security system on.

"It so happens I'm not going anywhere. My evening of bridge was cancelled because of the snow."

"What about your children?" He heard a TV playing loudly in the background.

"Nanny took off as soon as she heard I'd be home this evening. She's visiting a relative in the hospital. The kids are watching a video."

"Go check on them, will you?"

With an exasperated sigh, May put the phone down and was gone for several minutes. "They're fine. The alarm system's on."

"Has it been on all the time up until now?"

"I suppose. Nanny's good about resetting it when she goes out."

"All right, you just stay there. I'm going to get officers outside."

He went through the same type of conversation with June, requested outdoor surveillance at both houses, and dialed Riverview Elder Care. Rhonda answered, and informed him that Jasmine was working in her office and didn't want to be disturbed.

"Use that buzzer intercom on her. I want to talk to her."

"If you insist," Rhonda said. After a minute she came back

to the phone and said, "She's not answering. I told you she didn't want to be disturbed."

"Get in there now and tell her I have to talk to her. If the office door is locked, get somebody to open it. Break it down if you have to."

Schultz heard the phone being set down hard on Rhonda's desk. She was doing everything she could to express her irritation with him, while still trying to cooperate with the law. Schultz was used to that kind of behavior, so she wasn't getting under his skin.

Several minutes passed. Schultz was still in the lynching room. He let his eyes wander while he was waiting. They fastened on a bulletin board with items haphazardly pinned up. He walked over to it. There were recent clippings about the Metro Mangler with parts underlined and comments written to the side, none of them flattering to the St. Louis Police Department. There were pictures of all members of the CHIP team, including some taken at their homes with a telephoto. Schultz winced when he saw several pictures of PJ and him kissing at the front door, in the car, sneaking a kiss outside Millie's, and one photo that showed his hand planted on PJ's ass. He knew he had to deal with their boss-worker-lover situation in the department, and soon. He was sure all members of the team knew about their relationship. Lieutenant Wall was probably waiting for them to work things out on their own, but wouldn't wait too long. What was on the bulletin board was going to force their hands.

There were also surveillance pictures of murder victims.

Schultz heard screaming through the phone, and his heart sank. He hadn't liked Jasmine, but he wouldn't sic April on anyone. The phone was knocked onto the floor and picked up.

"She's dead! Oh my God, she's dead!" Rhonda sounded

like she was on the edge of hysteria. Had she and Jasmine been close? Closer?

"Rhonda," he said, using a voice that assumed control. She sniffled and stopped yelling. "Is there a second phone line?"

"Yes. Oh my God!"

Schultz imagined that what she'd seen in Jasmine's office involved a lot of slicing and blood.

"Call 911 on the other line, Rhonda. Don't hang up on me. Come back to me as soon as you're finished."

She was back in a couple of minutes, her voice shaky but better controlled.

"Now I want you to make an announcement over the public address system and tell everyone to return to their rooms and stay there."

"We have a code for 'Intruder in the Building.' All the residents and guards know it. I'll use that."

When she came back, he told her to sit down on the floor behind her reception counter and wait for the cops. He stayed on the phone with her until he heard the police arriving. Anxious to go to them, Rhonda hung up on him.

Only then did he realize he'd left PJ standing in the snow at her car. He dialed her cellphone, but the call rolled over to voice mail. A little annoyed that she wasn't accessible, he sent an officer out to locate her.

Chapter 53

PJ awoke lying on the floor in a dark room. The floor was hard to the touch, and rough, probably tile. Sitting up, she felt dizzy. There was a painful spot on her head, and she could tell that blood had flowed down her forehead and all the way to her neckline. Her hands were tied behind her back. Waves of pain were chasing each other up her leg from her left ankle.

There was a line of light coming in under a door. Her head spun, and she saw double strips of light. She wasn't ready to move, but wasn't ready to wait in a confined shooting gallery for April to return.

April! How long have I been out?

Everyone could be dead. May, June, Jasmine. And any collateral damage, like Mary Beth. April wouldn't hesitate to wipe out anyone who stood between her and the women who'd stolen her life. *A bloodthirsty Cinderella.*

There were children in the house.

PJ tried to stand and found that she couldn't. Her leg was twisted under her, with sharp jabs from her ankle. She rolled onto her stomach. Her injured left ankle smacked into the floor as she did so, sending bolts of searing pain up to her hip. She lay still, trying to bring her breathing and heart rate down. Then she began to inch her way across the floor. With her good foot, she could get leverage on the rough tiles. Scraping along slowly, she made it to the door and stopped to rest. Then, grimacing, she braced her back against the door and slowly worked her good foot back toward her. Her leg and arm muscles trembled with the effort, and her left foot dragged painfully. Her fingers spread, she walked up the door a fraction of an inch at a time. Once she got her rear several inches off the floor, it got a little easier.

Standing up with all her weight on her right foot, leaning against the door, she again stopped to rest. PJ was very aware that every minute that went by increased the chances of multiple deaths in the house, if it wasn't too late already. And of April coming back to finish her off.

Twisting the knob, she found it turned freely, but there had to be a lock somewhere else, because the door wouldn't budge. She used her shoulder to feel around on the wall in the spot where there would normally be a light switch, right inside the door. She flicked it on with her tongue, wondering if she was going to get shocked, like sticking her tongue in a wall socket.

No shock, just lots of light. Blinded, she pinched her eyes shut, then opened her eyelids just a little, getting a view of the room through narrow slits. What she saw startled her enough that her eyes flew open.

Blinking hard against the light, she realized she was in a storage room for sex toys. There were shelves lined with dildos of all sizes, shapes, and colors. Strap-on dildos were hung on hooks. There was a rack of clothing with all kinds of sexy lingerie, skimpy little nurse and maid costumes, and men's thong underwear, pouches covered with sequins or feathers, even a leather thong with spikes on the pouch. Hanging on the wall were two life-sized inflatable dolls, one open-mouthed female and one amply endowed male.

May was so indignant when she found out about June's fore-play album. Hell, this is an entire foreplay warehouse.

Checking her leg, PJ saw bone fragments barely poking through the skin at her ankle. It was a compound fracture and no way was it going to bear her weight. Yet she had to move.

PJ studied the room carefully. Relief washed over her when she saw what she was looking for: tools. There was an old, rusty toolbox, unlocked, tucked under one of the shelves.

Hoping that box wasn't empty, she reversed the procedure she'd used to stand, sliding the last several inches and landing hard, jolting her body enough to take her breath away. Inchworming on her back across the floor, she came to the box. Sitting up, her back to the box, she tugged on the handle and worked the lid of the box open. Grappling around blindly, she found the narrow, toothed blade of a hacksaw. Exultant, she pulled the saw out and looked around for a place to anchor it. A shelf at the right height had separated from its support board, pulling the nails apart. Scooting around on her butt, she got to the right spot and inserted the blade. It took her several tries, but finally it seemed firmly anchored.

She pulled the rope—clothesline?—that bound her wrists back and forth over the hacksaw. A number of times she slipped and the teeth bit into the skin of her wrist.

I wonder when my last tetanus booster was.

A few more strokes and her hands were free. The first thing she did was check her pockets for her cellphone. Not there. She remembered tossing it into the back seat of her car.

It was easier to move across the floor with the full use of her hands. She went to the toolbox, and what she wanted was right on top: a hammer and screwdriver, probably used in building the storage shelves and left to grow rusty. *Left to save my life.*

Leaning against the wall by the door, she removed the door's hinges by tapping up each pin. The door was held, probably by a hook and eye on the outer side, but she would be able to rotate the door to get out. There was a stab of pain from her ankle, enough to sicken her stomach and cause her to vomit. She'd hit her foot against the doorframe and felt bones grinding inside. The pain lessened enough to focus again.

Now for a weapon. She tucked the hammer and screwdriver into her waistband and considered the hacksaw blade. Was it worth going back for?

A noise came from upstairs, a soft crying. *No. Go now!*

She was about to leave when she noticed the broom standing in one corner. Leaning against the wall, she worked her way around to it, grasped the broom head, and twisted it off. She had a cane. Better mobility meant she could get to the kids faster.

Armed and leaning hard on the broomstick, she swung the door open, careful not to make noise with it. That's when it hit her. She was going after a vicious killer with rusty carpenter's tools, a household cleaning item, a broken ankle, and a likely concussion. Fear and anger vied for control of her emotions. She shoved the fear down into a little corner where giant spiders, child abductors, and all of Dean Koontz's books lived.

PJ limped out to find that she wasn't far from the front door. She could see Mary Beth's body lying in the entry foyer. To her right was the dramatic marble staircase she'd never climbed. When Mary Beth took her on tour, they'd used the staff's rear stairs. It was up that staircase she needed to go now.

PJ made her way there and sat on a step. She went up the stairs backward, lifting her rear one riser at a time, trying to keep her ankle from impacting the stair. Near the top, the hammer in her waistband worked itself loose and clattered down a couple of steps. The noise reverberated in the two-story stairwell. She felt very exposed. If attacked on the stairs, she was at a terrible disadvantage. The only thing to do was keep moving and hope the hammer's noise sounded louder to her because of her proximity than it did to someone up on the second floor.

She made it to the top and stood up, with the aid of the massive stair rail and her broomstick. She entered into a lengthy hallway that had several doors. PJ was looking for the kids, for May, for April, and for a phone. She made a right turn, went down a short distance, and tried the first door on her right. It opened to reveal a small room with a nightlight burning. The light was enough for her to see boxes stacked almost to the ceiling. She checked the contents of one that was open, and found it packed to overflowing with children's clothes. May said that Frank worked with children's charities, and here was the proof of a dead man's philanthropy.

She spotted a wall phone. Eagerly she made her way over to it and picked up the receiver. There was no dial tone.

April has been a busy little bee here since killing Mary Beth.

PJ had been so close when that happened that she heard the impact of the bullets tearing into Mary Beth, or imagined that she did. Either way, she'd be hearing that sound for the rest of her life. Mary Beth had lost her daughter to leukemia, Schultz said, and now she'd died a violent death. There was no trace of her left on earth, nothing to connect her to the future, no one to remember her.

Mom always said you weren't dead as long as a living person remembered you. Maybe I can do that for Mary Beth.

She heard a noise, and froze in place. There was a sound of scuffling on a wooden floor, and something falling with a thud. The source was close. Her breath barely whispering in and out of her lungs, she moved to the door as quietly as she could. Halfway there, the room started reeling. Closing her eyes, she waited it out, willed the nausea down, and floated in the pain coming from her head and her ankle. Time passed before she could move again, and then she made it to the door.

She listened with full concentration, then put her face out in the hall for a quick look. The hall was empty.

PJ eased into the hallway and moved down, listening for more noises. The next door down had children's drawings stuck up on it, and just as she got there, there was a scraping sound coming from behind the door. Her heart plummeted all the way to her feet. It had to be the children's suite. She had a sickening feeling that April was in there.

Too late, too late.

She put her hand on the doorknob and turned it.

Chapter 54

"Shit, where is that woman?" Schultz said.

"Are you referring to your boss?" Anita gave him a hard glare.

"I know she wants in here," he said. "Probably thought she was going to bust the door down herself. So she goes off and takes a nap or something?"

"The officer will find her."

Just then, the man Schultz had sent in search of PJ came back onto the front porch and stuck his head in the door. "No luck," he said. "Are you sure she's here?"

"Of course I'm sure," Schultz said. He thought of their parting. "You need to find Officer Daniels, a woman; I don't know her first name. She parked the car we arrived in. She'll at least know what direction the doctor took off in."

I can't believe she could get lost at a crime scene.

Dave came up and told him about a locked storage area he'd found in the basement, and thought Schultz should be there when the door was forced. Schultz trotted off after him.

It turned out to be the place that solved the time of death puzzle. Arlan Merrett was kept captive in a four by six closet for four days. There were manacles bolted high on the wall. Schultz stood in place and stretched his arms up. He was a big man, over six feet like Arlan, but Schultz wouldn't have been able to keep his feet on the floor while fastened in the manacles. That was all he needed to know about the conditions of Arlan's captivity. Others would fill in the details for him later.

Schultz tried PJ's cellphone again. He wanted to make sure she knew that the woman who'd been arrested was most likely not April. Her phone was turned off, and that alarmed him. He sent word that he wanted to talk to Officer Daniels— now. He went up to the porch to wait for her, and it didn't take long.

"Daniels, what's going on with Dr. Gray? Have you seen her since we arrived?"

"I got your question twenty minutes ago and I sent back an answer. I guess I should have come in person."

Damn straight.

"She left about an hour ago."

"Left? To do what?" A chill started walking up Schultz's spine.

"She didn't say."

"Was she alone?" *April could be anywhere.*

"As far as I know, yes," Daniels said. "The windows were covered with snow. I couldn't see inside very well. I spoke to her. Come to think of it, she seemed to be choking on her words a little. Said she was catching a cold."

"Jesus," Schultz said. He whipped out his phone and called June's house. She answered, nervous from his last call, and tried to ask a lot of questions that he didn't have time for. He cut her off and called May. He got an out-of-service message, and knew immediately where PJ was, and where April was. An overwhelming sense of dread hit him.

Dave was nearby. Schultz yelled to him, "Send backup to May's house, secure that area. Nobody leaves. Extreme caution. Stealth approach until I get there." Then he was charging down the steps, running flat out through the snow. He stopped at the first cruiser he came across, hopped in, and told the startled officer to take him to Lindell and Kingshighway.

Chapter 55

The doorknob turned and PJ eased the door open a crack. What she saw was nearly enough to stop her heart.

There was a young boy tied to a chair, his mouth covered with duct tape, blood on his cheek and nose. *Brian.*

He turned in her direction and she was afraid the boy would give her away, but his eyes were wide, vacant with fear.

Hoping the door wouldn't squeak, PJ pushed in a little further. There was the girl, Amelia, tied and taped. A scratch on her arm bled freely. Tears ran down her face. Her eyes were very aware, and locked on something low in front of her.

There was an odd singsong voice in the room, like a tape of children's songs.

The fear that permeated the room washed over her and left an unclean feeling behind. Unclean or evil. There was a large mirror set low on the opposite wall, at the height a child would need to get a full-body view. Reflected in it PJ saw April, and it was a horrifying sight.

April was sitting on the floor, a teddy bear in her lap. She was rocking back and forth, and with each forward motion, she plunged a knife into the teddy bear.

Amelia whimpered, and that made PJ realize what her heart had already decided: she was going into that room to put a stop to whatever deranged plan April had. The only things left to decide, where when, and how.

Dizziness struck again, and PJ leaned against the wall until it passed.

The door was open about an inch. The girl's eyes pulled away from watching April stab her teddy bear and suddenly spotted PJ. Amelia stiffened and stared. PJ quickly put a finger to her lips and made sure Amelia could see it through the narrow opening of the door. The girl caught on immediately, and shifted her eyes away from the door. She whined louder and rocked her chair onto its back legs and then let it thud down on the floor. She was drawing April's attention to her.

"Stop that, girl," April said, not taking a break from stabbing the bear. "Wouldn't want to wake your mommy, would we? That'll come later. I've got her this time. 'Woman goes berserk, kills own children.' Too bad you kids won't be around to see your pictures in the paper."

May's still alive, then.

April dropped the bear and stood up with the knife. Amelia started to thrash around in her chair.

PJ pulled the screwdriver from her waistband. It was time to make a stand for the kids. She pushed hard on the door, sending it crashing into the wall, and charged into the room, moving as fast as she could, leaning on the broomstick. Startled, April turned in her direction, but PJ was already on her, slamming into her bodily, slashing with the screwdriver at April's eyes. The screwdriver raked across April's face and across one eye. April screamed. Knocked off balance, she still managed to grab PJ, so they both fell to the floor. Grappling with each other on the floor, April kicked PJ's ankle, then did it again. Blackness edged PJ's vision, and the room began to swirl and fade. She was sinking into unconsciousness.

If she blacked out now, she was signing her death warrant and perhaps three others. She fought back the pain and the encroaching blackness. PJ still held the screwdriver, and she plunged it upward blindly, hoping to hit a belly or chest. She didn't make contact with flesh. April had rolled away, but was coming back on hands and knees. The side of April's face was bloodied, one eye bulging and torn. PJ's first jab had done its work.

Fighting the urge to close her eyes and give up, PJ lashed out with the broomstick and was rewarded with a solid crack on April's arm. April backed up out of reach of the broomstick. Then she did what PJ was desperately hoping she wouldn't. April turned her back on the adult attacker and went for the girl, knife ready to flick away a life.

PJ straightened out her body as well as she could, tucked the stick in close, and rolled, spinning on an axis from head to toe. As soon as she was close enough, she uncoiled and used all of her strength to swing the stick into April's back. Howling, April fell forward. The broomstick broke with a resounding crack, leaving PJ with a short, sharply pointed wooden stake. She stabbed it into April's calf, deeply penetrating the muscle. April screamed and scrambled away. When she got near the door, April pulled herself up on it and limped out to the hall, leaning on the wall as much as she could.

PJ reassured herself that the children were okay, if frightened, and then crawled over to the door. April could return, and with a gun. All PJ had left was the screwdriver, and she didn't think she could throw it with any accuracy. She was near the bottom of her reserves of strength, but knew she had to hold on.

April was at the top of the stairs. The woman gave her a look of wild, venomous hatred, pulled the stake out of her leg, and threw it at PJ. Then April started down the stairs, clinging to the rail for support.

A scream, a horrible scream, the sound of the hammer bouncing from step to step, the sound of someone tumbling, followed by a sickening crack.

By the time PJ got to the top of the stairs, April was twisted and broken at the bottom of the stairs, but alive. The hammer lay next to her. April's feet must have tangled with the hammer PJ had dropped, causing both person and tool to roll down the steps.

April's uninjured eye locked on PJ and pleaded mutely for help. PJ bumped carefully down the stairs, then was past the urge of wanting to move at all once she reached the bottom. If she was going anywhere else, it would be on a stretcher. She noticed that her cellphone had fallen out of April's pocket and was lying near the woman's head. Cautiously, she reached for the phone, nearly blacking out as she stretched to pick it up. April, unable to move, couldn't stop her.

She opened her phone to call 911. Then she closed it, deciding that there was no rush. PJ sat there on the steps and watched April's life slowly slip away.

Chapter 56

"I want that door open now," Schultz said. "Lives are in imminent danger."

"You got it, Detective. Stand back."

Shotgun blasts dug into the beautiful oak door at May's house. In about thirty seconds, the scarred, ten-foot door hung by one hinge at the top. Officers from the backup cruisers poured into the opening, weapons drawn, looking for the woman Schultz described as "armed and very dangerous, take no chances."

They nearly tripped over a body in the foyer. Heart in his throat, Schultz saw that it wasn't PJ, but was bad anyway. It was Mary Beth, a woman whose strength he admired. He felt for a pulse and found none. Sure that the next body was going to be PJ's, he charged after the officers, who'd gotten ahead of him when he stopped to check for a pulse.

There was another body at the base of the sweeping, marble staircase, broken, blood pooled on the shiny floor.

But it wasn't her. He caught sight of PJ sitting on the stairs, her leg bloody and stretched out in front of her, her eyes fastened on the corpse.

Weapons were trained on PJ, who wasn't responding to orders to lie on the floor.

"Don't shoot! One of ours!" Schultz came hurrying up. Her appearance was shocking. There was blood in her hair, a fragment of bone jutted from her leg at the ankle, and she looked as though she'd lost a fight with a bulldog. He took her pulse with one hand and lifted her chin with the other. The gesture reminded him of PJ lifting Shower Woman's head, and bile rose in his throat. That woman was irretrievably

360

gone. His woman still had a pulse.

Thank God.

Wailing sirens announced the arrival of the ambulances he'd called for.

Recognition lit her eyes. "Leo?"

"Yes," he said. He clasped one of her hands in both of his, protecting it, wanting to hold her but fearing that would make her injuries worse.

"Children upstairs to the right. Don't know where May is," she said. Every word seemed to take a focused effort. When she'd said them, she closed her eyes and collapsed. Schultz caught her before she hit her head on the cold marble, and he was immensely grateful that it wasn't a cold slab in the morgue she was heading for.

Chapter 57

"Guess who got a speeding ticket today?" Dave said.

The team was in PJ's office. Wrappers littered her desk from the deli lunch they'd had. Her crutches stood in the corner. She had a stool next to her desk with a pillow on it, and her knee-to-toe cast was propped up. The compound fracture had needed surgery, so she had screws and plates in her ankle. Schultz had said they were two of a kind, since one of his feet was bolted together too.

"I'm no good at guessing games," PJ said. "Just tell me. Anita, please turn on that fan behind you."

I'm never going to air out the onions and jalapeños. Why didn't we eat out instead of carry in?

"The driver of a black Blazer," Dave said.

"*The* black Blazer?"

"Speeding on Market Street. Said she was in a hurry to get to Union Station."

"A hot sale going on?" Anita said. "Wait, *she?*"

PJ could see that Dave was clearly relishing the information no one else had gotten hold of yet. *How could we? It feels like we've been eating sandwiches in here since breakfast.*

"*She.* June Marie Merrett. Apparently she confessed to the traffic cop right there on Market. The woman's on the edge."

"We knew that already," PJ said, thinking back over her conversations with June. "Why was she after me? I was trying to solve her husband's murder. You'd think she would want me on the job."

"It was because you had uncovered evidence of her husband's affair with tantalizing Fredericka. She really didn't know. Then when she found that gift that she thought was for her, and it turned out to be sexy lingerie in Fredericka's size, it all crashed in on her. She thought you'd be blabbing about it everywhere and besmirch the memory of her beloved."

"You're kidding, right?" PJ said. She was waiting for everyone in the room to burst out laughing, having a joke at her expense.

"It's true," Dave said.

"So she couldn't stand to have her true love bubble burst," PJ said.

Poor guy probably didn't stand a chance against Fredericka. All those hours working late in her loft.

"I can't believe she was still driving that Blazer," Anita said. "Didn't she know it could be linked to the attempts on PJ's life?"

"You'd be amazed what people keep after committing crimes," Schultz said. "People are damn cheap."

When the group broke up, PJ had them take the food wrappers and other assorted trash out with them. It probably ended up in the trashcan in the men's room across the hall, where the smell would be a big improvement.

Schultz stayed behind, and closed the door. PJ's eyebrows went up when he locked it.

"Leo, I admire your enthusiasm, but I'm not up to lap dancing," PJ said. She rapped her knuckles on her cast.

"It's not what you think," he said. "I just didn't want an audience."

He came over to her, leaned heavily on the desk, and dropped to one knee. Pulling a box out of his pocket, he opened it and held it out to her. It was a diamond ring, an incredibly beautiful one.

"I love you and I want to spend the rest of my life with

you," he said. "Will you marry me?"

Damn you, Leo, we never worked it all out, we never had the Talk.

She looked at the ring and tears welled up in her eyes. *Can I say no to a man who left a rose on my pillow?*

"Those had better be tears of joy, and I hate to rush you, but my knee isn't gonna take much more of this," he said.

Yes. Yes. Yes. Yes.

"Yes."

He slipped the diamond ring on her finger and kissed her hand.

"What are we going to do, Leo? I'll ask for reassignment," she said, answering her own question.

"I have an idea about that," he said. He pulled something else out of his pocket and handed it to her.

It was a business card, and on it, in confident raised black ink, it said:

Leo Schultz, Private Investigator
Criminal Investigations
Cold Cases are my Specialty
No Damn Divorces

Afterword

Forensic animation has become a popular tool in courtroom presentations. An animation is a rendering of an expert's testimony on a monitor, set in motion and utilizing lighting and shading to make the elements appear three-dimensional. Since the early 1990s, dozens of companies have sprung into existence offering animations of everything from car accidents to airplane crashes to homicides. Instead of having a medical expert drone on about the angle of firing and position of the victim, a savvy prosecutor can create a computerized animation sequence that is accompanied by the expert's explanation. Complex testimony becomes straightforward when reduced to visual terms.

Additionally, there is far more emotional impact in showing a bullet traveling in *Matrix* fashion toward a victim, the victim falling to his knees and being shot again, point-blank, than there is in having an expert recite the same events. Jurors are being converted into witnesses to the crime rather than passive listeners as attorneys tap into familiarity—conditioning might not be too strong a word—with television.

Computer simulations are different from the animations now in widespread use in that simulations allow the introduction of extrapolative evidence that is not a strict rendering of expert testimony. Simulations project logical outcomes, called scenarios, based on input provided to the computer. Alternative theories about how the crash occurred or the victim was killed can be played out in real time. Trial judges now rule on the acceptability of computerized presentations on a case-by-case basis. Judges seem more and more accepting of straightforward animations to help an expert witness make a point. Scenarios, because of their speculative nature and ability to captivate and convince a jury, can be excluded as prejudicial.

Developing scenarios about homicides sounds a lot like the investigative process already done by law enforcement personnel. Detectives have been doing this with their minds, chalkboards, and stray bits of paper for a long time. Recording the crime scene has gone from drawings to photographs to videos to panoramic three-dimensional images that allow an investigator to return to the scene of the crime on his office computer. There's still one problem, though. The actual crime is in the past. The investigator is looking at the results and making inferences, some based on fact, some on experience, and some on a cop's instincts.

It's a small leap of the imagination—but a large leap of technology—from there to fully immersive virtual reality (VR) crime scenes that not only allow the investigator to watch a crime unfold but to participate in it as the criminal, victim, or witness. Immersive means that the investigator wears gear that isolates him from the real world as the computer creates a life-sized world he can experience by exploring. The investigator actually remains in one place while the virtual world moves around him. A close representation of what the killer saw and heard can be achieved, and the investigator can try out new theories on the fly. Senses beyond sight and hearing are in the works to enhance the experience. Interaction with the virtual world is vital to the experience. If a knife is on the kitchen counter, an investigator can grab it and stab the victim.

The virtual reality techniques in this book are almost all possible today, even though they may seem futuristic. One twist I have added is the use of artificial intelligence (AI) coupled with the virtual reality, so that the computer can creatively suggest ways that the crime might have been committed. The computer has become an investigator on the case—a partner with an off switch.

Forensic virtual reality is on the way to becoming an accepted law enforcement tool, just as psychological profiling was in the 1970s and DNA fingerprinting was in the 1980s. There are hurdles to overcome in terms of cost, acceptance by law enforcement personnel, and admissibility as courtroom evidence. If a police department has to organize a community fund-raiser to buy bulletproof vests or a trained police dog, it isn't likely that the department will be pushing for the equipment and staff needed for a state-of-the-art forensic VR program. As costs come down and acceptance rises, forensic VR will be added to the detective's tool bag just as onboard computers are showing up in police cruisers. PJ Gray and Leo Schultz might be fictional pioneers, but within a decade or two, they will have plenty of real-life counterparts.

It isn't difficult to see immersive VR in use as detectives formulate theories. It's much harder to imagine the progression from the investigative side to the prosecutorial. Picture this: jurors fully immersed in a crime scene, standing right there in the living room with the defendant watching every blow and blood spatter as he beats his wife. Will judges ever allow it, and what defendant would stand a chance if so?

While virtual reality is an interesting aspect of this book, it is really about the people on both sides of the homicides: the human dynamics of crime-solvers and the killers they hunt.

S.K.

About the Author

Shirley Kennett is the author of six books, including the thriller *Burning Rose* and several suspense novels featuring PJ Gray, single mom, psychologist, and pioneer in the field of forensic virtual reality. Shirley has been a mystery fan as long as she can remember, which may have had something to do with growing up in a converted turn-of-the-century funeral home. A member of International Thriller Writers, Mystery Writers of America, Sisters in Crime, and the American Crime Writers League, Shirley lives with her husband, two sons, and several cats in the St. Louis metropolitan area. Email her at sak@shirleykennett.com.